INTRIGUE

Seek thrills. Solve crimes. Justice served.

Smokey Mountains Graveyard
Lena Diaz

K-9 Missing Pesron
Cassie Miles

MILLS & BOON

SMOKEY MOUNTAINS GRAVEYARD
© 2024 by Lena Diaz
Philippine Copyright 2024
Australian Copyright 2024
New Zealand Copyright 2024

First Published 2024
First Australian Paperback Edition 2024
ISBN 978 1 038 90764 6

K-9 MISSING PERSON
© 2024 by Kay Bergstrom
Philippine Copyright 2024
Australian Copyright 2024
New Zealand Copyright 2024

First Published 2024
First Australian Paperback Edition 2024
ISBN 978 1 038 90764 6

MIX
Paper | Supporting
responsible forestry
FSC® C001695
www.fsc.org

Published by
Harlequin Mills & Boon
An imprint of Harlequin Enterprises (Australia) Pty Limited
(ABN 47 001 180 918), a subsidiary of HarperCollins
Publishers Australia Pty Limited
(ABN 36 009 913 517)
Level 19, 201 Elizabeth Street
SYDNEY NSW 2000 AUSTRALIA

Cover art used by arrangement with Harlequin Books S.A.. All rights reserved.

Printed and bound in Australia by McPherson's Printing Group

Smokey Mountains Graveyard
Lena Diaz

MILLS & BOON

Lena Diaz was born in Kentucky and has also lived in California, Louisiana and Florida, where she now resides with her husband and two children. Before becoming a romantic suspense author, she was a computer programmer. A Romance Writers of America Golden Heart® Award finalist, she has also won the prestigious Daphne du Maurier Award for Excellence in Mystery/Suspense. To get the latest news about Lena, please visit her website, lenadiaz.com.

Visit the Author Profile page
at millsandboon.com.au.

DEDICATION

This book is dedicated to Dr. Tomas A. Moreno and Dr. Lenka Champion. One restored my sight. The other helped restore its clarity. A year and a half after going blind in one eye, I can see far better than I ever thought would be possible again. I am forever grateful to you both.

CAST OF CHARACTERS

Asher Whitfield—A cold case investigator employed by a private firm called Unfinished Business. Asher uses his skills from his previous career in law enforcement to solve cases that East Tennessee police forces don't have the time or resources to work.

Faith Lancaster—Fellow UB cold case investigator, Faith often partners with Asher. While trying to solve the disappearance of a young single mother, they stumble upon the private cemetery of a serial killer.

Daphne Lancaster—Faith's younger college-aged sister was raised by Faith after their parents died. Very much aware of Asher's long-standing infatuation with her older sister, Daphne encourages him to do something bold that will make Faith finally see Asher as more than just a really good friend.

Chief Russo—Chief of police of Gatlinburg, Tennessee. The hunt for a serial killer strains his relationship with UB and may jeopardize the case.

Jasmine Parks—Single mother who went missing five years ago. Was she the victim of a serial killer as many believe? Or was there more to her disappearance?

Leslie Parks—Jasmine's twenty-year-old sister was only fifteen when Jasmine went missing. Now she's at the center of the investigation.

Chapter One

Faith Lancaster wasn't in the Smoky Mountains above Gatlinburg, Tennessee, for the gorgeous spring views, the sparkling waters of Crescent Falls or even hunting for the perfect camera shot of a black bear. Faith was here on this Tuesday morning searching for something else entirely.

A murdered woman's unmarked grave.

If she was right, then she and Asher Whitfield, her partner at the cold case company, Unfinished Business, were about to locate the remains of beautiful bartender and single mother of two, Jasmine Parks.

Five years ago, almost to the day, Jasmine had disappeared after a shift at a bar and grill named The Watering Hole, popular for its scenic views and a man-made waterfall behind it. Instead of returning home that night to her family, she'd become another sad statistic. But months of research had led Faith and Asher to this lonely mountainside, just a twenty-minute drive from the home that Jasmine had shared with her two small children, younger sister and her parents.

Faith shaded her eyes from the sun, trying to get a better look at the newest addition to the crowd of police lined up along the yellow tape, watching the techs operating the ground-penetrating radar machine. Once she realized who'd just arrived, she groaned.

"The vultures found out about our prediction and came for the show," she said.

Beside her, Asher peered over the top of his shades then pushed them higher up on his nose. "Twenty bucks says the short blonde with the microphone ducks beneath the crime scene tape before we even confirm there's a body buried here."

"You know darn well that *short blonde* is Miranda Cummings, the prime-time anchor on Gatlinburg's evening news. Toss in another twenty bucks and I'll take that bet. Only I'll give her less than two minutes."

"Less than two?" He arched a brow. "Deal. No one's that audacious with all these cops around."

No sooner had he finished speaking than the anchor ducked under the yellow tape. She tiptoed across the grass wet with morning dew, heading directly toward the group of hard hats standing by the backhoe.

Faith swore. "She's the kind of blonde who gives the rest of us a bad name. What kind of idiot wears red stilettos to traipse up an incline in soggy grass?"

"The kind who wants to look good on camera when she gets an exclusive."

"Well, that isn't happening. She's about to be arrested." She nodded at two of the uniformed officers hurrying after the reporter and her cameraman.

"Double or nothing?" Asher asked.

"That they won't arrest her?"

"Yep." He glanced down at her, an amused expression on his face.

"Now who's the idiot?" Faith shook her head. "You're on."

The police caught up to the anchorwoman and blocked her advance toward the construction crew. She immediately aimed her mic toward one of the officers while her equally bold cameraman swung his camera around.

"Are you kidding me?" Faith shook her head in disgust. "Are men really that blind and stupid? They're fawning all over her like lovesick puppies instead of doing their jobs."

Asher laughed. "They're fawning all over her because she's a hot blonde in red stilettos. You want to go double or nothing again? I can already picture my delicious steak dinner tonight, at your expense."

"I'm quitting while I'm behind. And she's not *that* attractive."

His grin widened. "If you were a man, you wouldn't say that."

She put her hands on her hips, craning her neck back to meet his gaze, not that she could see his eyes very well behind those dark shades. "You seriously find all that heavy makeup and hairspray appealing?"

"It's not her hair, or her face, that anyone's looking at." He used his hands to make an hourglass motion.

She rolled her eyes and studied the others standing behind the yellow tape like Asher and her. "Where's the police chief? Someone needs to put an end to this nonsense."

"Russo left a few minutes ago. Some kind of emergency at the waterfall on the other side of this mountain. Sounds like a tourist may have gotten too close and went for an unplanned swim."

She winced. "I hope they didn't hit any rocks going over. Maybe they got lucky and didn't get hurt, or drown." She shivered.

"You still don't know how to swim, do you?"

"Since I don't live anywhere near a beach, don't own a pool, and I'm not dumb enough to get near any of the waterfalls in these mountains, it doesn't matter." She motioned to the narrow, winding road about thirty yards away. "Our boss just pulled up, assuming he's the only one around here who can afford that black Audi R8 Spyder. Maybe he'll get the police to escort the press out of here. Goodness knows with his history of helping Gatlinburg PD, Russo's men respect him as much as they do their own chief. Maybe more."

Asher nodded his agreement. "I'm surprised Grayson's here. I thought he was visiting his little girl in Missouri. Now that she knows he's her biological father, he visits as much as he can."

"I'm guessing his wife updated him about the search. He probably felt this was too important to miss."

"You called Willow in on this already?" he asked.

"Last night. She's with the Parks family right now, doing her victim's advocate stuff. It's a good thing, too, because it would have been terrible for them to hear about this search on the news without being prepared first."

"Kudos to you, Faith. I didn't even think about calling her. Then again, I didn't expect the word to leak about what we were doing up here this morning. It's a shame everyone can't be more respectful of the family."

She eyed the line of police again, wondering which one or ones had tipped off the media. None of her coworkers would have blabbed, of that she was certain. "At least Willow can tell the family there's hope again."

"That we'll find Jasmine, sure. But all that will prove is that she didn't accidentally drive her car into a pond or a ravine. I doubt it will give them comfort to have their fears confirmed that she was murdered. And we're not even close to knowing who killed her, or how."

"The how will come at the autopsy."

"Maybe. Maybe not."

She grimaced. "You're probably right. Unless there are broken or damaged bones, we might not get a *cause* of death.

But if she's buried up here, there's no question about *manner* of death. Homicide." She returned their boss's wave.

Asher turned to watch him approach. "As to knowing who's responsible, we're not starting from scratch. We've eliminated a lot of potential suspects."

"You're kidding, right? All we've concluded is that it's unlikely that anyone we've interviewed was involved in her disappearance and alleged murder. We still have to figure out which of the three hundred, thirty-five million strangers in this country killed her. Almost eight billion if we consider that someone from another country could have been here as a tourist and did it."

He crossed his arms. "I'm sticking to my theory that it's someone local, someone who knew the area. Out-of-towners tend to stick to the hiking trails or drive through areas like Cades Cove to get pictures of wildlife. There's nothing over here to attract anyone but locals trying to get away from the tourists."

"I still think it could be a stranger who travels here enough to be comfortable. We shouldn't limit our search to Gatlinburg, or even to Sevier County."

"Tennessee's a big state. How many people does that mean we have to eliminate, Ms. Math Whiz?"

"The only reason you consider me a math whiz is because you got stuck on fractions in third grade."

"I'd say ouch. But I don't consider it an insult that I'm not a math nerd."

"Nah, you're just a nerd."

He laughed, not at all offended. She reluctantly smiled, enjoying their easy banter and the comfort of their close friendship. As handsome and charming as he was, it baffled her that he was still single. She really needed to work at setting him up with someone. He deserved a woman who'd love him and appreciate his humor and kind heart. But for the life of her, she couldn't picture anyone she knew as being the right fit for him.

"Play nice, children." Grayson stopped beside them, impeccable as always in a charcoal-gray suit that probably cost more than Faith's entire wardrobe. "What have I missed?"

Asher gestured toward Faith. "Math genius here was going to tell us how many suspects we have to investigate if we expand our search to all the males in Tennessee."

"No, I was going to tell you *if* we considered all of Tennessee, the total population is about seven million. I have no idea how many of those are male."

Grayson slid his hands in the pockets of his dress pants. "Females account for about fifty-one percent of the population. Statewide, if you focus on males, that's about three and a half million. In Sevier County, potential male suspects number around fifty thousand." He arched a dark brow. "Please tell me I'm not spending thousands of dollars every month funding this investigation only to narrow our suspect pool to fifty thousand."

They both started talking at once, trying to give him an update.

He held up his hands. "I was teasing. If I didn't trust you to work this cold case, you wouldn't be on it. Willow told me you may have figured out where our missing woman is buried. That's far more than we had at the start of this. If the case was easy to solve, someone else would have done it in the past five years and Sevier County wouldn't have asked us to take it on. Give me a rundown on what's happening. I'm guessing the German shepherd is part of a scent dog team. And the construction crew standing around is waiting for guidance on where to dig. The guy pushing what looks like a lawnmower—is that a ground penetrating radar machine?"

Faith nodded. "The shepherd is Libby. She is indeed a scent dog, a cadaver dog. Although Lisa, her handler, prefers to call her a forensic recovery canine." She pointed at various small clearings. "Lisa shoved venting rods in those areas to help release potential scent trapped under the ground to make detection easier."

"It's been five years," Grayson said. "I wouldn't expect there to be any scent at all."

"Honestly, Asher and I didn't either. But after our investigation brought us here as the most likely dump site, we contacted Lisa and she said there would absolutely be scent. One study showed cadaver dogs detecting a skeleton that had been buried over thirty years. And Lisa swears they can pick up scent fifteen feet deep."

"Impressive, and unexpected. I'm guessing those yellow flags scattered around mark where the dog indicated possible hits. There are quite a few."

"A lot of flags, yes, but Lisa said it amounts to six major groupings. As good as these types of dogs are, they can have false positives. Other decomposing animals and vegetation can interfere with their abilities. And scent is actually pulled up through the root systems of trees, which makes it more difficult to find the true source. There could be a hit in, say, three different areas. But the decomposition actually originated from only one spot. Thus, the need for the ground penetrating radar. Lisa recommended it, to limit the dig sites. Asher called around and found a company already in the area." She motioned to Asher. "Where'd you say they were?"

"A cemetery near Pigeon Forge. The GPR company is ensuring that an empty part of the graveyard doesn't have any old unmarked graves before a new mausoleum is erected. Originally, I was going to ask a local utility company to bring over their GPR equipment. But what I found online is that it's more effective if the operator has experience locating the specific type of item you're searching for. Kind of like reading an X-ray or an ultrasound. The guys from the cemetery know how to recognize potential remains because they tested their equipment on known graves first. To find the unknown, you start with the known."

"Bottom line it for me," Grayson said.

Asher motioned to the guys wearing hard hats. "As soon as the radar team tells us which of the flagged sites has the most potential, the backhoe will start digging."

"How soon do we think that will happen?"

"Everybody stay back," one of the construction workers called out as another climbed into the cab of the backhoe.

"Guess that's our answer," Faith said.

Lisa and her canine jogged over and ducked under the yellow tape to stand beside Faith. Asher held up the tape for the GPR team as they pushed their equipment out of the way. The anchorwoman and her cameraman were finally escorted behind the tape as well.

Thankfully, they were a good distance away—not for lack of trying. The blonde kept pointing in their direction, apparently arguing that she wanted to stand beside them. No doubt she wanted to interview the radar people or maybe the canine handler. But Lisa had asked the police earlier to keep people away from her dog. By default, Faith and the small group she was with were safe from the reporter's questions.

For now at least.

Their boss formally introduced himself as Grayson Prescott to the others, thanking them for the work they were doing for his company. And also on behalf of the family of the missing woman.

"How confident are you that we'll find human remains

in one of the flagged areas?" Grayson asked the lead radar operator.

"Hard to say. We didn't check all of the sites since the sediment layers in those first two areas seem so promising. They show signs of having been disturbed at some point in the past."

"Like someone digging?"

He nodded. "There's something down there that caused distinctive shaded areas on the radar. But false positives happen. It's not an exact science."

"Understood."

The backhoe started up, its loud engine ending any chance of further conversation.

The hoe slowly and surprisingly carefully for such a big piece of equipment began to scrape back the layers of earth in the first of the two areas. Ten minutes later, the men standing near the growing hole waved at the operator, telling him to stop. They spoke for a moment then loud beeps sounded as the equipment backed up and moved to another spot to begin digging.

Faith sighed in disappointment. "Guess hole number one is a bust."

"Not so fast," Asher said. "They're signaling the forensics team."

A few minutes later, one of the techs jogged over to Faith and Asher, nodding with respect at Grayson.

"We've found a human skull. That's why they stopped digging. We'll switch to hand shovels now and sifting screens to preserve any potential trace evidence and make sure we recover as many small bones as possible."

Faith pressed a hand to her chest, grief and excitement warring with each other. She'd been optimistic that their research was right. But it was sad to have it confirmed that Jasmine had indeed been murdered. She'd only been twenty-two years old. It was such a tragedy for her to have lost her life so young, and in what no doubt was a terrifying, likely painful, manner.

"You don't see any hair or clothing to help us confirm that the remains belong to a female?" she asked.

"Not yet, ma'am. An excavation like this will take hours, maybe days, because we'll have to go slowly and carefully. But as soon as the medical examiner can make a determination of gender, the chief will update you. Since the GPR hit on those two sites, we'll check the second one as well. Natural shifts underground because of rain or hard freezes could have moved some of it. We also have to consider that the body might have been dismembered and buried in more than one area."

She winced. "Okay, thanks. Thanks for everything."

He nodded. "Thank *you*, Ms. Lancaster. Mr. Whitfield. All of you at UB. Whether this is Jasmine Parks or not, it's someone who needs to be recovered and brought home to their loved ones. If you hadn't figured out an area to focus on, whoever this person is might have never been found."

He returned to the growing group of techs standing around the makeshift grave. Hand shovels were being passed around and some of the uniformed police were bringing sifting screens up the incline.

"Looks like our work here is done," one of the radar guys said. "We'll load up our equipment and head back to Pigeon Forge."

"Wait." Asher pointed to the backhoe operator, who was excitedly waving his hands at the techs. "I think you should check out all of the other groups of flags too."

Faith stared in shock at what one of the techs was holding up from the second hole.

Another human skull.

Chapter Two

The sun had set long ago by the time Asher, Faith, Grayson and Police Chief Russo ended up in UB's second-floor, glass-walled conference room to discuss the day's harrowing events. Asher glanced down the table at the power play happening between Russo and Grayson. Across from him, Faith gave him a "what the heck is going on" look. Just as confused as Faith, all he could do was shrug his shoulders.

Russo thumped his pointer finger on the tabletop, his brows forming an angry slash. "Six bodies, Grayson. Your investigators led my team to the graves of six people. I want to know how that happened and who the hell their suspect is, right now. I don't want to wait for them to cross their t's and dot their i's in a formal report. The media's already all over this and I need something to tell them. Make your investigators turn over their files to my team so we can run with this."

Grayson leaned forward, his jaw set. "And this is why I refused your request for Asher and Faith to go to the police station. You'd be grilling them with questions as if they were criminals. Treat them with respect or the next person you'll speak to is Unfinished Business's team of lawyers. And you won't get one more word about what UB has, or hasn't, found in relation to this cold case."

Faith cleared her throat, stopping Russo's next verbal volley. "Can we please bring down the temperature a few degrees? We all want the same thing, to figure out why our belief that Jasmine Parks was buried on that mountainside turned into the discovery of a serial killer's graveyard. Because that's exactly what we've got here, a serial killer. No question. And now that his personal cemetery is all over the news, we have to expect he's already switching gears and making new plans. He could change locales, go to another county or even another state and start killing again—unless we work together to stop him."

"Unfinished Business will do everything we can to bring the killer to justice," Grayson said, still staring down Russo. "But if Gatlinburg PD can't be civil, we'll continue this investigation on our own."

The staring match between Russo and Grayson went on for a full minute. Russo blinked first and sank back against his chair as if exhausted. He mumbled something beneath his breath then scrubbed his face, which was sporting a considerable five-o'clock shadow.

Grayson, on the other hand, seemed as fresh as he had when he'd first stepped out of his Audi this morning. He could use a shave, sure, but there wasn't a speck of lint on his suit and the stubble on his jaw gave him a rugged look that appeared more planned than accidental.

Asher didn't know how his boss always managed to look so put-together no matter what was going on around him. Kind of like Faith. She, too, looked fresh, as beautiful as always, while Asher's suit was rumpled and his short dark hair was no doubt standing up in spikes by now. Russo was just as bad, maybe worse. He seemed ready to drop from the stress of the unexpected discoveries in his jurisdiction.

The chief held up his hands as if in surrender. "Okay, okay. I may have been too harsh earlier."

"*May* have been?" Grayson shook his head. "You practically accused Asher and Faith of being the killers."

Russo winced and aimed an apologetic glance at the two of them. "I didn't mean to imply any such thing."

"Russo," Grayson warned.

"Okay, all right. At the time, the implication was on purpose. It seemed impossible that you two could have stumbled onto something like that without some kind of firsthand knowledge. Still, I know you both better than to have gone there. It was a knee-jerk reaction. My apologies." He frowned at Grayson. "Talk about overreacting, though. You sure are touchy tonight."

"With good reason. I cut short a visit with my little girl to come back here. And then the police chief acts like a jerk instead of being grateful that Asher and Faith's hard work is going to bring closure to six families who have never known what happened to their loved ones."

Russo's expression softened. "I'm glad you're finally getting to establish a relationship with your daughter after thinking she was dead all these years. How old is she now?"

Grayson still seemed aggravated with his friend, but his voice gentled as he spoke about Lizzie. "She's about to become a precocious, beautiful, nine-year-old. And she's delighted to have two sets of parents around for her upcoming birthday. Twice the presents."

The chief laughed. "I imagine it will be far more than twice with you as her dad."

"Actually, no. Willow and I have come to a co-parenting agreement with Lizzie's adoptive parents. They didn't know she'd been abducted when she more or less fell into their laps as a baby. And they raised her all this time, giving her a loving, secure home. I don't want to upstage them or even try to replace them. Willow and I are being careful about not trying to outdo them in the gift department so that we don't unduly influence her toward us because of material things. We want her to stay grounded and continue to love the Danvers and, hopefully, grow to love us as well. But not by trying to buy her affections."

"You're a better man than me. I'd use every advantage at my disposal to win my little girl over, including suing her foster parents for custody. But I sure do admire that you're putting her interests above your own."

Grayson's mouth twitched in a rare smile. "If you're trying to soften my disposition with flattery, game well-played. I can't stay mad at you for long. Too much water under that bridge." He motioned to Asher and Faith at the other end of the table. "It's getting late and every one of us will be besieged tomorrow by reporters and families of missing persons wondering whether their loved ones are among the dead who are still being dug up on that mountain. Asher, Faith, just answer the chief's main question now and we can reassemble bright and early tomorrow to brief his team about the rest of the investigation. Does eight o'clock work for you, Russo?"

He nodded. "I'll limit my entourage to two of my best detectives and one crime scene tech so we can all fit in your conference room with your full team. Appreciate the cooperation."

Grayson nodded as if the two of them hadn't come close to blows a few minutes earlier.

Asher glanced at Faith, silently asking for her help. He couldn't remember the chief's main question at this point.

She took mercy on him and filled in the gap. "The chief wants to know how we knew where to dig."

"Right. Thanks. I got lost there for a minute."

"That's why I work with you. To keep you straight," she said, deadpan.

"And I appreciate it." He winked, earning another eye roll and a quick wave of her hand, signaling him to hurry up.

"The best answer to your question, Chief, is that it was geographical profiling. But it wasn't traditional profiling. We only had one victim to work with, not sets of data from several different victims. We couldn't extrapolate and come up with a good hypothesis of where the killer might live, which is traditionally how we'd use geographical profiling. Instead of focusing on what we did, or didn't, know about the killer, we created a geographic profile of our victim. We found out everything we could about her and built complex timelines for what she did every day in the three months before she disappeared. It was a painstaking process and involved performing dozens of interviews of just about anyone who'd known her."

Russo and Grayson were both sitting forward, looking as if they were about to pepper him with questions that would probably have them there until midnight. Hoping to avoid an inquisition, Asher hurried to explain.

"Our goal, initially, was to determine Jasmine's routine and mark all of the spots that she frequented on a map, from her home, to her work, where she bought groceries, where her doctor and dentist were, friends' homes, movie theaters she favorited—"

"You're talking victimology," Grayson said.

Asher was always impressed with how much his billionaire businessman boss and former army ranger had picked up on police procedures since starting his cold case company a few years ago. Back then, he'd had one purpose—to find out who'd murdered his first wife and what had happened to their infant daughter who'd gone missing that day. And he and Willow—a former Gatlinburg detective—had done exactly that. In truth, his knowledge of police procedures rivaled both Asher's, as a former Memphis detective, and even Faith's, who'd received numerous commendations as a detective in Nashville.

"Victimology, exactly. We'd hoped to zero in on the locations in her routine that would lend themselves the most to allowing an abductor to take her without being seen—which, of course, is what we believe happened. We came up with three most likely locations. From there, we worked as if we were the bad guy, scouting each one out to see how we would have kidnapped someone in that area and where we might have taken them."

Grayson frowned. "Maybe it's my lack of law enforcement background. But this isn't making sense to me. Not yet anyway."

Faith exchanged a nervous glance with Asher before jumping into the conversation. "What Asher's saying, in his adorably convoluted way, is that we came up with one main potential crime scene for the abduction as our working theory."

Asher grinned, wondering if she realized she'd said *adorable*. Slip of the tongue most likely. Nothing personal toward him.

Unfortunately.

"Instead of our theory leading to a suspect," she said, "it led us to ask questions about what would happen with the body after he killed her. There was really only one area near that location that made sense—a place not frequented by tourists, with very little traffic around it, close enough to the abduction site that the risk of being caught while transporting a victim in his car was low. It made sense that he'd take her into a wooded area, do whatever awful things he wanted to do, then dispose of her in the same location. Thus, the mountainside we were at this morning."

Grayson interjected another question before either Faith or Asher could cut him off. "What made you so confident in your theory that you arranged to have a cadaver dog, a ground penetrating radar team and Russo's techs all waiting there for a discovery that might not have happened?"

"It wasn't as bold as you think," Asher said. "We went over and over our theory, doubting our conclusions. We even spoke to one of our FBI profiler contacts about what we'd come up with. His suggestion was to get a cadaver dog out there first, which is what we did. Lisa and her forensic canine came out a few days ago and she was confident there was something there. Based on her track record, we went to Chief Russo. He agreed to send techs and officers out this morning in case the GPR team came up with a potential gravesite. Lisa had the dog rerun the route once everyone else showed up and it alerted on the same areas."

Russo swore. "You didn't explain this flimsy geographical profiling theory when we spoke. You said your months of investigating had you confident that was where Ms. Parks was buried. Sounds to me like you're lucky we found anything at all and I didn't waste all of that manpower for nothing."

"Russo," Grayson warned again.

The chief held up his hands. "Okay, okay. Your theory proved out. But finding a veritable graveyard of victims was never something I anticipated. *None* of us expected it. I get that. But when it happened, I wasn't prepared to deal with the fallout. That dang anchorwoman." He shook his head. "My guys should have escorted her out of there the minute she arrived. This whole thing is blowing up all over the news, along with that tourist's accidental death at Crescent Falls this morning." He shook his head in disgust. "First time we've had a death there in over twenty years, but now everyone's raising Cain saying it's not safe."

He eyed Grayson again, his expression a mixture of aggravation and stress. "A killer's graveyard found a football field's length from where a hiker drowned today is horrible for tourism. The park service is going to conduct a full-blown safety study of Crescent Falls. I'm getting calls from the tourism council, the mayor, and even the governor, asking when all of this will be resolved. Even TBI is threatening to park themselves on my doorstep."

Faith leaned forward in her chair. "Calling in the Tennessee Bureau of Investigation isn't a bad idea. We believe that one of the six bodies is Jasmine Parks. But we don't have a clue who the others might be. If TBI can explore missing person cases and narrow down the timeframes and locales to give a list of potential IDs to the ME, that could jumpstart the victim identification process."

Grayson was nodding his agreement before she finished. "That's a good idea. We could drive that part through Rowan, our TBI liaison. I'll alert him tonight and ask him to attend our meeting tomorrow morning. Sound good, Russo?"

"Works for me. This all started because we don't have the budget to work our cold cases. Now we suddenly have six to look into and everyone demanding action." He eyed Grayson. "Speaking of resources—"

"You'll have our full support. If necessary, I'll bring in contract investigators to temporarily expand our team. That's standard procedure here when the scope of work increases like this. We can ramp up quickly. TBI can do some of the grunt work for both of our organizations. And we'll coordinate the logistics together, you and me, so we can impact your budget as little as possible. Fair enough?"

Russo's brow smoothed out and he actually smiled. "More than fair. Thanks, Grayson. I owe you."

"That's how I prefer to keep it."

Russo laughed and stood. "I'll see you all in a few hours.

Hopefully, tomorrow will be a better day than this one was." He opened the door and strode toward the stairs.

Asher and Faith stood, ready to follow Russo.

"Just a minute." Grayson crossed to the glass wall that looked down on the main floor below with its two-story-high ceiling. What would have been called a squad room at a police department was affectionately called the war room by Unfinished Business's investigators.

He watched as Russo headed through the empty room, everyone else having gone home for the night. And he waited as Russo went into the parking lot, the view through the one-way glass walls allowing those inside to see out but no one outside to see in, even with the lights on. It was only once Russo's car was backing out of his parking space that Grayson turned around, an ominous frown on his face and his eyes the color of a stormy night.

"No one leaves this conference room until you tell me why you both just lied to the chief of police. And to me."

Chapter Three

Asher watched Grayson with growing dread. "What makes you think we're lying?"

"Don't even go there with me. I was in Special Forces and learned interrogation techniques from the best. I've also been playing in the big leagues in the business world for years. I know when someone's not being straight up. You and Faith just told a whopper with that story about using a new type of geographical profiling. What I want to know is why."

Faith's green eyes were big and round as she met Asher's gaze. Both of them slowly sank back into their chairs.

"Wanna draw straws?" Asher asked her.

"Coward. I'll tell him." In spite of her brave words, she seemed nervous as she answered Grayson. "We really did try to do what we said, map out everywhere our missing person had been, her usual routine at least. And we tried to figure out what areas made sense as the best ones where she'd have gone missing. But, well—"

"There were too many," Asher said. "With no witnesses to the abduction and no forensic evidence. We hit a wall. Couldn't make any headway."

"So we, uh, we…" Faith swallowed hard and squeezed her hands together on top of the table.

Grayson's brow furrowed. "I've got all night. But I'd rather spend it at home with my beautiful wife than in a conference room trying to draw the truth out of two of my extremely well-paid employees. I deserve the truth and I want it. Now."

She let out a deep breath then the confession poured out of her in a rush. "We sent letters to ten serial killers in prison and offered a deal. If they'd put us on their visitation list and agree to speak to us, we'd go see them. In exchange for their opinions on which of our potential locations would make the best dump site, we'd put four hundred dollars in their prison accounts."

Grayson stared at her a long moment then cleared his throat. "And how many of these despicable murderers took you up on this bribe?"

She chewed her bottom lip before answering. "All of them."

Another minute passed in silence. Then, his voice deadly calm, Grayson said, "Let's see if I have this straight. You gave four thousand dollars of my money to the scummiest excuses for human beings so they would give you their *guesses* on which of the areas in Gatlinburg they would choose to dump a body. Is that what you're telling me?"

She winced. "Sounds way worse when you phrase it that way. But, um, yes. That's basically what we did."

He blinked, slowly, then looked at Asher. "Let me guess. This was your harebrained idea?"

Asher cleared his throat. "Actually, I believe it was."

Grayson leaned back in his chair. "And how many of the sites they chose did you send the cadaver dog team to?"

"How many?" Asher asked. "Total?"

"That's what the phrase *how many* means. *In total*, how many sites did the cadaver K-9 sniff out before you hired an expensive ground penetrating radar team, construction workers with a backhoe and, on top of that, lie to Chief Russo that your brilliant deductive reasoning determined that mountainside this morning was most likely where our missing person's body would be located?"

Asher stared up at the ceiling as if counting. Then he straightened his tie. "Um, pretty much it was—"

"One," Faith said. "Just the one. The dog hit on it and we felt confident that we were going to find…something. If we told Russo about asking serial killers for opinions, he'd have laughed us out of his office, in spite of the cadaver dog. So we exaggerated the geographical profiling theory in case he asked questions. We needed something to make it seem more—"

"Legit? Reliable? Worth a substantial expenditure of resources in spite of how busy Gatlinburg PD is and how tight Russo is with his budget? Since the whole point of us taking on this cold case was to keep him from having to use his funds and resources, you do realize I'll have to reimburse him for his expenses from this morning?"

Faith clenched her hands together on the table. "We believed strongly that our—"

"Educated guess?"

"We believed we had a high probability of finding Jasmine Parks. And we were somewhat desperate for a break in the case. So, we, um, we lied. And, yes, we cost Unfinished Business—you—a lot of money today. But wasn't it worth it, sir? By all accounts, the clothing and jewelry found on one of the skeletons makes it seem highly likely that we've found Ms. Parks. Plus, we've found other missing people."

"That doesn't sound like an apology for lying to the chief of police and your boss."

She glanced at Asher. "In our defense, sir, we never intended to lie to you. We didn't expect you to even be there today. Our hope was that after we located Ms. Parks's remains, no one would care how we did it."

Grayson stared at her a long moment, his eyebrows arching up toward his hairline. Then a deep rumble started in his chest. His shoulders shook and he started laughing so hard that tears rolled down his cheeks. Still chuckling and wiping away tears, he pushed back his chair and headed for the conference room door.

"Willow's going to love this one." He laughed again as he left the room.

Faith stared at the closed door, her eyes wide.

Asher turned in his chair to watch Grayson cross the war room below, his cell phone to his ear as he no doubt updated his wife about what had happened. "I hope this means we're not fired." He turned around. "Maybe we should have taken advantage of his amusement and went ahead and told him how much that GPR team cost."

"Oh, heck no." Faith stood. "We'll let that one slide in under the radar with the rest of the team's monthly expense reports and hope he never notices."

He stood and held the door open for her. "Now who's the coward?"

She lightly jabbed his stomach with her elbow, smiling at his grunt as she headed out the door.

He hurried to catch up to her as she descended the stairs. "Where are you off to so quickly? Got a hot date?"

"Yep. His name is Henry." She headed across the room to her desk and retrieved her work computer and purse from the bottom drawer.

"Ah. Your laptop. Henry Cavill. If you're going to name a piece of metal and plastic, couldn't you come up with something more exciting than the name of some scrawny actor? Cavill. Seriously. He's so two years ago."

"So is my laptop. Let me guess. You think I should have named it Asher?"

"It does have a nice sound to it."

She rolled her eyes and headed toward the open double doors just a few steps from the exit. Asher tagged along with her.

"I think you've rolled your eyes at me a hundred times today. It's getting a little old."

"Then maybe you should stop doing things that make me want to roll my eyes."

"Ouch."

A low buzzing sounded from her purse. She stopped at the building's main exit and pulled out her phone.

Asher moved to the door. "Sorry, princess. Are you waiting for me to open this for you? Allow me—"

"Wait." She stared at her phone, her face turning pale.

He stepped toward her, frowning. "What's wrong?"

In answer, she turned her phone around. "I had my News Alert app set to buzz if any local updates went out. This is from a local evening newsbreak."

Asher winced at the picture on the screen. "Poor Jasmine. Poor Jasmine's family. It was bad enough when the news vultures paraded her pictures on TV this afternoon. Here they are doing it again. We don't even have confirmation from the medical examiner that it's her. I mean, you and I both know it is, based on her jewelry and—"

"Asher. Look at that picture again."

He frowned and took the phone from her. Then he saw it, the name beneath the photo. He blinked. "No way."

Faith's eyes seemed haunted as she stared up at him. "The odds against this happening have to be astronomical. What the heck is going on? How is it even possible that a handful of hours after we find Jasmine Parks's body, her younger sister is abducted?"

Chapter Four

Faith yawned as she pulled into the parking lot of Unfinished Business the next morning. It had been a late night for her and Asher. Or, rather, an early morning. They hadn't left UB until after three. They'd pored over their files and explored the databases at UB's disposal to gather every bit of information that they could about Leslie Parks, the younger sister of Jasmine, who'd been only fifteen years old when Jasmine went missing. But nothing they'd found gave them a clue about who might have taken her. And they hadn't discovered anything to tie the two abductions together.

Other than the obvious—that they were sisters—their age difference meant their lives had been more or less separate and different. Leslie had been a sophomore in high school when Jasmine got her job bartending. It wasn't like they'd frequented clubs together or hung out with the same friends. That left two distinct possibilities.

Either whomever had abducted Leslie was a completely different person than the one who'd abducted Jasmine.

Or both abductors were the same person.

The first option seemed ludicrous even though it was technically possible.

The second was terrifying.

Had the person who'd taken Jasmine kept an eye on her

family all these years, waiting for the perfect opportunity to hurt them again? Had the perpetrator decided that he wanted to destroy the family's relief at finding their daughter's body by visiting more horror and pain on them? Faith couldn't even imagine the sick, evil mind of someone who'd want to do that.

She yawned again and pulled to a halt at the end of the third row. She'd never had problems finding a parking space here before. Unfinished Business was located near the top of Prescott Mountain, owned by Grayson Prescott, whose mansion was essentially the mountain's penthouse. No one else lived in this area and UB was the only business up here. People who came to UB were employees, law enforcement clients, or experts assisting them with their cases. So why was the parking lot full?

"Serves me right for sleeping late, I suppose." She sighed and drove her sporty Lexus Coupe out to the main road and parked on the shoulder. Just as she was getting out of her car, Asher's new black pickup truck pulled in behind her.

She leaned against her driver's door, waiting for him.

"Morning, Faith. Did your army-green toy car get a flat or something?" He eyed her tires and started toward the other side of her car.

"Just because you traded your old car for a shiny new truck doesn't mean you should make fun of my Lexus. It's metallic green, not army green. And the only reason it seems small to you is because you're so tall. It's perfect for a normal-size person."

He leaned over the other side. "I'm normal size. You're pint size." He winked then stopped in front of her. "No flat. What's the problem? Need me to wind up the hand crank on the engine?"

"Ha, ha. There's nowhere to park. The lot's full."

He glanced at her in surprise then scanned the lot behind them through a break in the trees. "Can't remember that ever happening before. Guess Russo brought more of his team than he said he would."

"I think it's more than that. Look at the placards around the license plates on some of those SUVs up close to the building. They name one of the big rental car companies. My guess is TBI sent a bunch of investigators, maybe even the FBI if Russo invited them in on the case. Six bodies discovered all at once lit a fire under law enforcement."

"That and a pushy local anchorwoman," he grumbled.

"I thought you liked all that makeup and hairspray?"

"I liked her curves, and those sexy stilettos. Doesn't mean I like *her*."

Faith laughed. "Then you're not as hopeless as I thought."

"Gee. Thanks."

She smiled and they headed through the lot toward the two-story, glass-and-steel office building perched on the edge of the mountain.

"Let's hope that fire gets them cooperating and working hard to find Leslie Parks before she ends up like her sister," Asher said.

"Let's hope. Maybe they'll let us in on the action to find Leslie since we've been investigating her sister's case for several months."

"I'm sure they will. Who else is better qualified? And finding her quickly is urgent."

Three hours later, Faith and Asher were forced to stand out of the way in the war room as the TBI director, Jacob Frost, and an army of TBI agents used the power of a warrant to confiscate Faith's and Asher's work laptops and their physical files and flash drives from their desks.

Fellow investigator, Lance Cabrera, and their team lead,

Ryland Beck, stood with them near the floor-to-ceiling wall of windows on one side of the cavernous room. Faith wasn't sure if they were there for moral support or to keep her and Asher from attacking the TBI guys. Other UB investigators—Ivy, Callum, Trent, Brice—tried to work at their desks amid the chaos. But from the way they kept glancing around, they were obviously distracted. How could they not be? The agents were like locusts, buzzing around and swarming the entire room.

"I'm so mad, I could spit." Faith glared at any TBI investigator dumb enough to glance her way as they ransacked her desk.

"Yeah, well," Asher said. "It is what it is."

"How can you be so nonchalant about this? They pick our brains in the conference room for hours, have us review every detail of our investigation. And then they shove a warrant in our faces and steal our files. On top of that, we're ordered not to work the case anymore. These idiots are going to use our hard work to give them a jumpstart. Then once they solve this thing and catch the bad guy and, hopefully, rescue Leslie, it will be all glory for them and nothing for us." She shifted her glare to Ryland. "Stop trying to edge in front of me as if you think I'm going to draw down on these guys. I'm not that stupid. I'm way outgunned."

His eyes widened. "You're outgunned? Is that the *only* reason you aren't pulling your firearm?"

"It's the main one," she practically growled.

He swore beneath his breath.

Lance laughed and clasped Ryland on the shoulder. "I think that's my cue to leave this to our fearless leader."

"Gee, thanks for the help," Ryland grumbled.

Lance only laughed again and headed to his desk.

Asher grinned. "Look on the bright side, Faith. With all of these suits on the case, and the resources they can bring to bear, they've got an excellent chance of solving this thing and rescuing Leslie. I don't like being pushed aside any more than you. But if it means saving a life, I'll bow out gracefully."

She put her hands on her hips. "Have you forgotten that the TBI worked Jasmine's case when it was fresh? And yet here we are, five years later, finding her body for them. What makes you think these yahoos will do any better with her little sister's disappearance?"

Ryland eyed Asher. "Gun-toting Annie Oakley here does have a point."

Asher's smile faded. "She does. Unfortunately." He glanced up at the glass-enclosed conference room at the top of the stairs on the far end of the room. "Grayson is still arguing with Russo and Frost about this hostile takeover. Maybe he'll make them see reason and keep UB involved."

A few moments later, Grayson yanked open the conference room door and strode to the stairs. His face was a study in anger as he took them two at a time to the ground floor.

Faith crossed her arms. "Looks like Russo and Frost saw reason." Her voice was laced with sarcasm. "Good call on that one, Asher."

"I can't be right all the time. It wouldn't be fair to you mere mortals."

She gave him the side-eye. "Careful. I'm in a really bad mood."

"Darlin', when are you not in a bad mood?"

Her eyes narrowed in warning.

"Follow me," Grayson ordered without slowing down as he passed them.

"O…kay," Asher said. "Come on, Faith. Ryland, where are you going? The boss said to follow him."

"I'm betting he meant the two of you. Good luck." He grinned and headed for his desk.

"Traitor," Faith called after him.

He waved at her from the safety of the other side of the room.

"That's it. I'm going to shoot him." Faith reached for her pants pocket.

Asher grabbed her arm and tugged her toward the door. "Shoot him later. The boss is waiting."

They rushed to catch up. Grayson was standing in the elevator across the lobby, texting on his phone and leaning against the opening to keep the door from closing. When they reached him, he gave them an impatient look as he put his phone away. "Nice of you to join me."

"My fault." Asher practically dragged Faith inside.

She said a few unsavory things to him, yanked her arm free, then immediately regretted it when it felt as if she'd ripped her skin off. "Ouch, dang it."

"Well, I didn't expect you to yank your arm or I'd have loosened my hold. I just didn't want you to jump out of the elevator and shoot anyone."

Grayson briefly closed his eyes, as if in pain, then punched the button for the basement level, one floor down. It was the only part of the building underground. But it had the absolute best views since the entire back glass wall looked out over the Smoky Mountains range.

In spite of that view, Faith could count on two hands the number of times she'd been down there. The basement was where the forensics lab was located, as well as the computer geeks. She didn't speak biology or chemistry and, other than knowing how to run her laptop, she didn't speak tech either. Well, unless she counted Asher. He reminded her of Clark Kent, about as bookish as they came but also tall, broad-shouldered and decent-looking. Okay, more than decent. He put both Clark Kent and his alter-ego to shame in the looks department. But Asher was the only person who spoke technology that was patient enough to word it so that it made sense to her. There just wasn't any reason for her to go down to the basement level and listen to other techies.

As the elevator opened, she looked out at the many doors on the far wall with some trepidation. "Grayson. Why are we here?"

She and Asher followed him as he strode down the hallway to the glass wall at the end.

"Where are we going?" she whispered to Asher.

"Since we passed the lab entrance and the storage rooms, I'm guessing the nerd lair."

She let out a bark of laughter then covered her mouth. This wasn't the time for laughing. Not when a young girl's life was at stake, if she was even still alive. And not when her own desk upstairs was being violated, her laptop stolen, more or less—warrant or no warrant. Just thinking about it had her blood heating again.

Grayson stopped at the last door and glanced at them over his shoulder. "Wait here."

When the door closed behind him, Faith whirled around. "What the heck?"

Asher shrugged as if he didn't have a care in the world and leaned against the wall beside the door, his long legs bracing him as he stared out at the mountains. His navy blue suit jacket hung open to reveal his firearm tucked in his shoulder holster. It had Faith longing to pull hers from the pocket of her black dress pants to head upstairs and set a few people straight. She eyed the elevator doors, wondering if she had enough time to do that before Grayson returned.

"Dang. Absolutely gorgeous," Asher said, recapturing her attention.

Since he was looking at her now, she blinked, not sure what to say.

He grinned and motioned at the windows. "We should make the IT department come upstairs to the war room and let us take over their subterranean paradise."

She glanced toward the view that she'd only barely noticed, then shook her head. "Nah. Too distracting. Grayson knew what he was doing when he put us facing the parking lot."

His grin widened as he continued to look her way. "Definitely distracting. I'll agree with that."

She shifted uncomfortably, her face heating. "Um, Asher, what are you—"

"The view." He motioned to the windows. "I agree it would be hard to focus on work with that to look at all day."

Her face heated with embarrassment. For a moment there, she'd misread him and thought he was actually flirting. Really flirting, not the teasing he normally did. She cleared her throat and leaned back against the opposite wall. "I wonder how the computer guys manage to maintain their focus."

"They don't strike me as the outdoors types. I doubt they even notice."

"I'm told they get used to it." Grayson stepped through the door that neither of them had noticed opening. Once again, he motioned for them to follow him to the elevator.

Faith gave Asher a puzzled look.

He shrugged, seemingly as perplexed as she felt. Before she could recover, he grabbed her hand and towed her after him.

Grayson leaned out the door. "You two coming or not?"

"Coming," they both said as they hurried inside.

"Where to now?" Faith asked.

Grayson's jaw tightened.

"Sorry, sorry. I've obviously aggravated you." She pressed the button for the first floor. Since the only thing on the second floor was the catwalk around the war room that led to Grayson's office and the large conference room, it was rare that anyone ever took the elevator to the second floor.

He sighed heavily. "I'm far more aggravated at the situation than at either of you. Russo shouldn't have called TBI without our liaison talking to them first so we could arrive at an agreement. Instead, he made his own arrangement with TBI, letting them wrestle our case away. I'd bet a year's profits from all of my companies that you two could figure out who this serial killer is way before those bureaucrats." He glanced first at her then at Asher. "That is, if you were allowed to work the case. Which, of course, you're not."

The elevator doors opened and he strode into the lobby. But instead of heading into the war room, he continued toward the exit.

Again, Faith and Asher hesitated, not sure whether they were supposed to follow him or not.

"Uh, boss," Asher said. "Did you want—"

"Hurry up." Grayson flung one of the double doors wide and jogged down the steps. At the bottom, he turned and looked up at them. "Faith, did you bring a purse today?"

She blinked. "Um, I'm female, so, duh." Her face heated. "I mean yes."

"Go get it."

"Go...what?"

Asher gently grasped her shoulders and turned her toward the building. "Get your purse, darlin'."

She sighed and hurried to the war room. The TBI jerks had finished ransacking her desk and had everything they were taking boxed up and on a dolly. Lucky for them, they weren't in punching range. After retrieving her purse, she headed outside.

"Where are you two parked?" Grayson asked when she reached the bottom of the steps.

Asher motioned toward the road. "We didn't leave UB until after three and both got here later than we intended this morning. There wasn't a single parking spot to be had. Both of us are on the shoulder of the road."

Grayson's jaw flexed. "They'd better hurry and get out of here while I'm still in a good mood."

Asher choked then coughed when Grayson frowned at him.

Grayson headed for the road, and this time they didn't hesitate to follow but were forced to jog to catch up. Once they reached Faith's car, she leaned against the driver's door, slightly out of breath. The fact that Asher, who'd jogged with her, wasn't even breathing hard had her regretting that she'd missed so many workouts to focus on the case these past few months.

"Boss, please," she said between breaths. "What's going on? Are we in trouble? Are you...are you firing us?"

For the first time that morning, he smiled. "Why would I fire two of my best investigators?"

Faith gave him a suspicious look. "You tell everyone they're you're best investigators."

"That's because it's true. I only hire the best. And, no, I'm not terminating your employment."

Asher leaned beside her against the side of the car. "Yesterday you were pretty upset when you found out we'd—"

Faith elbowed him in the ribs, not wanting him to remind their boss about a sore subject.

He frowned and rubbed his side.

Grayson chuckled, which had Faith even more confused.

"You two are *officially* ordered to stand down, to not investigate the Parks cold case in any way. The case, after all, belongs to Gatlinburg PD, and they've rescinded their request for us to work on it. We'll no longer have access to any of the physical evidence. That's all being transferred out of our lab back to Gatlinburg PD's property room, or TBI's, if they decide to take it into their custody. And all of the files are being stripped from your computers and the physical files confiscated. I'm supposed to ask whether either of you have any additional files, printed or electronic, at your homes."

Faith's face flushed with heat. "This is ridiculous, Grayson. We're not children, even if we tend to bicker back and forth. It's just how we are, like brother and sister."

Grayson's brows rose and he glanced sharply at Asher in question.

Asher cleared his throat. "Exactly. Brother and sister. You were saying, Grayson?"

Grayson hesitated then smiled again. "I was asking whether you have any files, because, *per our contract* with TBI and all the eastern Tennessee counties that we work with, we always defer to law enforcement regarding their cases. They remain the owners and can fire us at any time, which is what they're doing on this particular one. Therefore, *since Russo and Frost told me to ask you*, not to mention the warrant they got, I'm *required to do so*. Think very carefully before you answer because I have to pass your answer along to them. *Do you have any more files pertaining to the Parks case?*"

Faith tried to decipher the odd stresses he'd put on various words and phrases. Since when did he care if Russo told him to do something? Or even if he had talked a judge into giving him permission to take their data? Grayson always did what he felt was best, no matter what. It kind of went with the territory of being a billionaire and not worrying where your next paycheck was coming from.

She pictured her home office with reports and notes on the Parks case arranged in neat stacks on the top of her desk and filed in drawers. There was even a large map on the wall with the geographical profiling information they'd worked on. She probably had more documentation there than she had at UB. Still, there were quite a few files she didn't have copies of. If she wanted to sneak and continue to work the case, she'd have to spend considerable time reconstructing that missing data. But Grayson was ordering them to stop. Wasn't he?

"Faith?" Grayson prodded. "Nothing about the Parks case is at your home. Right?"

"To be completely honest, in my home office there—"

"Isn't anything on this case," Asher interjected. "Neither of us keeps copies of files at home. Ever."

That was a whopper of a lie, since they *all* kept information on active investigations at their homes to save time. Grayson knew that. It wasn't a secret. Having the data at home allowed them to jump on tips and take any documents they needed with them to conduct interviews or further their research without having to go to the office first.

Asher continued his lie. "Absolutely no notes, pictures, affidavits from witnesses, recordings of some of our interviews, maps, theories, plans for future interviews, or copies of any of the files that TBI confiscated here at UB." He gave Faith a hard look. "Isn't that right?"

She frowned. "Well, actually, it's—"

"Excellent," Grayson said. "I can truthfully tell Russo and the TBI that you told me that you don't have anything related to the Parks investigation outside of the office. I hope you're beginning to understand the situation."

Faith blinked, the lightbulb finally going off beneath Asher's hard stare. "As a matter of fact, it's suddenly becoming clear, sir. Confusing, but clear. If that makes sense."

"Glad to hear it. We've been ordered to no longer work this investigation. If we do, we could suffer legal consequences. All of us. And the future of UB could be at risk." He frowned and glanced back at the building. "Or, at least, the way that UB operates today, with quite a bit of control leveraged by those we contract with."

His look had hardened and he mumbled something else beneath his breath that had Faith thinking he was already revamping their future contracts in that business-savvy brain of his.

He smiled again. "We all know what a...*stellar* job the TBI and Gatlinburg PD do with cold cases. I'm *officially* ordering both of you to stand down. Again, do we understand each other?"

Since the whole reason UB existed was that Gatlinburg PD and TBI *hadn't* done a great job and Grayson's first wife's murder had gone unsolved for years, Faith definitely understood him now. "Crystal clear, sir."

Asher nodded his agreement. "Loud and clear. Sometimes Faith is a little slow but she catches up eventually."

Grayson laughed. "You're going to pay for that remark."

"He certainly is." She glared her displeasure.

"I can handle her."

She gasped with outrage.

"Hold that thought." Grayson took out his wallet and handed Faith a platinum-colored credit card. The thing was heavy and actually made of metal. She'd never seen a credit card that fancy before. "As compensation for this disappointment, I'm sending both of you on vacation. Use that card for anything you need. Don't file expense reports or contact anyone else at UB about your...vacation. After all, the police and TBI might be here off and on while working the Parks investigation. I wouldn't want you interfering with that in any way. Still clear?"

They both nodded.

"Take however much time you need. When you feel like you might want to come back, for whatever reason, rather than come to UB, come up to the house. In fact, I'd appreciate it if you check in with me every now and then with a status of your...vacation."

Faith stared at the credit card in her hand. It was probably the kind with no spending limit. The kind people used to purchase multimillion-dollar yachts without blinking an eyelash. Her hand shook as she carefully tucked the card into her purse and zipped it closed.

"One more thing." He reached into a suit jacket pocket and held up a flash drive. "Since you'll be out of the office for a while, I had IT put copies of some upcoming cases on there, just in case you wanted to review them before coming back to work."

Asher swiped the flash drive before Faith could. "Thanks, boss. We'll take it from here. We won't come back to UB until you tell us to."

"Enjoy your vacations. And be discreet."

Asher pressed a hand to his chest as if shocked. "Discretion is my motto."

Faith snorted. "More like your kryptonite. Don't worry, Grayson. I'll keep him in line." She quirked a brow. "I can handle him."

Asher grinned.

"See that you do." With that, Grayson strode toward the building.

Faith eyed the flash drive in Asher's hand. "What do you

think's really on that? Obviously something about the Parks case, but what?"

"Backups. Every night IT backs up the network."

"How do you know that?"

"I know a lot of things you'd be surprised about. I'm not just a handsome face."

She laughed.

He rested an arm on top of her car, facing her. "If I'm right, everything that TBI just took away has now been given back to us. I hope you didn't have visions of white sandy beaches and views of sparkling emerald-green water dancing in your head. This is a working vacation. We're going to secretly continue the Parks investigation. And, hopefully, we'll figure out the killer's identity in time to send an anonymous tip to the police so they can rescue Leslie."

Faith snatched the flash drive. "My house is closer than yours."

Chapter Five

Asher stepped inside Faith's foyer with her then moved into the family room while she locked the front door.

"Ash!" Suddenly his arms were filled with soft, warm curves as a young woman threw herself against him. "It's been too long." She squealed as she continued to hug him.

"Uh, hey, Daph. Need to breathe here," he teased as he gently extricated himself from her grasp. Just in time, too, because Faith was now glaring at him from beside her younger sister. "If I'd known you were home from that joke you call a university, I'd have come over much sooner."

"Hey, my Tennessee Vols can smash your Memphis Tigers any day."

"Says the sophomore who still hasn't been to her first football game."

Daphne rolled her blue eyes, reminding him of Faith, who tended to roll her eyes when she was exasperated—which was often. But where Daphne's eyes were blue, Faith's were sparkling emerald-green that lit up whenever she smiled. And even though she and her sister both had blonde hair, Faith's was darker, a shade she called dirty blonde. Asher called it pretty.

"I don't have to go to boring games to show school spirit."

He laughed. "I suppose not. Why aren't you in Knoxville? I thought you were taking classes over the summer semester."

"Finals finished up a week ago and I have another week before summer classes start. I figured I'd catch up with some friends and grace my big sis with my amazing presence."

It was Faith's turn to roll her eyes.

"I head back a week from tomorrow," Daphne continued. "I told Faith to tell you I was home."

"I must have forgotten." Faith's tone clearly said she *hadn't* forgotten. "And his name is Asher, not Ash. Want a soda anyone? Water?" As if deciding the crisis of Asher holding her sister had passed, she moved into the kitchen area and opened the refrigerator.

"I'm good," Daphne said. "I know Ash would like a high-test soda. But since you only have diet drinks around here, get him a water."

Asher chuckled. A cold bottle of diet cola was soon thrust into his hands.

"Asher doesn't drink the hard stuff anymore," Faith said. "He's trying to watch his weight." She stood beside her sister, a water bottle clutched in her right hand.

"That can't be true, Ash. You hiding some extra pounds beneath that suit jacket?" Daphne started to run a hand down his flat stomach.

Faith knocked her hand away. "We have work to do. I thought you were meeting some of your high school buddies for lunch."

Daphne's eyes widened and she pulled her phone out of her jeans' pocket to check the time on the screen. "Shoot. They'll be here soon to pick me up. I need to finish getting ready. Don't worry, Ash. I'll say bye before I leave." She waved at him and headed down the hallway toward the back of the house.

As soon as Daphne was out of earshot, Faith said, "Leave my sister alone."

"Whatever do you mean? We were just catching up."

"She's jailbait. Don't. Touch."

"I think you're confused about what that word means. Daphne's twenty, a legal adult."

"I'm not confused at all about the definition of jailbait. It means that if you touch her, I'm going to jail. Because I'll shoot you."

He chuckled. "Careful, darlin'. Your jealousy is showing."

"I'm serious, *Ash*. My sister is off limits. It would make things too…awkward working with you."

He leaned down to her, enjoying the way her eyes widened and her breath hitched in her throat. True to her stubborn personality, she refused to back away, which was what he'd counted on. When his lips were mere inches from hers, and her expression had softened from anger to confusion, he turned his face to the side and whispered in her ear.

"You going to stand there all day, Faith? We have work to do."

He headed for her home office on the front right side of the house, chuckling when he heard her swearing behind him and jogging to catch up.

Seeing the empty spot in the middle of the incredibly neat and organized stacks of paper on her desk, he paused and turned around. "Organized chaos, as usual. But also kind of bare-looking without your work laptop to put there."

"TBI jerks." She paused beside him. "I'll have to dig up Daphne's old laptop, the one she ditched after I bought her a new one for school. Hopefully, I can find a power cord that fits."

"I still can't believe you never use a personal computer when you aren't working. Everyone has a computer in this century."

"It keeps me sane not going anywhere near one when I'm

not working. I'm a TV girl in the evenings. It's called relaxing, recharging. You should try it. You work way too hard."

"Maybe you can teach me this TV concept—after we do everything we can to save Leslie."

She blinked, her eyes suspiciously bright. "Poor Leslie. She's twenty, Daphne's age. Just two years younger than her sister when she disappeared. She has to be so scared. Assuming he hasn't already—"

"He hasn't. I don't think so, anyway. If it's the same guy who took Jasmine, then he's toying with the family. He'll keep her alive long enough to send them pictures or a token of some sort to prove he has her, so he can cause them more pain. If it's not the same guy, it could be a copycat. He heard about the first daughter on the news and decided to go for his fifteen minutes of fame by taking the other daughter. Again, if that's the case, I would think he'd keep her alive until he milks all the attention out of this that he can get. Either way, I choose to believe that we have some time. Not a lot, but we might have enough to find her before it's too late."

"That's not usually the case in abductions, especially if it's an abduction by a stranger."

"True. But with all the media attention on this one, it's automatically different. The statistics don't talk to this particular situation. I say we have a chance."

"I pray you're right. The odds of finding anyone alive more than a few hours after being taken like this are abysmal."

"But not zero."

Her smile was barely noticeable, but a smile nonetheless. "Not zero." She squeezed his hand in thanks before looking down at the stacks of paper on her desk.

He let out a slow breath and focused on not revealing how that touch, that barely-there-smile, affected him. She didn't think about him the way he did about her. There was no changing it. And even if he were to try, now was the worst possible time.

She rifled through one of the stacks of paper, somehow managing to keep it aligned and neat at the same time. "To believe it's the same guy who abducted Jasmine, we have to accept that he's stayed in the area all this time. That supports your theory that her abductor was a local. Of course, that burial ground we discovered pretty much confirms it, unless all of the victims there were part of a spree of killings done years ago and the killer moved on somewhere else. Maybe he was just passing through, if that's what killers like him do. Someone completely unrelated to the original incident abducted Leslie. Coincidence."

"That's a hell of a coincidence." He leaned against a corner of the desk, careful not to disturb her papers, and crossed his arms.

"Yeah. It would be. Let's toss that aside for now, assume he *is* local, is still around."

"Same guy."

She nodded. "Same guy who killed Jasmine. Although, we're making leaps of logic without evidence. We don't have confirmation from the medical examiner that we've found Jasmine among all those bodies." She shivered and ran her hands up and down her arms. "If it wasn't for the media, no one would even realize that we suspect Jasmine is among the dead. The timing of Leslie's abduction is too quick, just a few hours after the first media report that mentioned Jasmine. That makes me think this really is a crazy, devastating coincidence. Lightning doesn't strike twice in the same place." Her eyes were unfocused, her thoughts directed more inward than on anything in front of her.

"World War Two, the Sullivan brothers."

She frowned and looked up. "The Sullivan brothers?"

"Five brothers who all died in 1942 during the Second World War. Lightning does sometimes strike twice in the same place. Or *more* than twice in the Sullivan case."

"And this is why I'm not a history buff. Stories like that are too depressing."

He smiled. "I'll try to keep my depressing historical references to a minimum in the future."

She smiled, too, the shadows of grief lessening in her eyes. "It's actually impressive how much trivia you store in that amazing brain of yours."

He waggled his eyebrows and flipped his suit jacket open, resting his hands on his belt. "If you think my brain's amazing, you should see my—"

She lightly tapped his arm. "Stop it. You're such a guy. Be back in a few. *If* I can find that dang computer and the cord." She hurried from the room.

He sighed at her inability to see him as more than a friend. His jokes fell flat, his lamebrain attempts to get her to see him as…more, never seemed to gain traction. He was about to sit in one of the two office chairs that Faith kept behind the desk because they worked together so much, but Daphne entered the office.

"'You're such a guy,'" she mimicked her sister. "The woman's blind. You need to jump her bones before you're both in retirement homes."

He coughed to cover a laugh. "And you need to quit stirring the pot. Faith doesn't think about me in that way. I doubt she ever will."

"Then do something to open her eyes. Something outrageous. I'm no longer living at home. She can't use me as an excuse to make *you* go home when you're here working late.

There's absolutely nothing to stop you two from going at it like rabbits except that she's an idiot."

He coughed again, nearly choking at her amusing audacity. "Daphne, you really do need to stop—"

The sound of footsteps on the hardwood floor outside the office heralded Faith's return. After setting a power cord and a bright pink laptop on the desk, she hesitated, eyes narrowed suspiciously as she glanced back and forth between them. "Why did you both stop talking when I came into the room? What's going on?"

"Nothing. Unfortunately." Daphne winked at Asher then pulled her sister close for a quick hug and kissed her cheek.

Faith stepped back, a serious look on her face. "No barhopping. It's too dangerous. Come back here if you and your friends want to drink. If the worst should happen, leave bread crumbs—not actual bread, of course, but some kind of clue to help me find you. You're going to the mall, right?"

"The mall? Seriously? I'm not sixteen anymore. And it's not barhopping, it's plain, clean, having fun. Everyone goes to bars—men, women, young people, old people. It's a place to unwind, catch up, stop off on your way home. You really need to loosen up."

"Daphne—"

"Relax, smother-mother. I wouldn't want you to have a heart attack worrying about me. We're just going to a movie." She wiggled her fingers at Asher. "Have fun, you two. Don't do anything I wouldn't do."

Faith shook her head as her sister jogged out the office door. "Don't stay out too late. Text me once you get there and before you leave. And make sure that Find My Exasperating Sister app is turned on this time."

Daphne raised a hand in the air without looking back. A

moment later, the sound of the front door closing had Faith letting out a deep sigh.

"She's going to be the death of me."

He shoved his hands in his pants pockets, mainly to keep from doing something dangerous—like pulling Faith in for a hug. "If you get this worried when she's in town with people she knows, how do you survive when she's at school with thousands of strangers?"

She shuddered. "Don't remind me. It's hard, harder than you can imagine. She's like my own kid. I practically raised her."

In spite of his misgivings about her potential reaction, the lost look on her face had him taking her hand in his. "You were about her age now when your parents died, weren't you?"

She nodded, tightening her hand in his rather than pulling away, probably not even realizing it. But he felt that touch all the way to his heart, and only wished she'd accept more.

"She was a preteen, a baby in my eyes. I'm surprised my whole head hasn't gone gray just getting her to this stage. I'll probably never have children of my own. The worrying would likely kill me."

"Oh, I don't know. Maybe if you ever meet the right guy, you'll change your mind."

She shook her head. "Fat chance of that. I'm always working or trying to recover from working by bingeing TV shows. Heck, I spend more time with you than anyone else. When would I ever have a chance to meet a guy?" She chuckled and tugged her hand free. "Come on. We've—"

"Got work to do. I know." His heart was a little heavier as they rounded the desk.

Chapter Six

Faith smiled as Asher walked into the office several hours later carrying a plate of sandwiches, a bottle of water for her and a diet cola for him. "You're going to make some lucky woman an amazing husband someday. She'll enjoy being waited on. You certainly spoil me."

He gave her an odd look then smiled, making her wonder what that look meant. "Make any breakthroughs while I was slaving away in the kitchen?" He set the plate and drinks down to one side, away from the color-coded folders and papers on the desk.

"Not yet. I can't believe it's been…" She glanced at the time display on her phone on the corner of her desk and grimaced. "Over four hours since we started researching Leslie Parks and we still don't have a clue about what happened to her. It would help if TBI and Gatlinburg PD weren't so stingy about sharing their info. If it wasn't for the news reports, we wouldn't even know that she was abducted from her home."

"Speaking of news reports, the TBI press conference is supposed to start soon." He took the remote from one of her desk drawers and turned on the TV beside the massive map on the far wall that they'd used when trying to find Jasmine's grave.

After turning on closed captioning and muting the sound,

he took the largest of the two ham and cheese sandwiches he'd made and enthusiastically began scarfing down his very late lunch, or early dinner since it was past four in the afternoon.

Faith shook her head. "I don't know how you don't get fat."

"Why?" he asked around a mouthful. "It's just a sandwich. No chips or cookies."

She motioned toward hers. "Twice the size of my sandwich and you're a third of the way through in one massive bite."

He took a drink before answering. "I'm hungry. Besides, I'm twice your size. Of course, I eat twice what you do. I'm surprised you don't blow away in a strong wind. I'll be even more surprised if you finish half of your sandwich."

She took a large bite just to prove him wrong and then promptly ruined her point by choking on her food.

He laughed and pounded her back until she waved him away, begging for mercy. Her eyes were watering as she coughed in between laughs.

Finally, she drew her first deep breath and wiped her eyes. "Serves me right for trying to compete with you."

"I'll always win," he promised. "No matter what the contest."

"I'm pretty sure there are more ticks in my win column than yours right now."

He shook his head. "No way. You still owe me over our bet about that anchorwoman."

"Dang. I forgot about that. I guess we're eating steak tonight. Well, maybe not tonight. Not with it this late already. And time's our enemy with Leslie missing."

His expression turned serious. "Rain check. Definitely. Hopefully, by this time tomorrow, we'll—"

"Asher. Turn up the sound. The press conference is starting."

He grabbed the remote. "Look at Frost, front and center.

Always wants to preen for the cameras, even when he has nothing to say."

"The camera loves him just as much as he loves it," she admitted.

He gave her the side-eye. "If you like the stoop-shouldered, gray-haired, senior type, I suppose."

She laughed. "He has a sprinkling of gray, enough to make him look debonair. And he's not a senior or stoop-shouldered."

"If you say so."

About ten minutes later, he held up the remote. "Heard enough of this nonsense?"

"Definitely."

He muted the sound again. "In spite of all their talking, what they actually have is a big fat nothing."

"That's my take, too," she said. "Basically all they did was confirm what we already knew—that she was abducted from her home. The abductor sure is bold."

"Calm, cool, able to snatch a young woman from her house in broad daylight without anyone noticing. That's not the act of a first-timer. He's confident, patient. I guarantee he's done this before."

She sat back beside him, arms crossed. "That supports the theory that he's the same perpetrator who took Jasmine. Five years later, more mature, confident, experienced."

"Agreed. Maybe we've been going at this all wrong. We've been approaching it like we do all our cases, trying to gather as many facts about the victim as we can and build a time-line. That hasn't gotten us anywhere and it's what TBI and Gatlinburg PD are doing—Investigation 101—by the book. Let's throw the book away, make a leap in logic. We already assumed that Jasmine was one of the bodies. Let's assume we also know we're dealing with the same perpetrator and see where that takes us."

"What if we're wrong and we waste time chasing that theory?"

"Then we'll be no worse off than we are now. We have nothing to show for all the hours we've been working. Come on. Grayson wanted us to work on this because we know the case. Let's use that experience, jump in where we were on Jasmine's investigation and see where it leads."

She sat straighter. "You're saying build off our geographical profiling we were already working on."

"Absolutely. If it's the same guy, then he's lost his favorite burial grounds. He needs somewhere new. A place he can take his victim that's secluded, quiet, and offers options for… whatever he wants to do."

She rubbed her hands up and down her arms again. "A place where he can dispose of the body, too, just like we theorized in Jasmine's case."

"A theory that proved true. Same guy, same—"

"Habits," she said, feeling more enthusiastic now.

He pushed back from the desk. "I'll get the map."

"I'll clear some space."

He strode across the room and carefully pulled the three-foot-wide map off the wall where they'd taped it months earlier.

She stacked their papers and folders into neat piles on the floor.

He grinned as he waited. "Even when you're in a hurry, you're organized."

"Cleanliness is next to godliness." She frowned. "Wait. Wrong quote." She shrugged, brushed a few crumbs off the desk and then dumped them in the garbage can while he smoothed out the map on top.

"Colored pens?" he asked.

"Here, on my side." She opened the bottom left drawer

and selected two markers. "Red this time? We used blue for Jasmine."

"Works for me." He took one and they both got on their knees on their chairs and leaned over the map. "We know the Parks live at the same address as they did when Jasmine went missing. So we can start with a red circle around that."

She drew a large circle around the house that already had a blue circle from when they began noting areas where the first sister had been known to frequent. "I wish we had time to talk to our convicts again."

"Let's cross our fingers that we can use the same reasoning they told us about to think like Leslie's abductor. Our theory is it's the same guy, so he'd have the same thought process."

"Right. Scary to make all these assumptions without facts, but I'm game to try." She drew another red circle around a horse ranch business for taking people on trail rides in the Smoky Mountains foothills.

He seemed surprised by what she'd circled. "Stan's Smoky Mountains Trail Rides. We talked through all the tourist traps when making our first pass on the map for Jasmine. I can't imagine Leslie's abductor trying to sneak her past people lining up for trail rides."

"We're trying to think outside the box, right? The TBI and police are covering the box. They're following standard protocols, performing *knock and talks*, canvassing Leslie's neighborhood trying to find someone who saw something out of place, noticed some stranger in an unfamiliar car, that kind of thing. We did all that with Jasmine and found nothing. No one in her neighborhood or even the immediate surrounding area had any useful information to help with the investigation."

He was starting to look as enthusiastic as she was feeling. "You're saying skip all that, because we covered it once already, again assuming we have the same perpetrator. We cover the places outside law enforcement's current search zone, places they won't get to anytime soon."

"Now we're on the same wavelength again." She tapped the circle she'd just drawn. "This place seems promising to me. It's not all that far from the burial site and yet has many similarities. Familiar types of surroundings and advantages could place this in the killer's comfort zone. That's what the convicts told us, that they typically had specific types of territories they considered theirs, places where they felt secure. That's where they hunted."

"And where they buried their dead."

She grimaced but nodded her agreement.

He ran his fingertips across the map, exploring the topography symbols that showed many of the waterfalls in the area, major trails, elevations of the various foothills and mountains. It also showed the roads in the vicinity of the stables. "I rarely go out that way, don't even remember this place. It's not on a main thoroughfare between Gatlinburg and Pigeon Forge, or any other towns. There wouldn't be much traffic to worry about. And there should be pull-offs since it's in the foothills, safe places where someone can park their car to take pictures of the mountains."

"Places where a killer could pull off the main road and no one would think anything of it. He could park in one of those and walk Leslie onto the trail-riding land."

He considered the map again then gave her a skeptical look. "Theoretically, sure. But the land around that ranch has rough terrain, steep climbs. I don't see anyone making it up those foothills without a horse, which is kind of the point of running a trail-riding business there. Leslie's picture is all over the news. Her abductor wouldn't want to risk someone seeing him try to lead her into the mountains. The weather is mild today, perfect for sightseeing or riding. That place has to be crawling with tourists right now, even if it is getting late in the day. I say we skip the horse ranch and look down this main road for something more appealing to our killer. Someplace more isolated."

"I'd agree with you, except that today is Wednesday. This particular business is only open on weekends. No tourists to worry about."

He arched a brow. "You sound sure about that. I know you didn't call them to schedule yourself a trail ride. You hate horses."

"I don't hate them. They hate me."

"You got bucked off as a kid and stepped on once as a teenager. Deciding all horses hate you because of those two minor incidents is rather extreme."

"Minor? You should have seen the bruises I had from being thrown. They lasted for weeks. And the beast who stepped on my foot broke two bones. It still hurts sometimes, all these years later."

He grinned. "One of these days I'll get you on a horse again and you'll change your mind."

"No way. Unlike you, I didn't grow up around them. And I don't intend to do anything to change that going forward."

"Back to my original question. Why do you know so much about this place?"

"Daphne's been visiting, remember? She went trail riding with some of her friends last week. I did some of the research for her, called around, made the reservations. She didn't want to wait for a weekend, so we marked this place off her list. She ended up at a place in Pigeon Forge."

"Makes sense. What doesn't make sense is for a trail-riding business to only be open two days a week. Seems like they'd lose a ton of money limiting their options like that in a town that lives and dies by the tourism dollar."

"I asked Stan Darden, the owner, about that when I called. He said he and his son, Stan Darden Junior, used to run the place seven days a week. But the father is retiring and downsizing. It's just the two of them now during the week, taking care of the remaining horses. They have others who help on weekends, earning enough for him to help offset the maintenance costs. That's the only reason he keeps it open anymore, so he can afford to keep his horses."

"I wonder what the son thinks about his dad essentially letting the business die instead of giving it to him. Regardless, I agree we should take a look. With only the two Stans around during the week, our perpetrator could easily park down the road, like we said, walk Leslie onto the property, maybe staying in the tree line on the peripheral edge. Once he's out of sight of the main house and doesn't see any activity at the stables, maybe he takes her into an empty stall or tack room. If he's comfortable with horses, he could even take a couple out and escape into the foothills with her. The roadblocks the state police likely have on the main highways in and out of the area won't stop someone on horseback from escaping through the woods. How far is this place from the Parkses' residence?"

"About twenty minutes, like where he took Jasmine. It's just in a different direction from her home. But get this—it's only five minutes from his makeshift cemetery, in the same geographical area where he feels comfortable. If TBI or the local cops aren't considering this ranch, I believe we should."

"Agreed."

She wrote a note on the map, naming the ranch as their first place of interest. "What other promising locations should we focus on?" She ran her finger on the map down the road past the trail-riding place, studying the names and descriptions they'd put on it earlier. "Maybe this house here. It's isolated. No neighbors anywhere around to speak of. I can search property records, see if it's occupied full-time or a vacation rental. It's one of the places we were going to research next for Jasmine if the scent dog hadn't hit on our original location."

When he didn't respond, she glanced at him. He seemed to be lost in thought as he stared at the map, his brows drawn down in concentration.

"Faith to Asher, come in. What's going on in that brilliant but math-challenged mind of yours?"

"What?" He glanced up, seemingly surprised. "Oh…the stables. There's something bothering me about those." He drummed his fingers on the table. "Stables. Horses. I heard something earlier, somewhere."

"About horses?"

He nodded. "I can't remember where, or why…wait. The news. That's it." He grabbed the remote control.

"What, Asher? Tell me."

"The press conference, after it was over. There was a story on the ticker the news runs along the bottom of the TV about some stables. But I didn't pay attention to what it said." He pressed the rewind button until the feed was at the end of the press conference. Then he fast-forwarded and reversed several times, frowning at the TV. "Yes, there." He pressed Play.

She stared up at the screen, reading the captions. "Blah, blah, blah…okay, same stables I circled. A horse broke out of its pen this morning. They're warning motorists in that area to be careful in case the horse wanders onto the road."

"Not exactly, darlin'. *Two* horses went missing."

She frowned. "Okay, two. But they said the horses broke out of a pen. They didn't say *went missing*."

"No. They didn't. *I'm* saying it. What if they didn't break out? What if someone *took* them and made it look like the horses escaped on their own? Not long after Leslie was abducted?"

She checked their notes on the map, around the red circles, the distances between them. "When did the horse thing happen?"

"Early this morning. The owner, or whoever was checking on the horses, realized they were gone around ten."

She stared at him. "Leslie went missing just after nine. Twenty minutes from the horse place."

He smiled. "Stables."

"Whatever. That's enough time for our perpetrator to drive there—if they did go to this place—leave his car on a pull-off, steal the horses and—"

"Force her at gunpoint or knifepoint to ride up into the foothills. He doesn't have to know the area. The horses do. They're trained to follow the trails. Once he gets high enough, far enough, he could go off-trail, take her somewhere isolated where no one ever goes."

They both stared down at the map, considering the possibilities, talking about other potential hiding places. But they kept coming back to the stables.

"It's a long shot," he said. "We have no evidence either way, just supposition."

"And it assumes the killer is comfortable with horses."

"He's comfortable outdoors, has been in this area for years. It's not a huge leap to assume he could be familiar with horses given that there are so many horse-riding businesses around the Smokies. But, honestly, even a novice could handle a trail horse. That's the whole point. They're docile and trail-trained so tourists who've never sat on a horse before are safe around them. Once you're on their back, they practically guide themselves."

"You'd still need a saddle. A novice wouldn't know how to put one on. I sure wouldn't."

"If he chose this place, he either has the background to prep the horses or—"

"He forced one of the ranch hands to do it. Or, I guess it would be the son, or father, since they're the only ones there during the week."

He shook his head. "That didn't happen or the news would have said that. They always go with the most sensational story angle. Someone being forced to saddle some horses would definitely be a bigger story than a small note about motorists watching out for horses on the loose. I'm a transplant around here. Horses didn't escape all that often where we lived, if ever. You've told me your family visited here a lot on vacations. How common is it for this kind of thing to happen? Ever heard of that on the Gatlinburg news before?"

She stood. "No. Never. We need to check this out. Now. We should call the TBI. Let them handle it. Goodness knows they can wrestle up a lot more manpower than we can to search for her. Maybe they can get a chopper up and—"

"Scare Leslie's horse into plunging down the side of a mountain? A trail horse is docile, but it's still a horse. A chopper could spook it. Regardless, do you honestly think the TBI would put even one person on this if we called? What would we tell them? That we're working a case we're not supposed to be working? That we drew some circles on a map and guessed that some horses that got out of their stalls *might* have been taken by the bad guy? With absolutely no proof whatsoever? What do you think they'd do with that information?"

She frowned. "They'd laugh us off the phone. Then they'd complain to Grayson that we broke the rules of UB's contract with law enforcement, not to mention the warrant. They'd try to get us fired. Or worse, arrest us."

"And while they're comparing jock straps to see whose is bigger, Leslie is all alone with a serial killer. Maybe she's at these stables, maybe not. But so far, that's our best educated guess. If Leslie was Daphne, what would you do?"

She grabbed her purse from near one of the stacks on the floor. "You drive. I'll call Grayson."

Chapter Seven

As Asher's truck bumped along the pot-holed gravel road into Stan's Smoky Mountains Trail Rides, he shook his head in disgust.

Faith straightened in the passenger seat from studying their map. "You see something?"

"Neglect. That barn on the left must house the stables. Doesn't look like it's seen a paintbrush in decades. Paddocks beside it are muddy and full of weeds. Only thing to recommend this place is that pond and the gorgeous waterfall coming down from those foothills at the end of the pasture. It's probably a great location for selfies. Tourists might come here just for that, especially if there are more falls up the mountain where they go trail riding. As for everything else, run-down is a nice way to describe it. Look at the fence around the pasture. Half the rails are broken or missing, with large gaps between a lot of the posts. No wonder some horses got out. It's probably not the first time."

"So much for our theory that the killer stole them."

"I still want to talk to the owner, get his take on it. If he's home."

"I doubt it," she said. "I must have called him five times on the way here. It rolls to voice mail."

"Doesn't surprise me that he doesn't bother checking his messages all that often. By the looks of this place, I don't think this Stan Darden guy is all that worried about attracting new business."

"He answered when I called last week. Maybe that was lucky timing on my part."

Asher's hands tightened on the steering wheel. "Or maybe something has happened to him."

Her worried gaze met his. She folded the map and put it in the console between their seats. "I'm guessing that building off to the right is the office. Might double as their house too. None of the other outbuildings seem big enough for anything besides storage."

Sure enough, when he pulled his truck up to the small, weathered, single-story building, a rusty sign on the faded blue door proclaimed it as the Office.

He cut the engine and popped open his door. "You want to call about that place down the road you marked on the map? Find out if it's occupied or not while I see if someone will answer the door? We can check the other place when we're done here."

"If we don't find Leslie."

"If we don't find Leslie, yes. You said Grayson was sending Lance to help us search. Can you call him first, get an ETA?"

She pulled her phone from her pants pocket. "Will do."

By the time he reached the office door, his boots were mired in mud and the hems of his dress pants were suffering the same fate. He sorely regretted not changing out of his suit before they'd headed out here. But that would have meant a trip to his house, in the opposite direction. They didn't have time for that.

He tried the doorknob, but it was locked, which made sense since the place only did trail rides on weekends. But if this was also their residence, he'd expect to see some dirt or mud on the front stoop from them going in and out. The stoop was one of the few things around that seemed clean.

Maybe Stan Senior and Stan Junior were both in the stables and hadn't taken a phone with them. Seemed odd, but if they were mucking stalls, the possibility of a phone falling and getting dirty or even trampled by a horse might make them think twice about taking it along. That would explain them not answering Faith's calls on the way here. They could even be in town, maybe enjoying an early dinner. There weren't any vehicles parked on the property, at least from what they'd seen driving up.

Several knocks later bore no results. The place was quiet, seemingly deserted. He stepped to the only window on the front and tried to peer between the slats of the blinds. They'd been turned facing up, no doubt for privacy. All he could make out was the ceiling fan's blades slowly turning. Looking back at the truck, he motioned to Faith that he was going to take a circuit around the building.

As he walked the perimeter, he checked for any signs that would indicate that someone had been there recently. Everything appeared to be in order, no evidence of a break-in, no trampled-down grass.

When he hopped back inside the truck, he said, "It doesn't appear that anyone's been here in the last few days."

"Someone had to have been at the stables this morning to report the horses missing."

"If they were, they didn't go to the office. Keep a careful eye out. Nothing we've found so far rules out that our perpetrator took the horses."

His jaw tightened as the truck bumped across the gravel toward the dilapidated barn. "I sure hope the owner takes better care of his animals than he does his property. Did you find anything out about the place down the road that we want to check?"

"I spoke to the owner and his wife, who live there full time. Neither of them have seen anything unusual. And they have dogs, lots of them, by the sound of the barking in the background. Mr. Pittman, the husband, said the dogs run loose on his property. If anyone had been out there, he'd have known about it."

"We can probably move that place lower on our list of potential spots then. What about Lance?"

"He's on his way. But he won't be here for another forty-five minutes or so."

"Forty-five? He doesn't live that far from this place, fifteen minutes at the most if he takes the highway route."

"He was out of town conducting an interview when Grayson called and told him to come back. The rest of our team is either at UB or working other critical investigations. Do you want me to ask Grayson to send someone else?"

Asher thought about it then shook his head. "No. I'm sure Grayson weighed priorities when he assigned Lance to help. No doubt TBI and Gatlinburg PD are all over him right now and he has to be careful with appearances in regard to Leslie's case. Lance is the right guy for this. He and I go riding every now and then. If we do end up on horseback in the mountains, he'll be an asset."

Her slight intake of breath had him glancing at her as he parked by the barn. "You okay?"

"Um, fine. I just…didn't think about us actually, you know—"

"Riding a horse?"

"Yeah. That."

He smiled. "If we find evidence to support our theory that the bad guy might have taken Leslie up into the foothills above this place, how did you think we were going to go after him?"

"I guess I didn't think that far ahead." She drew another shaky breath.

He gently squeezed her hand. "Don't stress over that possibility. Let's take it a step at a time and see if we find evidence to lead us in that direction. Okay?"

She gave him a weak smile.

He led her along the least muddy, cleanest path he could find to the entrance but she was still cursing up a storm by the time they stopped.

"Why didn't we change into jeans before we left?" she grumbled. "These pants are ruined."

"You can take them off if you want. I don't mind."

She laughed. "You're impossible. And, no, I'm certainly not going to walk around a bunch of smelly animals bare-assed."

His throat tightened. "Does that mean you're not wearing any—"

"It *means* mind your own business. You're not getting me to take off my pants."

He couldn't help grinning at the embarrassed flush on her face.

"Shouldn't we be looking for shoe prints, or something?" Without waiting for his reply, she stomped into the building.

Asher chuckled and followed her inside.

She hesitated a few feet in, her nose wrinkling. "That smell. Ugh. I don't know what Daphne likes about horses. This same smell was all over her when she got home after riding with her friends the other day. Took two cycles in the washing machine to get rid of it."

"It's the smell of freedom. The freedom to go anywhere you want, see the sights, enjoy nature as it was meant to be enjoyed."

"I can enjoy it just fine with my two feet on the ground. And no horsey odor."

He laughed.

A shadow moved off to their right. He and Faith immediately drew their guns, pointing down the darkened aisle between two rows of stalls. There was a tall, brawny man standing in the shadows, a horse not far behind him.

"Show yourself," Asher demanded.

"Whoa, hold it. Don't shoot." He stepped into the light shining through the open door of the main entrance, his jeans faded and dirty, his blue-plaid shirt just as faded but relatively clean. He held both of his hands up in the air. His brown eyes were wide with uncertainty as he glanced back and forth at them. "If you're here to rob me, there's no cash on hand. I swear."

"Who are you?" Asher demanded as he and Faith continued to aim their pistols at him.

"The owner. Well, future owner. My dad, Stan Senior, owns this place. I'm Stan Junior. He's going to turn the place over to me once I get enough sweat equity built up." He shook his head as if embarrassed he'd shared so much. "Would you mind putting those guns away, or at least pointing them in another direction? I'm not armed and I swear I won't fight you. Nothing here is worth my life. Take whatever horses you want. You can get decent money for some of them."

While Asher wondered at Stan Junior's categorization of his dad turning over the business when Stan Senior had told Faith he was downsizing it, Faith called out, "Let's see your ID."

His dark eyes flicked to her with a flash of annoyance. "DUI. Lost my license. I haven't bothered yet to get one of those identification cards."

"You live here? On the property?" Asher asked.

His gaze returned to Asher. "You're kidding, right? In that dilapidated building Pop calls an office? No way. I live with my girlfriend in town. Dad drove me here this morning to feed the horses. That's when we discovered the gate was open and a couple of trail horses missing. He called it in and left me here to handle the search." He mumbled something unflattering about his father under his breath. "Why are you asking about this and pointing guns at me? What the heck is going on?"

Asher studied the blond-haired man, noting the tension around his eyes. Of course, anyone having guns pointed at them would be worried. That alone didn't mean he was hiding anything. "Where's Stan Senior?"

He rolled his eyes much like Faith tended to do. "My old man? Who knows? Probably off spending my inheritance. Maybe he went back to his place in Pigeon Forge. It's a heck of a lot nicer than anything around here." A flash of anger crossed his face. "Way nicer than me and Rhonda's place in town. You going to rob the place or not?"

The man was either a really good actor or he was the thirtysomething-year-old, entitled brat he appeared to be. Asher glanced at Faith. She subtly nodded, and they both holstered their weapons.

"We heard some horses went missing this morning," Asher explained. "We came by to see if they'd been located yet and whether you think they went missing on accident or on purpose."

Relief flooded the man's face as he dropped his hands to his sides. "You're cops? Why didn't you start with that? Dad called you guys hours ago. It's about dang time someone came out to help instead of just talking to us on the phone. Do you have any idea what a twelve-hundred-pound animal can do to a car if it runs out in the road?" He frowned. "Wait a minute. On purpose? You think someone stole them?"

"You don't?"

He shrugged. "Hadn't really considered it before. I suppose it's possible. Shouldn't you be taking this down? Writing up my statement or something?"

"We're not police officers," Asher said. "We used to be, but now we both work in the private sector."

Stan's brows drew down in confusion. "Private sector?"

Asher gestured to Faith. "This is my partner, Faith Lancaster. I'm Asher Whitfield. We work on cold cases for a company called Unfinished Business."

"Cold cases, huh? What's that got to do with our failing trail-riding operation?" Again, he sounded aggravated, as if his complaints about the place were an ongoing argument with his father.

This time it was Faith who explained. "We were investigating a cold case, but got sidelined to work on a recent abduction. The missing horses story on the news got us wondering if the perpetrator might have taken them to head into the mountains with his captive."

His eyes widened. "Cool. I mean, not cool that someone got kidnapped or whatever. But thinking they could be at our place might put us on the map, know what I mean? Could be good for business."

Asher clenched his jaw. He didn't like this guy one bit. "More importantly, a woman's life is at stake and we're trying to find her."

"Oh, yeah. Of course. What can I do to help?"

A whinny sounded behind him in the near darkness.

Stan let out an exasperated breath. "Coco's calling. I just got her saddled and she's getting impatient." He headed down the darkened aisle.

Asher strode after him, not wanting to let him out of his sight.

Faith followed, but stayed well out of reach of the impressive bay mare standing in the middle of the aisle, a white blaze on its face and flashing white stockings on its legs.

"Now that's a nice piece of horseflesh." Asher couldn't resist smoothing his hand down its velvety muzzle, earning a playful toss of the mare's head and a gentle nudge against his shoulder.

Stan tightened the cinch on the mare's girth. "She's one of two bays. The other over there is Ginger. Do I sense another equestrian aficionado in our midst?"

Asher chuckled. "Aficionado might be too strong a word. But I grew up around horses. I know quality when I see it. This mare is gorgeous. Not what I expected in a trail-riding operation."

"They wouldn't be here if it wasn't for me. Dad's stock is the usual docile, follow-the-leader kind most places around here use. I insisted on getting a couple of decent mounts for the two of us when we need to ride the fence line or chaperone tourists up into the foothills. The bays are just as sure-footed as a trail horse, but they're bigger, stronger, with more stamina."

He roughly patted Coco's neck, causing her to nervously shy away. He frowned and yanked the reins, making the mare grunt in protest and forcing her back beside him.

Asher stiffened, instantly on alert. For a man who worked with horses daily, Stan didn't seem all that good with them. Asher exchanged a quick glance with Faith and saw his suspicions mirrored in her eyes.

"I don't mean to be rude or whatever," Stan said. "But neither Dad nor I have seen anyone else out here today. And I haven't seen any signs of a break-in. I'm guessing the horses got out on their own. And If I don't get going soon for round two of my search for them, I'll lose what daylight I have left."

"Round two? If you've been searching for them and haven't found them yet, why did you return to the stables?" Asher asked.

Junior gave him an impatient look. "I've been searching all morning. I was hungry and tired. Any other *important* questions?"

"Take us with you," Asher said.

Stan's eyes widened. "What? Why?"

Faith put her hand on Asher's arm. "I'm fine waiting here. Once Lance arrives, I can update him and send him after you two."

"Um, hello," Stan said. "What are you talking about? Who's Lance?"

"Lance Cabrera, a guy we work with. Give us a minute," Asher said. "Saddle that other bay and a trail horse."

"But why—"

"We believe the man who abducted a woman this morning may have stolen your two horses and is in the foothills above your ranch right now. If you go up there by yourself and stumble across him, your life is in danger. You can be our guide and let Faith and me take care of any trouble that comes along."

Junior's eyes widened, but he didn't argue anymore. Instead, he ducked into what Asher supposed was a tack room and hurried out with another saddle. "Give me a few minutes."

After he headed into the other bay's stall, Faith whispered, "Asher, don't ask me to do this. I can't get on one of those things."

Stan stuck his head out of the stall. "If you're worried the bay is too spirited, I've got a four-year-old gelding that's as calm as can be."

"We won't need the gelding," Faith insisted.

"Yes. We will."

Faith frowned.

Stan Junior disappeared back into the stall.

Asher led her a few feet back up the aisle, out of Stan's earshot.

She shook his hand off her arm. "You're not talking me into this. I'm not riding that, that, that…"

"Horse?"

"Gelding." She shuddered. "Sounds even scarier than the word *horse*. What does that even mean?"

"A gelding is a male horse that's been castrated."

Her eyes widened. "Castrated. How cruel."

"It's no more cruel than neutering a dog to avoid unwanted litters of puppies who end up being euthanized. Besides, castrating a horse makes it more docile, easier to control. And it helps keep the peace in the stables. Trust me, you don't want randy stallions trying to kick down their stalls to get to the mares all the time."

"So I take it a gelding would be your ride of choice?"

He grinned. "Hell no. I'll take a randy stallion any day of the week. That fire and attitude makes riding much more of a challenge."

Faith waved a hand as if waving away his words. "We're getting off track. I'm not going to ride one of those things." She crossed her arms. "And you're not making me."

If it had been anyone else, he'd have laughed at her childish-sounding words. But this was Faith. And he could see the fear in her eyes that she was struggling so hard to hide.

Asher gently pulled her arms down and took her hands in his. "It's okay. I'm not going to try to force you to ride a horse—"

"Good. Because I don't want to have to shoot you."

He smiled. "That's kind of the point, though. The shooting part. I need backup, someone who's as good a marksman as I am—"

"Pfft. I'm way better."

"Perhaps."

"I always beat you at target practice."

"I'd say it's more fifty-fifty. Regardless, I need backup." He glanced toward the stall where Stan was working before meeting her gaze again. "You're the only other qualified person here right now to help me if things go bad."

"That's not fair. You're trying to guilt me into going with you."

"No. I'm making sure you're aware of the facts and that your horse prejudice doesn't blind you to them."

She swore.

"If Leslie is up there," he said, "and I find her, I'll need your help to make sure we can rescue her and that the bad guy…" Again he glanced toward the stall. "Doesn't get a chance to hurt her—or worse. I need your skills and expertise, Faith. I know how hard this is for you. And I wouldn't ask if it wasn't important. But if you stay here and I get into trouble, the time it takes for you or someone else to reach me might mean compromising Leslie's safety."

Her face turned pale. "Lance is on the way." She jerked her phone out and checked the screen. She winced. "Thirty minutes, give or take."

"Okay."

Faith blinked. "Okay?"

He feathered his hand along her incredibly soft face. "It's okay. You stay here. When Lance arrives, tell him which way we went. Send him after us."

A single tear slid down her face and she angrily wiped it away. "You know darn well I'm not going to stand around

for thirty minutes while you go up there without backup."
This time it was her turn to look toward where Stan was sad-
dling the other bay. She lowered her voice. "And we both
know you might need backup sooner rather than later. Something's off with Stan."

"I agree," Asher whispered.

She sighed heavily. "Get me that stupid gelding."

He grinned. "That's my girl." He pressed a kiss to her forehead. "Thank you, Faith."

She made a show of wiping his kiss away. "I hate it when
you use psychology on me. Thank me with an expensive
dinner, assuming I survive this escapade. This cancels out
the steak dinner I owe you, by the way."

The sound of metal jangling had both of them turning to
see the other bay, Ginger, being led out of her stall to stand
beside Coco.

Stan glanced their way. "I'll get the gelding and—"

"Never mind," Asher said. "Ms. Lancaster will ride double
with me. The guy coming to back us up can saddle the gelding himself. Like you said, there's not much daylight yet. We
need to get going."

"Backup? Cops?"

"The coworker I mentioned before. He's already on the
way—"

Stan suddenly vaulted into Coco's saddle and jerked her
around in a circle toward the open doors behind them.

Asher swore and sprinted after him, yanking out his pistol. "Stop or I'll shoot!"

Stan kicked Coco and they took off outside.

Faith ran to the doors beside Asher, her pistol drawn like
his, both of them aimed toward the fleeing figure of Junior
on horseback, racing toward the foothills.

She swore. "We can't shoot a man in the back."

"I'm more worried that if we kill him, and he's got Leslie up in those foothills, we may never find her." Asher shoved his pistol into the shoulder holster beneath his suit jacket and jogged back to Ginger. As soon as he stuck his foot in the stirrup, the saddle slid off the horse and slammed to the floor, sending up a cloud of dust and hay.

Faith ran over to him, waving at the air in front of her face. "What happened?"

Asher grabbed the girth strap, swearing when he saw it cut in two. "He sliced the strap that secures the saddle." He shoved the useless saddle to the side, yanked off what looked like a rug from the horse's back and then pulled Ginger to the nearest stall.

He reached for the top of the stall's wooden slat wall, but his suit jacket pulled tight across his shoulders. After shucking it off and tossing it aside, he was able to climb the wall to mount the horse.

Faith rushed toward him then scrambled back again to give the horse a wide berth. "Asher! What are you doing? You need a saddle—"

He slid onto the horse's back and yanked the reins free from the post, gently patting her neck to settle her down. "No time. Odds are that Stan Junior, or whoever he is, has Leslie. If he hasn't killed her already, he's about to. Unless I can stop him." He clucked to the mare and turned her around to face the exit.

"Wait!" Faith bravely moved to the side of the horse again, standing her ground even when the horse tossed its head. Faith extended her hands toward him. "Swing me up, or whatever. You said we'd ride double."

"Not now. I'm sorry, Faith. It would slow me down." He kicked the mare's side and sent her racing out of the stables at a full gallop.

Chapter Eight

Faith clenched her fists in frustration as she watched Grayson in his business suit, minus the jacket, clinging to the back of the huge red horse, scrabbling over rocks and up the hillside. Soon, they disappeared into the trees. The man was fearless. And competent in ways she'd never imagined. Who rode bareback up a mountain at a full run? Chasing a man who may or may not be a killer?

With no backup.

She cursed herself for the coward that she was and whirled around. Whipping out her cell phone, she strode back inside the building and punched one of the numbers saved in her favorite contacts list. As she held the phone to her ear, she peered into the first stall. A doe-eyed red horse, much smaller than the ones that Stan and Asher were riding, stared silently back at her. Was that a gelding? How was she supposed to recognize a gelding? She bit her lip, then leaned down and peered through the wooden slats. She couldn't even tell if it was a boy or a girl, much less whether it had been castrated.

Jogging to the next stall, she looked in. This time a gray-and-white horse stared back at her, the dark spots on its rump reminding her of one of those spotted dogs. What were they called? Dalmatians maybe? It was pretty and seemed nice.

But it was too big. She couldn't even imagine the terrifying view from its back. On to the next stall.

The phone finally clicked. "Hey, Faith. Sorry it took so long to answer. I was—"

"Lance. How soon will you be here?"

"Nice to talk to you too. I'm guessing another fifteen minutes or so. Traffic in town is crazy with all the tourists—"

"Forget the tourists. Step on the gas. Asher's all alone on the mountain chasing the guy we think is the killer. He needs backup. And I…" She cleared her throat. "I couldn't get on a damn horse and help him."

"I'll be there as fast as I can." The engine roared. Horns honked. The phone clicked.

Faith shoved it in her pocket and hurried down the line of stalls, looking at each horse. There were eight in all. Every single one of them was intimidating. But the first horse was the smallest. She prayed it was the gentle gelding.

Running back to the first stall, she was relieved to realize the horse already had the leather thing on its head. She glanced around for the reins. There, hanging on a hook right outside the stall. It was a long leather strap with a clip on one end. That must be it. She grabbed it and opened the door with trembling hands.

"Here, horsey, horsey." She held out her hand. The horse nickered softly. "Well at least you aren't trying to bite me. Good sign, right? We're going to be friends, okay?" Forcing herself to shuffle forward, she reached out then gently feathered her hand down the horse's neck as she'd seen Asher do earlier. The horse didn't seem to mind. It turned its head and shoved its nose into a metal can hanging from the wall, then snorted.

Drawing a deep breath, Faith inched forward then quickly

clipped the rein to the round metal ring at the end of the leather contraption on the horse's head. It didn't even flinch.

She let out a breath and smiled. "This isn't so bad. Come on, horsey, horsey. This way." She gently tugged the rein. The horse snorted again, as if disappointed, but it left the metal bucket and docilely followed her out of the stall.

Faith looped the rein around the same metal hook it had been hanging from earlier and the horse patiently stood waiting.

Even though she was feeling more confident, she knew there was no way she'd be able to stay up on a horse without something more than its mane to hold on to. She glanced at the saddle Stan had sabotaged. She needed something like that, only smaller. Something she could actually lift. Hadn't Stan pulled that saddle out of one of the rooms on the other side of the aisle?

Yes, there. The door on the end. She ran to it and yanked it open. Her heart sank when she saw the jumble of leather reins and saddles stacked all around and hanging from hooks on the wall. She had no idea which one to try. But all of the saddles closest to the door seemed too big and heavy. There had to be something more manageable for her, lighter, or she wouldn't even be able to get it on the horse.

Near the end of one of the stacks was exactly what she'd hoped to find, a small, lightweight saddle. It looked odd, with two knobs sticking up on the end, not at all like the one Stan had used. But she supposed a saddle was a saddle, and she'd be able to hold on to both the knobs if she needed to. She hefted it, relieved that it weighed no more than a large sack of potatoes, and carried it to the waiting horse.

"Now what?" She looked at the horse, who looked at her, perhaps a bit skeptically. Then it closed its eyes and proceeded to ignore her.

"That's fine," she said. "Just stand there like that. Let me do the work. Don't move, okay?"

She sent up a quick prayer then tossed the saddle up on the horse's back. It whinnied in alarm and bumped against the stall. Faith spoke calming, nonsensical words and managed to keep the saddle from sliding off. As soon as the horse settled down again, she went to work trying to figure out how to keep the saddle from falling off. The amount of buckles and pieces of leather were confusing. But she knew there was one big strap that was supposed to go around its stomach. Asher had called it a girth strap, hadn't he?

Running over to the saddle that Asher had tried to use, she studied the sliced piece of leather. Keeping that picture in her mind, she ran back to the horse and figured out which strap seemed about the same.

A few minutes later, she stood back to admire her handiwork. Everything looked right, as near as she could tell. And when she'd tugged on the saddle, it'd stayed in place.

"Okay. Now, how do I get up?"

The horse aimed a sleepy glance at her then closed its eyes again.

"You're no help," she grumbled. Asher had climbed the boards of the stall to get on his horse. Without any stools or ladders in sight, she supposed she'd have to do the same thing. It took several tries, but finally she gingerly lowered herself down on the saddle. The horse didn't move at all.

She chuckled with satisfaction. "Boy, will Asher be surprised. Let's get this party started, Red. Is that a good name for you? Asher needs us." She patted its neck before tugging the other end of the rein off the hook where she'd hung it. Something wasn't right. It was clipped to the horse's headgear on one side, but the other end had a handle of sorts, not a clip. Didn't Asher's reins hook on both ends?

She wound the rein around her hand to shorten it and then experimented by tugging it. The horse dutifully turned around, facing the exit doors.

Faith shrugged. Maybe she wasn't doing it exactly right, but it was working.

"Yah, horsey."

It didn't move.

She wiggled in the saddle. "Come on. Giddy up, Red. Let's go."

The horse turned its head and gave her the side-eye.

"Great. I picked the broken horse. Come on. Go." She wiggled in the saddle again. "Go, dang it. Come on."

"Faith, stop!"

She turned in the saddle to see Lance running toward her. The horse decided at that moment to move. It trotted out the stable doors with Faith desperately sawing back on the rein. Red jerked to a stop and started turning in a circle.

Lance was suddenly there, grabbing the rein from her hands and pulling the horse to a stop again. "Faith, what the heck are you doing? Trying to kill yourself?"

"I'm trying to help Asher. I told you he needs backup." She frowned. "How did you get here so fast?"

"Ran every light in town. Come on, let's get you off of there."

She gladly let him pluck her from the saddle. But instead of him vaulting up and heading into the mountains, he turned and jogged back to the stables with the horse in tow.

Faith stood for a moment in shock then jogged after him. When she ran inside, she was even more surprised to see her saddle falling to the floor and Lance shoving the horse inside its stall.

"Lance, stop. Don't waste time being picky about which horse you use. Asher needs you."

"That's why I'll grab a horse big enough to support me without buckling under my weight. I'll use a saddle I can sit in, not an English sidesaddle." He shook his head. "Why they even have one of those at a trail-riding place is beyond me. Instead of a lunge line and a halter with no way to steer the horse, I'll use reins and a bridle. For goodness' sake, have you never ridden a horse before?"

"A couple of times. Didn't end well," she admitted.

"No kidding."

She crossed her arms and moved out of his way as Lance led a larger, dark brown horse out of the next stall.

"Tack room?" he asked.

"If you mean where are the saddles and stuff, in there." She pointed to the door at the end.

He strode inside. A moment later, he emerged carrying one of the big heavy saddles, a small rug and a handful of leather with metal jangling from it.

"Can you call Asher and get GPS coordinates for me?" He spoke soothingly to the horse and tossed the rug on its back.

"I don't want to distract him or give his position away if he's trying to sneak up on the bad guy. But I can use my Find Asher app and tell you exactly where he is."

He chuckled as he settled the saddle on the horse's back. "You have an app on your phone to locate Asher?"

"More or less. It's the same app I use for my sister. It'll locate his phone."

"Works for me." His fingers moved with lightning speed as he buckled and tugged and adjusted the fit of the saddle. A few minutes later, he'd ditched the leather contraption—the halter, she remembered he'd called it—and replaced it with another that looked almost exactly the same except that it had metal hanging off the end that he slipped into the horse's mouth, and rings on both sides to hook leather straps to it.

Now she understood why her rein hadn't looked right. It wasn't a rein. It was whatever that lunge line thing was that he'd mentioned. She clenched her hands, embarrassed that she'd done everything so wrong. But also grateful that Lance had gotten there when he had and knew what he was doing.

He hoisted himself into the saddle and turned the horse using a subtle motion of his legs without even using the reins he'd looped over the front of the saddle. He held his phone and arched a brow. "Coordinates?"

"Oh, yeah. Right. Texting them to you now."

His phone beeped and he typed on the screen, nodded and slid his phone into his shirt pocket. "Text me the coordinates every few minutes. I'll adjust my path accordingly. And call Grayson, give him an update. I didn't get a chance to call him during my Mario Andretti race here."

Before she could answer, he looped the reins in his hand and kicked the horse's sides. It whinnied and flew out of the building.

After watching to make sure Lance was going up the same trail that Asher had, Faith headed inside and pressed the favorites contact for Grayson. He answered on the first ring.

"Faith, it's about dang time I got an update. What's the situation? Found any evidence of our abductor or Leslie being at those stables you were checking out?"

"Maybe, maybe not." She updated him on everything that was happening as she carried the English sidesaddle, as Lance had called it, back into the tack room. As she answered Grayson's questions, she idly fingered the various pieces of equipment hanging from the walls, wondering what they were. One she recognized: a whip. She was glad that neither Asher nor Lance had used one of those on their horses. When she reached the end of the large, messy room, she stumbled on something on the floor and fell against the wall. When she looked down to see what she'd tripped over, she sucked in a sharp breath.

"What's wrong?" Grayson demanded.

She bent to flip back the rest of the little rug. Her hand shook as she lifted another, larger rug beside it. "Oh, no."

"Faith? What is it? Speak to me."

"Based on their physical resemblance, I think I just found the Dardens—Stan Senior and the real Stan Junior. They're dead."

Chapter Nine

Asher knelt to study the hoof prints in the dirt. They appeared to be fresh, and they were about the same size and depth of the prints his bay was leaving. He was on the right track. He just hoped he reached Stan before Stan reached Leslie.

He was about to mount his horse again when a whinny sounded through the trees. Close by, maybe twenty, thirty yards. And since he didn't hear the sound of the horse's hooves, it must be stopped. Easing his gun out of his shoulder holster, he held it down at his side, leaving his bay to munch on the grass beneath the trees as he crept through the woods.

A few moments later, he heard another sound. A whimper. His hand tightened around his pistol and he sped up, as quiet as possible but as quickly as he could. There, up ahead, through a break in the trees, he saw what he'd been looking for. Leslie. She was alive, thank God. Naked, she was standing on a five- or six-foot-long piece of log, cowering back against an oak tree, her head bent down with her hair covering her face. But he didn't need to see her face to know it was her. The height, weight, dark curly hair, the mahogany color of her skin…everything matched the missing girl's description.

Asher peered through some bushes, looking for Stan or his horse. His arms prickled with goose bumps as he continued to wait. Everything about the situation—that whinny, Leslie whimpering against a tree in a small clearing—screamed setup. It was a trap. But where was Stan?

Another whimper had him looking at Leslie again. Even from a good twenty feet away he could tell that she was shivering, the air up in the mountains a good fifteen, maybe twenty, degrees cooler than in the valley. He scanned the surrounding area again. He desperately wanted to run into the clearing and help her. But if he got ambushed and killed, that wouldn't do her any good. She'd still be Stan's prisoner.

Where the heck are you? Where are you hiding, you lowlife?

And then he saw it. A rope, mostly hidden by leaves and small branches, trailing along the ground in the middle of the clearing. One end snaked into the trees on the far left side. The other went directly to the piece of wood Leslie was standing on. It was tied around it.

He jerked his head up, looking above the girl. Sure enough, a second brown rope that almost completely blended in with the bark of the oak tree ran around from the back of the tree down behind Leslie. Asher realized immediately what was happening. Stan had tied that rope to a branch in the back of the tree, the other end around Leslie's neck. Sure enough, the sound of another whinny had the girl lifting her head revealing the hangman's noose around her neck.

Stan had led him there to watch him kill his victim.

A wicked laugh sounded from the shadow of the trees, making Asher's gut lurch with dread.

"Show yourself, Stan. Or are you a coward?"

"I'm no coward, Investigator," he yelled from the shadows. "But I'm not stupid either. You'll let me go to try to save the girl." He laughed. "If you can."

The rope attached to the log grew taut, as if someone was

pulling on it. "Yah! Go, go, you stupid nag," Stan yelled to his horse.

Asher swore and sprinted through the bushes and into the clearing, running full-out toward Leslie. The sound of horse's hooves echoed through the trees. Leslie's eyes widened with pleading and fear as he ran toward her, her skin turning ashen.

The rope snapped against the ground.

The log jerked forward.

Leslie screamed as her feet slipped out from beneath her.

FAITH COULD BARELY breathe with all the testosterone surrounding her. Didn't the TBI hire any women these days? In spite of Frost's agents pushing in on her from all sides, she refused to give up her front-row position at the hood of Frost's rental car. Chief Russo had spread a map on top of it and everyone was crowded around as he and Frost gridded out the search area for the nearby foothills. While no one had heard yet from Asher, Lance had texted Faith an update not long ago that he was on Asher's trail and hoping to team up with him soon in the search for Leslie and her abductor.

The roadblocks that Russo had set near the Parkses' residence were in the process of being moved closer to the stables. Frost discussed the possibility of getting a chopper into the air with infrared capabilities, and whether they could get it in position before dark.

Faith cleared her throat. When that didn't get their attention, she rapped her knuckles on the hood. "Director, Chief, we—Asher and I—discussed a chopper earlier and he was worried it could spook the horses. I understand your men who volunteered to search on horseback are skilled in riding. But a spooked horse is still dangerous, especially if our missing woman is on it. I don't want anyone getting hurt, especially Leslie Parks."

One of the special agents frowned at her. "Look, lady—"

Grayson shoved his way in beside her, frowning at the agent. "That's Ms. Lancaster to you. She's a highly decorated, former police detective, who, as a civilian investigator, has solved half a dozen cold cases that various Tennessee law enforcement agencies, including the TBI, couldn't."

It was hard not to smile as the man's face turned red, but Faith managed it, somehow.

Effectively dismissing the agent, Grayson turned his back on him and addressed Russo and Frost. "If Asher thought it was too dangerous to bring in a helicopter, I trust his instincts. As to the search, your people and mine are anxious to saddle up and follow Detectives Whitfield and Cabrera's trail, but you've blocked access to the tack room. We're losing daylight, and we potentially have an innocent victim up in those mountains, as well as my men, who may need backup. Instead of waiting any longer for the medical examiner to arrive and remove the bodies, why not have your crime scene techs get the equipment that we need out of that room right now?"

Frost's brows drew together. "We can't risk messing up the crime scene. A defense attorney could argue it's contaminated and have any evidence we collect thrown out. We wait for the ME."

Faith rapped her knuckles on the hood again. "You won't even have a perpetrator to bring to court if he gets away while everyone's standing around planning. There's no telling what he could be doing to his captive. We don't even know if Asher and Lance have found her, or the perpetrator. They need our help. We need to get moving."

Grayson gave her a subtle nod of approval and turned his intimidating stare on his friend, Chief Russo.

Russo gave him a pained look. "Okay, okay. We'll nix the chopper idea, for now at least. And we'll stop waiting for the ME. We've already photographed the room. The bodies are at the far end. My techs, and only my techs, will pull out whatever equipment is needed. The fewer people in the crime scene, the better. Contamination is a real concern."

Grayson motioned to Ivy Shaw, one of the UB investigators who'd driven out because of her experience with horses. She nodded and ran toward the building's side entrance, waving for the rest of the half dozen agents and UB investigators who'd volunteered to search via horseback to follow her.

Frost obviously wasn't happy with Russo's decision, but it was the chief's jurisdiction. So he didn't argue. "I'll finish mapping out search grids for those who will follow on foot. Ms. Lancaster has the GPS information. Someone borrow her phone or load up her app, whatever it takes so that both search teams can use the coordinates to find Whitfield and Cabrera."

The sound of a vehicle's tires crunching on the gravel road announced the arrival of the long-awaited medical examiner's van. It pulled up to the main entrance to the stables a good thirty feet away.

Russo plowed through the crowd around the car to reach the ME. Faith stepped back, rounding the hood of the vehicle to follow them into the building.

A hand firmly grasped her arm, stopping her. Grayson. She glanced up in question.

He let go and shook his head. "I know you've been frustrated at the wait, but everything's in motion now. Give the ME and techs the space they need to get the equipment out and protect the evidence at the same time. We'll be saddled up and off on the hunt soon."

"'We'? Are you planning to go along? You ride?"

He gave her one of his rare smiles. "I'll let the younger guys handle this one. But, yes, I ride every now and then. Willow and I both do. We really need to get you over your fear of horses. You're missing out on a lot of fun."

She stared at him, her face growing hot. "Who told you?"

"You did. By your reactions when giving me the update about what happened earlier. You glossed it over, saying Lance arrived and wanted to head after Asher instead of you. But I know that if you were comfortable riding you'd have been right beside Asher instead of following later."

Her face burned even more, realizing that he knew she'd been a coward.

He put his hand on her shoulder. "Stop feeling guilty for not going with him. It made far better sense for a skilled horseman like Lance to tackle the job. You'd have been a liability."

"Gee. Thanks."

He squeezed her shoulder and let go. "Just keeping it real, Faith."

She reluctantly smiled then critically eyed the rag-tag deputies and TBI agents who'd said they could ride. None of them inspired the confidence that her fellow teammates did, or her former army ranger boss. But at least they knew the difference between a lunge line and reins—not that she'd ever make that mistake again. "They need to hurry up."

"It won't take long to reach him. Your GPS app will guide them, and they won't have to go slowly like I'm sure Asher had to initially while searching for a trail to follow. How far away is he now?"

She checked her phone and frowned. "That doesn't make

sense. What's he…he's turned around. He's coming back *toward* us, fast."

Grayson bent over her shoulder to look at the screen. "At that speed, it won't take long for him to get here." He looked up at the foothills. "Contact Lance. See if he knows what's going on. If he doesn't, risk contacting Asher. He's obviously not trying to be quiet or careful anymore. It's not like we'll give away his position by making his phone buzz."

Her fingers practically flew across the screen as she sent Lance a text. Daphne would have been proud of her newfound fast texting abilities. Apparently, stress improved her typing skills.

When Lance didn't text her back, she speed-dialed his number. She tried Asher, as well, with the same results. "Neither of them is texting or picking up. I don't like this. Something's definitely wrong. Asher is pushing his horse too fast, taking risks in the rough terrain."

She checked the GPS again, her stomach sinking. "Asher's riding *recklessly* fast. Do you think Fake Stan could be chasing him?"

Grayson shook his head no. "Asher wouldn't run from a fight. Maybe the trail went cold and he's hurrying back to get a search party together before dark."

She studied the trees at the top of the ridge. She didn't doubt Asher's bravery. He wouldn't run from a fight, *unless it was the only option left*. Maybe he was hurt and had no choice. His gun could have jammed. Or Fake Stan could have ambushed him and—

"He's fine, Faith. They both are. Stop worrying. That's an order."

She clenched her fists in frustration. "You can't make someone quit worrying by ordering them to stop."

The clatter of hooves had both of them turning to see the

search party finally emerging from the barn. Seven horses were saddled and being led outside. As they mounted, one of them lifted his phone and called out to her. "Ready for those coordinates, Ms. Lancaster."

She hurried over and gave him the information. "But you might want to wait. Looks like Asher is on his way back. He should be here any minute."

Flashing lights had her turning again to see an ambulance pull up beside the van. She whirled back toward Grayson. "Did you call for an ambulance?" She ran to his side. "You heard from Asher, didn't you, but didn't tell me? He's hurt. I knew it. He—"

"Faith, no. I haven't heard from Asher. Russo asked for the ambulance earlier in case we find Leslie, as a precaution. Are you this worried about Lance too? Or is it just Asher?"

She blinked. "Both of them, of course. They're…they're my teammates. And friends. Why would you even ask?"

"No reason." But his amused tone said otherwise.

Russo shouted from the stable doorway for Grayson.

"Better see what he wants." He jogged toward the chief.

Faith watched him go as she pondered his question. *Are you this worried about Lance too?* In all honesty, no, she wasn't. But that didn't mean anything, not really. She cared about both of them. They were her coworkers, her friends. She didn't want either of them hurt. Was Asher special to her? Yes. Of course. They were close, *best* friends. But that was only natural since they worked together much more often than they did with anyone else. Their team leader, Ryland, tended to assign both of them to the same cases when an investigation required more than one investigator. It was because they complemented each other's skill sets. Together, they got results quicker than apart. It didn't mean there was something more to their…relationship. Not the way Grayson's tone had implied.

She shook her head. He was acting as if she had a crush on Asher, or maybe he had one on her. That idea had her chuckling. Asher often flirted with her. Grayson must have taken it wrong. It was Asher's way of teasing her.

Wasn't it? Had Grayson seen more to the flirting, like maybe that it was…real?

No, no. She wasn't going down that path. She was tired and concerned for both men. That's all it was. She was way overthinking this because her emotions were raw. Period.

She clenched her hands at her sides as the search party trotted across the weed-filled pasture toward the foothills. They must have decided not to wait for Asher. She just hoped they weren't really needed, that he would be here soon, and that he was okay.

And Lance, of course. She hoped he was okay too.

A big red horse emerged from the trees at the top of the nearest ridge.

"Asher," Faith breathed, relief making her smile for a moment, until she realized how recklessly he was urging his horse down the rock-strewn incline. From her vantage point, it looked like the horse would tumble off a ledge with every hop-skip step it took.

Behind him, Lance followed on the big brown horse, his gun out as he kept turning and looking at the trees behind them. Faith looked up at the trees, unable to see anything in the gloom beneath the thick forest canopy. Were they being pursued as she'd feared?

The two men met up with the search party halfway across the pasture. Asher turned slightly to say something to Lance. That's when Faith caught the gleam of the late afternoon sunlight on Asher's golden, *naked* skin. She'd seen his shirt and thought he was wearing it. Now, she realized he wasn't. It was draped around a petite woman sitting on his lap, her head pressed against his chest.

Faith's breath caught in her throat. Was that Leslie Parks, so still and unmoving against him? Why would she need Asher's shirt? The obvious answer was that Leslie didn't have any clothes of her own, which had Faith wishing she could kill Fake Stan right now, assuming Asher hadn't already.

When his horse shifted slightly, she got a better look at the shirt. Her stomach churned with dread and fear.

Grayson came up beside her and rested his hands on top of the fence. "He found her. Son of a… He really did it. You both did. You found her."

"She hasn't moved, not once. Her eyes are closed too. And the shirt she's wearing, it's—"

"Covered with dark splotches." His voice was tight with worry as he straightened. Neither said the word both of them were thinking, the word that thickened the air with tension.

Blood.

The shirt was covered with blood.

Please let her be alive. Please, God. Let her live.

A moment later, Ivy and the group of men on horseback raced toward the hill, heading in the direction that Asher and Lance had just come from.

Asher clutched Leslie against him and urged his horse forward again, probably using his legs to guide it the way Faith had seen Lance do earlier. Lance rode up to Asher's side and motioned to Leslie. Whatever he was saying made Asher's mouth tighten in a hard line, but he didn't say anything.

His own face a study in anger and concern, Lance urged his horse forward, reaching the open gate ahead of Asher. He glanced at Grayson before stopping by Faith.

"Get the EMTs, Faith. Hurry."

The urgency in his tone had her running to the ambulance, even though she wondered why he didn't ride his horse over there and alert them himself. Once the EMTs had their gurney out with the wheels down, and had placed their boxes of supplies on top to follow her, she turned to see where Leslie and the others were. They were only about fifteen feet away.

"Be careful of her neck," Asher warned.

Lance had dismounted and stood beside Asher's horse, helping him lower Leslie into the waiting arms of the EMTs as they rushed over. As soon as they put her on the gurney, her eyes fluttered open and she moaned.

"She's alive," Faith whispered, smiling in relief.

Lance said something to the EMTs. Asher shook his head, looking angry. The EMTs both nodded at him before rushing toward the ambulance with Leslie.

Faith ran to the horses to congratulate Asher and Lance, and ask about Fake Stan. But her mouth went dry and logical thought was no longer possible as she finally got a good look at Asher up close, astride the big horse. Half-naked, incredibly *buff* Asher. Where had all those rippling muscles come from? Had they been there all along and she'd never noticed? She couldn't help admiring his equally well-defined biceps. Had she ever seen his biceps before? When would she have had the chance? He was always wearing long-sleeved dress shirts and suits.

Her greedy gaze drank in the small spattering of hair on his chest and the long dark line of it going down his flat belly to disappear beneath his pants. Goodness gracious. Asher was *hot*!

She swallowed and forced her gaze up, fully expecting him to have noticed her practically drooling over his body. No doubt he'd tease her mercilessly over that. But he wasn't even looking at her. His eyes were half closed, his face alarmingly pale. And Lance and Grayson were holding on to his upper arms on either side of the horse, as if they were afraid he was about to fall.

Her stomach dropped. She'd been so intent on ogling him that she hadn't realized that something was wrong, terribly wrong. She stepped closer to his horse, stopping just shy of its head and those huge square teeth.

"What's wrong?" she asked. "Asher?"

"Let's pull him down on this side," Lance said to Grayson, ignoring her question. "Careful."

Fear seared Faith's lungs as they pulled him sideways out of the saddle.

He staggered then crumpled to the ground in a slow-controlled fall, with Lance and Grayson helping him. But instead of laying him down, they held him up in a sitting position.

"I've got him," Grayson said. "Tell one of those EMTs to get back here, now, in spite of Asher insisting they look after Leslie first."

Lance jumped up and ran to the ambulance.

Faith dropped to her knees in front of Asher. "What's wrong? Asher, look at me." His eyes were closed now. He seemed to be concentrating on just…breathing. "Grayson?" Her voice broke as she scooted to Asher's side and started to slide her arm around his shoulders.

"Faith," Grayson warned. "Don't touch his back."

She froze then leaned over to see behind him. The haft of a large knife protruded from beneath his left shoulder blade.

She sucked in a startled breath. "Asher. Oh, no." Her hands shook as she gently cupped his face. "Whatever happened, it will be okay." A single tear slid down her face as she kissed his forehead. "It's okay. We'll take care of you." She glanced over her shoulder toward the ambulance. "Hurry, Lance!"

When she looked back, Asher's eyes were open and staring into hers. They were glazed with pain, his breaths shallow and labored. But in spite of his obvious pain, his mouth quirked up in that smile she knew so well.

"We found her, Faith. We found Leslie. Alive." His voice was gritty, barely audible. "He told her he killed Jasmine, that he was going to kill her too." Asher drew a ragged breath, turning even more pale as he struggled to speak.

"Don't try to talk, Asher," she pleaded.

"Had to…" Asher rasped. "Had to grab her, hold her up. The noose would have snapped her neck." He choked and dragged in an obviously painful breath.

Faith stared in horror, the word *noose* sickening her. But her curiosity would have to wait.

"That's when he threw the knife."

"Stop talking, Ash. Just breathe. In, out, in, out." Her hands shook as she stroked his short dark hair back from his forehead.

His smile widened. "You called me Ash."

"Did I? My sister's bad habits are rubbing off on me. It won't happen again."

His answering laugh turned into a cough. Frothy, bright-red blood dotted the corners of his mouth.

Her gaze shot to Grayson. His answering look was dark with concern. He grasped Asher's upper arm tighter with both hands, carefully supporting him. "Faith, call 9-1-1. Get a medevac chopper out here. *Yesterday.*"

Chapter Ten

A slow, rhythmic beeping and the sound of muted voices tugged Asher up through thick layers of lethargy. He struggled to open his eyes, but the feat seemed beyond his abilities. His eyelids were too heavy, like a weight was pulling them down.

Tired, so tired.

Everything ached. His chest and back were on fire. A sharp piercing pain stabbed him with each breath he took. Did that mean he was alive? Where was he? Who was talking?

Most of the voices seemed familiar. He lay there in a fog of pain and confusion, desperately trying to capture snatches of the conversation to figure out what was happening. The last thing he remembered after getting Leslie to safety was Faith calling him Ash. It was the first time she'd ever done that.

Faith.

That was one of the voices he heard. Smart, beautiful, frustrating Faith. She was here. But where, exactly, was here?

Beep. Beep. Beep.

"Pneu…mo…thorax." Faith's voice. "What the heck is that?"

"A collapsed lung. The knife the assailant threw went into his back and…"

The voices trailed off. Waves of confusion threatened to push him under.

No. He needed to wake up. Hospital. He must be in a hospital. The unfamiliar voice had to be the doctor, talking to Faith and… Grayson. And Lance. Those were the other voices he was hearing. He struggled to capture more of the conversation.

"—missed any major organs…"

More murmurs he couldn't catch.

Beep. Beep.

"—But will he be okay?" Faith's voice again. "Will he make a full recovery? Will he be able to walk…"

Be able to walk? Had the knife that Stan had thrown hit his spine? He tried to move his legs, wiggle his toes. He couldn't. Raw fear sliced through him.

Wake. Up.

"I think he's in pain." Faith's soft, warm hand gently clasped his. "Please, give him something to take the pain away."

No, no medication. Need to wake up. What's wrong with my legs?

Another beep. The fire eased. He let out a deep breath, no longer feeling as if his lungs were going to burst out of his chest.

"Can you hear me, Asher?" Faith, her hand still clasping his. He wanted to squeeze it, stroke her fingers with his. But he couldn't. Would it be possible to feel her hand touching his if he had a spinal injury? Maybe he was just too drugged up to move. He had to know. He struggled again to open his eyes.

"It's okay, Asher," she said. "Don't fight the drugs. Rest. If you can hear me, you're in a hospital, in Knoxville. The chopper brought you to the Trauma Center at the University of Tennessee Medical Center—"

Beep.

"When you saved Leslie from being hung by her captor's trap, and he threw his knife at your back, it pierced a lung and—"

And *what*? If he could just open his eyes. *Wake up!*

"Doctor, he's restless. I think he's still in pain. Please. Help him."

No. No, don't. I have to know.

Liquid sleep flooded his veins. If he could yell his frustration, he would have as the darkness swallowed him up again.

BRIGHT LIGHT SLANTED across Asher's eyelids. He turned his head away, raising his arm to block it out.

His arm. He'd raised it. He tried to open his eyes. The lids twitched, as if in protest. But then they opened. He could finally see. As he'd suspected before, he was in a hospital room, lying in a bed, with an IV pole to his left. That must be the beeping he'd heard, or maybe the monitors just past it, showing his vital signs. The bright light was the sun glinting through the shades on the window to his right. There was no one else in the room. Faith was gone.

A pang of disappointment shot through him, followed by a cold wave of fear. *Will he be able to walk again?* Faith's words ran through his mind. Drawing a shallow breath that, thankfully, was far less painful this time, he tried to move his toes. The sheet over his feet moved up and down. He laughed with relief then sucked in a sharp breath at the fiery pain that seared his lungs.

When the pain finally dulled, he took a tentative, shallow breath. It still hurt, but not nearly as much as when he'd laughed. He was still groggy, exhausted. This time, he didn't fight the pull to sleep. He closed his eyes and surrendered.

It was dark when he woke again. The sun had set long ago. But once his eyes adjusted to the darkness, the lights from the IV pump and other equipment in the room was enough for him to make out some details.

To his left was an open door, revealing the dark outline of a sink and a toilet. Another narrow door to the right of that was likely a small closet. The wall stopped a few feet beyond that, no doubt leading to the alcove that concealed the door into his hospital room.

Asher slowly turned his head on the pillow, trying to make out more details he hadn't really paid attention to earlier. There was a digital clock on the far wall, announcing it was nearly midnight. Beside it, a small impossibly old-fashioned-looking TV was suspended from the ceiling. An equally old and uncomfortable-looking plastic chair was tucked against the wall. It was a typical private hospital room, small but efficient. And when he finally looked all the way to his right, he noticed something else. Or rather, some*one*.

Faith.

He smiled, his gaze drinking In the soft curves of her beautiful face as she lay sleeping, curled up in a reclining chair pulled close to his bed. Her shoulder-length hair created a golden halo above her head, glinting in the dim lights from the equipment. And there was something else he could just make out, the thick, pink blanket tucked around her. It looked suspiciously like the one he'd given her last Christmas as a joke, knowing she hated pink. She'd graciously thanked him and he'd laughed, assuming she'd toss it in the garbage as soon as he'd left. And yet there it was.

He wanted to wake her, to see her green eyes shining at him, her soft lips curve in that smile he loved so much. He wanted to thank her, for being there for him. And he wanted to know what was happening with the case.

Was Leslie recovering from her injuries? Had the TBI and police caught Stan? With their combined manpower, the roadblocks, and with Stan only having about a thirty-minute head start, they must have captured him. Asher had desperately wanted for him and Faith to be the ones to bring Stan to justice. But as long as the killer could no longer hurt anyone else, that's what mattered. For now, it was enough. It had to be.

Chapter Eleven

Faith shifted into a more comfortable position on the side of Asher's hospital bed. He sat a few feet away in the reclining chair eating breakfast, frowning at her. He'd barraged her with questions the moment she'd entered the room. And she had a few for him as well. But she'd refused to discuss anything other than reassuring him that Leslie Parks was in good condition and home with her family. Since this was Asher's first solid food since being admitted to the hospital, Faith wanted him to eat as much as possible. He needed to regain his strength. He'd obviously lost weight. And he was still far too pale for her peace of mind.

He washed down some scrambled eggs with a sip of water, glaring at her the whole time.

"Okay, okay," she relented. "You've done really well and haven't tried to murder me while waiting to interrogate me. I'll take that as a win. Two more bites and we'll talk. Big bites."

"You're worse than my instructor at the police academy," he grumbled.

"I'll take that as a compliment."

"It's not."

She laughed. "Eat."

He wolfed down the rest of his eggs then tossed his fork onto the tray. "Enough. Where's our killer being held? Did TBI take him into custody or is he in the local jail?"

Her amusement faded. "Unfortunately, neither. They never managed to catch him."

He choked on the water he'd just sipped.

Faith started to rise to check on him, but he held up a hand to stop her. "I'm okay," he rasped then cleared his throat and shoved the rolling tray away from his chair. "How the hell did he get away?" He coughed again, his eyes tearing from the water going down the wrong way.

"We can discuss all of that in a minute, when you recover from almost drowning from a straw."

His eyes narrowed in warning.

"It's so good to see you out of bed and finally lucid," she added, her cheerfulness returning. "How are you feeling this morning, by the way?"

"Angry and disgusted. How did the TBI and police screw this up? Stan only had a half hour's head start in rough terrain. They should have closed down that mountain until they found him. What day is it anyway? How long have they been searching for him?"

"I'm fine. Thanks for asking. In spite of several uncomfortable nights sleeping on that recliner waiting to see if my partner would ever wake up." She grabbed the pink blanket that she'd left on the foot of his bed last night and covered her legs. "Is this room cold to you? Maybe I should adjust the thermostat—"

"Faith."

"Normally, if you took that tone with me, I'd be out that door and wouldn't come back without an apology and some serious groveling. But I'm feeling exceedingly generous right now. I guess almost losing your best friend does that. I'm very glad you didn't die, in spite of how irritating you're being this morning."

He rolled his eyes.

She laughed. "Getting my bad habits?"

He inhaled a deep breath then winced.

She was immediately off the bed, tossing the blanket behind her. Leaning in close, she gently pressed her hand against his forehead, the same way she'd checked him for fever dozens of times over the past few days as he'd slept. "How bad is the pain? I can call the nurse and ask her for—"

He grabbed her by the waist and pulled her onto his lap.

She blinked up at him, so astonished that she didn't immediately try to get up.

His arms wrapped around her like a vise, making the decision for her. She was trapped, unless she wanted to wiggle and push her way off him. In his weakened state, it wouldn't be that difficult. But she didn't want to cause him any pain, either, so she let him win this round.

She tapped his left arm where some tubing was taped against the back of his hand. "Careful. Don't mess up your IV."

"I don't even need one. I should pull the thing out and be done with this place. They've kept me so drugged up, I haven't been able to think clearly, let alone stay awake long enough to get any information. If you hadn't showed up a few minutes ago, I was going to start calling everyone at UB until someone gave me an update on the case. I'm not letting you go until you answer every question I have. First, what are they doing to try to catch Stan—"

She covered his mouth with her hand.

This time it was his turn to look surprised.

"The most important question," she corrected him, "is about your prognosis. Do you even know what happened? What injuries you have? Have you spoken to the doctor?"

He pulled her hand down. "I haven't spoken to anyone, except you, and the guy who delivered my breakfast tray. I feel okay. I can wiggle my toes. And I got from the bed to this chair without any help, so I figure I'm going to live."

She blinked. "Wiggle your toes?"

He smiled. It was a small one, but the fact that he was smiling at all was huge.

"I was worried earlier," he said. "I think it was the first day, after surgery. You asked the doctor about me being able to walk again and—"

"You heard me?"

He nodded.

"I'm so sorry." She gently pressed a hand to his chest. "I should have been more careful in case you were able to understand me even with all those drugs in your system. The knife the bad guy threw at you missed your spine, as you've obviously figured out. It punctured your lung, which is why you had such a hard time breathing. It'll take a while to fully recover. And they had to stitch up muscles, so you have to be careful. I definitely shouldn't be on your lap—"

He tightened his hold. "You're not escaping until we're through talking."

"You do realize that I could make you let me go by punching you in the chest."

"But you won't. Because you don't want to hurt me."

"Yes, well. Friends don't generally hurt friends. So there is that. Your prognosis is excellent. It was scary there for a while, touch and go, because you'd lost a lot of blood. You were bleeding internally, in addition to the collapsed lung. But Grayson had them fly you up here so the trauma-one team could take care of you."

"They should have flown Leslie up instead of me."

"Leslie wasn't in nearly as bad a shape as you. She was terrified, shell-shocked. But physically she only suffered some bruises and minor cuts and scrapes. We got to her before he did his worst. She has you to thank for that. You saved her life, very nearly getting killed yourself." Her hand tightened against his chest. "Lance told us what you did. He arrived in that clearing right as it was happening. You saved Leslie from being hanged. And you threw yourself between the perpetrator and his knife. You shouldn't have taken chances like that. You nearly died."

"I did what I had to do. We're both alive. That's what matters. Leslie told you he's our guy, right? That he killed Jasmine too? She whispered to me that he hated Jasmine because she ruined everything, that she was going to tell the police about him. That goes along with our theory, that Jasmine saw something she shouldn't have. Put two and two together, figured out he was bad news. That's all Leslie said, though. I couldn't really talk and she just sort of...stopped. Are you sure she's okay?"

"She's okay. Promise."

He gave her a curt nod, looking relieved. "We need to find Stan and put him away before he hurts another woman."

Faith stared up at him. "You really haven't spoken to anyone about the case, have you?"

"If I did, it was in a half-awake state and I don't remember anything."

"Well, I'll answer your very first question, about how long you've been here. Since Thursday evening. Today is Sunday morning, so that's—"

"I slept for almost three days?"

"The doctor wanted you to be still and rest to let your body heal. You weren't quite in a drug-induced coma, but close. It was scary to watch you sleeping so deeply, so long."

His eyes widened. "You were here the whole time?"

Almost every single minute. "Of course not. I was here off and on. I wanted to make sure you were okay. That's what friends do."

Asher frowned down at her then sighed. "Well, as your *friend*, thank you for looking out for me."

"You're very welcome. Now, may I get up?"

INSTEAD OF LETTING her go, his arms tightened. "Tell me about the hunt for Stan first."

"Stan Darden Junior isn't our serial killer. The guy you went after, the man who took Leslie, we don't know his real name yet."

"I was worried that might be the case. But I'd really hoped he was Stan. At least that way we'd know his identity. More importantly, the real Stan would be okay. He's dead, isn't he?"

She nodded. "We found him and his father in the tack room."

"Good grief. I got a saddle out of there and didn't even notice. Where were they?"

"Hidden under some horse blankets behind some piles of equipment at the very back. There's no reason you would have noticed. Lance pulled some stuff out of there and didn't see them either. The only reason I discovered them was because I was anxious while waiting for you and Lance and went exploring."

He gently squeezed her waist. "I'm sorry you found them. I'm sure it wasn't a pleasant sight."

She stared up at him. "I'm a cop, or I used to be. It goes with the territory. Are you sure you didn't hit your head?"

"I must have. Goodness knows it wouldn't make sense otherwise for me to worry about you, us being just friends and all."

The bitterness in his tone had her studying his face.

"What?" he asked.

"Are you in pain? You don't seem…yourself."

"I've been sleeping for three days and have been shut out of my own investigation. Of course I'm not myself."

"*Our* investigation. And no one shut you out. I was just going to tell you that Lance has been filling in, helping me, while you're recovering."

He frowned. "Has he really?"

She frowned back. "Yes, of course. No reason to get surly about it. He's not trying to steal the case. He wants to help us."

His jaw tightened, but he gave her a crisp nod. "What have you both found out? Anything?"

"A lot and nothing, kind of like where you and I were. It's been one step forward, two steps back. Lance worked with Gatlinburg PD to put together a timeline of events based on cell phone records and neighbors who saw Stan Senior and the real Stan Junior the morning that Leslie was taken. Our theory that the abductor drove Leslie to one of the turnoffs near the ranch and parked his car there is correct. They found the car, but it was stolen."

"Of course. It being his own car would have been way too easy."

"It's not a total dead end. The car was taken in a neighborhood about ten minutes from Leslie's home. Since no other vehicles were found ditched around there, the belief is he walked to that location from his own place, or hired a car to drop him off."

"He wouldn't have hired a car. Too easy to trace."

"I agree. So does the TBI and Russo. They're canvassing that neighborhood with a sketch of the perp based on my and Leslie's eye-witness accounts. Now that you're up and about, I'm sure that Russo will want to send his sketch artist here to see what you remember so they can refine the drawing."

"Not necessary. You're better at details like that than me. I doubt I can add anything."

She smiled. "Was that a compliment?"

"Nope. Just a fact."

"Oh, brother."

He grinned.

She laughed. "It's good to see the old Asher is still in there somewhere." She smiled up at him, relieved. But as he stared down at her, something changed. His eyes darkened, his face tightened. And for the first time ever around him, she felt...confused, unsure, and a little afraid of whatever this...this tension might mean.

Asher was her friend, her best friend. She treasured that closeness and didn't want to lose it, or change it. She was already struggling not to see the image of his drool-worthy chest every time she closed her eyes. What she really needed to do was to get off his lap and put some distance between them before they crossed a line they could never uncross.

Before she could figure out how to extricate herself without hurting him, he tightened his arms around her. And then he was kissing her. It happened so fast, like him pulling her onto his lap, that she didn't react immediately. Her mind was in shock. This was *Asher*. His mouth was actually on hers. His very warm, insistent, and unbelievably *expert*, lips were doing sensual things that had her toes curling in her shoes.

A little voice of warning cried out somewhere in her dazed mind telling her to push him back, get up, and stop this insanity. But that voice became a whimper of pleasure as he deepened the kiss. This kiss eclipsed every other kiss she'd ever had or even dreamed of having.

She didn't want to push him away. She wanted...more. More of his mouth on hers. More heat. More... God help her, she wanted more *Asher*. Her fingers clutched at his hospital gown, pulling him closer as she pushed her soft curves against his hard planes. Their bodies fit together as if made for each other. Even the evidence of his arousal pressing against her bottom wasn't enough to make her stop. She was helpless to do anything but *feel*.

When she pressed the tip of her tongue against his mouth, he groaned and swept his tongue inside. Heat blistered through her, tightening her belly. Every reservation, every lingering doubt was viciously squashed into oblivion. She refused to pay attention to the warnings, the doubts. She didn't want to think right now. All she wanted to do was to enjoy him, to answer every stroke with one of her own, every ravenous slide of his mouth with an equally wild response.

His warm, strong hands speared through her hair as he half turned, pressing her back against the recliner. When he broke the wild kiss and his warm mouth moved to the side of her neck, she bucked against him, her fingers curving against his shoulders. Her heart was beating so fast she heard the rush of it in her ears. Trailing her hands down his hospital gown, she caressed his mouthwatering chest muscles, and continued the long, slow slide of her fingers toward his impressive hardness pressing against her hip.

A knock sounded on the door, followed by a vaguely familiar voice. "Mr. Whitfield, it's the doctor, making rounds."

Reality was a bucket of ice water, snapping Faith back from the precipice. She practically leaped off Asher and whirled away from him just as the doctor stepped inside, a stethoscope hanging around his neck.

His brows rose. "Should I come back?"

Faith's cheeks flamed. She absolutely refused to look at Asher. "No, no. I was just, uh, leaving."

"Faith, don't go," Asher called out. "Please."

Mortified about what she'd done, what she'd almost done,

with *Asher*, she grabbed her purse from the vinyl chair on the other side of the room and escaped out the door.

ASHER SWORE AND leaned back against the chair.

The doctor gave him a look of sympathy. "Bad timing. Sorry, pal. But at least you appear to be doing better. This is one of the few visits where I've caught you fully awake." He sat on the side of the bed where Faith had been only moments earlier. "I'm Doctor Nichols, in case you don't remember."

"I have a vague recollection of hearing that name before. Faith told me I've been here since Thursday, three days. I would have thought it was only one."

"You've been heavily sedated to keep you from moving around too much. The man who stabbed you in the back used a two-inch-wide serrated hunting knife. Thankfully, it only nicked your left lung, otherwise those jagged edges would have shredded it. But it did a number on the muscles in your back, damaged some nerves, collapsed the lung."

"That explains why everything hurts. Thanks for patching me up." He glanced at the door, silently willing Faith to return.

"I can get the nurse in here to give you more pain meds."

"No, no. They just put me to sleep. I need to talk to my coworkers and get updates on the case I've been working. But thanks. Thanks for everything. Sounds like you saved my life."

"I can't take all the credit. There was another surgeon with me, and an excellent trauma team to help pull you through. It's a good thing your boss insisted on medevac. You'd lost a lot of blood and were fading fast. It's doubtful you'd have survived an ambulance ride and subsequent treatment at a hospital without a level-one trauma team."

"I appreciate everything, believe me. But I'm ready to go home. When can I get out of here?"

"Don't mistake the fact that you were able to move from the bed to a chair to mean you're ready to be discharged. You're not."

Asher frowned at him. "I have a job to do, a killer to catch. I really need to get out of here."

"Ignore him, Doc. He's a terrible patient." Lance strode into the room, nodding at the doctor before smiling at Asher. "Good to see you finally back from the dead. Gave us all quite a scare."

Lance clasped his shoulder then moved back. "Sorry to interrupt. Faith told me you were awake and I wanted to see for myself. Please, finish whatever you're doing, Doctor."

Nichols looked back at Asher. "When you got here, you had a pneumothorax—a collapsed lung. By itself, that usually requires a good week at the hospital so we can monitor for any breathing issues or signs of infection. But, on top of that, you had major surgery to reconnect muscles and repair nerves. If you get out of here before *next* Sunday, I'll be surprised."

Asher swore and proceeded to argue with the doctor.

After a few minutes back and forth, Nichols shook his head. "This isn't a negotiation, Mr. Whitfield. I understand you're involved in an important investigation. I'll release you as soon as possible. But it won't be one minute before I deem it safe for you to go home."

Once the doctor conducted his exam and left, Asher eyed Lance. "You have to help me."

"No way. I'm not breaking you out of here. I won't have that on my conscience if something goes wrong. You're here like the doc said, until it's safe for you to leave."

"We'll see about that," Asher grumbled. "You said you spoke to Faith. How is she?"

"Hard to say. She was in a hurry to leave, said she had an errand. Barely stopped in the waiting room long enough to let me know you were awake. Did something happen between you two? She seemed upset."

He squeezed his eyes shut. Damn. He hadn't meant to upset her. He'd gotten caught up in the moment and had finally done something outrageous, as Daphne had encouraged him to do so many times. Had he opened a door with Faith? Or slammed it shut?

"Asher? You okay?"

Hell no. "I'm fine. Tell me about the search for the killer. Faith said you were working on the timeline. When did he get to the ranch? Why was he in the stables when Faith and I got there? Where was Leslie when he was in the stables? How—"

Lance held up his hands, laughing. "I can see why Faith was in such a hurry to get out of here. You probably drove her nuts with all your questions." He crossed the room and grabbed the extra chair, then sat in front of Asher. "Since you didn't call the bad guy Stan again, I'm guessing you heard the *real* Stans, junior and senior, were murdered and stuffed in the back of the tack room long before you and Faith arrived."

"I heard. I'd hoped to stop this guy before he hurt anyone else."

"Don't beat yourself up. The cops had five years to find him. You and Faith found him in a few months. We've got his description, a BOLO out on him. Every law enforcement officer in eastern Tennessee will be on the lookout, with the picture the sketch artist made after talking to Leslie and Faith. They swabbed the hilt of that knife he threw at you and sent it away for DNA testing. That could break the case wide open."

"Only if he's in the system already."

"Pessimist." Lance chuckled. "We also know, thanks to both you and Faith, that he's good with horses. Maybe he's employed at one of the horse-riding operations around Gatlinburg or Pigeon Forge."

Asher glanced at the door again, worries about Faith making it difficult to focus. Or maybe it was the drugs. It was getting harder and harder to stay awake.

"I wouldn't characterize our killer as being good with horses," Asher said. "He doesn't have the patience or empathy for them. Not surprising for a sociopath. I admit I bought into him being Stan, though. He spun a detailed convincing story about his dad and girlfriend, and him inheriting the business. Either he got that info from the real Stan before killing him, or he's a good actor."

"Probably both. We'll never know how much time he spent, or didn't spend, talking to Junior before killing him. Unless we catch him and he confesses, gives us details. The girlfriend part seems to be made up. None of Stan's friends were aware of him dating anyone, let alone living with them as he'd told you and Faith."

Asher nodded. "What about Leslie Parks? Physically, I'm told she's more or less okay. But we both know she had to have gone through hell."

Lance's smile faded. "No doubt. Thankfully, he didn't have a lot of time with her, relatively speaking. From what he told her, he was planning on holding her for days, maybe weeks, torturing her before killing her. Considering what could have happened, her physical injuries are minor. Psychologically…well, I can't speak to that. I'm sure it's going to take a long time and some intense therapy to move past this, if that's even possible."

Asher refused to glance at the door again, not wanting to

clue Lance in to just how worried he was about Faith. He really needed to talk to her. But what would he say? How could he fix this? Did he even want to? He didn't want to go back to the friend zone. He wanted her right where he'd had her, in his arms. Hell, he wanted far more than that.

"You okay, buddy?" Lance asked.

"Just thinking about the case," he lied. "What about the other bodies we found in his Smoky Mountains graveyard? Have they been identified yet?"

"As expected, Jasmine Parks is one of them. They've identified three of the others so far. No known cause of death, unfortunately, since all the ME had to go on were skeletons. No knife marks on any of the bones to indicate stabbing. No bullet holes or shell casings." Lance pulled out his cell phone. "I'll pull up the latest update."

Chapter Twelve

Once again, Faith was saying goodbye to her little sister. It was bittersweet since they hadn't seen much of each other during Daphne's college break. Work, as it often did, had interfered.

Daphne slung her backpack over one shoulder and leaned into the open passenger door of Faith's Lexus. Her orange-brick dorm at the University of Tennessee towered like a monument behind her. "Thanks for the ride, sis. Give Ash my love when you visit him at UT Med today. You're taking him home soon, right? Hasn't he been there for almost a week?"

"Today would be a week. They flew him up last Thursday. I'll tell Ash*er* you said hello when I see him."

"Give *Ash* a kiss for me too." Daphne winked, laughing when Faith gave her an aggravated look.

Faith watched her sister until she safely entered the dorm. Then she turned the car around and headed back to the main road. She wouldn't see her baby sister again until next week, when she returned to Knoxville to take her out for pizza at one of the campus hangouts. It was a tradition. Faith did her best never to miss pizza night, although the day of the week they chose depended on both of their schedules.

While Daphne sometimes called Faith her smother-mother instead of her big sister, she was mostly teasing. She understood Faith's longing to see her only blood relative, especially because Faith's career, her glimpses of the dark side of humanity, made her worry so much about Daphne's safety. The only reason Faith hadn't switched to a job in Knoxville when Daphne decided to go there for school was that Daphne had made her promise not to. Their compromise, in exchange for Faith paying Daphne's tuition, was that Faith could text her whenever she wanted. What Faith really *wanted* was to text her sister several times a day to make sure she was okay. But she didn't want her sister to resent her. So she kept it to one text a day. Most of the time.

The two of them had always been close, and that had only solidified after they'd lost their parents. They'd had no one else to lean on except each other. It was the main reason Faith had given up her career as a police detective in Nashville when the opportunity at Unfinished Business had come along. The move to Gatlinburg had been a smooth transition, since it was like a second home anyway. Their family had vacationed there dozens of times over the years. But mainly she'd made the move because cold cases would be much less dangerous than active homicide investigations. She and Daphne were already, technically, orphans. She didn't want Daphne having the extra burden of losing her only sibling. Faith wanted to be Daphne's rock, to be the one person she could always rely on and trust. That was why Faith was struggling with guilt as she drove down the highway. She'd broken that trust by lying about Asher. He wasn't in the hospital.

He was already home.

He'd been discharged yesterday, Wednesday morning, several days ahead of the doctor's prediction. Lance had told her that the doctor gave in because he was weary of Asher's constant requests to go home. Lance had been the one who'd driven Asher back to Gatlinburg.

If it wasn't for Lance's updates, she wouldn't have known

what was going on. She hadn't been brave enough to visit Asher herself, not since that earth-shattering kiss. She hadn't taken his calls, either, or replied to his texts. She was a coward, avoiding the inevitable, having a face-to-face discussion about what had happened between them. If it was up to her, she'd never have that discussion.

She wanted, needed, the closeness, the friendship that the two of them had always shared. The thought of crossing that line had never even occurred to her until that devastating kiss. Well, it had really first occurred when she'd seen his naked chest. But it was only a fleeting thought at that time and she'd quickly discarded it. Now, having sipped at the well of Asher, she wanted to dive in and let him consume her.

She tightened her hands on the steering wheel. This obsession with him had to end. Yes, they'd crossed the friendship line. And she'd glimpsed something truly amazing on the other side. But she also knew what had happened to several of her friends who'd dated coworkers. Inevitably, if the relationship didn't work out, things ended awkwardly and they lost the friendships they'd once treasured. One of them would end up transferring to another department to escape the awkwardness of seeing each other every day. There wasn't another department to transfer to at UB. And even if there was, Faith had no interest in that. She didn't want to *never* see Asher again.

She cherished their closeness, the teasing, being able to finish each other's sentences. She craved it, needed him in her life. And she was terrified that if they pursued…more… she could lose him completely. The idea of him not being around was devastating, unthinkable. That's why she desperately wanted to repair the damage that had been done. She had to try to put things back the way they used to be.

Tomorrow morning, the entire UB team was having a

mandatory meeting at Grayson's mansion. Their boss had specifically ordered her to be there. He knew she'd hit a brick wall on the case without Asher there to bounce ideas back and forth. And he'd no doubt heard that she'd stopped visiting Asher at the hospital. For the sake of the investigation, he wanted their partnership repaired ASAP.

Their killer was still on the loose. No one had a clue who he was or where he might be. The DNA and fingerprints from the knife had yielded no hits on any law enforcement databases. And even though blasting the composite sketch of the killer across the media had resulted in tons of tips, none of them had panned out so far. It was Grayson's hope that she and Asher could work their magic, build on their research, and figure out once and for all how to stop the killer. That meant she had to clear the air between the two of them *today*.

Somehow.

Over an hour later, Faith pulled her Lexus up the familiar, long, winding driveway to a two-story log house teetering on the edge of one of the Smoky Mountains. In the past, she'd looked forward to the view from the two-story glass windows off the back of the house. Today, she dreaded it. But there was no turning back now. Asher was standing at the front picture window, looking out at her, no doubt alerted by his perimeter security system that a car had turned into his driveway.

After cutting the engine, she grabbed her backpack of files on the Parks case. All too soon, she arrived at the nine-foot-tall massive double doors. Before she could knock, one of them opened.

A disheveled, bleary-eyed Asher stood in the opening. He was barefoot, wearing sweatpants, dark blue ones that matched the blue button-up shirt he had on, no doubt because trying to pull a T-shirt over his head would have been too painful.

He hadn't shaved in days. And it didn't look as if he'd even brushed his hair this morning. Had *she* done that to him? Or was he in pain? Goodness knew his body still had a lot of healing to do.

"Faith. Hello." His deep voice was short, clipped, bordering on cold. He made a show of glancing over her shoulder. "Your wingman, Lance, isn't with you?"

Her cheeks flushed with heat. "That tattletale. I told him not to let you know that he was feeding me updates. I just wanted to make sure you were okay."

"You could have done that by visiting me yourself. Or at least responding to one of my texts."

She held her hands out in a placating gesture. "I'm here now."

Friendly, welcoming, smiling Asher was nowhere to be found. Instead, a stoic stranger blocked the entryway, his expression blank, unreadable.

Her heart seemed to squeeze in her chest as she realized she'd made a terrible mistake. Avoiding him hadn't salvaged their relationship. It may very well have destroyed it.

Regret had her blinking back threatening tears. "We need to talk." When he didn't move or speak, she added, "Please?"

Still nothing. Was he going to shut the door in her face? She waited, hating how awkward things were between them right now. It was an unfamiliar feeling, the exact kind of feeling she'd been trying to avoid by not letting their relationship change.

Clearing her throat, she hoisted the backpack higher on her shoulder. "Okay, well, I guess I'll see you at Grayson's tomorrow. Sorry I didn't call first. I'll just—"

He sighed heavily and turned away, heading toward the back of the house. At least he'd left the door open. It was a start.

ASHER STOOD WITH his back to the two-story windows in the great room, watching Faith enter. It took every ounce of self-control he had not to run to her, pull her in for a hug, a kiss, anything to reassure himself that he hadn't destroyed his chance with her. Because, surely there was a chance, or had been, based on the way she'd responded to his kiss.

He very much wanted her in his life. But he didn't want to return to the friend zone. Having tasted heaven, he craved it and refused to settle for anything less. He'd already wasted two years pretending, of listening to her chat about her dates with other men as if he was one of her girlfriends. It never seemed to occur to her that there was a reason he never dated, that he didn't pay attention to any woman but her. All this time he'd been hoping that she'd finally open her eyes to what was right in front of her. Well, he was done with that. He couldn't live like this anymore. Something had to give.

She set her backpack on the dining table at the far left end of the open room, and glanced around as if she hadn't been here hundreds of times. The true detective that she was, she noticed the setup of bagels and pastries on the kitchen island that he normally kept empty.

"I know you didn't set up that pretty display. And I'm pretty sure that fancy cake dome didn't come from your kitchen. Did Ivy stop by and bring that?"

He crossed his arms and leaned against the side of the stone fireplace. "She came to visit. Everyone from work has come by. Except you."

Faith winced.

"But," he continued, "Ivy didn't bring that over. My mom did."

Her eyes widened, sparkling emerald green in the sunlight coming in through the back windows. "I thought your parents were in France, visiting some friends."

"They'd still be there, if it was up to me. I didn't want to worry them. But Grayson called them. They flew in Monday."

She glanced around, as if looking for signs of them being there. "They aren't staying with you?"

"They left an hour ago, heading back to Florida."

"Tampa, right? Your dad always entertains me with stories about his fishing excursions there and—"

"Why are you here, Faith?"

She winced again then started toward him, stopping a few feet away. He had to admire her for that. He'd been an unwelcoming ass so far and she was facing him head-on. That's the Faith he was used to, not the one who'd run earlier this week.

"Why are you here?" Asher repeated, not sure what to expect. Was this an official goodbye? Had he scared her so much she was quitting her job, leaving Gatlinburg? Maybe going back to Nashville? The thought of that sent a frisson of fear through him. But he wasn't backing down. In the few minutes that she'd been here, he'd made his decision. Going backward wasn't part of it.

She took his right hand in both of hers. "You look tired. Do you feel okay? Any trouble breathing?"

"I'm sure I look as ragged as I feel. The pain's at a steady four now. But that's much better than the eight or nine a few days ago. I imagine I'll live."

"I'm so sorry you're hurting. Do you want to sit down? Can I get you some pain meds?"

"I'll get them myself once you tell me why you're here."

She sighed and gently ran her thumb over the back of his hand. "You know you're my best friend in the whole world, right?"

That soft slow stroke of her thumb was killing him. He had to force himself not to tighten his grip, pull her to him and seek another taste of heaven.

"I used to think I was your best friend," Asher said. "Now I'm not sure."

"My fault. I treated you horribly. It's unforgivable, really, to leave and not come back. I should have been there for you. That's what friends do. They take care of each other. I didn't do that. And I'm sorry, deeply sorry. Do you think you can forgive me?"

"No."

Faith blinked and tugged her hands free. "No?"

"There's nothing to forgive. You ran because you were scared. I get that. And I respect, and appreciate, that you finally came back to face me."

A look of relief crossed her face. "Thank you. I was worried I'd ruined everything. That you wouldn't want to be around me anymore. Your friendship means everything to me and I don't want to destroy it because of one moment of insanity between us." She laughed awkwardly. "I don't know how it happened. We were both tired, and I know you were in pain and…well, let's just put that behind us and pretend it didn't happen. I brought my case files with me and we can—"

Asher stepped closer, forcing her to crane her neck back to look at him. "I refuse to pretend that amazing, scorching, earth-shattering kiss didn't happen. I've been trying to make you see me as more than a friend for almost two years now. We clicked right away, had fun together. I get that you were glad to have someone welcome you and show you the ropes at a brand-new job. But we started off wrong. I was patient, too patient, and never let you know how I really felt. Well, I'm letting you know now. My interest in you has never been just as a friend. I want you, Faith. And I'm not going to pretend anymore that I don't. I'm done with pretending."

When she simply stared at him, in obvious shock, he decided not to pull any punches. He laid it all out in the open so there would never be any misunderstandings again.

"While we're working, I'll do my best to keep it professional. But when we're off the clock, or having that downtime you mentioned, we're just a man and a woman. And this man very much wants to treat you like a woman, in every way. If you can't deal with that, you can run again, go home. I'll ask Grayson to assign me another partner to help with the Parks case."

Her cheeks flushed. "Assign someone else? It's my case too. I'm not going to stop working on it. You're not replacing me, not on this investigation."

"Then you have a choice to make. Work with me, knowing my feelings for you are anything but…tame. Or we let Grayson decide which one of us continues working on the Parks investigation and which one gets reassigned to something else."

Her hands fisted at her sides. "I don't want to risk him reassigning me. You don't play fair."

He leaned down until their faces were only a few inches apart. "Darlin', if I played fair, I'd never get what I want. To be perfectly clear, what I want is you. In my bed."

Her face flushed an even brighter red as she took several steps back. "Well, I can tell you right now. *That's* never going to happen. And you're not kicking me off this case."

He smiled. "Good to know, about the case. That means we'll continue to work together day in and day out until we solve this thing. You'll have plenty of time to realize you're underestimating yourself."

Her brows drew down in confusion. "Underestimating myself? What do you mean?"

He moved close again, so close that her breasts brushed against him. "You've had a taste, a very small taste, of how good it could be between us. And, like it or not, you're curious. You're wondering just how much better, and hotter, it could get. And one day…maybe not today, maybe not for a while yet, you'll want to scratch that itch."

Her mouth fell open in astonishment.

"When you reach that point," Asher continued, "when you decide you've wondered enough and are ready to discover just how good it will be between us, all you have to do is crook that pretty finger of yours and I'll come running."

Her jaw snapped shut and she smoothed her hands down her jeans. "Well, then. I'll be careful not to…crook my finger. I wouldn't want *you* to get the wrong impression. Now, if you're through feeding that tremendous ego, we both have work to do. On the case."

"Of course. After you." He motioned in the direction of his office.

She grabbed her backpack from the table, then headed down the hallway.

When the door closed behind her with a loud click, he swore beneath his breath and strode into the kitchen to grab some pain pills. Shaking his head as he popped a couple out of the bottle, he swore again. What had gotten into him? He knew the answer to that. Daphne. Faith's sister had pushed him, over and over, telling him to be bold, to do something outrageous to let Faith know how he felt. Well he'd done that and more.

He'd been waiting far too long, moving at glacial speed. Either she'd decide she wanted him or she wouldn't. But he was through spending his life trying to make her notice him.

If it was meant to be, great. If not...well, he'd cross that bridge if it came to that. They'd work the case, hopefully solve it. Then it was up to her. If the answer was no, or even to wait longer, he was done.

His bruised ego applauded his decision. But his heart was already mourning the expected end, that Faith would never care about him the way he cared about her.

He glanced down the hallway toward the closed office door. Then he returned to the kitchen and grabbed a bottle of beer from the fridge. He didn't care that it was technically still morning. As the saying went, it was five o'clock somewhere. He popped the top, grimacing at the pain in his back as he tilted the bottle.

Chapter Thirteen

It had been a concerted effort yesterday, but Asher had done his best to *behave*, to act professionally and as platonically as possible so that Faith wouldn't feel uncomfortable. They'd spent the day poring over her research, and that of TBI and Gatlinburg PD, from when he'd been in the hospital. And they'd brainstormed various theories, not that they'd made much progress. She'd gradually relaxed and they'd fallen into their old routine of easy camaraderie. It was a good day, far better than he'd expected when it began.

When she'd fallen asleep at his desk in the early morning hours, he'd wanted to carry her down the hall to the guest room. But his still healing shoulder wouldn't cooperate. Instead, he'd urged a mostly-asleep Faith to shuffle to the couch with his help. He couldn't get her to go the extra distance to the guest room without her sleepily threatening to shoot him. Chuckling, he'd tucked the infamous pink blanket around her, the one she'd left at the hospital when she'd run out. He'd been curious about how she'd react when she woke and saw it. Her laughter the next morning had him smiling when he heard her from his master bath where he was brushing his teeth.

She'd gone home to shower and change, leaving the pink blanket neatly folded over the back of the couch. He hadn't tried driving since getting hurt but he was thinking he'd have to either give it a try or call Lance for a ride to Grayson's mansion for the morning UB meeting. But Faith had surprised him by pulling up and offering her services as his chauffeur.

Approaching Grayson's mansion was just as awe-inspiring this morning as it was every time Asher saw it. Honey-colored stone walls sparkled in the morning sun. A giant portico shaded much of the circular drive out front, with enough space for half a dozen cars beneath it.

Massive windows that Grayson had added in a recent renovation reflected the trees and English gardens out front. They were made of bullet-resistant, one-way privacy glass, just like the windows at Unfinished Business. And they went floor to ceiling in every room.

"How many square feet do you think this place is?" Faith asked as she parked behind Lance's white Jeep. "You could fit four or five homes like mine inside, and my house isn't exactly tiny."

"No clue. I've never asked. Have you ever seen the whole thing?"

"Don't think I have, actually. Maybe we should ask for a guided tour someday."

"In our spare time?"

She smiled. "Maybe we'll have time for a real vacation one day, instead of the fake one we had to work for the Parks investigation." She cut the engine.

"We?"

Her smile faded. "I mean, you know, both of us, our own vacations. I didn't mean to—"

He gently squeezed her hand. "I was teasing, Faith."

"Oh. I knew that."

He grinned.

She rolled her eyes.

"I've missed this," he said. "A day isn't complete without you rolling your eyes at me."

"Well, now that I know how much you love it, I'll be sure to do it more often."

He laughed and they both got out of her Lexus and headed inside.

As he closed one of the double doors behind them, which was even larger than the ones at his place, he leaned down next to her ear. "I'm always surprised when a stuffy English butler doesn't answer the door here. But then, Grayson doesn't stand on ceremony, in spite of all his money. He's pretty down to earth."

"He's not what people expect, that's for sure." She took a turn around the magnificent polished wood and marble entryway. "I think he's got a dozen employees running this place. But half of them are elderly and have lived here longer than he has. It's more of a service he's giving them than the other way around, making sure they can live out their days in style instead of being relegated to some retirement home."

Willow stepped out of the double doors to the left that led to the library. "And if he hears you talking about how wonderful and kind he is, he'll turn ornery and resentful. He's not good at taking compliments."

Faith hugged her. "I'm so glad the two of you ended up together. You're the perfect couple, yin to his yang and all that."

"He's perfect for *me*, that's for sure. Now, let's get this party started. You're the last two investigators to arrive. The rest are already here—Ryland, Lance, Brice, Trent, Ivy. Even Callum put his current case on hold to be here for the meeting. He drove in from Johnson City last night. The only one missing is our resident TBI liaison. Rowan is negotiating the access to evidence in some of our cases but will be here later. No need for us to wait. There's a breakfast buffet set up in the library. After that, we'll get down to business."

The library was exactly that, a two-story-high room that was filled with books. But it was also the equivalent of a family room with groupings of couches and recliners in several different areas. Or, they would have been, except that some of the groupings had been combined into one big U-shaped cluster in the middle of the room for the meeting.

On the opposite wall to the windows, the buffet that Willow had mentioned was set up. It contained an obscene amount of food running the gambit from fruit and bagels to eggs, biscuits and gravy. To a stranger, it might seem wasteful. But everyone at UB knew the truth. Nothing went to waste here. Grayson was generous and shared everything with the staff and any of the temporary workers in the gardens. No doubt the kitchens were bustling right now to ensure that everyone got plenty of fresh, delicious food. And if there ended up being too much for the staff and their families, it would be taken to a local food bank.

True to Faith's caring nature, in spite of the prickly exterior she often showed the world, she fussed over Asher, making sure he ate far more than he really wanted.

"You have to regain your strength," she said, bringing him a second glass of orange juice. "And you need plenty of vitamin C to help your muscles heal."

He eyed the glass without enthusiasm. "I guess that explains why you're trying to get me to drink a gallon of this stuff. I don't really care much for orange juice, to be honest."

"Doesn't matter. It's good for you."

Lance, sitting on a nearby couch, started laughing.

Faith narrowed her eyes. "What's so funny?"

He shrugged, still grinning. "Just beginning to understand why your sister calls you a smother-mother."

She gasped. "Who told you that?"

He pointed at Asher.

"You *didn't*." She crossed her arms.

He started drinking the juice to avoid answering.

She sat back, her expression promising retribution later.

He couldn't help grinning when he finally set the juice down. But before Faith could make him pay, Grayson and Willow stood.

"Thank you all for coming here," Grayson said. "Rather than have this status meeting in the conference room at the office, I wanted to have it at our home because this is a special occasion. Asher, thank God, is with us today when he came close to dying a little over a week ago. Willow and I are both extremely grateful that you're on the road to recovery and back with the team."

Everyone clapped and cheered. A few whistled. Asher shook his head, motioning for everyone to stop.

Faith subtly moved her hand on the couch between them, gently pressing her fingers over the top of his hand.

He glanced at her in question and she simply smiled. He knew she was thanking him, as the others were. But her private gesture moved him more than all the others combined.

Before Asher could say anything, Grayson cleared his throat and the noise died down.

"I'll add one more thing," Grayson said. "Asher risked his life to save the life of another. That's rare. Even more rare is for someone to help another by *actually* giving them the shirt off their back."

Asher groaned at the corny joke.

"Willow and I would like to compensate you for your loss." Grayson pitched something at Asher.

He caught it against his chest, shaking his head when he realized what it was.

A shirt.

Soon, shirts were being tossed at him from everyone there, the last from Faith, who was laughing as it landed on top of the small pile of clothes on his lap.

"Very funny, everyone," he said dryly. "Hilarious." He made a show of checking the tag on one of them and tossed it at Lance. "Someone must have meant that one for you. It's a small."

Lance, who was just as big as Asher, tossed the shirt back. "Then it's definitely for you, little guy."

Faith started folding the pile of shirts.

"Thanks, darlin'," Asher whispered.

She avoided his gaze but subtly nodded.

"All fun aside," Grayson said, "we're all busy and have a lot of work to do. Ryland, you want to give your status first? We can end with Faith."

He nodded and began updating the team on his current case. They each gave updates, as they normally did each morning whether at UB or via remote link, depending on where each of them was working that day. They bounced ideas off each other and made suggestions. When it was Asher's turn, he gave a quick summary of what had happened when Faith zeroed in on Stan's Smoky Mountains Trail Rides as a potential place for Leslie Parks to have been taken.

"You know the rest. We were lucky to find Leslie. But, unfortunately, the killer got away. Faith can tell you what happened after that since I was out of commission for a bit."

"He totally glossed over the details that some of you haven't heard," she said. "The perpetrator strung up Leslie with a noose around her neck. He had her stand on a log and had a rope tied around it, with one end trailing into the woods where he was hiding. As soon as Asher found Leslie, the perp yanked the rope. Asher dove at Leslie, grabbing her legs against the tree just as the log upended her. If he hadn't done that, her neck would have snapped. Then the coward in the woods threw his knife at her to finish the job. But Asher twisted his body in between the knife and Leslie, again saving her life. Leslie told me that knife was headed straight for her heart. Even with the knife embedded in his back, puncturing a lung, Asher managed to get the noose off Leslie and mount a horse with her to bring her back to the stables."

Willow, seated with Grayson across from them, went pale. "I had no idea just how bad it was up there. Good grief. We really are lucky you survived, Asher."

"I appreciate it. But it's over. I'm doing fine." He motioned to Faith. "You worked up a timeline based on yours and Gatlinburg PD's research. Want to tell them about that?"

She took mercy on him by taking over, speaking to all of the research she'd done in the past handful of days.

"The perpetrator walked Leslie into the stables, stole the two horses and forced her to ride up into the foothills. He was rough, slapped her around, gave her some shallow cuts with that same knife. Mostly, he terrified her, telling her the awful things that he was going to do. Thankfully, he never got to the point of carrying out those plans. Asher rescued her before the perp could assault her in the way he'd planned."

Ryland leaned forward in his chair to Faith's left. "Why did he return to the stables and leave her up in the foothills? And why kill the two he left in the tack room?"

"Leslie said that when Stan Darden Junior rode into the foothills searching for the horses, he stumbled right onto them and saw Leslie tied to that tree, being tortured. Stan, again, the real one, tried to intervene. But the perp got the better of him and stabbed him. Stan was able to stagger to his horse and take off, presumably to get help. You can all pretty much guess what happened after that. Our bad guy took off after Stan. He caught him and butchered him at the stables. Then he did the same to Stan's father when the noise alerted him and he came outside looking for his son."

Ivy winced across from Faith. "How awful. That poor family."

"I know." Faith shook her head. "It's so sad. Such a useless waste of life."

Asher took up the tale. "It appears that he was getting a fresh horse, hiding the bodies and grabbing supplies so he could head deeper into the mountains with Leslie at about the time that Faith and I arrived."

Faith nodded. "Leslie hasn't spoken to anyone aside from me that first day. We were both together because the police wanted us to help the sketch artist make a composite of the man who attacked her. Immediately after that, she gave me the basics that I just told you. But after that, she stopped talking, wouldn't even speak to the detectives on the case. I think she's been in shock, unable to face the trauma of what happened. I'm hopeful that she'll agree to speak to Asher and me, given that he saved her life. Willow, as our victim advocate, you've already made inroads with the family. Do you think you could speak to them, see if Asher and I can interview Leslie? Today if possible?"

"Absolutely. Her well-being will be my first priority, of course. But if she's up to it, and her family agrees, I'll let you know right away."

"That's all I can ask for. Thanks."

Willow smiled.

At that moment, Rowan Knight arrived. Nodding at Asher, he went directly to Grayson and handed him a piece of paper. They spoke for a moment before Rowan turned to leave. On his way out, he tossed a shirt at Asher and grinned as he hurriedly left.

Asher chuckled and added the shirt to the pile that Faith had set between them just as Grayson handed the paper to Faith.

"The medical examiner," Grayson said, "with the help of a forensic anthropologist, identified the final two victims. Those are their names, brief descriptions including limited background information on them, as well as their last-known addresses."

Faith summarized the findings for everyone, reading the pertinent details out loud. "Victim number five identified as June Aguirre, female, Hispanic, twenty-six years old. She was single, had a steady boyfriend—Nathan Jefferson. Lived in Pigeon Forge. Occupation, branch manager of a credit union. Disappeared on her way home from work in downtown Gatlinburg and was never seen again. That was five years ago." She blinked. "Wow, she disappeared one *day* before Jasmine Parks."

Asher frowned. "That's a heck of an escalation, from about six months between our earlier victims and only one day between those last two. Definitely something we need to pay attention to. What about cause of death? The ME couldn't come up with one on the other victims. Anything on June Aguirre?"

Faith reread the short summary then shook her head. "Manner of death, homicide. Cause of death, undetermined." She flipped the paper over. "Victim number six is Brenda Kramer, female, white, twenty-three. Also single, with a steady live-in boyfriend—Kurt Ritter. She was a lifelong resident of Gatlinburg. After high school, she took two years off to travel. When she came back, she began attending business school. She was one year from graduation when she disappeared one night after partying with friends. Her boyfriend said she never made it home. That was seven years ago. And before you ask, cause of death again is undetermined." She grimaced. "This is weird. Some smooth river rocks were found in the victim's pocket. Could that be significant?"

"Were there rocks found with the others?" Grayson asked.

"Not that I recall. Asher?"

"I'll double-check, but I don't think so. I remember one of the victims had really hard dirt caked on what was left of their clothes. The ME speculated it might have been mud at the time the body was buried. That could mean two of the victims had been in or near water shortly before their deaths. Or it could be as simple as someone hiking and picking up rocks. And the other getting caught in the rain and getting muddy before they were kidnapped. I'm not seeing how rocks or mud can help us, but we'll note it, see if it ties into anything else we've found."

Grayson crossed his arms, his brows pulled together in a frown. "Seems thin, agreed. I know it's been years since the murders and the only thing the ME has to go on are skeletons, but can't we get her to at least speculate about possible causes of death? Like strangulation? Isn't that a common COD in serial killer cases?"

Asher nodded. "It's actually one of the most common ways serial killers murder their victims. But usually that breaks some bones in the throat, and that will be found during the autopsy. Since none of our victims had their hyoid bone broken, strangulation doesn't seem likely. Lack of tool marks or splintered bones on any of our victims also makes it seem unlikely they were stabbed. There weren't any bullet holes in any of the bones, no bullet fragments. So shooting is highly unlikely."

"What about poison?" Grayson asked. "There was some hair found with some of the victims. Can't they test the hair for toxins? I seem to remember hearing that hair continues to grow for some time after death. If that postmortem hair contains toxins, could it prove someone ingested some as a cause of death?"

Faith smiled. "Changing professions, boss? Wanting to become one of your investigators?"

"I don't want to work that hard," he teased. "But I'm as frustrated as I'm sure you and Asher are. Just asking questions that come to mind."

"They're good questions. Questions that Asher and I have discussed as well. Or, we did, when discussing the earlier victims. With June and Brenda added to the mix, I'm sure we'll rediscuss all of that. Poison is one of the things we can't rule out. Even with hair growth after death, to have enough concentration of toxins in that hair to detect would only happen if the poison took a long time to kill the victim. The heart would have to be pumping long enough to circulate toxins all over the body and to end up in hair follicles in large enough concentrations to detect. I can't see a serial killer dosing victims over a long enough period of time for the poison to show up in postmortem hair deposits."

Asher nodded his agreement. "It's also rare for men to use poison to kill. That's more of a female killer's method of choice. We know our killer is a white male in his early thirties. That matches our latest FBI profile on him, and the eyewitness accounts—namely Leslie's, Faith's, and mine. The profile also said he's likely single, never married, and has difficulty holding down a steady job. He'll resort to hourly, cash jobs, possibly outdoors, like landscaping or construction. That goes along with his comfort up here in the mountains. This location is his domain, where he feels most at ease. He likely started killing in his mid-twenties, which would go right along with our first victim having been killed seven years ago. As often happens with serial killers, there was likely a trigger at that time that sent him over the edge from hurting and murdering women in his fantasies to actually doing it."

"Don't forget the trauma he believes the killer suffered during his childhood, as a preteen or early teen," Faith added. "That supposedly had a major impact on his world outlook, maybe even began his hatred for women. It might help explain his depravity, but I don't see how that helps us figure out who he is other than looking for some kind of childhood trauma in any background searches we do in the hopes of narrowing any potential suspect lists down."

"Faith and I speculated that hanging could be his go-to for how he kills, since he tried to hang Leslie Parks," Asher said. "But she called the ME about that possibility shortly after we rescued Leslie. That's when the medical examiner explained about the hyoid bone and lack of any other broken bones in our victims. With hanging, it's possible *not* to break the neck. But she believed it unlikely that at least one of the deceased wouldn't have showed some kind of bone injury if they were all hung. Then again, we're assuming our killer is consistent with how he kills. Most are. But some do change it up. They learn from their mistakes, adjust their weapon of choice."

"What about a signature?" Lance asked. "Even if a serial killer changes how he kills, there's usually one thing, a ritual or whatever, that's always the same. It could be as simple as how he binds his victims, or that he kisses their forehead before killing them. Is there anything at all you've been able to piece together as his signature, given that you only have the skeletons, some hair, and fragments of clothes and jewelry?"

Faith shook her head no as she handed the paper to Asher. "With so little to go on as far as physical evidence in each of the graves, we don't even have a theory about his signature.

It's something we debate often but neither of us has anything concrete to offer there."

She motioned toward the paper that Asher was studying. "These two latest victim identifications, on top of the information we have on the others, means that the killer's first victim was Brenda Kramer. The rest, in order of when they were killed, are Natalie Houseman, Dana Randolph, Felicia Stewart and June Aguirre. Jasmine Parks is the last victim, five years ago. There aren't any other bodies in that makeshift graveyard. TBI brought in their own scent dog team and reexamined the entire mountainside with ground penetrating radar. Six victims, total. He kills one every five to six months, then his last two only one day apart. After that, nothing. One thing I want answered is why he escalated from his routine of about six months between kills to one day between his last two."

"No clue about the one-day-apart thing," Lance offered. "But I didn't think serial killers stop killing by choice. Either they die, are incarcerated, or incapacitated in some way that makes it impossible for them to continue. Have you explored the incarceration angle?"

"We have," Asher told him. "We actually hired a computer expert for that because we had a massive amount of data on intakes and releases of prisoners from the Tennessee prison system to analyze. He wrote a program that compared all of that data with the dates that our victims were killed and the gap since Jasmine's disappearance and Leslie's abduction. Some of the more recent convicts to be released could theoretically have abducted Leslie. But our computer guy was able to exclude most of them because they were incarcerated during times when some of the other victims were killed. We ended up with only five potentials and were able to rule them out because their photos don't match our killer."

"That thorough analysis pretty much proves he wasn't incarcerated during that time gap," Lance said. "Unless he was incarcerated in another state, which I'd consider a low probability given that he's choosing and murdering people here. He's comfortable, knows the area. Maybe he hasn't stopped killing at all and is burying the more recent bodies in another personal graveyard, perhaps on another remote mountainside."

"Possibly," Asher said. "But it's all speculation without any facts at this point. It's rare, I agree, that a serial killer stops or *increases* the amount of time between kills. Generally, the time decreases as the desire to kill grows stronger and they can't resist it as long. But there are known documented exceptions. One is the BTK killer—Bind, Torture, Kill—out of Park City, Kansas. He killed several victims months apart and then went years without killing anyone before he started up again."

"Regardless of whether our killer did or didn't...pause," Faith said, "we know he's killing again. He would have killed Leslie for sure if you hadn't stopped him. This is one of those areas Asher and I have discussed, and we both lean toward your way of thinking, Lance. We believe there probably is a second graveyard somewhere. We just haven't found it yet."

Grayson shook his head. "Russo and Frost will go ballistic if that's the case. But it's not like I can tell them there may be more bodies without having an idea of where to look."

Asher shrugged then winced when pain shot up his back. He breathed shallow breaths until the pain began to subside then continued. "I'd be comfortable saying the second graveyard, if there is one, would be in the area we already speculated about in our earlier geographical research. If you draw a circle of about twenty-minutes' travel time around the graveyard we already found, I'd bet big money that if he does have another burial site, it'll be in that circle."

"Absolutely," Faith said.

Asher went on. "If most of us agree that there's probably another graveyard, maybe we should get TBI involved, at least. The police don't have the resources to hunt for it. But TBI sure does. We could share our geographical theories and research, and they could go on a wild-goose chase, if that's what it is. Let them decide whether or not to look into this theory. They already pulled all the missing person cases of females in a thirty-mile radius of Gatlinburg for the past ten years to help the ME identify the victims we already have. They can use those as a starting point, see which cases don't have any good suspects already and focus on those as potentially being the work of our serial killer."

Grayson crossed his arms. "Why would they want to do that? Shouldn't they focus on the known victims first, see if that can help lead them to the killer?"

"They're already doing that," Faith said. "So are we. And none of us has gotten anywhere. New cases, new to us anyway, might offer links we haven't seen before, some new evidence that might break the case wide open."

"When you put it that way, it makes sense. I'll pitch that to Russo and Frost."

"Can you also pitch them getting any evidence from the two newly identified victims to our lab?" Asher asked. "I know there wasn't any viable DNA and no hits on the national database for the fingerprints found on the knife the perp used to stab me. Maybe we'll get lucky and get a hit off of evidence found with Kramer's or Aguirre's bodies."

Ryland joined the conversation. "You mentioned hits on the national database, AFIS. What about local law enforcement that might not be linked to AFIS, or that has minor, even nonviolent arrest records they've never bothered to enter into the system. Maybe Ivy or Lance can pursue that angle. You two are wrapping up a major case right now. Can one of you finish that up and the other pursue the fingerprints?"

Ivy glanced at Lance. "I can probably take it. You okay doing the wrap-up?"

"No problem. And I'll help you as soon as I'm done."

Asher smiled. "Thanks. That's a great idea. Fingerprints are as good as DNA if we can get a hit."

Ryland pulled out his cell phone. "I'll text Rowan to contact the TBI about pursuing those other missing person cases. As for the rest of UB helping you two…unfortunately, most of us are heavy into some pretty urgent cases ourselves right now. Contact Ivy if you come up with anything urgent for her to pursue."

Lance motioned with his hand. "Don't hesitate to call me if there's something you need help on. If I can fit it in, I will."

Asher glanced at Faith in question. "Victimology on the two newly identified victims?"

"Absolutely. That would be perfect. Lance, Ivy, add that to your to-do list if and when you can assist. I'm sure that even working this on a limited basis, you can pull together information on Aguirre and Kramer faster and better than TBI and Gatlinburg PD combined."

Lance laughed. "You're laying it on thick there, Faith."

She smiled. "Maybe a little. Anything you can find on them and send to Asher and me would be appreciated. That will allow us to focus on Jasmine and Leslie and any clues we can glean from the other victims that we've already been studying."

"Sounds like we have a plan," Grayson said. "Asher, do you need Faith to provide any further updates on what she's worked on while you were in the hospital? I know it's early and this is the first time you've seen each other since you were released from the hospital—"

"Actually," Faith said, "I brought him up to speed last night."

"At my place," Asher said. "She slept over."

She gasped. "On the couch! Alone!"

He grinned.

Several of the others started laughing.

Grayson coughed and glanced at a wide-eyed Willow.

Faith narrowed her eyes at Asher, in warning.

He chuckled. He was fine airing his attraction to her out in the open, even if Faith wasn't. Heck, everyone at UB had probably known for a long time how he felt about her. She was the only one he'd foolishly hid it from, waiting for her to wake up and give him some kind of signal.

"I'm glad you're both together again," Grayson said.

Faith's eyes widened. "Working, you mean."

He arched a brow. "What else would I mean?"

Her cheeks flushed pink and she crossed her arms as the others laughed again.

Willow lightly punched Grayson's arm and gave him a warning look. "I think what my husband meant to say is that he's glad you're an investigative team again."

"Absolutely," he said. "That's what I meant." He winked at Willow.

Faith's face flushed even redder. If Asher survived the car ride back to his house, he'd count himself a lucky man.

Ryland addressed Lance and Ivy. "Keep me in the loop when you update Asher and Faith. If anyone else on the team frees up, I'll send them your way."

"Thanks, Ryland." Faith's cheeks were still flushed. "And thank you, Lance and Ivy. I appreciate any help I can get on this. Even from Asher, for what little that's worth."

He grinned at her teasing. She sat a little straighter, getting back into the groove of bantering with him and taking his humor in stride. It felt good. And when he winked again, and this time she actually smiled, it felt even better.

He was going to enjoy this. And he was going to give it his all—to the case and to his pursuit of Faith. He'd take nothing less than a win in both arenas.

Chapter Fourteen

Last Sunday, Faith had been visiting Asher in the hospital in Knoxville. This Sunday, she was with him again. But they were in her car driving to Pigeon Forge and distant parts of Gatlinburg that she'd never been to before, doing what she'd called knock-and-talks when she was a police officer. They'd been visiting people from the lives of June and Brenda, looking for anything to link them to the other victims.

So far, talking to Nathan Jefferson about June, and to Kurt Ritter about Brenda, the only link they'd found was that June used the same grocery store as one of the earlier victims.

"What's next?" Faith asked as she headed back toward downtown Gatlinburg.

"Lunch? I'm starving."

"Finally getting your appetite back?"

"Been trying to lay off the pain pills so I don't get addicted to those things. Seems like my appetite's rising with the pain level."

She gave him a sharp look. "If the doctor was worried about addiction, he'd have told you to stop taking them. He didn't, did he?"

"Not in so many words. But I researched the medication. I know the dangers. And I don't want to end up hooked. Stop worrying. If the pain gets much worse, I'll take something over the counter. But I'm through with prescription meds."

She thought about arguing, but the smother-mother teasing still smarted. And even though she was struggling to forget their scorching kiss and to think of Asher as only a friend again, she also didn't want to be thought of as a "mother" in any capacity to him.

Their relationship had become way too complicated. She could barely sleep at night, tossing and turning, thinking about him. Thinking about every *inch* of him. The thoughts she had were waking her up in a sweat the few times she did get to sleep. She was surprised she hadn't caught the sheets on fire with the fantasies that she was having. And every single one of them revolved around him.

Faith cleared her throat and tried, again, to focus. "Where do you want to eat?"

"You okay? You seem a little flushed."

She flipped the air conditioner vent toward her. "It's a little warm today. Where do you want to go?"

He didn't appear to believe her excuse, but he didn't push it. "You in the mood for a burger?"

"I'm always in the mood for a burger. Johnny Rockets? Smokehouse Burger?"

"You read my mind. Can't remember the last time I had one of those amazing creations."

"Probably last Christmas, is my guess. Daphne was at her then-boyfriend's family's house and your parents were off on another trip. To Italy, I think."

"Yep, Christmas was Italy. The summer before that was Spain."

"Oh, yeah. I remember the Spanish candy they brought back. *Huesitos.* I loved the white-chocolate ones. Anyway, since we were both alone, we decided to find a Chinese place and drown our sorrows together."

He grinned. "The Chinese place was closed but Johnny Rockets was open. I'd forgotten about that."

"I'll never forget. You stole my onion rings."

He laughed. "You weren't going to eat them anyway. You couldn't even finish your cheeseburger."

She pulled into a space in front of the diner with its yellow, red and blue sign above the door declaring it the home of The Original Hamburger. "We've had some good times, haven't we, Asher?"

"Yes. We have. And I wish you'd call me Ash."

"No way. Too intimate. If I start calling you that, you'll know something's wrong."

"You called me Ash at the stables."

"I was under tremendous stress. You were hurt. Like I said, something was wrong."

He laughed and they headed inside.

Several hours later, they were back at his house, sitting at the dining room table, this time with both their laptops open. She stared at the pictures of all six victims on her screen then stretched and sat back. "I don't get it. This serial killer is breaking all the rules."

"Rules? Like what? Waiting six months between most of his kills, then possibly killing no one else for the past five years?"

"I'm not even pursuing that angle right now. I've been studying the victims, looking for similarities, and I'm not finding many aside from him choosing only female victims. Serial killers usually kill the same race as them. Our killer is white, but his victims are white, Black, and Latino. We've estimated him as mid-thirties. But his victims' ages range from early twenties to early forties. I could overlook all of that if they had similar physical features of some type, like if they all had straight dark hair. But they don't. I can't get a lock on this guy. My former life as a Nashville detective didn't give me much experience hunting this type of predator. You took some FBI serial killer courses at Quantico. What's your take on these inconsistencies?"

"I learned just enough to be dangerous. But one thing that they taught me is that a large percentage choose victims because of things they have in common that don't have to do with their physical attributes. It could be as simple as occupation or geography, and opportunity. Each one fulfills a specific need in him at the time that he kills them."

"That doesn't help me at all."

He shrugged then winced.

"When was your last pain pill? Over the counter or otherwise?"

"It's been a while. I'd hoped to avoid taking any more meds. But I'm ready to wave the white flag and grab a couple of Tylenol."

She wished he'd take something stronger. It wasn't like him to reveal that he was in pain, so he was probably in far more pain than he was admitting. She tapped her nails on the tabletop while he headed into the kitchen. "I haven't heard from Willow today. Have you?"

"Not a peep. Leslie must be really having a hard time if Willow can't convince her to talk to us." He downed some pills with a glass of water.

"She's the only known survivor of this killer. Something he said, or did, could be the key that ties everything together. And she may not even realize she holds that key."

"Don't pin your hopes on her. She may *never* speak to us. We have to figure out a path without her."

Faith sighed. "I know, I know." She waved at her computer and the pictures of the victims, guilt riding her hard that she hadn't yet figured out how to get justice for them. "It's so much easier said than done."

"We need a break, a distraction to get our mind off this, even if only for a few minutes. Then we can come at it fresh."

"A distraction sounds good. What would that be?"

"I can think of something to distract you." The teasing tone of his voice had her glancing sharply at him. When she saw he was holding up a half gallon of chocolate ice cream, she started laughing.

"Gotcha." He winked. "With or without whipped cream?"

"Duh. Definitely with. I'll help. You don't need to be scooping that with your back still healing." She headed into the kitchen and grabbed the scoop while he got out a couple of bowls.

"I'm guessing your mom bought this for you," she said as she filled their bowls. "She always loads you up with junk food every time she visits."

"I wouldn't have it any other way." He grabbed the whipped cream and put two dollops on top of each of their bowls.

She stared at the chocolate mountains. "What was I thinking? That's more than we could both ever eat."

"Speak for yourself." Asher took a huge spoonful and shoved it into his mouth.

She laughed and did the same, although she went for a much smaller spoonful. They both stood at the island, shoving empty calories into their mouths.

"I'm totally going to regret this tomorrow," she said. "When I get on the scale. Maybe you should finish mine. You still have some pounds to put back on."

"Don't mind if I do." He shoved his empty bowl away and pulled her half-eaten one to him.

She rinsed his bowl, put it in the dishwasher, and then turned around. She froze at the sight of him licking his spoon.

His eyes darkened as he stared at her and slowly slid the spoon into his mouth. Her own mouth went dry as he scooped up some more and swirled his tongue around it before consuming it, all the while his heated gaze never leaving her.

"Stop, stop." Her voice was a dry rasp. She closed her eyes, blocking him out, and took a deep breath then another and another.

"Stop what, Faith?"

His tone had her eyes flying open. "Oh, my gosh. How do you do that?"

"Do what?"

"Lower your voice that way. You sound like…like—"

"Like what?"

"Like…sex! Just. Stop." She ran past him down the hall to the guest bedroom and slammed the door behind her.

ASHER DROPPED THE spoon into the bowl, at a loss for what had just happened. He'd made her mad and didn't even know how he'd done it. He'd been enjoying the ice cream and break from the case when he'd noticed the alluring sway of her bottom as she'd rinsed the bowl. When she'd turned around, his gaze had fallen to her lips and all he could seem to think about was the feel of them when he'd kissed her, the heat of her mouth when he'd swept his tongue inside.

The curve of her neck had him sucking on the spoon as he'd thought about sucking that soft, perfect skin as he'd done in the hospital. And her breasts, so soft and firm, pressing against his chest. Her words, asking him to stop, had truly surprised him, brought him crashing back to reality. His voice sounded like sex? He didn't even know he had that superpower. How could he not do something in the future if he didn't even know how he'd done it in the first place?

He scrubbed his hands across his face, cursing the situation. He was frustrated, in pain, and on edge. Nothing in his life seemed to be going right these days, either professionally or personally. And he was just plain tired.

Since it was too early for bed, Asher did the only other thing he could think of to try to ease his aches and pains and take his mind off all the stress, if only for a few minutes. He headed into his bedroom and strode into the bathroom to take advantage of his steam shower.

Washing away the aches and pains was much easier than washing away his worries about the case, and Faith. Even though they didn't have the answers they wanted on the investigation, they'd done so much digging that he felt they had to be close to a resolution. That's how these things typically went. Days, weeks or even months of work with little to show for it and all of a sudden that one puzzle piece would appear that made the entire picture come together. As for his relationship with Faith? That was still very much a puzzle. And he wasn't as optimistic that he'd ever find the missing piece.

After towel-drying himself, he wrapped the towel around his waist and headed into the bedroom for some fresh clothes.

"Oh...oh, my... I'm sorry."

He turned at the sound of Faith's voice. She stood at the foot of his bed, holding her phone, eyes wide as she stared at his towel. He glanced down, just to make sure he was covered, then strode to her, stopping a few feet away.

Her gaze jerked up to meet his, her cheeks that adorable shade of pink they turned whenever she was embarrassed.

"I didn't mean to... I mean I did, but it's still early-*ish* and I thought you had come in here to grab something and I... Oh, gosh, I'm sorry." She whirled around.

He gently grabbed her arm, stopping her. "Faith. No harm done. What's wrong?"

She drew a deep breath and turned. "An email from Ivy.

She sent me a file of open missing person cases in Gatlinburg. There are a depressingly large number. Most are old, several years. But one is recent, two days ago. I opened it and…well, look." She held up her phone.

Asher frowned. "I think you're showing the wrong picture. That's June Aguirre."

"No. It isn't. It's a woman named Nancy Henry. They aren't even related, but they look as if they could be twins. Just like Leslie and Jasmine could have been twins if it wasn't for their age difference. Please tell me what I think is happening isn't happening. Did our guy take her?"

He took her phone and studied the screen. "You're right. They could be twins. But we shouldn't jump to conclusions. It could be a huge coincidence. For all we know, she may have run off with her boyfriend or gone on a trip without telling whoever reported her missing."

"I know, I know. But what if she didn't? What if our guy is responsible? What if he's furious that we took his trophies, the bodies he'd buried. And he wants to replace them with look-alikes? Have you ever heard of a serial killer doing that?"

"No. Doesn't mean they wouldn't or haven't. I don't think we should panic and alert anyone without something more than a hunch. We need to look at those other missing person files."

"There are a lot. It will take hours."

"We'll put on some coffee. We're going to need the caffeine."

Her gaze fell to his towel for a moment before she took her phone. "I, um, I'm sorry about…earlier. The ice cream incident. I'm…on edge. Saying really stupid things right now. It wasn't you. It was me. I really am sorry."

He grinned. "The 'ice cream incident'?"

"Don't make fun of me."

He pressed his hand to his chest. "Never."

She smiled. "I really am sorry, for the stupid things I said. And for slamming my door like a child."

"Does this mean my voice doesn't sound like sex after all?"

Her eyes widened. "I, um—"

"Kidding. And I shouldn't tease you when you're this serious. I'm sorry too. It was a misunderstanding."

Her gaze dropped to his towel again. "Right. That's all it was. A…misunderstanding. I'll get that coffee going." She ran from the room.

He stared at the empty doorway, more confused than ever—about the case, and especially about Faith. So much for his shower clearing his mind.

Several hours later, with a quick, light supper behind them and numerous phone calls with Lance and Ivy, they finally had their answer about the look-a-like theory. He set his phone down on the dining room table and sat back, rolling his shoulders to ease the ache from hunching over the computer for so long.

"It was a good theory," he said. "Worth looking into. At least we know that Nancy Henry is safe and sound." He grinned. "Even if she did run off with a new boyfriend and ghosted her old one. Russo's canceling the missing person's report now."

She shut her laptop. "I wish his people were that diligent about closing out paperwork on their older missing person cases. We chased after two other look-alikes for hours before finding out they were both found within days of the reports being filed and no one canceled the alerts. We're back to nothing."

"No, we're back to reexamining what we have, taking a

fresh look. Something will shake out. When nothing makes sense, go back to step one."

"Victimology," she said.

"Exactly. It's too late to start on that now. Let's both get a good night's sleep and come at this fresh in the morning. You're welcome to stay over again, in the guest room this time, not the couch. You'll be much more comfortable there."

"I think I'll take you up on that. I'm too tired to drive home. Thanks, Asher."

"Of course. Anytime."

They both stood and headed in opposite directions, him to the main bedroom on the left side of the house, her to the guest room on the right.

"Hey, Asher?"

He turned around. She was still in the opening to the hallway on the other side of the great room. "Yeah?"

"It was a good day. I mean we didn't solve the case. But we worked hard, explored a lot of angles."

He smiled. "It was a good day."

"Asher?"

He chuckled, wondering why she was acting so timid all of a sudden. "Yes, Faith?"

"Thank you. Thank you for...for being my friend."

His stomach dropped at the dreaded *friend* word. Keeping his smile in place was a struggle. "It's my pleasure."

She smiled, looking relieved. Then she headed down the hall, away from him.

He fisted his hands at his sides as he stared at the now-empty hallway. Suddenly the idea of facing his very lonely bedroom was too much. Instead, he headed into the kitchen and grabbed a cold bottle of beer.

Chapter Fifteen

Asher blinked and looked up at the ceiling above his bed. Something had woken him. He turned his head then sat straight up, startled to see Faith standing a few feet away, twisting her hands together.

"Faith, hey. Is everything—"

"Kiss me."

The fog of sleep instantly evaporated, replaced by a fog of confusion. He scrubbed the stubble on his face. "Sorry, what?"

"Kiss me, Asher. I can't sleep. I need to get you out of my system. I have to stop thinking about what happened between us. You have to help me forget."

"You want me to help you forget that we ever kissed? By kissing you again?"

"Yes. No. I mean…yes. Just…kiss me, okay? If you don't mind?"

"Oh, I definitely don't mind. Can I brush my teeth first?"

"No. Yes, yes, probably a good idea. Go ahead. Hurry."

He started to the flip the comforter back then hesitated. "You might want to turn around."

"Why? I don't…oh. You mean you're…"

"Naked as the day I was born."

She whirled around.

He chuckled and grabbed some boxers from his dresser before heading into the bathroom.

When he came back out, he left the bathroom door open to provide better light. Not that he expected her to still be there. He figured she would have lost her nerve and run off again. Once again, she'd surprised him. She was still there, standing by the bed, wringing her hands. He padded across the carpet to stand in front of her.

"Still want to do this?"

"Yes, I… You don't have a shirt on."

"You want me to put one on before I kiss you?"

"Yes. No."

He grinned. "Are you even awake?" He waved his hand in front of her face. "Are you sleepwalking? Because you aren't making much sense and that's not like you at all."

"Believe me, none of this makes sense to me, either, except that I can't sleep because all I do is think of your damn golden gorgeous chest and your mouth and your tongue and…just do it. Kiss me."

He settled his hands around her tiny waist and leaned down.

"Wait." She pressed her hands against his chest, sucked in a breath as if she'd been burned and then snatched her hands away. Her breathing quickened as she stared at his chest, her gaze trailing down to his boxers. She squeezed her eyes shut and took a deep breath. "No tongue. Just a quick soft kiss on the lips."

"Faith."

"Yes?"

"Look at me."

She frowned and blew out a breath before opening her eyes. "What?"

"Explain it to me again, why you want me to kiss you? Not that I don't want to. Believe me, I do. But I don't want you to regret this later. I'm not sure you're thinking straight right now."

"I'm thinking as straight as I possibly can. I've been doing nothing but think for the past few hours. This is the only solution that I can think of."

"To get me out of your system?"

"Yes! I have a theory."

"A theory."

"I believe that I've built up that earlier kiss in my mind, made it seem way more…incredible than it actually was. If I have something to compare it to, I think I'll realize it was just the shock of it happening in the first place that has me in a dither."

He tried hard not to laugh. "You're in a *dither*? Is that what this is?"

"Don't laugh at me. This is serious."

"Of course. Forgive me. You want a quick soft kiss to make you forget the other kiss. Got it. Are you ready?"

She drew a shaky breath. "Ready. Oh, and I brushed my teeth too. It's all good."

He laughed. At her frown, he said, "Sorry."

"Just do it." She tilted her mouth up toward him and closed her eyes.

He slid his arms around her and gently pulled her against his chest.

Her eyes flew open.

He lowered his mouth to hers.

"Wait. No tongue. Remember, just a quick soft kiss."

"No tongue. Got it."

"Stop laughing. I hear laughter in your voice."

He arched a brow. "Would you rather hear sex in my voice?"

"No. Good grief, anything but that. Just hurry up, I need to get this over with."

"Ouch. My ego just limped off somewhere."

"Sorry. We're just friends, remember? I need to get things back the way they are."

"By having me kiss you."

"Exactly, we—"

He swooped down and kissed her, wildly, dragging his mouth across hers, nibbling on her lips.

She gasped against him and pushed at his chest, stepping back. "That wasn't soft!"

"Sorry. Should I try again?"

"Hang on a sec." She closed her eyes, frowned, then opened them again. "It didn't work. You definitely did it wrong."

"Because you're still not thinking of me as just a friend?"

"Exactly."

He grinned.

"It's not funny."

"It kind of is, actually."

"Once more. Soft. Not…wild like that. A quick soft kiss. That should do it."

"One quick soft kiss coming right up."

She pressed against his chest. "No tongue."

"Scout's honor."

"You weren't a Scout."

"I could have been."

"But you weren't. No tongue. Promise."

"Promise."

She gave him a suspicious look then relaxed her shoulders and closed her eyes again. "Let's get this over with. I really need to get some sleep tonight."

He was laughing when his lips touched hers. True to his promise, he gave her a gentle, tender kiss that about killed him not to deepen. When he ended the kiss, he inhaled a shaky breath, shocked at how such a brief, chaste touch had affected him.

Faith kept her eyes closed, her breaths sounding a bit uneven. When she finally looked up at him, the dazed look on her face had him instantly hardening. If she risked a quick glance down, there'd be no doubt about what she was doing to him.

He cleared his throat. "Did that work?"

She considered then slowly shook her head, looking disappointed. "Not even close. There's only one more thing I can think of to try."

"I can think of several things."

She put her hands on her hips "I don't mean that. We're definitely not doing *that*."

"Pity."

She blew out a frustrated sigh. "I need you to kiss me one more time."

His erection was becoming painfully hard now. He grimaced.

"Are you in pain? Do you need me to get you a pill?"

"No I'm… I'm fine. What kind of kiss this time?" Good grief, it sounded as if he was offering her up a menu.

"I think, in order to wipe out the memory of our first kiss, you're going to have to kiss me like that again."

His erection jerked. He cleared his throat again. "Like the first time? In the hospital?"

"Please. If you don't mind. I really think reality won't live up to the fantasy. That's my hope anyway."

His throat tightened. "You fantasize about me?"

"Just kiss me. I need a good night's sleep and—"

He covered her mouth with his and swept his tongue inside. He slid one hand in her thick hair, tilting her head back for better access. The other, he slid down her back to the curves he'd wanted to touch for so very long, pressing her against him. He expected his hardness to shock her into running away.

Instead, she moaned and fit her body more snugly against his, cradling him with her softness.

It was like a switch had turned on inside both of them. The kiss at the hospital was incinerated by this one. Both were wild to touch, to taste, wanting more, and more, and more. He whirled her around, pressing her against the bedpost, worshipping her mouth with his, tasting her sweetness, her sassiness, everything that was Faith. Lava flowed through his veins, burning him up. For the first time since he'd been stabbed, the constant pain in his healing back faded into oblivion. All he felt was *Faith*.

He lifted her bottom, fitting her even more perfectly against him, moving his lips to the side of her neck. She shivered and moaned, bucking against him. Holding her with one arm beneath her bottom, he raked back the comforter and began to lower her to the bed.

Her eyes flew open. "Stop!"

He immediately set her on her feet and stepped back, even though it nearly killed him. "Are you sure?"

"Yes! We can't... I mean I want...but we can't...damn it." She stared up at him in shock and pressed a hand to her throat. "That kiss didn't work *at all*."

He motioned to his straining erection. "It worked for me."

Her eyes widened as she looked down. She stood transfixed, then slowly stepped toward him, her hand raised as if to stroke him.

He started to sweat, yearning for her touch, waiting, hoping.

She suddenly snatched her hand back. "What the hell am I doing?" She swore a blue streak and ran out of the room, cursing the entire time until the door down the hall slammed shut yet again.

He groaned and rested his forehead against the cool bedpost, struggling to slow his racing heart. More than anything, he wanted to follow her, to get on his knees and beg if he had to. Faith. She'd always been in his heart. Now she was in his blood. He wanted her so much he ached. And there wasn't a damn thing he could do about it.

He drew a ragged breath and strode into the bathroom for yet another shower. A cold one.

WHEN THE MORNING sun's rays slanted through the plantation shutters in Asher's bedroom, he was already dressed and ready to start the day. He'd chosen jeans and a loose, button-up shirt as he'd been doing since his confrontation with the perpetrator up on the mountain. His back was too stiff to make shrugging into a suit jacket remotely comfortable.

He tapped his fingers on his dresser, dozens of other useless minutiae running through his mind. None of it mattered. None of it was what he cared one bit about. All he was doing was putting off the inevitable. Facing Faith this morning and seeing what kind of a mood she was in today.

Would she blame him for whatever the hell had happened last night? Walk out? Tell him they were done? No longer friends, no longer work partners, nothing? Or would she smile and lighten his heart, be the friendly, fun woman he loved so damn much? Or would she be a mixture of the two? The only thing he knew for sure was that standing in his bedroom avoiding a potential confrontation wasn't going to make things better. And it wasn't going to solve the case either. He had to face Faith head-on and go from there. Somehow.

He strode to the door and pulled it open, almost running into Faith. He grabbed her shoulders to steady her, then let go.

"Faith. Good morning. Are you—"

"It's Willow." She held up her phone. "Leslie Parks is ready to talk to us."

Chapter Sixteen

Faith had never been more grateful for a phone call than this morning when Willow told her that Leslie was ready to talk. She'd been dreading facing Asher after last night. There was no way she could pretend anymore that she thought of him as just a friend. But she was still so shocked at the turn of events that she didn't know what to do.

She was a coward twice over, again not wanting to have an honest, tough conversation. Thankfully, he must have picked up on that and he hadn't even brought up what had happened. But how long would he wait? And how long was it fair to keep him waiting? It wasn't a secret how he felt about her. He deserved to know how she felt about him. But how *did* she feel? He'd been firmly in the best friend category for nearly two years. Thinking of him in any other capacity was…confusing. And it had her on edge.

After going home for a shower and change of clothes, she'd returned, ready to take him to the Parkses' home. Her already high anxiety went off the charts when he said he was going to drive his truck instead of being chauffeured in her car. He'd insisted it had been long enough, that he needed to give it a try to see how it went. The only reason she'd backed down and didn't argue was that he'd readily agreed if it was too difficult, too painful, he'd pull over and let her drive.

When they reached the Parkses' neighborhood and turned onto their street, Asher groaned and pulled to a stop. "News-hounds. They're camped outside Leslie's home."

Faith fisted her hand on the seat. "That pushy brassy-blonde anchorwoman's leading the pack. I can practically smell her hair spray from here. Every time I see her it makes me want to dye my hair brown."

He chuckled. "I'm sure Miranda Cummings is a very nice person. You should give her a chance. Maybe you two could become great friends."

"Not even in my worst nightmares. What's the plan? Sneak in from the backyard? We could call ahead, let the Parkses know."

"That would only give the media more fodder for gossip if someone spotted us. I don't want to give them a video clip for their prime-time broadcast. And I can't imagine Grayson being happy seeing us climbing over a fence on the news, even if we do get the homeowner's permission."

"Good point. The direct approach it is."

"Should I take your gun, to keep Miranda safe?"

"Probably. But I'm not giving it to you."

He smiled and drove farther down the street. But he was forced to pull to the curb a good block away because there was no available space any closer. "Looks like we're hoof-ing it from here. No shooting, Faith."

"If she thrusts a microphone in my face, I'm not respon-sible for my actions." She smirked and popped open her door.

Asher jogged to catch up and she immediately slowed, glancing at him in concern. "I'm sorry. I didn't mean to make you hustle like that. How's your back? Breathing okay?"

He surprised her by putting his arm around her shoul-ders. "Getting better all the time. See? I couldn't do this a few days ago."

She ducked down and gently pushed his arm off her shoulders. "And you can't do it today either."

"Spoilsport."

She laughed. He smiled. And her world was right again. At least until they reached the walkway to the Parkses' home and the anchorwoman recognized them.

"Don't look now," she whispered. "The bulldog and her cameraman are running over as fast as her stilettos will allow."

"Then we'll just have to run faster." He winked and grabbed her hand, tugging her with him, double-time, up the path.

Faith didn't even have a chance to worry about his injuries or try to stop him. She had to jog to keep up with his long-legged strides. But they made it to the front door before Cummings and her cameraman could maneuver around the other media to cut them off.

The door swung open and Mr. Parks waved Faith and Asher inside, firmly closing the door behind them.

He shook his graying head. "Danged rude reporters. They haven't left since the day you found our Jasmine. Neighbors have to bring us groceries so we don't get mobbed going outside. The police had people out here the first couple of days. But then they left, won't do a thing about it."

Faith took his hands in hers. "Mr. Parks, we're so sorry for your loss. We truly are, and everything you and your family are going through."

He patted her hand, smiling through unshed tears. But before he could respond, Mrs. Parks ambled into the foyer. "Lawd, Ms. Lancaster. You don't have anything to apologize for, you or Mr. Whitfield. If it weren't for both of you, we'd never have gotten our Jasmine back. We were finally able to give her a proper burial. And thanks to you, Mr. Whitfield, our baby, Leslie, is home safe and sound. If we'd lost both of them, I just don't think we could have made it. You saved our little family."

Faith held back her own tears as Mrs. Parks hugged Asher. She was probably the only one who noticed him slightly stiffening when Mr. Parks squeezed his shoulder and patted him on the back. But just as Faith took a step forward to warn them to be careful, he gave her a subtle shake of his head. She understood. These people had suffered one of the most painful losses possible, the loss of a child. If hugging him or pounding his back gave them some comfort, his physical pain was a small price to pay.

The four of them sat in the modest family room for a good half hour, with Asher and Faith being showed the family albums and listening to the couple reminisce about their precious Jasmine.

Mrs. Parks grabbed a stack of pictures from an end table and fanned them out on top of the last album. "These are from her funeral. I don't think we could have gotten even one more person in the church if we tried. And look at all those flowers."

Faith looked at every picture then carefully stacked them again and handed them back to her. "Jasmine was obviously well loved. She must have been a very special young woman."

"Oh, she was. She definitely was. Her two babies are half grown now and just as smart and precocious as she was." Her smile dimmed as she exchanged a suffering look with her husband. "'Course, we don't get to see them near as often as we'd like to. Their daddy moved an hour away from here."

Her husband patted her shoulder. "We see them once or twice a month. They're healthy and happy and love their nana and papa. That's what matters."

"I suppose." She didn't sound convinced.

Faith reached across the coffee table and squeezed her hand. "I'm sure no grandparents feel they get to see their grandchildren enough."

"Honey, you got that right. Can I get either of you some coffee, some pie? I made apple pie last night when Leslie said she was thinking about calling Mrs. Prescott this morning, just in case. You have to try my pie."

Faith glanced at Asher for help.

He leaned forward, gently closing the last photo album. "Maybe we can have a piece of pie to go. Right now we'd really like to speak to Leslie, if she's still okay talking to us. It could really help with the investigation. We want to get justice for Jasmine, and for what Leslie went through. It's also urgent that we catch this man before he hurts someone else."

"Oh, goodness. And here I've been rattling on and on." She dabbed at her eyes. "Charles, check on Leslie. See if she's ready."

"I'm ready, Mama," a soft voice said from the hallway off to Asher's right. She nodded at Faith and gave Asher a tentative smile. "You're the man who saved me."

He stood and smiled down at her, offering his hand.

When she took it, instead of shaking it, he held it with both of his. "And you're one of the bravest young women I've ever met. You're a survivor, Leslie. Don't let what this man did define you. You're going to go on and do amazing things with your life."

Her eyes widened and she seemed to stand a little straighter. "You think so? You think I'm brave?"

"I know so."

She cleared her throat and nodded at Faith, who'd moved to stand beside him. "I don't think I know anything that will help you catch him. But I'll answer any questions that you have, if I can."

"Thank you," Faith said. She looked around the small house. "Is there somewhere we can go to talk privately? No offense, Mr. and Mrs. Parks. It's just that sometimes survivors feel more comfortable talking without their loved ones in the same room."

They exchanged surprised looks, but Mr. Parks overrode whatever his wife was about to say. "Of course. Leslie, take them to Jasmine's room. They might want to see her pictures anyway. You can answer any questions they have about her too."

Leslie didn't seem enthusiastic about his suggestion. But she waved Faith and Asher to follow her down the hall. The last room on the left was a surprising combination of adult and child. The full-size bed on one wall had a contemporary, grown-up feel with its country-chic bedding and subdued tones. But the other side of the room boasted a bunk bed with bright blue football-themed blankets and pillows on top, and a fluffy pink comforter with white unicorns dancing all over it on the bottom.

"I never come in here since…" Leslie's voice was small, quiet. "Mama cleans it every week as if she expects Jazz to come through the door and pick up where she left off."

"I can tell she loves both of you very much." Faith motioned to the big bed. "Do you think it would be okay if we sit on her bed so we can talk?"

Leslie shrugged then sat. "Don't guess it matters now. She's in Heaven. I wonder if mama will keep cleaning the room."

Per the plan that Faith and Asher had worked out on the way over, Faith did most of the talking. They figured it would be easier for a woman who'd been victimized by a man to talk to another woman. Asher pulled out a chair from the small desk along a wall with a collage of pictures and spoke up just a few times to ask questions that Faith didn't think to ask.

To Faith's disappointment, the only thing Leslie told them that was new information was that the killer had zapped her with a Taser to abduct her when she was out walking in her neighborhood. She'd have to remember to tell Chief Russo so he could send someone back to where Leslie had been abducted to search for the tiny Anti-Felon Identification confetti tags that shoot out of Tasers when fired. If the killer had legally purchased the cartridges used to deploy the darts, the tags would trace back to him. But she wasn't hanging her hopes on a legal purchase.

Leslie also said the man who'd abducted her had zip-tied her wrists together and then threatened her with a large, wicked-looking knife—likely the same one that he'd used to stab Asher—to get her to do what he'd wanted.

When Leslie couldn't think of anything else to tell them in response to their questions, Faith pulled the stack of photos out of her purse that she'd printed off before leaving Asher's home.

"Leslie, would you mind looking at these? I know it's been five years since your sister went missing, but if any of these people seem familiar, let me know. We're wondering whether your sister knew any of them. Their names are on the back of each picture."

Leslie dutifully looked through the photos and read each name. When she handed them back, she shook her head. "I don't recognize any of them. But I didn't hang with her and her friends. She was older than me. She'd graduated high school before I even started. I'm sorry. I guess I haven't been too helpful."

"You've been a huge help. We don't know which details will be important until the case all falls together."

Leslie nodded, but didn't seem convinced.

Asher leaned forward, his elbows resting on his knees. "Leslie, you were with your abductor for several hours. The sketch you and Ms. Lancaster helped the police artist draw is very good. But it's impressions, thing like how he spoke, certain word choices he might have used that stood out, things that don't show up in a sketch that might help us too. Faith and I spoke to him. But we weren't with him all that long. Neither of us picked up on anything unique or different that might make him stand out. Is there anything at all that you can think of that we may have missed?"

She started to shake her head no then stopped. "Well, it's probably not important."

"What?" Faith asked. "Tell us."

"I'm sure you noticed too. Maybe not him." She motioned to Asher. "But you probably did. His eyebrows."

Faith blinked. "Uh, his eyebrows? What about them?"

Leslie rolled her eyes and Faith suddenly realized how irritating that could be. Maybe she should work on trying to break that annoying habit herself.

"They were dark," Leslie said. "You know, really dark. Guys don't pencil their brows, at least none that I know. His blond hair didn't match his brows." She shrugged. "Like I said, probably doesn't help. But I think his natural hair color is a very dark brown, like his eyebrows. He either bleached his hair lighter or he was wearing a wig as a disguise."

A knock sounded on the open door and Mr. Parks stood in the entry. "Everything going okay?"

Asher stood. "Yes, sir. I think we're finished. We appreciate you allowing us to come into your home. And thank you, Leslie. You've been very patient with our questions."

She smiled, and Faith noticed the hero worship in her eyes. Asher had earned a life-long fan when he'd rescued Leslie.

There might even be a little infatuation going on there. Faith couldn't blame the young woman. She was in the throes of a major crush on Asher herself. And still so shocked she didn't know what she was going to do about it.

Asher motioned to the large photo collage on the wall above the desk. "Mr. Parks, would you mind if I snap some pictures of those? Just the ones of your daughter, Jasmine, and her friends?"

He shrugged. "Help yourself. She sure had a lot of friends, a lot of people who loved her." He smiled and tapped one of the pictures that showed Jasmine and four other young women in a bright yellow raft going over a four-foot water-fall that began a series of small rapids, probably class twos, maybe a few threes, too, just enough to make the trip exciting without being too dangerous for beginners and intermediate rafters. All of the women were smiling and appeared to be having the time of their lives.

"That there is the first time she ever went white-water rafting," Mr. Parks continued. "See her sitting right up front, holding that rope instead of a paddle? That's some kind of trick the guides show them, riding the bull or something like that. She wasn't afraid at all and jumped up front to give it a try. 'Course her best friend told me the secret, that she fell into the water right after the guide took that picture." He chuckled. "She'd have hated it if I knew that." His smile disappeared and his expression turned sad. "Come on, Leslie. Let's give these nice people a few minutes to take their pictures."

Faith exchanged a sad smile with Asher then helped him by moving some of the photos out from behind others so he could get good shots of all of them.

It took another half hour to extricate themselves from the home. Mrs. Parks was obviously going through grief all over again with the discovery of her oldest daughter's body. And she desperately needed to talk about her. Asher was far more patient with her than Faith, who'd been trying to edge them toward the door much sooner than he did.

When they did finally leave, they had an entire apple pie in a large brown paper bag. They'd tried to turn it down, but when it became clear that Mrs. Parks would be offended if they didn't take it, Asher had graciously accepted her gift and kissed her on the cheek.

Faith grinned at him once they got through the media gauntlet and were back in his truck heading down the road.

"What?" he asked. "Did I miss a joke somewhere?"

"I just think it's cute."

"Cute? You think *I'm* cute?"

"No. I mean yes. No secret there. You're an extremely handsome man. But I'm talking about the Parks women. It's cute that both of them have crushes on you."

"I sure hope not. Can we go back to that part about you thinking I'm extremely handsome?"

"Nope. Your ego's healthy enough as it is." She held up her phone. "And I'm busy trying to reach my baby sister."

"Your daily text?"

"Not every day."

"Mmm-hmm."

"Seriously. I try not to hover."

He laughed. "I can't imagine what you think hovering looks like."

"Whatever. I just worry about her. One text a day isn't hovering. It's caring."

"So you admit it's daily."

"I'm through with this conversation." She scowled as she stared at her phone. "She hasn't answered yet."

"Give her a few seconds."

"It's been far more than that. I texted her on the way to the Parkses' house. That was almost two hours ago."

"If you're really worried, why not call her?"

She checked the time. "No. I think she's in her chem class right now. I'll wait." She set the phone beside her. "Did you catch anything I missed in what Leslie told us? I didn't feel as if we learned anything new. Well, except that maybe our killer dyes his hair. Or wears a wig. I suppose that's something."

"It's a good reminder not to get thrown off by hair color if we see someone who fits his description in any other way. But, I agree. Nothing really new. I do want to review those pictures I took in her bedroom. Most of them appeared to be from the bar where she worked. I'd like to review them closely to see whether our killer could be in any of the background shots. Maybe he's been at that bar before and that's how he zeroed in on her as his target."

"Can I see your phone?"

He pulled it out of his jeans' pocket and gave it to her.

She flipped through the snapshots he'd taken of Jasmine's photos. Nothing stood out. The pictures taken at The Watering Hole, the bar where she'd worked, didn't reveal anything surprising. It was just a bar. Not one of the sleazy ones, more like a bar and grill. The grill part took up one side and the bar the other. Jasmine looked so young and happy, posing with other young people who could have been friends or patrons, or both. It was so heart-wrenching knowing her life would be cut short not long after many of these had been taken.

Faith was about to hand the phone back to Asher when something in the background of one of the shots caught her attention. She tapped the screen then enlarged the shot.

"No way."

"You found something?"

"Maybe." She grabbed her own phone, flipped through her photos, then stopped and compared it with one on Asher's phone. "It's her. June Aguirre is in one of the background shots. And if I'm not mistaken…give me a sec." She flipped through more photos on both phones until she could compare two more shots. "Asher, another one of our victims is in this picture, at The Watering Hole, where Jasmine worked. It's victim number three, Dana Randolph. That makes three of our victims so far—Jasmine, June and Dana. I think we've found our link."

Chapter Seventeen

"Dana Randolph," Asher said. "The married mother of two? She's at the bar?"

"Sort of. I mean yes. She's definitely there. But I don't think she's barhopping. It appears that she's sitting with her family at that high-top table. The kids certainly favor her. You know how when a restaurant is really busy, they offer to seat you in the bar area to eat? I think that's why she's there."

"Nothing about the bar came up in any of our interviews with victims' families."

"We've been trying to build timelines, come up with places everyone frequented. If they didn't go to this place very often, it might not have even occurred to them. This could be the tie-in we've been looking for. Maybe our killer is a regular and picks his victims there. When we interviewed the staff at the bar who were there when Jasmine worked there, we were focused on friends and enemies, anyone she knew and interacted with a lot. Every single person we checked out from that bar failed to raise red flags."

She set both phones down and shifted to face him as he turned the truck onto the long winding road up the mountain to his house. "I can almost see the gears turning in that mind of yours. You have a theory?"

"A possibility more than a theory. Something to check

out. What if none of the people we looked into at the bar came up as persons of interest because the killer was never after Jasmine?"

"Okay. You lost me there. Explain that one."

"You've seen two of the victims in the crowd, assuming that second one really is Dana Randolph. That's a heck of a coincidence that three of our six victims had been to that location. If we can prove the other three had at least been there, that's our link."

"I'll bet I can prove all six have been to the same fast-food chains too."

He smiled. "You've got me there. However, the bar where Jasmine worked isn't a chain. It's the one location. And it's not in downtown Gatlinburg with all the tourist spots. It's more out of the way, a place for locals. I think it's unlikely it's just a coincidence that they've all been there before. I think that's where the killer saw them and decided to go after them."

"All right," she said. "I'll go with that, for now. How does that explain your earlier statement that Jasmine was never a target? Wait. I think I know where you're going with this. The others were a target, but Jasmine saw something she wasn't supposed to see? Like maybe she started realizing some of the missing person stories she was seeing on the news were of people she'd seen in the bar, and she'd seen them all with our killer. He killed her to keep her from talking."

He nodded. "Possibly. Like I said, the theory could be far-fetched. But it does fit the evidence. It would explain why no one mentioned anyone fitting our killer's description as being one of her friends, or a regular who caused problems. If he didn't interact with her, if he kept to the background to try not to be noticed, then he wouldn't be on anyone's radar who knew her."

"That really does fit," she said. "The last victim before Jasmine, June Aguirre, went missing one day before her. Maybe Jasmine saw the killer with June, didn't think anything about it at the time. But the killer knew she'd seen him and decided to make sure she couldn't tell anyone once June's disappearance hit the news. It makes sense with what we know, or think we know anyway. What about Leslie, though? How does she fit in this? Why take another victim from the same family?"

"The media hasn't made a secret that we found his victims' graves because we were trying to find Jasmine. If the theory holds that he killed Jasmine because she saw him take June, or even because he believed she was beginning to suspect him for some other reason, that could make him even angrier that because of Jasmine again, he's lost his private graveyard."

She nodded. "He was angry at Jasmine all over again, so he wanted to hurt her. But with her gone, the next available outlet for his anger at her was to hurt someone she loved. Leslie."

Asher parked beside her car in the garage, grabbed the bag with the apple pie, and followed her into the house. "We need to review those pictures more in-depth and set up interviews with the bar staff again, those still working and the ones who no longer work there who knew Jasmine."

Faith chewed her bottom lip as she looked down at her phone again.

"Daphne still hasn't responded to your text?"

"Nope. I'm getting really ticked off about it too. She knows how much I worry."

"Go see her." He set the pie in the refrigerator. "I mean it. It's almost time for your weekly pizza night anyway. Reinterviewing everyone from the bar is going to take days.

You heading to Knoxville to see your sister isn't going to jeopardize the investigation. I'll get Lance to help me. And Ivy's still tracking down those fingerprints. Maybe she'll get a hit soon."

"Are you sure? I mean I'd feel like a heel taking off right now. But I keep thinking about how guys that get out of prison sometimes go after prosecutors, judges, even their own defense attorneys, wanting revenge for them having gone to prison in the first place. This guy knows you and I are on his trail because of the stables. And it's been no secret in the media that we're the ones who discovered his grave-yard and took away his trophies, the bodies of his victims. What if he goes after us, after our families, out of revenge?"

"I think that's a stretch. But you should still check on Daphne in person. It's the only way you're going to reassure yourself that she's okay. Do you want me to go with you? Or one of the others from UB?"

She shook her head. "I appreciate the offer. But, no. Some-one needs to direct the others, explain what we've found, our theory. I'll head to her dorm, yell at her for letting her phone battery die, or whatever, and worrying me. Then I'll join you at the bar. Two and a half hours max. I'll still be able to help you with those interviews." She dug her keys out of her purse and headed toward the garage.

Asher stopped her with a hand on her arm. "Did you check that Find My Sister app on your phone?"

"It's turned off."

"Have you ever known Daphne to turn it off?"

"Only once, back when she was in high school. I lit into her for it and she's never done it again. Ever."

"I'm going with you. You can call Grayson about your concerns on the way to Knoxville."

She blinked back threatening tears of gratitude. "Thanks,

Asher." Without even thinking about it, she wrapped her arms around his waist and hugged him. When she realized what she was doing, and that her arms were pressing against his healing injuries, she stiffened in shock. "I'm so sorry. I'm probably hurting you."

She started to pull back but he tightened his arms around her. "I'm fine. You need to stop worrying about me so much."

She hesitated. "I'm not hurting you?"

"Just the opposite. I'd like to stand here forever holding you. But I know you're worried about your sister." He kissed the top of her head again then sighed and stepped back. "Let's go."

They'd just gotten into his truck when her phone buzzed in her purse. She gasped and held up a hand to stop him from backing out of the garage. "It's Daphne. She finally texted me."

He leaned over and started laughing when he read the screen.

She gave him an aggravated look. "It's an endearment."

"Smother-mother's an endearment?"

"It is!"

"Sure. Okay." He grinned.

"Whatever. Just give me a minute to see if she really is okay." She reread the text.

Hey, smother-mother. Sorry—my battery died. Is something wrong?

Faith typed a reply.

Everything is fine. Just worried when no answer to my texts or call.

"Go see her, Faith. It'll make you feel better."

She almost denied it, but he was right. Seeing her sister, safe and sound in person, would calm her nerves. And maybe, just maybe, they could talk out her confusing feelings about Asher. Daphne might tease her. Okay, she'd definitely tease her. But in the end, she would hopefully help her see things more clearly, figure out what she should do.

"If you're sure, I think I'll take you up on that," she told him.

"Of course. I'll head to the bar and start setting up interviews. I can show the picture on my phone to the owner, see if it jogs his memory about regulars back then, even if they didn't pay attention to Jasmine. If Lance can't help, I'll get Ryland to send some others out there, even if he has to pull in some temporary consultants. We'll get it done. Don't worry about the case. Do what you need to do."

She took his hand in hers. "You really are a wonderful friend and partner, Asher. Thank you."

He gave her a pained look then nodded. "Call if you need me."

Her heart twisted at that look. But she didn't have time to try to sort things out with him right now. She really needed to see Daphne, to rid herself of this nagging feeling that things *weren't* okay, in spite of the text.

Asher backed out of the driveway while she idled in his garage, texting Daphne again before she got on the road.

Daphne, where are you?

My dorm. Why?

Stay there. Don't let anyone in. If anything seems off in any way, call security.

You're scaring me.

Don't be scared. It's just a case I'm working. Has me uneasy. I'm coming to see you.

Oh brother.

I'll make it up to you. Pizza on me.

Sounds good.

And turn your Find My Annoyingly Independent Little Sister app back on.

Have to plug it in first. Battery almost dead.

She was halfway to Knoxville when the last text that Daphne had sent flashed in her mind again. Something about it was bothering her. She pulled to the side of the highway to reread it.

Battery almost dead.

That didn't seem right. She scrolled to one of the earlier texts.

Sorry—my battery died.

Bad word choice or something else? If her battery had died, the assumption was that she had it plugged in so she could text Faith after that. So why, after Faith asked her to turn on her app, would she then say her battery was *almost* dead?

"You're overreacting, Faith. You're overreacting."

But even as she said the words out loud, her fingers were flying across the keyboard, sending another text.

Daphne. Call me.

Nothing.

Faith tried calling her sister.

No answer.

She texted again, called again. Still nothing.

She turned on her app. A few seconds later, it stated Daphne's phone could not be found. What was going on?

Suddenly a text came across, with a picture.

She screamed and immediately swung her vehicle around, almost crashing into a car that had to swerve to avoid her. Ignoring the honking horn, she slammed the gas, fishtailing until her wheels caught and shot her car back down the road toward Gatlinburg.

Her hand shook so hard she struggled to press the favorites button on her phone for Asher. When it finally buzzed him, he answered on the first ring.

"Everything okay?"

"No. God, no. I'm heading back to Gatlinburg. Asher, he's got her. He's got Daphne."

"Hold it. Slow down. I can't understand you. Try again."

She clenched a hand on the steering wheel, her knuckles going white. "It's *Daphne*. That bastard has her. He texted me a picture of her, bruised, bleeding. Oh, God, Asher. I recognized the background in the photo. The killer's got Daphne *in my house*."

Chapter Eighteen

Faith swore in frustration as she yanked her car to the side of the road a good two blocks from her home. There were dozens of police cars parked along both sides, their red and blue lights flashing off the bushes and trees that covered the mountain. Several unmarked, dark-colored SUVs, likely the TBI, were scattered around, some parked in her front yard. Her driveway was taken up by a big black SWAT truck. Farther down the road, on the far side of her property, an ambulance waited.

Her stomach churned at the image branded in her mind of Daphne's bruised and blood-streaked face. She'd hoped the police would have rescued her by now. But part of the SWAT team was just now creeping up toward the front door. Others headed around the side of the house, no doubt to cover any exits—not that there were any. There was no backyard. Her home, like so many in the Smokies, looked like a typical one-story ranch in front with an expansive yard. But the back was on stilts, drilled into solid bedrock deep in the mountain. The basement didn't have any doors out back, just a few, small, high windows that let in light. The only real access to that basement was through the stairs inside the house.

She checked the loading of her pistol, then shoved it back in her pants pocket and took off running toward her house.

She'd only made it halfway before at least a dozen officers surrounded her, guns drawn, ordering her to stop.

Holding her hands in the air, she froze. "I'm Faith Lancaster. That's my house. My sister's inside."

"Show some ID," the nearest policeman ordered.

She swore, wishing some of them were cops she knew. There wasn't time for this. "My purse is in my car, back there."

"Check her for weapons," he told another policeman.

"Oh, for the love of…my pistol's in the front right pocket of my jeans. Yes, it's loaded. I'm a former police officer, a detective with Nashville PD. I work for Unfinished Business now."

She wanted to shout at them to let her go. But she knew how out of control and dangerous things could get really fast. Everyone was hyped up on adrenaline and. She endured a humiliating pat-down after one of them took her pistol away.

"There, I'm unarmed now. Please, let me go. I need to talk to the SWAT commander. I need to know what's happening. I can give him intel on the layout of my house and—"

"They already have intel on the layout of your house. I gave it to them."

She turned at the sound of Asher's voice. Grayson and Russo were with him, ordering the police to lower their weapons.

"Asher, thank God." She ran to him and grabbed his hands in hers. "What's going on? Why haven't they gone inside yet? Have they got eyes on Daphne—"

He squeezed her hands and pulled her to the side, leaving the bosses to deal with the group of anxious police.

"They had to secure the scene first, get a negotiator to try to make contact."

"What? Are you kidding? He's a freaking sociopath. Forget negotiations. Get my sister out of there!" She reached for her gun then stopped. "One of the cops took my pistol. I need to get it back and—"

"And nothing. We'll worry about that later. Faith, listen to me. SWAT's about to go in. You need to wait out here and—"

"I'll go with you. I can help. Just need my gun." She frowned and looked around for the cop who'd taken her pistol. The police were all huddling behind the cars parked in her yard now, using the engine blocks for cover as they aimed their pistols at the house. "What are they doing? Daphne's in there. Tell them to put their weapons down."

He lightly shook her and she looked up in question.

"Faith, we're going in, right now. You need to fall back, get somewhere safe to wait this out."

She frowned as he motioned at someone behind her. "We? You're going in too?" Her eyes widened. "Wait, you're wearing a SWAT vest. Hell, no. Asher, what are you thinking? You can't go in there with the SWAT team. Your back—"

"Is fine. And you know damn well I was SWAT before I switched to detective work. I need to do this, for you, for Daphne. God willing, I'll protect her and bring her out in just a few minutes. But you have to calm down, get to cover and—"

"No. *No.* If anyone's going in there, it's me. Give me your gun and I'll—"

He glanced past her again. Suddenly strong arms wrapped around her middle, anchoring her arms against her sides.

She bucked, squirming, trying to break the hold. "What the…let me go."

Asher jogged across the front lawn, away from her, weapon drawn, joining the SWAT members on the porch.

"Get your hands off me now!" She tried to slam the back of her head against whoever was holding her.

Swearing sounded in her ear. "Stop fighting me, Faith. It's Lance."

She immediately stopped. Then he picked her up and jogged with her arms still clasped against her sides. She kicked with her legs, twisting and desperately trying to get loose.

"Lance, damn it. Where are you taking me? That's my sister in there."

"Which is why—ouch, stop kicking me! You're too emotionally involved to help. You'll only endanger her. Seriously, Faith, will you knock it off?"

He stopped with her beside the last police car in the long line of them parked against the shoulder and finally set her on her feet. As soon as he let go, she took off running.

He swore and grabbed her again. He yanked her up in the air and stuffed her into the back seat of the patrol car, then slammed the door.

She screamed bloody murder at him and pounded on the glass. "Let me out of here!"

He leaned in close. "It's for your own good. I'll let you out as soon as the place is secure."

She could barely hear him through the thick, bulletproof glass. She pounded on the window again in frustration then showed her appreciation with a rude gesture.

He mouthed the word *sorry*, then jogged back to her house to join the others watching the SWAT team.

Faith had never been so frustrated in her life. A little voice in her head told her that Asher and Lance were right in keeping her from trying to go in and rescue her sister. But her heart told her she couldn't wait and do nothing when Daphne was in danger.

As she watched from almost too far away to see the action, her front door was busted in and the SWAT team, along with Asher, ran into the house.

Her shoulders slumped in defeat. Daphne's life, her safety, was now completely out of her hands. She dragged in a deep, bracing breath and pulled her phone out. She wasn't about to sit in this police car while they—hopefully—brought Daphne out. She needed to be right there for her and ride with her in the ambulance.

Please let her be okay. Please.

She thumbed through her favorites in her contact list, searching for Lance so she could tell him to let her out of the car.

The back door swung open.

She jerked her head up. Before she could even react, a policeman reached in and grabbed her phone out of her hands and tossed it into the woods.

"Hey, what are you—" She stared in horror at the face staring back at her. Stan. No, not Stan. Fake Stan, the killer. As her stunned mind finally realized what was happening, she drew back her fist to slam it into his jaw.

The door swung shut and her fist struck the window. She swore, shaking her aching hand, blood trickling down her knuckles.

The driver's door jerked open. He hopped into the driver's seat, closing the door on her screams for help.

He glanced at her in the rearview mirror through the thick plexiglass that separated them. And smiled.

THE HOUSE WAS eerily quiet. And clean, neat, as it always was. Nothing seemed out of place, as you'd expect if a madman had busted inside and kidnapped someone. Everything seemed…off.

Asher knew his job, to wait for the team to clear the main

level before accessing the basement. But he also knew that a young woman he and Faith both loved very much was right now at the mercy of a killer. He'd seen the picture that Faith had sent him and knew right where she was when the picture had been taken. He wasn't waiting one more second to help her.

He sprinted into the kitchen and rounded the end of the row of cabinets to the staircase behind the wall that led to the lower level.

Ignoring one of the SWAT members frantically motioning from across the room for him to wait, Asher headed downstairs. Although he desperately wanted to take the steps two at a time and sprint into the basement to rescue Daphne, he also knew that getting himself killed wouldn't help her. So, instead, he stealthily moved down the stairs, gun out in front of him, avoiding the spots he knew from experience would creak. At the bottom step, he ducked down behind the wall that concealed the stairs so his head wasn't where the killer would expect if he shot at him. Then Asher quietly peeked around the wall.

Daphne was tied to one of the support posts about twenty feet away. Her mouth was duct-taped and her hands were zip-tied above her head to the post. Her ankles were zip-tied together, but not to the post. She was wearing shorts and a T-shirt, both dotted with blood in a few places, probably from the small cuts on her face that had dripped onto her clothes. Her chest was rising and falling with each breath she took. She was alive.

His mind cataloged all of those details in a fraction of a second as he swept his pistol back and forth, looking for the killer.

The sound of something knocking against a pole had him swinging back toward Daphne. She was twisting her tied feet back and forth, hitting the pole. Her eyes were wide and frantic above the gag as she watched him.

Seconds later, several SWAT team members emerged from behind the wall that concealed the stairs. He motioned to them to secure the basement and ran to Daphne. She seemed desperate to tell him something and every instinct in him was screaming to pull off her gag. The feeling that all was not as it seemed, that had hit him the moment he'd entered the house, was now an all-consuming feeling of dread.

He loosened the edge of the duct tape on her cheek. "This is going to hurt, Daph."

She nodded.

He ripped the tape off in one long swipe.

She gasped at the pain, sucking in a sharp breath.

"Where's the man who did this to you?"

She blinked, tears running down her face. Then her eyes widened again. "Asher, where's Faith? Where's my sister?"

"She's outside. She'll greet you when we get you out of here. Are you hurt anywhere else besides your face?"

She ducked away from his hand when he tried to brush the hair out of her eyes. "Are you absolutely sure Faith's safe?"

He frowned. "Safe? What are you—"

"It's a trap," she said. "All of this. I'm bait, to get Faith here. It's her he wants."

"Ah, hell." Asher took off running, taking the stairs two at a time and sprinting through the house. At the ruined front door, he paused, only to make sure none of the police outside mistook him for the killer and opened fire.

"Clear," he yelled, motioning inside.

Russo ordered his men to lower their weapons and they started running toward the house.

Asher sprinted down the porch steps, searching the groups

of TBI agents and other police until he spotted Lance with Grayson, standing behind one of the police cars a short distance away. He ran up to Lance, dread and worry making his blood run cold when he didn't see Faith and didn't hear her swearing at him for not allowing her to go into the house.

"Where is she?" he demanded, turning in a circle before whirling back around. "Lance, where's Faith?"

"I put her in the back of a patrol car to keep her from interfering."

"Where? Show me."

Lance frowned. "Is Daphne not okay? Is that why you're—"

"Daphne's fine. She was bait. He wants Faith. Where the hell is she?"

Lance's eyes widened. "The last police car, way down there." He pointed and Asher took off running again.

His heart slammed in his chest, his healing lung and back protesting with twinges of pain as he raced down the row of cars. Each one was empty, lights flashing but no one inside. When he reached the last car and looked through the back window, he fisted his hands and whirled around.

Lance and Grayson both stopped in front of him, gasping for breath.

"She's not here. Is this the right car?" Asher demanded.

Lance's brows drew down. "Well of course it—wait, no. No, it's not. This is one of the Sevier County Sheriff's cars. The last one was a Gatlinburg PD patrol unit. It's…it's gone."

Grayson whipped out his phone and stepped away from them.

Lance motioned at some of the police, drawing their attention. As they jogged up to them, Asher pulled out his own phone.

"I never use this thing," he mumbled as he opened an

app. "Hopefully I can figure out…there. Right there, that dot. That's her."

Lance stepped beside him, looking down at the screen. "Is that Faith's infamous find-Asher app?"

"She calls it a number of different things, depending on who she's tracking. She made me put it on my phone to track *her* in case we ever got split up. Her phone is that dot. It's not moving, it's…" He jerked his head up. "Right over there. In the woods."

He and Lance both drew their weapons and rushed to the trees. They swept their pistols in an arc, each covering the other as they followed the blinking dot on his phone. Less than a minute later, Lance swore and crouched over the bloody body of a man dressed only in his underwear. He pressed his fingers against the side of his neck and shook his head. "He's gone. Throat's slit. He's not our perpetrator."

"He's a policeman. I met him earlier." Asher bent down and picked up a small brightly colored piece of paper with a number written on it.

Lance stood. "What is that?"

"AFID. Anti-Felon ID confetti tags. Some Taser canisters shoot them along with the darts to help identify who pulled the trigger on a Taser. It's only useful if the ID numbers trace to a legal buyer though."

"This guy was Tased then his throat slit. Why?"

Asher checked his phone again then stepped around the body and walked a few more yards into the woods. His stomach sank with dread. "I found Faith's phone." It lay discarded on a bed of leaves and pine needles.

Lance stood and crossed to him. "Oh, man."

The sound of shoes crunching on leaves and twigs had Lance and him whirling around, guns drawn.

Russo held his hands up. "Hey, hey. Only friendlies here.

Everyone holster your guns." The uniformed police officers with him slowly put away their weapons. Lance and Asher did the same.

Grayson stepped around Russo and stopped in front of Lance and Asher. "What have you…oh, no."

Russo knelt by the body. "Sweet, Lord. It's Sergeant Wickshire."

Asher glanced down at Faith's phone then at Grayson. "It was a setup from the beginning. Daphne said the man who abducted her didn't want her. He told her she was bait, to draw in Faith. We played right into his hands. He must have killed Sergeant Wickshire, took his uniform, then drove off in the car with Faith in the back seat. She was supposed to be safe there. Instead, we delivered her directly into the hands of her enemy. And because of me, she doesn't even have her gun to defend herself." His voice broke and he took a steadying breath. "We have to find her. We have to find her before it's too late." He ran back toward the road with Lance and Grayson running after him.

Chapter Nineteen

This time when he ordered her to stop, just past a group of pine trees, Faith did. Running right now wasn't an option, not when he'd already proved he wouldn't hesitate to Taser her. When he'd opened the rear door of the police car, she'd jumped out and taken off. But he'd been prepared. The twin dart wounds on her back attested to that. And if that wasn't enough incentive, the lethal knife sheathed at his side was more than adequate to keep her following orders.

At least until she could figure out how to escape without getting killed.

"Head uphill, up the path."

She hesitated, thinking about all the scary movies she'd seen where the too-dumb-to-live heroine went up instead of down, sealing her fate.

The razor-sharp tip of his knife pressed against her back, cutting into her flesh. She gasped and arched away from it, then started up the incline.

One step, two, three. The sound of his footfalls joined hers, following behind. He certainly wasn't dumb, staying close enough so she couldn't escape but far enough back so that she couldn't simply whirl around and shove him down the mountain.

Being helpless and forced to pin her hopes on someone

else coming to her rescue was a foreign and uncomfortable feeling. But the way things looked, if no one figured out where she was and helped her, she wasn't going to make it off this mountain alive.

In spite of her longing for one of her UB teammates or the police to find her, she silently prayed that Asher didn't. Oh, she knew he'd try. If the roles were reversed, she'd do everything in her power to find him too. But even though to most people he might seem healed and back to normal, she'd seen his winces of pain often enough to know the truth. He wasn't at a hundred percent, which made him vulnerable. She didn't want him risking his life to save hers. She'd rather die than have that happen.

That realization had her blinking back tears of shock. Good grief. When had he become so important to her? She'd always treasured his friendship. But now he was so much… more. In spite of her determination to not risk the loss of their friendship to a romantic relationship, she'd utterly and completely failed.

She loved him.

Completely.

Hopelessly.

Loved him.

Please, God. Don't let Asher be the one to come for me. Let it be someone else, or no one at all. Protect him. Keep him safe.

"Quit daydreaming. Move." The knife pricked her back again.

She swore and started up the mountain.

RUSSO AND GRAYSON stood with Asher, discussing the circles he and Faith had drawn on the map currently spread out on the hood of his truck. Asher was explaining the colors of the circles and which ones he recommended that the police focus on as phase two of their search for the missing police car, and Faith. Everyone available was searching for her, and had been for the past forty-five minutes or so. But they'd found nothing. They needed a more focused approach, to think like the killer, and find her before it was too late. That was why Asher had stopped his seemingly fruitless searching and raced back to his house to grab the map.

He couldn't even consider that they wouldn't find her and save her. Even now, just the thought of her not being around left a big, gaping hole in his future. Who was he kidding? Without her, there *was* no future as far as he was concerned. Hell, if she wanted to be only friends and couldn't see him as anything else, he'd take it, pathetic as that was. He'd rather be her friend than to lose her completely. What mattered most was that she was happy. And safe. God, he wanted her safe.

He motioned above them, speaking loudly to be heard. "Chopper's been over this area for several minutes now. Heard anything from them yet? That police car has to be close by, even if the killer ditched it for another car. Otherwise, your men would have found some witnesses who saw it go down the mountain."

Russo grimaced.

Grayson exchanged a surprised look with Asher. "Russo, don't start holding back information now. Faith is our teammate, our family. We deserve the truth. We *need* the truth if we're going to find her."

The chief let out a deep breath. "I know, I know. I just don't want to get anyone's hopes up. The chopper pilot thinks he saw sunlight glinting off something in the woods just around the curve at the bottom of the mountain, before the stop sign. My guys are checking it out right now."

"Get us an update," Grayson told him. "Now. Every minute counts."

"On it." Russo pulled out his phone to make the call.

Asher's own phone buzzed. He checked the screen. "It's Lance. I have to take this." He stepped away from the hood, holding his hand over his left ear so he could hear Lance over the sound of the helicopter circling above.

"Lance, tell me you have something."

He listened for a moment then swore. "Don't give up. Someone at The Watering Hole has to know this guy. You're using the police sketch, right? Telling people to picture him with dark hair, too, not just blond? Someone there has to know him, or remember him, maybe what he drives in case he hid that car and used it after ditching the patrol car. Get me a name."

"We're pulling out all the stops, doing everything we can." Lance updated him on what the other UB investigators were doing to help. "We'll find her, Asher. We will."

He swallowed against his tightening throat. "I know. I just pray to God we're not too late."

A solemn group of police officers stepped out of the woods, escorting the medical examiner's team as they finally brought Sergeant Wickshire's body to the ME's van.

Asher's stomach sank as he watched the body bag being loaded. The idea of Faith in one of those shredded his heart. He turned away, still on the phone.

"Lance, check with Ivy. See if she's made any headway with those fingerprints. If we can just get this guy's name, we can figure out where he lives, what he drives, talk to people who know him and can give us insight on places he frequents."

"I'll call her right now. Hang in there, Asher."

Grayson rounded the hood and leaned back against the side of Asher's truck. "They found the police car. It's empty."

Asher nodded. "I figured. Any evidence inside? Anything to tell us what happened? Where they went?"

"There were tire tracks that don't match the police car. One of their forensic guys said they appeared to have been made from a car, not a big truck or SUV. Looks like he hid it there, planning all along to escape in a police car then switch vehicles. What I don't get is how he could have foreseen Faith being put in that last car, well away from where all the police were gathered."

"Easy enough to predict," Asher said. "Every officer in the area would have rushed up here to try to catch the serial killer and rescue his latest victim. Anyone who's ever seen police activity like that knows there will be tons of cars and the cops themselves will all congregate around the action. Police rarely lock their cars in a situation like that. They leave the keys in them in case someone needs to move some of the vehicles out of the way."

"I follow what you're saying," Grayson said. "Since Faith was personally involved, she'd have been kept way back from the action. Which is exactly what happened."

"And we made it even easier for him by putting her in the back of a police car." He shook his head, hating himself right now.

"There's one other thing that Russo told me, about the cop car they just found." Grayson gave him a sympathetic look. "There were some of those confetti ID tags on the ground."

Asher squeezed his eyes shut a moment, a physical ache starting deep in his chest. "He used a Taser on her, probably the same one he used on Sergeant Wickshire. When I catch this guy, I'm going to tear him limb from limb."

"I'll pretend I didn't hear that." Russo joined them. "We've got TBI agents searching those areas you circled on that map. I took pictures of it and sent it to them. Law enforcement volunteers are driving in from neighboring counties to help so we can cover more territory more quickly."

Grayson clasped Asher's shoulder. "What else do you want us to do? Anything. Name it."

Asher raked his hand through his hair. "I don't… I don't know. Damn it. I hate this. I have to do something."

"You already are. You searched up and down the mountain like the rest of us, then rallied the troops and got everyone more organized. You've given her the best chance possible."

"I have to figure this out, figure out where he has her." Asher strode to the front of his truck and grabbed the map off the hood.

Grayson and Russo stepped back as he hopped inside and started the engine. When Grayson tapped on the window, Asher swore and rolled it down. "What?"

"I don't think you should be driving right now. You're upset and—"

"Damn straight, I'm upset. Faith is out there, somewhere, with a sociopath who's killed nine people so far, that we know of. I'm heading up to this sicko's cemetery. Finding it was the trigger for him to go after Leslie. It's probably why he went after Faith too. He blames her, and me, for taking away his personal dumpsite. That location means something to him. There has to be a clue up there, something we've missed, something we haven't thought of."

Russo called out to him as he and Grayson hurriedly backed up to let him turn around in the yard. "My men already searched that area. There's nothing there."

"There has to be. There *has* to be." Asher slammed the accelerator, kicking up dirt and sending his truck racing down the road.

Chapter Twenty

Russo's men had definitely been to the makeshift graveyard. Their fresh shoeprints showed they'd scoured the place, conducting a thorough search. But Asher did his own search anyway. He was more focused on specifics, like finding more of those neon-colored confetti tags shot from the Taser when fired. And he'd also been looking for bread crumbs. Not real bread crumbs, but some kind of sign that Faith had been there. She was smart and careful. If there was any way at all to leave any kind of trail to prove she'd been there, and to give someone else something to follow, she'd do it. But he hadn't found anything to indicate she'd been there.

So much for his theory that the killer would have brought her to this particular mountain.

He dropped to his knees and spread the map out on the ground. It had been the foundation of Faith's and his investigation. It had yielded them the missing Jasmine and her sister. It was proof that they'd done their homework, knew the killer's habits to some degree. The clues had to be right there in front of him. He just had to figure out how to identify them.

Everything to do with this case was concentrated in a twenty-minute travel radius from this mountainside. He'd explained that to Russo when he'd sent his men out searching. With this exact spot as the epicenter, all of the abductions could be placed within the large circle he'd made on the map. Every single one of them. This circle was the killer's comfort zone, where he hunted and where he buried his victims. He lived here, worked here, played his sick games here. So, where in this circle, was he now?

Think like the killer. Put yourself in his head. Where would you go to avoid the cops, knowing that killing a police officer means that every law enforcement agent within driving distance is going to join the manhunt?

I'd go somewhere I'm comfortable with, stay in my twenty-minute circle.

But the police were already looking in the places that they knew he'd been to before. That seemed like a waste of time to Asher. The killer already had his victim. The question was, where would he take her now that he had her? What place had special significance for him? What was the common thread between all of his victims that caused him to choose that special place?

Asher ran his fingers over the topographical symbols, studying the map as if he'd never seen it before. The names of the victims ran through his mind as he studied it. What did they all have in common?

The link that Faith had found between victims was the bar, The Watering Hole. Did something set it apart from other restaurants and bars, make it attractive as a hunting spot to the killer? What about it made it comfortable to him? All Asher could think of that was unique to that bar was the manmade waterfall behind it. Customers loved to take selfies and post them on social media in front of that waterfall. But there were hundreds of real waterfalls throughout the Smoky Mountains. That by itself didn't seem unique at all.

What else did he know about the victims themselves? Something that stood out?

Mud. Two of the victims' bodies had dried mud, or what the experts believed was originally mud, in their hair or on their clothes.

Another victim had river rocks in her pocket.

Jasmine liked to go white-water rafting. What about the others?

He accessed the cybercloud from his phone to read the latest reports his team had been uploading with any information they'd gathered for the investigation. Mini bios had been created for all of the victims. Asher quickly skimmed the ones for the remaining victims he didn't know as much about.

Natalie Houseman owned a boat.

Dana Randolph used to work at the Ripley's Aquarium in downtown Gatlinburg.

Felicia Stewart was an avid fisher. Her favorite spot to fish was off the dock in her backyard.

Some of them had visited or frequented The Watering Hole. The link between all of that seemed obvious—water. Each of the victims he'd just thought about had some kind of water in common. Was that a useless coincidence or a useful fact? Was it possible that the killer had some kind of fascination with water? He certainly seemed comfortable in the outdoors, as evidenced by his taking Leslie up into the mountains. Leslie…wait. There was a waterfall at the trail-riding place where they'd found her. And a pond. Water yet again. Was that another coincidence?

He ran his fingers across the map more quickly now, his instincts telling him he might be onto something. Too many things kept coming back to water of some form or another. There had to be a reason. Or was he off on a ridiculous, unrelated tangent?

Think, Whitfield. Think. What do you know about this guy?

All of his victims were women. Everything else about them varied. Young, older, Black, white, Asian. He didn't have a specific type of person he abducted, except, maybe, that they all had some kind of affinity for water either to work or play. Did the killer resent them for that? Or was it something he liked about them?

The idea that a serial killer would choose his victims because they boated, rafted, liked waterfalls or anything else to do with water seemed ludicrous. Then again, serial killer Ted Bundy chose his victims because they all had long straight hair parted in the middle. What could be more ridiculous than that?

He was onto something. He felt it in his bones.

It all went back to The Watering Hole. Asher knew the killer didn't have Faith at the bar. The place was crawling with cops and UB investigators. But the killer had picked out his previous victims there. Because he frequented the place. It was his hunting ground. He'd likely listened to conversations and discovered interests in his favorite attraction—water— as a part of some recreational activity. He'd chosen them at the bar, stalked them, figured out the best place to abduct them, killed them, then buried them on this mountainside.

Close. So close. The missing puzzle piece was here. He knew it.

He glanced around at the mounds of dirt where the graves had been filled in. Killing them, then bringing them here to bury them didn't feel right. It was a lot more work to carry a dead body than to force a live one where you wanted them to go. It made more sense that he'd kill them right here. But if that was the case, wouldn't he stick to his routine and...try to kill Faith here? There was another puzzle piece. Maybe he did kill them somewhere else and brought them here. But it was harder to move a dead body. Maybe he did it anyway, used a litter or something like that to pull them up the mountain. Seemed crazy to think he'd do that. But, hey, serial killers were crazy as far as Asher was concerned. Trying to understand them was next to impossible. But that didn't mean he couldn't predict what they'd do, not if he sifted through the evidence the right way. Setting aside the logistics question about moving bodies, he explored the next obvious question.

How did he kill the women?

The ME couldn't find an obvious cause of death. But Asher knew the most common way that serial killers murdered their victims was strangulation. Hanging was an obvious choice to strangle someone since he'd tried to hang Leslie. But without any bones broken in any of the bodies they'd found, it didn't seem to make sense that he would have hung them. That threat was exactly that: a threat he'd set up with Leslie to force Asher to choose between going after the killer or saving his victim. Hanging wasn't his method of choice for killing all of his victims.

No obvious stabbing or bullet wounds found with any of the victims. No broken bones. No blunt force trauma. Poison didn't seem likely, either, given their earlier discussion at Grayson's house.

He was left with suffocation of some kind. So how did you suffocate someone without breaking bones in their necks?

He blinked as he stared down at the map again. Water, water, everywhere. How do you take away someone's ability to breathe and explore your twisted fascination with water at the same time?

You drown them.

His phone buzzed in his pocket. He grabbed it without looking at the screen. "Asher."

"It's Lance. We struck gold. Just as you thought, the common link is the bar. Asher, we know who he is. There was a freaking picture of him on the wall, one of dozens of framed pictures showing crowd shots. I grabbed it and showed it to nearly everyone there. I got a name. And right after, I swear, to the very second, Ivy called. She's been visiting every Podunk police force in all the neighboring counties and got a fingerprint match from that knife. It was a small police station that didn't enter the fingerprints into AFIS because it was for a minor arrest, a traffic violation. He—"

"Lance, for God's sake, who is he? Tell me something to help me find Faith."

"Malachi Strom. Get this. He saw his father drown on a family trip when he was only twelve. Then his mother died seven years ago of leukemia. That's when the killings began. Maybe that was his trigger to start killing."

"Water. His father drowned? That's the link."

"Okay, you've lost me now."

Asher quickly explained his theory about water and that he'd drowned his victims.

"How is that supposed to help us find Faith?"

"I don't know yet. Obviously, we can't search every river, stream or waterfall in the county. My gut tells me that's where he's taking Faith, to some body of water. She can't swim, Lance."

Lance swore.

"You said his father drowned. Where did he die? Is it in our twenty-minute circle?"

"Oh, man. Hang on, let me see what Ivy sent."

Asher fisted his hand at his side, torn between frustration and hope as he waited. "Hurry, Lance. Hurry."

"This is it. Yes, yes! It's in that circle you gave us. Holy… it's on the other side of the mountain from the graveyard.

Crescent Falls. His father must be the person Russo said drowned there twenty years ago."

Asher's shoulders slumped as hope drained out of him. "He wouldn't have taken Faith there. On a day like today, that place is crawling with tourists."

"No, no, it isn't. Remember a tourist drowned there a while back, the day you found the graveyard? The park system shut it down until they can do a study on the safety measures. It's still closed."

"That's it. Has to be. Get everyone over to the falls. Get that chopper up there. And tell me everything you know about what happened to his father." Asher took off running.

The falls couldn't have been more than a football field away. But by the time Asher reached the parking lot, his healing lung was burning and he was having trouble taking a deep breath. His back ached, but it always ached these days, so he didn't pay much attention to that.

"You okay, buddy?" Lance asked over the phone. "Your breathing doesn't sound so good."

Probably because it wasn't.

Asher tried to take a deeper breath, but every time he did, it felt as if a knife was being stabbed into his lung all over again. Didn't matter. He couldn't let it slow him down, not with Faith's life at stake.

He stopped at the taped-off entrance to the path that visitors used to go to the top of Crescent Falls. Something neon orange on the ground caught his attention. One piece of Taser ID confetti. The Taser hadn't been fired here or there'd have been dozens of them. Instead, someone had specifically dropped one piece.

Faith. It had to be her. He was on the right track. She must have secretly pocketed some confetti after getting Tased beside the police car. She'd left him a bread crumb.

"Asher?" Lance called out. "Give me an update. Are you okay? Have you found anything?"

He studied the path that followed a steep angle up the mountain, winding around rocks and trees. The falls weren't visible from this vantage point. But he could hear them. He was close.

"This is the place. She's here. Tell everyone to hurry." He ended the call, silenced his phone, then ducked under the yellow tape and began jogging up the steep path toward the falls, as quickly as his burning lung and aching back muscles would allow.

Chapter Twenty-One

Faith stood in the knee-deep swirling waters at the top of the waterfall, just feet from the edge, her wrists zip-tied in front of her. Four feet away, the cold dead eyes of a sociopath stared back at her, one hand holding the Taser, the other a wicked-looking knife with a six-inch blade that was already stained with her blood. It was as if he was trying to come to a decision—Taser her yet again or gut her. Or maybe he was going to toss her over the falls and let the rocks and water do their worst.

She couldn't resist taking a quick glance at the edge. It was a twenty-foot drop, maybe more. If she did go over, and managed not to crush her skull or drown, she'd probably be swept to the second tier of the falls and go over again. The pool of water at the very bottom was much deeper than up here. It was where the tourist had drowned a few weeks ago. And that tourist's hands hadn't been tied. If she ended up down there, it was lights out.

Asher was right. She should have learned to swim a long time ago. Although how she could do that with her hands tied was beyond her, even if she knew how.

Asher. Daphne. The two most important people in her life. Just thinking about them had her tearing up. They would take her death hard, assuming Daphne was even okay. This lowlife had refused to answer her questions about her sister.

She'd begged him to tell her if he'd left her alive in the base-ment. His only response was a cruel smile that chilled her more than the water swirling around her legs.

It took all her strength to remain standing as the current pushed her ever closer to the edge. Her teeth chattered, the water brutally cold this high in the mountains. But Fake Stan, the killer she and Asher had been trying to find for months, seemed immune to it as he continued to watch her.

"What do you want from me?" she demanded, not for the first time.

And just as before, he said nothing. He simply kept star-ing at her with those dead eyes, making her want to vomit.

At least she had one thing to be thankful for. The gashes in her legs from the Taser barbs he'd yanked out no longer hurt. The freezing water had mercifully dulled that pain. Too bad it wasn't high enough to take away the throbbing aches in her back and stomach. The slices he'd made weren't deep enough to kill. But they hurt like hell.

She risked another quick look past the falls to the thick trees lining the steep path below that she'd been forced to climb. Beyond that, around several curves in that path, was a parking lot. But no one had been there when he'd driven into it. No sirens sounded in the distance. No police or friends from Unfinished Business were rushing up the mountain to rescue her. She was going to die, unless she could think of something else to try.

Like somehow freeing her hands so she could put up some kind of defense. The only way she could think of to free them was to cut the zip-ties. To do that, she needed a knife. He was the only one with a knife. Kicking it out of his hands was one option to try. But she'd likely be swept over the falls trying to get the knife. Either way, the end result was death.

As if finally making up his mind about how he was going

to kill her, he holstered the Taser. Then he slowly started toward her, fighting the current, his knife firmly in his right hand.

"Wait," she called out, forced to scoot her feet closer to the slippery edge to keep some space between them. "My sister, please. Tell me if she's okay. You used her as bait, didn't seriously hurt her. Right? Please tell me. I have to know."

He cocked his head like a bird looking at a worm right before it bit its head off.

"The knife usually scares them," he said. "They scream by now, try to run, get swept over the falls. Why aren't you screaming?"

Oh, God. This was how he'd killed all his victims? Forcing them over the falls? Revulsion and dread made her stomach churn.

"Will screaming make a difference in what you do to me?"

A cold smile curved his lips, sending a shiver through her soul. "It never has before." He raised the knife again.

She held up her hands. "Wait."

He lunged forward, the knife high over his head.

She fell backward into the water, desperately scrabbling away, searching for something to hold on to so she wouldn't get swept over the waterfall.

He yelled with rage, leaping at her just as the crack of a gunshot filled the air. Faith screamed and scrambled out of his way as he landed with a splash. He immediately pushed up on his knees, knife raised again.

"Faith! Move out of the way!"

She whirled around, astonished to see Asher running out of the woods toward them, gun raised.

"Faith, behind you!"

She twisted to the side, the killer's arms narrowly missing her as he fell into the water. She scrabbled away, desperately fighting the relentless current as it pushed her toward the edge. But the rocks beneath the surface were slippery and her bound hands so numb she couldn't grip them.

"Faith!"

Another gunshot sounded as she screamed and hurtled over the falls.

ASHER WATCHED IN horror as Faith fell over the waterfall. He splashed through the water to the edge. A guttural roar had him whirling around, gun raised. But the killer was on him before he could fire. They both fell back under the water, jarring the gun loose. The glint of the knife below the surface came slashing at him. Asher grabbed the other man's wrist, yanking hard.

Bubbles blew out of his attacker's mouth as he yelled underwater, the knife coming loose. He kicked at Asher, breaking his hold. They both surfaced, gasping for breath and climbing to their feet. But when the killer ran toward him, Asher ran for the edge of the falls. Faith was down there somewhere, in the water. And she couldn't swim.

He leaped out over the rushing water and fell to the pool below. He landed hard on the bottom then pushed to standing. It was only waist-deep. And there was no sign of Faith here. She must have gone over the second waterfall to the much deeper pond at the bottom.

Running as fast as he could toward the edge, he leaped again just as a splash sounded behind him. He fell to the deep pool below then quickly kicked to the surface.

"Faith!" he yelled. "Faith!"

He twisted and turned, desperately searching for her, hoping to find her on the edge of the pool. Nothing. No sign of her anywhere. He tried to take a deep breath, but his hurt lung had him gasping in pain. Swearing, he drew a more shallow breath and dove straight down. He pulled himself through the water as quickly as he could, both dreading and hoping to find her. His lungs screamed for air, forcing him to surface. He dragged in several shallow, quick breaths, then dove again.

There, on the far side. A shadow on the bottom. He kicked his feet, using the last of his air, refusing to surface no matter how much his lungs burned as he raced underwater. As he reached the dark shadow he'd seen, long tendrils of golden-brown hair floated out toward him. Faith.

He scooped her up and kicked for the surface.

Something slammed into his back. Fiery lava exploded through his veins. But he didn't stop. He kept hold of his precious burden and climbed to the surface. He breached into the air and whirled onto his back, pulling Faith into the crook of his arm, face up. As he kicked with his legs for the shore, he breathed air into her lungs over and over. Kick, breathe, kick, breathe.

He was almost there when a hand grabbed his leg and yanked him under the surface. He kicked out violently, smashing his foot against the other man's face. It broke his hold and Asher again surfaced, half dragging and half throwing Faith out of the water. She landed on her side, still unresponsive.

The water rippled around him, his only warning. He dove back under, grabbing the killer from behind, his arm around his throat. Asher yanked his forearm back in a swift lethal movement, crushing the man's windpipe. He went slack and Asher shoved him away and kicked for the surface again.

He crawled out of the water, feeling oddly light-headed and short of breath. Sirens sounded in the distance. Help was finally on its way. But was it too late? He reached Faith's side and rolled her onto her back; her beautiful face so pale and white, his stomach sank. He gave her three quick breaths, watching her chest rise and fall. Then he began chest compressions.

"One, two, three…" He kept counting, thirty chest compressions for every two breaths, as he'd been trained so long ago. Over and over, he pumped her heart, swearing at her, swearing at him, swearing at the man who'd done this to her, all the while pumping, pumping, breathing, pumping.

"Come on, Faith. Don't leave me. Breathe."

"Asher, Asher, move. Let them help her."

He blinked and realized he wasn't alone anymore. Lance and Grayson were both pulling at him as two EMTs jumped in to take over.

"She drowned," he told them. "She's got water in her lungs. I can't get her heart going. Please, you have to help her."

Grayson and Lance dragged him back as more first responders came to Faith's aid.

Asher desperately jerked sideways, looking back, but he couldn't see her anymore. There were half a dozen people surrounding her on the ground. "Let me go. I need to see her." He twisted and fought against their hold.

"Stop fighting us," Grayson ordered. "Let the medics help her. Where's Strom?"

Asher frowned, still twisting and trying to see Faith. "Who the hell is Strom?"

"Malachi Strom," Lance told him. "Fake Stan. Where is he?"

"Fish food." Asher motioned to the pond. "I crushed his windpipe. Do they have her heart going? Is she breathing?"

"They're working on her," Grayson said. "Stop moving for one damn minute. Is this Faith's blood? Strom's?"

Asher jerked his head back toward Grayson. "Faith's

bleeding? I didn't notice any cuts. But I was focused on trying to stop the killer."

"I have no idea." Grayson glanced at Lance. "I think this is Asher's blood."

"The rocks," Asher said. "Probably cut myself on the rocks. Is she breathing? Let me see her." He coughed, struggling to catch his breath. "My lung's giving me fits." He coughed again, everything around him turning a dull gray.

"Medic!" Grayson yelled. "We need help over here. This man's been stabbed."

Lance swore. "You have the worst luck with knife-wielding homicidal maniacs. We need an EMT over here! Hurry!"

"No, no, no. They need to help Faith." Asher heard himself slurring the words. But he couldn't see anything anymore. "Faith. Have to save…save her." Everything went dark.

Chapter Twenty-Two

Faith sat up in her bed, coughing yet again as she tried to pull the pillows up to support her better.

Asher hurried into her bedroom, a look of concern on his face. "What are you doing? You're not supposed to overexert yourself. Those were the conditions of the hospital releasing you to go home so early."

"Neither are you," she complained as she endured another round of his pillow-fluffing. Finally, she pushed at his hands to get him to stop. "Enough. I'm never going to get out of this bed if you and Daphne don't let me do things on my own. I need to build up my strength."

"Which is only going to happen if you rest. You died. You realize that, right? You died and they brought you back. If the water hadn't been so cold, you'd have had brain damage and you wouldn't even be here. You got a nasty bacterial infection from that water, on top of everything else, so you need to take it easy, give your lungs a chance to heal."

"You can turn that same speech on yourself. You were stabbed, again. Had a collapsed lung, again. You were worse off than me when they got you down from the mountain. The only reason you aren't still in bed is that you didn't catch the nasty bug I did, and you're too stubborn to lie down and rest."

He arched a brow. "Okay. If you insist." He lifted the comforter and slid in beside her.

"What are you doing?"

"Resting. That's what you said you wanted, isn't it?" He gave her an innocent look that had her laughing even though it hurt.

"How do you do it, Asher? You make me laugh even when I'm mad at you."

His expression turned serious. "You've been mad at me ever since you woke up in the hospital three weeks ago. I think it's time you told me why."

She pulled back and looked at him. "You don't get it at all, do you? You don't have a clue."

He held his hands out in a helpless gesture. "I really don't. What's wrong?"

"Other than that we were both almost killed by that… that…"

"Homicidal maniac? That's what Lance called him."

She nodded. "That fits. Malachi Strom. Even his name sounds evil." She shivered.

Asher responded by scooting up against her and putting his arm around her shoulders. "You shivered. You must be cold. Let me warm you."

She rolled her eyes, but the expression was lost on him since he couldn't see her face. "I still can't believe that Strom blamed his mother for his father drowning and went on a rampage after she died, trying to avenge his father. How can one traumatic event as a child make someone into a sociopath who sees all women as his enemy?"

"I don't think it did. I'm not a psychologist or an expert on this in any way, but I personally believe someone as evil as he was is born that way. Sure, environment and experiences play a role. But most people going through that same trauma wouldn't become a serial killer. His brain wasn't wired right. Period."

She shuddered again. "I'm just glad it's over. He's dead and buried now and I can stop thinking about him."

"And you can stop being mad at me? For whatever it is that I did wrong?"

She took his arm from around her shoulders and turned to face him. "What's wrong is that you were still recovering from being stabbed and you jumped off a freaking waterfall. Two waterfalls! How stupid is that?"

He stared at her a full minute before finally clearing his throat. "You're mad that I risked my life to try to save you?"

"Yes!"

His mouth curved up into the most beautiful smile she'd ever seen. "I love you too."

She blinked. "I didn't say that!"

"Sure you did. You care so much about me that you would have rather died than have me die. I feel exactly the same way. I love you too."

She sputtered into silence then shook her head. "I can't love you. I don't want to love you."

His smile turned into a look of commiseration. "I understand. You want to keep me in the friend zone. But it's too late. We passed that threshold when you stuck your tongue down my throat at the hospital in Knoxville."

She gasped. "You stuck yours down my throat first!"

"I remember it differently. But that's okay. We're past that now. Just look." He motioned at the comforter over both of them. "We're in bed. And it's not the first time we've spent the night together." He winked.

She sputtered again.

His look turned serious and he slowly pushed her back against the pillows, his body covering hers.

"Faith. We've been best friends for a long time. I know you're scared to lose that closeness. I understand it. And I know you didn't think you wanted to cross that line, to let things change. It was obvious. But the truth is I've been in love with you almost from the day I first met you. I zipped past that whole friendship thing and straight into wanting forever with you a long, long time ago."

She stared at him in astonishment. "Did you say...forever? With me?"

He nodded, his gaze searching hers. "My heart belongs to you, Faith. It always has, always will. I'm here to tell you I'll always be your friend, no matter what. But I can be so much more. I want you, Faith. I want you any way I can have you. But mostly, I want you happy. If making you happy means I have to pretend we're just friends, give you that illusion, I'll do it. But I really hope you can see the truth and embrace it."

She stared up at him. "The truth?"

He pressed a gentle kiss against her lips. "The truth that's in your heart. What do you really want, Faith? Tell me right now you don't want me in your heart, in your bed. Don't try to convince me. Convince yourself."

She started to tell him that, of course, she was fine keeping him as a friend, that she didn't want more.

But that was a lie.

She did want him, in every way—her heart, her soul and, most definitely, her bed. But there was one little problem remaining. "I'm scared, Ash."

His hand shook as he gently stroked her hair back from her face. "Whatever you're scared of, we can face it together." He smiled. "Because you called me Ash. I know you're in trouble now. You can't resist me, or your feelings for me. Remember that warning you gave me? If you ever call me Ash, you're in trouble?"

"At the time, I was thinking I could use Ash as a code word if I was kidnapped or something."

He grimaced. "Let's not mention kidnapping again."

"Agreed. But that doesn't take away my real fear."

"Which is?"

This time it was her turn to frame his face with her hands. "That something could happen to you, that I'll lose you. If I let myself love you, give myself to you completely, in every way, how will I ever survive if the worst happens?"

"Ah. So that's it. You love me so much, you don't ever want me to leave. I can live with that."

She laughed. "How do you always change something serious into something funny?"

He grinned. "It's a gift." His smile faded. "I can't promise you that I won't die before you. What I can promise is that as long as there's breath in my body, I will love and cherish you. Take a leap, with me. A leap of—"

"Don't you dare say a leap of Faith. That is beyond corny."

"Then how about a leap of love? Marry me, Faith Elizabeth Lancaster. Marry me and I'll never leave you, so long as we both shall live."

Tears suddenly threatened as she stared up at him in wonder. "Ash, you wonderful, gorgeous, stubborn man. What in the world am I going to do with you?"

"Love me, Faith. Just love me."

And so she did.

* * * * *

K-9 Missing Person
Cassie Miles

MILLS & BOON

Cassie Miles, a *USA TODAY* bestselling author, lived in Colorado for many years and has now moved to Oregon. Her home is an hour from the rugged Pacific Ocean and an hour from the Cascade Mountains—the best of both worlds—not to mention the incredible restaurants in Portland and award-winning wineries in the Willamette Valley. She's looking forward to exploring the Pacific Northwest and finding mysterious new settings for Harlequin Intrigue romances.

Visit the Author Profile page
at millsandboon.com.au.

DEDICATION

For all the fantastic, talented K-9 dogs. And, as always, for Rick.

CAST OF CHARACTERS

Mallory Greenfield—Part owner of Reflections, an art gallery near Aspen, she's devastated by the disappearance of her mom.

Shane Reilly—Former award-winning skier, he's started a new career as a private investigator and is hired by Mallory.

Elvis—The black Labrador retriever with an Elvis-like sneer is K-9 trained for search and rescue in the mountains and as an attack dog.

Gloria Greenfield—Mallory's mom.

Amber DeSilva—Mallory's sister, whom Mallory has never met before.

Conrad Burdock—He's searching for Gloria but wants to find the fabulous blue diamond he suspects she has with her.

Felix Komenda—An artist from Sierra Leone who knows Gloria and raised Amber.

Chapter One

At the base of a seven-hundred-foot granite cliff, Shane Reilly adjusted his sunglasses and stared at the rock climbers from the Aspen/Pitkin County Search and Rescue team as they made their descent. On the way down, they scrutinized every inch, looking for a scrap of material, a blood smear, a hair clip—anything, any trace of the woman who had gone missing four days ago.

To get to this position at the foot of the cliff, Shane had driven down a steep one-lane service road. His assignment was to search this wide flat canyon where a scrawny creek wound through leafless shrubs, scruffy pines, rocks and patches of October snow that glittered like diamonds in the afternoon sunlight. If the missing woman had dared to hike through this desolate terrain, she must have been desperate to make her getaway. If she'd fallen…he was looking for a dead body.

Head tilted back, he studied the jagged rock face and mentally mapped the route he would have taken if he'd been hired by a group for a day of extreme skiing in the areas outside the groomed slopes. A decade ago, when he was still in his teens, Shane loved being dropped by helicopter into uncharted mountain territory and maneuvering his way down. Then he turned pro and had to be more careful. Skiing had been his life. Until the crash.

He lowered his gaze. The rugged territory had already been surveyed by drones. This effort was a more detailed search—the specialty of Shane's partner, Elvis. The seventy-two-pound, black Labrador retriever kept his tail in the air and his nose to the ground, moving purposefully, searching. His sense of smell, which was ten thousand times more effective than a human, alerted him to the presence of skittering voles as well as elk, coyote and mountain lion. *Layers and layers of scent.* Using a T-shirt that belonged to the missing woman, Elvis could track her through an old-growth forest or across the Colorado high plains. With minimal instruction from Shane, the Lab had divided the wide ravine into quadrants as soon as they arrived. So far, Elvis hadn't shown any indication of a find.

"How are you doing?" Shane glanced over his shoulder to his backpack, where he carried a water jug and collapsible bowl for Elvis. All that sniffing could be dehydrating. "Thirsty?"

Without pausing, Elvis chuffed impatiently as if to say, "Hey, I'm working here."

"Yeah, yeah, don't mind me. I'm just the guy who buys that pricey kibble you like."

Shane always talked to his Lab and, frankly, wouldn't have been too shocked if the dog answered back. Elvis had been his best friend since they were introduced at the physical therapy clinic after the skiing accident. The doctors had told Shane he might never walk again, but Elvis—his assigned service dog—never gave up on him.

When Shane strode out the door from rehab, he brought Elvis with him. For the past two years, they'd undergone

SAR training together. Shane had started skiing again. Not professionally, just for fun. And he'd opened his own business. Most of the time, life was good.

Elvis raised his head, went into high alert and shook all over. His feet scrambled in the gravelly dirt, and he bounded toward the cliff face. At the edge of a tall arched boulder, he sat and froze in place, which was his signal for a find.

Shane dashed toward Elvis. Was this the missing woman or something else? If the dog had sensed danger, he would have been in attack mode. This find was probably harmless. Nonetheless, Shane was glad for the Glock 17 in the holster clipped to his belt. He drew his weapon. Couldn't ignore the possibility that the woman who had disappeared might have been kidnapped.

Gun in hand, he stopped beside Elvis. "Heel."

The black Lab stood at his left hip, ready and waiting for the next command from Shane, the alpha of their little pack.

"Whoever is behind that rock, step out," Shane said. "Show me your hands."

The woman who emerged with hands raised had long blond hair cascading past her shoulders almost to her waist. Even though she wore jeans and an oversize flannel shirt, she looked like an angel. *Thank you, Elvis, for finding her.*

Shane peeled off his Ray-Bans and asked, "Who are you?"

"Mallory Greenfield. The person you're looking for is my mother, Gloria."

Though she spoke clearly, he barely made sense of her words. Consumed by inappropriate desire, he yearned to tangle his fingers in those silky blond strands and kiss those full pink lips. *Get a grip, Shaney boy. Been too long since you've had a date.* "Why were you hiding in the rocks?"

"I didn't want to disturb your search. I'm wearing Mom's shirt, and I thought your dog might smell it."

"Which he did." He holstered his Glock. "You can put your hands down."

"Thanks." She jammed her fists into her pockets and frowned.

She was still beautiful, but her unhappiness disturbed him. "What's wrong?"

She glared, and he realized what a dumb question that was. Of course, she was upset. Her mother was missing. "Who wants to know?"

"I'm Shane Reilly." He reached down and patted the Lab. "This is Elvis."

"Why do you call him Elvis?"

"For one thing, he ain't nothing but a hound dog." Shane tried on a disarming grin. "And take a look at his mouth."

She leaned close to study the handsome dog's upper left lip. Elvis the dog mimicked the sexy sneer of his rock star namesake. Mallory looked from the Lab to Shane and back. Then, she gave an enthusiastic laugh that made the world seem brighter. "Does he sing?"

Shane gave a command that wasn't in the regular training manual. "Give us a song. And-a-one-and-a-two-and-a—"

Elvis tilted his head back and yipped.

Mallory applauded. Her scowl was gone. "Can I pet him?"

"He'll be disappointed if you don't."

After a few gentle pats on his round noggin and scratching under his chin, she fondled his floppy ears, then stroked from head to tail. She hugged Elvis, and he gave a happy murmur in the back of his throat. *Some dogs have all the luck.*

Without letting go of her new best friend, she glanced up. "I've heard of you, Shane Reilly. You were a pro skier, competed in the Olympics in downhill and slalom."

"And now, I'm retired."

"What do you do?"

"For one thing, I volunteer with Search and Rescue. Me and Elvis are getting pretty good at SAR." He gazed into her wide-set eyes, which were an incredible shade of turquoise blue. "And I'm a full-time licensed private investigator."

"Really?"

"Elvis was learning how to be a crime solver, and I figured I should do the same. Plus my father and brother are cops in Denver."

"Why didn't you join them?"

"I wanted to have free time for skiing, and you'd be surprised by how many people in Aspen need my services."

She stood, looked him up and down and stuck out her hand. "You're hired, Shane. I want you and Elvis to find my mom."

He grasped her small delicate hand in his and lightly squeezed. "Where do we start?"

"She left a note."

"What did it say?"

She reclaimed her hand and dashed a tear off her cheek. "It said, I'll be back."

Not much to work with, but he'd do anything to find Gloria Greenfield and bring a smile to Mallory's beautiful face.

TWO AND A half days later at the bitter edge of dawn, Mallory turned off her alarm before the buzzer sounded. She'd barely slept. Her mom was still missing. During the past six days, her mood had alternated between elation when a clue arose to panic when she feared Gloria was gone forever, and then to despair and exhaustion. *Where the hell has she gone?*

In thick wool socks, Mallory padded to her bedroom window and threw open the curtains. Snow battered the beveled panes. This marked the first real storm of the season, a cause for celebration in Aspen where the fiscal well-being of the town meant at least twenty-five inches of base and a fresh supply of champagne powder. Mallory's fortunes weren't directly tied to the weather, but her business also depended on tourists and skiers. She was a part owner of Reflections, an art gallery and coffee shop perched at the edge of the cliff where she'd met Shane and Elvis at the bottom. Though Gloria had founded the gallery, she delegated much of the responsibility to Mallory.

For the past several months, Reflections hadn't been doing well. They'd barely survived the COVID shutdown and were still struggling toward recovery, relying mostly on the sale of baked goods, coffee and tea. Though tempted to close the doors and devote herself 24/7 to searching for her mother, Mallory suspected that would be signing a death warrant for Reflections. She couldn't take time off for grief. People depended on her, and the business wasn't going to run itself.

After a quick shower, she plaited her hair into a long braid, tossed on her clothes, shoved her feet into snow boots and donned her parka, hat and gloves. She lived close enough to the gallery that she was able to slog through the knee-high drifts and unlock the rear door. In the mud-room outside the kitchen, she changed from her boots into green slip-resistant clogs, and then she started the early morning prep work—mixing, kneading and proofing the dough for fresh breads and pastries. With muffins and scones in the oven, she took a caffeine break and pushed through the swinging kitchen door into the coffee shop adjoining the gallery.

Sipping her favorite dark roast brew, she peered through a window at the unabated snowfall on the sculpture garden at the edge of the cliff. Was her mother out there, freezing and lost? Suffering from a delusion? Hiding from someone or something that would do her harm? Mallory pinched her lips together to hold back a sob but couldn't stop her tears. *Don't give up.* She had to keep believing that Gloria would come home safe and sound. Living without her was unthinkable.

Given her mom's eccentric and unpredictable nature, her disappearance could be based on a whim or a half-baked scheme. That was Uncle Walter's opinion. Not really a relative, Walter Pulaski had been in Mallory's life for as long as she could remember. Not only was he internationally known as a sculptor who worked primarily in marble from a local quarry, but he also provided Mallory with grandfatherly guidance, ranging from bedtime fables to advice on creating wood carvings of forest creatures and totem poles. The end products were inexpensive and sold well. Not that Mallory considered whittling to be a viable career.

Walter hadn't known where Gloria went. Nor had any of her other friends, employees or ex-boyfriends. Everyone had said, "You know Gloria. She'll turn up."

Mallory wasn't so sure.

She glanced down at her cell phone. *Call Shane.* She'd begun to look forward to their frequent talks and seeing the singing dog with the Elvis sneer. Right now, she wanted reassurance, needed to talk to a kind-hearted, understanding person. She flashed on a mental picture of Shane, who was big—about six feet two inches—and comforting. His sun-streaked brown hair fell across his tanned forehead. He had stubble on his chin. When he grinned, dimples bracketed his mouth. *Call him.* It was after seven o'clock, not too early.

She tapped his number on speed dial, and he answered immediately in a clear, wide-awake voice. "Are you at work?"

"Where else would I be at dawn?"

"You might find this strange, but there are people who actually sleep until eight. Sometimes even later."

"Mom always says there's plenty of time to rest when you're dead." *Not dead, oh, please, not dead.* Another spurt of tears spilled down her cheeks. "This weather has me worried."

"I understand," he said. "You're right to worry. But I got to tell you, I love snow."

Of course, he did. He used to be a pro skier. Before they'd officially met, she'd seen him on the slopes and admired his form. He looked good on skis and even better close up. His hair was perpetually rumpled but not messy. Thick black lashes circled his caramel-brown eyes. Thinking of him gave her a much-needed distraction. "Can you come over today?"

"How about now? I bet you've got fresh muffins in the oven."

"Now is fine." Better than she'd hoped for, but she didn't want to come right out and tell him that she was smitten. There were already enough complications to deal with. "And why are you awake at this ungodly hour?"

"Doing cyber research on your mom. It's two hours later in NYC."

"Why are you researching New York?"

"An art connection to your gallery. I'm always working. A great PI never sleeps." He paused for effect. "Just ask Elvis."

At the sound of his name, the Lab gave a bark.

Shane responded, "That's right, isn't it? You're a great detective."

Mallory imagined the dog spinning in a circle, chasing his tail and wiggling his hindquarters. "Be sure to bring him along."

"You hear that, buddy? She can't help falling in love with you."

She groaned at the song reference. "Come to the kitchen door. It's unlocked."

As soon as she disconnected the call, she stared at the silent phone and wished she'd hear from her mom. The only texts she'd gotten this morning were from employees who would be late. On a typical weekday, at least one of the bakers would have shown up by now. Not that she needed help. The gallery and coffee shop didn't open until ten o'clock, and the monster snowfall would keep people away. Despite the need for paying customers, she hoped for a quiet day. No sooner had that thought registered in her brain than she heard loud thuds. Someone was pounding on the hand-carved doors at the entrance. A woman called out, demanding to be let in.

Mallory pocketed her phone, got to her feet and clomped across the gray-and-brown travertine tiles that reminded her of river rocks. She patted her cheeks, erasing every trace of moisture. Why had this person—this woman— come here? Did she have something to do with Gloria? *Oh, God, I hope so.* About time she'd catch a break.

The voice shouted, "It's cold. Let me in."

Mallory unfastened the dead bolt, unlocked the door and opened it. Outside, partially sheltered from the heavy snowfall by an overhanging eave, stood a tall woman in a black parka. A fur-trimmed hood hid her face.

She shoved against the door and stormed inside. "Thank God, I got here in time. He intends to kill you."

Chapter Two

After nearly a week of fear and confusion, Mallory didn't think she could be taken off guard, but this strange woman had hit her with an unexpected gut shot. Off-balance, Mallory staggered backward a step and bumped into an easel advertising the showing next week for the kindergarten through to fourth-grade classes she taught in the afternoon. She caught the poster before it fell and turned to the stranger. "Who wants to kill me?"

"Conrad Burdock. Actually, he's looking for your mother." The way her voice dropped when she said *mother* made the word sound like a curse.

Nascent hope shot through Mallory. Maybe something could be gained from this bizarre encounter. "What do you know about Gloria?"

"Quite a lot, actually. I'll tell you later. Right now, we've got to run, Mallory."

How does she know my name? "I've never heard of this Burdock."

"I'm trying to tell you. Don't be so stupid." The tall woman slammed the heavy door with a crash that echoed all the way up to the open beam ceiling. She adjusted the shoulder strap on a large leather messenger bag and focused on Mallory. "Listen to me. Do as I say and maybe, just maybe, you'll survive."

"Tell me what you know about my mom."

"First," the woman said, "you come with me."

"Into the blizzard?"

"Unless you can sprout wings and fly."

Now who is being stupid? Mallory pointed to her froggy green clogs. "I'm not dressed to tromp through the snow. If I agree to go outside with you, I have to change into my coat and boots. They're in the kitchen."

"Is anybody else in the kitchen?"

"I'm here alone. And I have muffins in the oven." When the woman unzipped her parka and pulled off her gloves, Mallory's gaze riveted to a gun holster clipped to her belt. The intruder's rude attitude took on a more sinister aspect, and she was grateful that Shane and Elvis would be here at any moment. She decided to stall until her backup arrived. "I want more information, okay?"

"We don't have time to play around. Get your damn boots."

Mallory had grown up dealing with difficult artists and angry customers and various other people her mom rubbed the wrong way. Her tone of voice took on a soothing tone, and she arranged her features in a conciliatory expression. She led the way along the carved half wall that separated the coffee shop from the gallery itself. "Back here, through the swinging doors."

"Nice place you've got here. Lots of polished wood and excellent sculptures."

"By Pulaski." Even under threat, Mallory couldn't help bragging about Uncle Walter.

"Walter Pulaski? I'm impressed."

"Reflections used to be a restaurant. All open space with the kitchen in the rear. Setting up the partitions and the lecture area took some work, but the end result was worth it." Over her shoulder, she said, "Doesn't seem fair. You know my name, but I don't know yours."

"Amber DeSilva."

"Like the gem?"

"Amber is a fossilized resin, not a gemstone." Though her voice oozed disdain, she stopped short of accusing Mallory of stupidity, again. "Don't you know me?"

Was she supposed to recognize this person? "Sorry."

At the kitchen door, she caught Mallory's arm and turned her around so they were face-to-face. "Look at my face. My eyes."

The color of her chin-length blond hair nearly matched Mallory's long braid. The symmetry of their features—upturned nose, wide mouth, square jaw—was similar. When Mallory gazed deeply into Amber's eyes, the green-blue color of her irises astonished her. An exact match to Mallory, but that was impossible. Nobody else had eyes like hers, nobody except her mom. The most notable difference between them was height. Mallory stood five feet four inches, and Amber had to be nearly six feet tall in her high-heeled boots.

Cautiously, Mallory admitted, "I see a resemblance."

Amber gave a snort. "Ya think?"

"Let's have a cup of coffee before we rush into anything." When she pushed open the kitchen door, the comforting aroma of baking breads and muffins wafted over them. "I really don't want to go outside again. It's freezing."

"You're not listening, damn it." Amber followed her

into the huge kitchen. "This is a matter of life and death. We have to find your mother before Burdock gets here."

"We're on the same page. I'm really worried about her and want to find her. Have you heard anything? Do you know where she is?"

Amber gave a short harsh laugh. "She didn't tell you that she was leaving, did she? Whisked away like magic. She's the queen of hocus-pocus. Ha! Doesn't feel nice to be left behind, does it?"

What was she talking about? "How well do you know my mom?"

"Oh, my God, you still don't get it. Look at me again. Look close."

Mallory took another glance and then shrugged. "Sorry."

Amber DeSilva framed Mallory's face between her hands and stared with her turquoise eyes. "Mallory, my love, I'm your sister."

Stunned, Mallory gaped. *Her sister?* Not possible! According to Gloria, her father died before Mallory was born, and they had no other living relations on either side. Either Amber had fabricated a weird, complicated lie or Gloria had a whole different life before she met Mallory's father. Conceivably she'd been married before and had other children. But why hadn't she mentioned another family?

"You must mean that you're my half sister." Mallory leaned forward, trying to get closer to the truth. "From an earlier marriage."

"Wrong! We have the same father, Raymond DeSilva, and the same mother, Ingrid DeSilva, who you call Gloria Greenfield. You know, I'd love to sit down for a sweet little chat with tea and crumpets, but we damn well don't have time. Get your buns out of the oven and put on your boots."

"How long have you known about me?"

"Only a few days. Once I had the name you were using, tracking you down was easy."

"I don't have a fake name."

Amber gave her a smug grin. "I'm sure Gloria filed all the fake paperwork. She spared no expense, stole enough to get the two of you started on a lovely new life. How sweet. How lovely. How selfish."

"How old are you?"

"I'm four years older than you."

My big sister. A strange feeling—a jumbled combination of joy and fear, happiness and dread—surged through her. She wasn't alone anymore. And her life was completely different.

MOST OF THE mountain roads and streets hadn't been cleared, but Shane drove his Lincoln Navigator SUV, a deluxe 4WD gift from a former sponsor, through the steadily falling snow with no skids, no slips, no problems. The full force of the storm was subsiding, and he guessed they'd get only eight to ten inches—significant but not crippling for Aspen.

In the rear of the SUV, Elvis rode in his specially designed pen where he could watch the snow from windows on both sides. He'd already been out this morning and raced around the fenced area behind Shane's cabin, tunneled into high drifts and buried himself under the glorious snowfall. Before Mallory called, Shane had taken the time to rub dry the dog's shiny black coat. Elvis still smelled doggy, but Shane didn't notice anymore. The Lab was his best friend, and it seemed rude to complain about his natural odor.

In the rearview mirror, Shane saw Elvis staring toward the front of the Navigator. His pink tongue lolled from one side of his mouth while the other side smirked. "We're going to see Mallory. You like her, right?"

A happy bark followed a shoulder shimmy.

"You understand, though, she's more my type than yours."

Elvis growled. He wasn't buying that logic.

"We could find a lady friend for you. Maybe a French poodle."

"Yip. Yip. Yip."

"Okay, three French poodles."

The Navigator rounded a final curve where snowplows had scraped off the parking lot in front of a strip mall and gas station. The art gallery came into view. Lights were on. A glow came from the north-facing windows nearest the entrance. The soaring eaves of Reflections resembled the bow of a clipper ship churning through the snowstorm toward the edge of a treacherous cliff that had claimed the lives of at least five rock climbers. A thick layer of snow piled on the slanted roof and on dozens of heavy marble sculptures in the garden.

Shane had visited plenty of museums and elite galleries around the world while on ski tours, and Reflections impressed him. Mallory's mom had done an outstanding job redesigning this structure, curating the displays and building a reputation. From what he'd heard, artists competed aggressively to be granted a showing here in Aspen, where ski bums rubbed elbows with rich and famous mountain residents.

He frowned to himself. Mallory wasn't going to like the information he'd unearthed in his latest online research. Much of his investigating happened on the computer, and he was skilled at navigating the ins and outs. Gloria Greenfield—art gallery owner and boho-chic free spirit—kept a relatively low-profile on social media with very few photographs. A cause for him to wonder what she was hiding.

Her life before Mallory's birth twenty-six years ago was sketchy. Her hometown in Texas had no records of her. The high school didn't have a photo of her in the yearbook, and the same held true for the art school she attended. Granted, computer data from that era wasn't always efficient or reliable, but he'd expected to fill in some of the blanks. The more questions he'd uncovered about her background, the more Gloria's disappearance smelled like something illegal and dangerous.

Outside Reflections, he saw an SUV parked near the front entrance. It seemed out of place. Shane doubted that the vehicle belonged to an employee. They usually entered through the kitchen where they could hang their coats and scarves in the mudroom before getting started. Tire tracks were still visible in the parking lot, indicating that the SUV hadn't been there for long. Too early for a customer or a friendly visit.

Shane followed a road at the edge of the parking lot and drove around to the rear where he parked. Mallory's car wasn't there, which was no big surprise because she often walked to work. He unlocked the compartment under the center console, removed his Glock 17, checked the clip and slipped the weapon into a belt holster. Not knowing what to expect, he needed to be prepared for anything.

Before entering through the kitchen door, he glanced down at Elvis. In spite of the Lab's high spirits, he was obedient. "Elvis, heel."

Instantly, the dog transformed into a SAR professional, sitting at Shane's side and waiting for further instruction. Shane placed his index finger across his lips. "Elvis, hush."

Confident that the Lab wouldn't make a sound, Shane entered the mudroom, shucked off his parka and drew his gun. *Ready for action.* Hearing voices from the kitchen at the back of the restaurant, he crept closer to the door that separated the mudroom from the kitchen, pushed it slightly open and listened. Elvis sat beside him, silent and alert.

The voice of a stranger said, "Your coffee smells good."

"I can make you a travel mug." That was Mallory.

"We don't have time. Besides, I don't expect your mountain coffee to be anywhere as delicious as my special brew in New York."

"This is an Ethiopian blend, fair trade and dark roasted."

"Don't care," said the stranger. "Hurry up and don't try anything cute. I don't want to hurt you, but you should know that I'm an excellent markswoman. Learned to shoot in Sierra Leone."

"Didn't you say just say you're from New York?"

"I often visited Africa with my father. He was a gemologist."

In his cyber research, Shane had learned that Gloria sold precious gems several years ago. A possible connection with this stranger from Africa. He recalled what he knew of conflict diamonds, also called blood diamonds, which were used to finance insurgents and warlords.

"I'm not going anywhere with you." Mallory's tone rang with determination. "Even if we are sisters…"

Shane swallowed his surprise. *Sisters?*

Mallory continued, "Why should I believe what you say? Why would some guy I've never heard of want to find Gloria and kill her?"

"Oh, my sweet, stupid Mallory. He doesn't care about Gloria or about you. Burdock is after the African Teardrop."

"What?" she gasped. "What do you know about the Teardrop?"

Supremely confident, the stranger continued, "A 521-carat, pale blue diamond that went missing at just about the same time my mother, Ingrid DeSilva, was killed in an explosion."

"What are you saying?"

"My mother—sorry, I guess that's *our* mother—faked her own death, disappeared and stole a small fortune in gems from *our* father, including the Teardrop. She couldn't sell or fence that particular diamond because it was too famous. Does any of this sound familiar?"

"Mom said the Teardrop was cursed."

"Well, she might be right about that. Conrad Burdock has already killed people in his search for that stone. He'll kill again."

Shane had heard enough. He stepped into the kitchen with his Glock braced in both hands. "Don't move."

Beside him, Elvis bared his teeth and growled.

When the tall blonde reached for her holster, Shane snapped, "Don't try it. Raise your hands over your head. Do it."

Though this wasn't the first time he'd faced off with a dangerous adversary, Shane did most of his sleuthing online or by interviewing witnesses. He'd taken training courses to get his license, and his brother, the Denver cop, had given him lessons on how to apprehend and subdue, but he was uncomfortable threatening a woman, especially a woman who looked enough like Mallory to be her actual sister. Still, he kept his Glock aimed in her direction as she lifted her hands over her head.

"It's okay," Mallory said. "She's not here to hurt me."

"Then she won't mind if you disarm her." He nodded toward the woman. "Take her weapon."

"Honestly, Shane. You're overreacting." Still, Mallory followed his instruction and approached the woman. "I'm sorry, Amber. I need to do what he says."

"Who the hell is he?"

Mallory unfastened the safety strap on the holster and carefully removed the Beretta. "His name is Shane Reilly, and he's a private investigator I hired to find Mom. Shane, this is Amber DeSilva, and she claims to be my sister."

"You never mentioned a sister."

"Because I didn't know about her," Mallory said.

Amber exhaled a frustrated groan and pointed toward her leather messenger bag. "I brought a laptop with me. You can look me up."

That would have been Shane's next move. Computer research didn't count as an infallible source for verification, but it gave something to start with. "Okay, sis. Are you carrying any other weapons?"

"I'm not. Trust me?"

"No."

She cocked an eyebrow. "Then I guess you'll just have to do a full body search."

If Mallory had issued that invite, he would have responded in a flash. He'd been longing to slide his hands over her body from the first moment he saw her, but she hadn't given him the okay signal.

"Quit fussing at each other," Mallory said. "Listen carefully, Shane, because I'm not going to repeat this."

She repeated the unbelievable story about Gloria stealing a fabulous gemstone and faking her death during the Civil War in Sierra Leone. He knew her Mom was eccentric, but this was over the top.

"Come on," Amber urged. "We need to hurry."

"Why?"

"I was careful to make sure Burdock's men didn't follow me from the airport, but they're smart enough to figure out the address of this place. It's not safe to stay here."

Or maybe she led these supposed bad guys directly here. Or maybe they didn't exist. He hadn't seen another vehicle out front. Shane lowered his weapon but didn't slide it into the belt holster.

"I should go," Mallory said. "If we don't, she's going to keep harping on it."

"Damn right, I am."

When Amber glared, Shane noticed the unusual turquoise color of her eyes—another indication of a sibling relationship with Mallory. Her story was bizarre, but it might be true. He had questions for her.

Amber dropped her hands and concentrated all her attention on her alleged sister. "This is important, Mallory. Do you know where the Teardrop is?"

"I only saw it once. I was probably ten and didn't realize it was real or valuable." Mallory ducked into the mudroom. "Let me change into my boots. If we hurry, we can get this figured out and be back here by opening time at ten."

"I'll drive," Shane said. "My car is more comfortable for Elvis."

"I'm guessing Elvis is your dog." Amber sneered. "Cute."

Hearing his name, the Lab perked up. But he didn't bounce over toward the tall blonde or even wag his tail. Apparently, Elvis didn't trust Amber, either.

Mallory emerged from the back room wearing her boots and parka. She carried ski gloves in her hands. "Let me lock the front door, and we can get going."

Shane heard the heavy front door crash open. Then came a shout. And the clatter of boots on tile.

Chapter Three

Amber's dire warning had come true. Or had it?

Was this a setup? Shane glanced past Mallory, who stood frozen in the middle of the kitchen and concentrated on Amber. Her haughty expression succumbed to panic. Tension and fear distorted her features. Amber was damn scared, and the people who'd charged through the front door had to be the ones who frightened her. Shane still didn't trust her motives, but he believed her terror was real.

They needed to move fast, before the intruders figured out that they were in the kitchen. While he kept his Glock trained on the swinging door from the gallery, Shane herded the women and Elvis toward the rear door. "Get in my car."

"Key fob?" Mallory held out her hand.

"It's unlocked."

"What if I want to start the engine?"

He handed over the fob. "I'll drive. Wait for me."

As soon as the women disappeared into the mudroom, he braced himself. For a brief moment, he considered stepping into the gallery and attempting to work out some kind of compromise, but the continued shouts and crashes indicated violent intent. These guys hadn't come here for a negotiation. This was a hostile assault.

The door from the gallery swung wide. Two men wearing black ski masks and heavy parkas charged into the kitchen. In a quick scan, they spotted Shane. Handguns raised, they aimed and fired. Four shots. Four misses.

He raised his Glock and returned fire. The taller guy yelped and fell to the floor.

Before his brain had time to process the fact that he might have killed a man, Shane pivoted and dove through the door into the mudroom. Grabbing his parka, he dashed outside.

Mallory hadn't waited for him to take the driver's seat. She sat behind the steering wheel with the windshield cleared and the engine running. *Smart move. He couldn't complain.*

He jumped into the passenger side. "Go."

Even though she wasn't familiar with Shane's 4WD Lincoln, she deftly maneuvered out from behind Reflections before one of the intruders burst through the back door and started firing at them. Bullets thudded against the rear of his car. In the back seat, Amber whimpered and wrapped her arms around Elvis, who had apparently forgotten that he didn't like this woman. He buried his nose in the fur-trimmed collar of her parka.

Looking over his shoulder, Shane saw the boxy outline of a Hummer crossing the parking lot and stopping at the rear door. How many of them were there? He'd seen two in the kitchen, including the guy who'd fallen, and a third must be driving the tank-like vehicle. Were there others? His Glock handgun didn't seem like enough defense. He asked Amber, "Did you pick up your Beretta?"

Her eyes were wide and frightened. "I have my gun."

"And you know how to use it, right?"

She swallowed hard. "I'm not a good shot from a moving vehicle."

"Nobody is," he said. "We might need the fire power later."

"I'll be ready."

Her trembling voice sounded anything but ready for a shoot-out. Oddly enough, Mallory—who appeared to be a peace-loving flower child—was the coolest person in their little combat group. She drove like a champ, skidding at the edge of disaster but not going too far. Her gloved hands rested steady on the wheel. When the Navigator reached the stop sign at the street that had been cleared earlier this morning, she executed a sharp left turn without slowing. Dangerous move but nobody else was on the road. They were headed into town.

Shane took his phone from his pocket. "Drive directly to police headquarters. I'll call ahead and let them know we're coming."

"No."

"Did you say no? You won't go to the police station?"

"Yes, I said no."

Her flat refusal didn't make sense. Mallory had worked with the sheriff and the police chief during the search for her mother, which meant she didn't have a built-in resentment against law enforcement in general. He kept his tone level and calm, which wasn't the way he felt. Shane was, after all, the son of a cop. "When somebody shoots at you, it's wise to tell the police. At least, let me call."

"No." She was more adamant.

From the back seat, Amber called out, "I see headlights following us."

If the thugs who attacked at Reflections were on their

tail, they had even more reason to contact the authorities. But Mallory had a different idea. At the next snowplowed road, she took a right and raced past four other cross streets to a stoplight. Through the thick veil of falling snow, he spotted the headlights behind them. At this distance, he couldn't tell if the other vehicle was a Hummer or not. "Why won't you go to the police?"

"Because I love my mother. I'll do anything for her."

"You care about Gloria. I get that." The bond with her mother ran deep and true. "But what does that have to do with police protection?"

"If half of what Amber told me is true, my mother broke the law. She faked her death and stole a fortune in precious gems. If we contact the police, there will be investigations and prosecutions. I refuse to be the person who sends Mom to jail."

She cranked the steering wheel and turned left again. Too fast. The back of the car fishtailed wildly. The moment she got the skid under control, she went left again, then drove back to the main road. She checked her rearview mirror. "Did we lose them?"

In the back seat, Amber and Elvis stared through the rear window. "I can't tell," Amber said. "There are a couple of other cars."

"We might be able to end this right away," Mallory said. "We're going to Mom's place. I remember where she hid the Teardrop after she showed it to me. Maybe it's still there."

"Not likely," Amber said. "Wasn't that several years ago?"

"Sixteen years. It's still possible."

Shane had no comment. Gloria's A-frame house had been their first stop when he signed on to be Mallory's PI.

Together, they'd searched for clues in her desk drawers, her closets, her bedside table and even her pantry. He'd learned quite a bit about her mother but nothing that pointed to her location. And he remembered the final stretch leading to the house. The road bordered a rugged granite wall on the left. The other side was a drop of a couple hundred feet. Not the sort of road to be driving on in a storm, especially not with bad guys on their tail. "This might not be the best time," he said.

"Can't hurt to try."

He knew she wouldn't be dissuaded. Mallory could be as sweet as a baby fawn but had the tenacity of a badger when she made up her mind. In that respect, she was somewhat like Gloria. The only way he could keep her safe was if he had control of the situation. Never again would he agree for her to be the one behind the wheel.

She dodged through a couple more changes of direction and circled around until she and Amber felt sure they'd lost the Hummer. Mallory set her course for her mother's A-frame house in a high canyon.

While the morning sunlight fought a losing battle with overcast skies, he peered in the direction of the ski runs on Aspen Mountain, which were obscured by a curtain of falling snow. The chair lifts and gondolas weren't open yet, but in a few short weeks, the slopes would be filled with skiers and snowboarders. Every year since he'd turned eighteen and moved to Aspen full-time, he'd looked forward to opening day. This season, he hoped Mallory would be with him, flying downhill and soaring over moguls. He wanted to hear her laughter ringing in the frosty air, to see the roses in her cheeks and the sparkle in her turquoise eyes.

She guided his Navigator into the series of winding turns that led to Gloria's house. When they entered the stretch with the steep drop on the passenger side, he held his breath and slammed his foot down on the floorboard to press an invisible brake. A treacherous ride but no one appeared to be chasing them.

Covered in several inches of snow, the odd-shaped house—partly A-frame with a couple of gables and a wall of glass on one side—reminded him of a fairy-tale dwelling. A place where elves and fairies might live. He told Mallory not to park in the driveway where they might get stuck in the snow. "We don't want anybody to pull in behind us and block our way out."

He swiveled his head and looked at Amber in the back seat. "Have you disabled your cell phone so your location can't be traced?"

"How would I do that?"

Inwardly, he groaned. Amber acted like she was tough and worldly-wise. A lot of bluster, but she had very little idea of what it took to be on the run, evading the alleged villain. What was his name? Conrad something? "Give me the phone."

"You're not going to erase my contacts or anything, are you?"

There were several apps to block locators, but he opted for the quick-and-easy method. "I'm turning it off and taking out your battery. When you need to make a call, let me know."

Mallory parked uphill, off the side of the unplowed road. Though their tracks through the snow couldn't be hidden or erased, their position was set for a quick escape.

Shane held out his hand for the fob. "You did good."

"I was born and raised in the mountains. I know how to drive through snow."

He took a moment to fasten his dog's flashy red leather harness with shiny studs. A little bit sexy and a little bit rock 'n' roll, it was perfect for a Lab named Elvis. Shane didn't hook the leash onto the harness, preferring to let Elvis bound ahead while they slogged through the snow to the rear door.

"The dog shouldn't be with us," Amber said. "He'll make noise."

"That's the point." Mallory kicked through snow that came almost to her knees. "He'll alert us to anybody approaching."

Shane didn't need a doggy alert to the danger he suspected wasn't far from them, but he liked having the seventy-two-pound black Labrador on his side in a fight. In addition to training as an attack dog, Elvis had killer instincts and a ferocious growl.

Reaching inside his parka, Shane rested his gloved hand on the butt of his holstered Glock while Mallory used her key to unlock the back door. She entered an open kitchen that was separated from a long dining room table by a counter where a collection of mushrooms—porcelain, wood and clay—were displayed. Doodads and tchotchkes filled every space in a design scheme that could only be described as chaotic but not unpleasant. He liked the house and wanted to meet the woman who lived there. A cozy warmth snuggled around him. The many windows on two sides of the kitchen, which must have been added on to the original structure, made him feel like they'd entered a snow globe.

"It's weird," Mallory said, "to be coming in here without hearing Mom's music. The greatest hits of the '90s."

"I remember." Amber's tone was uncharacteristically pleasant. "Lots of Madonna and Michael Jackson. She loved to dance the 'Macarena.'"

For the first time, Shane sensed that Amber's connection with Mallory might be the truth. Her unexpected appearance at Reflections had seemed too coincidental. And her story about a multi-million-dollar stolen diamond sounded like a fantasy. In spite of their matching turquoise irises, Amber had no proof that they were sisters.

"Watch me now." Mallory skipped into the front room in front of the long dining table. Humming tunelessly, she moved in a horizontal line, clapped her hands and returned in the opposite direction.

Elvis tried to match her steps, but it was Amber who faced her and provided a mirror image. At the end of the line, she said the magic words. "Can't touch this."

They went the other way. Together, they repeated the MC Hammer line. "Can't touch this."

Mallory laughed. "Did Mom teach you this dance?"

"Actually, it was Felix." She whirled, and her parka opened wide, revealing her belt holster with the Beretta tucked inside.

"Who's Felix?" Shane asked.

"A friend from Sierra Leone. He came home with Dad after my mother was supposedly killed in an explosion in Freetown. Their two-story office building burned for over forty-eight hours. Everything was incinerated. Most of the inventory of gems were lost."

"I didn't think diamonds could burn," Mallory said.

Amber stopped dancing. Her voice took on a smug,

superior tone as she explained, "Diamonds are made of carbon, like coal. So, yes, they can burn at extreme heat. Dad found a few intact. But the insurance paid for most of his loss."

Shane had another question. "Why didn't he keep the inventory in a fireproof safe?"

"He did," she said coldly. "The door to the safe was opened. Investigators believed that my mother opened it in the hope that she could rescue the gems, but she couldn't escape before the fire overwhelmed her. Before you ask, there was evidence of human remains but no way of identifying the victim. So long ago in a war zone, DNA testing couldn't be counted on. In the back of the safe, they found her wedding ring."

Mallory shuddered. "I know the story is untrue. Mom survived, and so did I. But it must have been horrible for you."

"It was." She flicked her wrist as if she could dismiss a lifetime of bad memories. "Felix helped. I was the only four-year-old in Manhattan with an extremely tall male nanny from Sierra Leone with tattoos up and down both arms. He told me all kinds of good stories about my mother. But I didn't believe a word."

"Why not?" Mallory gazed at her with deep sympathy.

"If my mother was such a wonderful person, why did she abandon me?"

Shane watched and cringed. If these two were, in fact, sisters, the differences between them made a stark contrast. A walking illustration of nature versus nurture, they shared genetics but had been brought up differently, and they wanted very different things. Heartbroken, Mallory desperately yearned to find and protect her beloved mother who had been the center of her life since birth. Amber couldn't care less about Gloria. She was after a big pay-off from the sale of the Teardrop and figured her mother owed her that much.

Mallory sighed. "I wish you could know her the way I do."

"Back at you," Amber said. "If you knew what she was really like, you might be glad she's gone."

"She'll come back. I just know she will."

"Don't be so sure. She might be—"

"Okay." Shane stepped between them to interrupt that thought. The possibility of her mom's death was already driving Mallory up a wall. "I think you ladies agree on a specific goal. You both want to find the diamond. And that means finding Gloria."

"Yes," Mallory said.

"An uneasy alliance," her sister chimed in.

"Let's get to it," Shane said. "Mallory, you said there was a hiding place somewhere in this house. Where is it?"

Returning to the kitchen, she peeled off her parka and got down on her hands and knees. Though her jeans weren't formfitting, her cute round bottom stuck up in the air, wiggling and distracting him. The more time he spent with her, the more common these moments of in-stant attraction became. Someday, he might be able to act on these urges. In the meantime, Elvis played surrogate for him, snuggling against Mallory, licking her face and bumping his hindquarters with hers.

In the back of a lower kitchen cabinet, she flipped a small latch and removed a fake wood wall to reveal a safe hidden behind mixing bowls and pans. "The combination is my birthday. I know because Gloria used it for everything."

The lock opened easily, and Shane wondered if this somewhat invisible but easily accessible spot was a good hiding place for a priceless asset. After fishing around in the opening, Mallory pulled out a small, square polished wooden box with dovetailed sides. "The Teardrop was in here. At least, I think so. It was such a long time ago. I might not be remembering correctly."

Amber snatched the box from her hand and tore off the lid. "There's nothing in here, not a thing. Damn, it was too much to hope we'd find it so quickly."

When she discarded the box on the floor, Mallory snatched it up. Sitting cross-legged on the kitchen floor, she probed the satin lining of the box, trying to find a clue or a note. A shred of evidence.

"Forget it," Amber snapped. "Your mother must have realized this was a lame hiding place and moved the diamond."

"You're wrong." Mallory peeled back the velvet on the bottom of the box. She smiled widely. "I knew there was a reason for coming here, a reason for searching."

"What?"

Mallory held up the small object she'd found in the bottom of the box. "A key."

Chapter Four

Mallory held the flat silver key by the cloverleaf top and ran her finger along the teeth on both sides. No logos or other markings, nothing except a six-digit number, which gave no indication of where the key might fit. "A safe-deposit box?"

"We can track that down," Shane said. "Where did Gloria bank?"

"She had personal and business accounts. A local bank where she got wire deposits and another in Denver." She paused and thought. "Oh, and I think there was something in New York that she opened on vacation. I've heard her talk about offshore banking, but that's probably not where she'd have a safe-deposit box. We should check with Uncle Walter. He knows more about her financials than I do."

Before she had finished speaking, Shane stopped paying attention. Elvis tugged at his sleeve and pulled him out of the kitchen toward the front windows of the A-frame section of the house. The interaction between man and dog reminded her of reruns from an old television show about Lassie, a collie with almost telepathic powers of communication. Under her breath, she mumbled the classic line, "What is it, boy? Did Timmy fall down the well?"

Shane rushed back to the kitchen. "We've got to go."

"What's wrong?" Mallory asked.

"The bad guys are here."

She joined him at the window. "Where?"

He patted the black Lab, who was positively vibrating with warning. "Elvis told me."

"Really?" Amber rolled her eyes. "Are we taking orders from the dog?"

"Stay here if you want," Shane said.

He picked up Mallory's parka and dragged her toward the back door. In seconds, they were outside, threading their way through snow-covered lodgepole pines and aspens toward where she'd parked his 4WD Navigator. A layer of snow had already accumulated on the car. With the sleeve of his parka, Shane wiped the driver's side window and the windshield. He got behind the steering wheel while she opened the back for Elvis and ducked into the passenger seat. Using the fob he'd taken from her when they arrived, he fired up the engine.

"Wait," Mallory said. "Amber isn't here."

"Her decision. And who knows? Maybe it's part of her plan. It's possible she's working with Conrad. The thugs in ski masks might answer to her."

"No way. Didn't you see how scared she was?"

"I don't trust your supposed sister," he said, "and I wasn't hired to protect her."

Before he could pull onto the road, Amber threw herself against the back door and leaped inside. "They're almost here. Coming up the front sidewalk."

Shane smoothly accelerated. "So Elvis was right."

"Yeah, yeah, your dog is brilliant." He reached into a pocket of his parka and took out a plastic sandwich bag.

"These are bacon treats. He loves them so don't be stingy, but don't give him all of them."

Around a curve about a hundred yards away, Mallory saw the Hummer that had chased them from Reflections. One man in a black ski mask limped behind the heavy-duty vehicle. He raised his handgun and aimed at them, but Shane was driving too fast for him to take the shot before they zoomed past. Still, he fired at their car as they sped down the road.

When a bullet thumped against the back, Shane winced. She knew how much he liked the Navigator, and the poor thing was taking a beating today. He swooped onto the treacherous part of the route, skirting the perilous drop on the driver's side. He asked, "How do I get to Uncle Walter's place from here?"

"At the bottom of the hill, you'll hit Meadow Ridge. Take a left." Directions to Uncle Walter's lavish château, part of an elite gated community, weren't complicated. She pulled her phone from a pocket and bypassed the apps Shane had installed a few days ago to disguise her signal. "I'll call ahead and let him know we're coming."

Consulting with Walter Pulaski felt like the smart thing to do. If anyone knew about Mom's secret identity, it had to be him. When she'd gone missing, he claimed ignorance regarding her whereabouts, but he confided in Mallory that Gloria—his long-time partner at Reflections—was troubled about the future of the art gallery and told him she had something of great value to sell. The African Teardrop?

She kept her phone conversation with him short, not wanting to give away too much before they talked face-to-face. She needed for him to look her in the eye and be completely honest even if he thought she'd be hurt. Also, she wanted Shane to be there. Not only was he good at asking questions that didn't occur to her—like knowing whether they should trust Amber—but he had investigative skills. He knew about internet searching, interrogations and legal issues.

Glancing across the console at his profile, she noted the sharp edges of his cheekbones, his stubborn jaw and cleft chin. Apart from the dimples at the corners of his mouth that appeared when he smiled, his features were chiseled and hard, almost obstinate. Not unlike his insistence on calling the police. No doubt, that was the right thing to do, and if any other person had disappeared, Mallory wouldn't have hesitated. But this was Gloria! She couldn't betray the woman who birthed and raised her.

While she directed him around the business area of town and into the hills, she made another call and talked to the guard outside Uncle Walter's gated community, warning him that she might be followed by men in ski masks driving a dark-colored Hummer.

"Don't you worry," he said. "I won't let anybody in who doesn't belong."

"Thanks, Henry. And I'd appreciate if you don't mention this to anybody, especially not the authorities."

"Just like your mama." He chuckled. "Don't worry, Mal. Your secrets are safe with me."

As soon as she ended the call, Shane asked, "Why are you dragging this guy in?"

"Into what?"

"Aiding and abetting," he said. "Sooner or later, we have to talk to the police."

From the back seat, Amber groaned. "For a private eye, you're not very adventurous. Why so law-abiding?"

Mallory answered for him, "His father and brother are both cops."

"Well, that explains it."

"Explains nothing," Shane said. "My goal is survival. The odds are better if we have the law on our side."

"Begging to differ," Amber said. "We're talking about a diamond worth twenty million, which opens a lot of doors to bribery. What makes you think the cops would help you?"

Mallory had to agree. Amber had a point—but could she be trusted?

The Navigator approached the tall wrought iron gates at the entrance to Wind Shadow, an exclusive area so high they could look down on everybody else. Mallory saw the road had already been cleared. Henry, the gatekeeper, sat atop a snowplow the size of a Zamboni blocking the way inside.

Mallory jumped out of the SUV and waved.

Henry responded and pulled the snowplow out of the way. As soon as Shane drove through, the obstacle returned to stop any unwanted guests from entering. Mallory waved again and shouted, "You're the best, Henry."

"No problem, cookie. Good luck finding Gloria."

In spite of his encouraging words, he sadly shook his head, which made her think the worst. Mallory responded with defiance, "She'll be back with a story to tell us all."

"That's the spirit."

She directed Shane past several spectacular homes to the swooping, curved driveway, scraped clean of snow, that led to Uncle Walter's stone and cedar chalet. His sculpture studio—the size of a barn with a huge door for transporting massive statues in and out—stood beside his three-car garage. Outside the front door was a massive marble sculpture of a woman in flowing robes and long hair spilling down her back while she reached toward the sky with an outstretched hand that could cradle the stars and moon. Her laughing face bore a remarkable resemblance to Gloria.

Shane parked in the driveway in front of the garage and turned to her. "You and Amber go on inside. Elvis and I will check the damage to my vehicle before we come in."

"Are you sure?"

"Elvis could use a break." The corner of his mouth lifted in a smile, activating his dimples. "And so could I. It's been a fraught morning, and it's not even nine o'clock."

His comment reminded her that she needed to put in a call to Sylvia who usually opened the coffee shop on weekdays. "We'll see you inside."

Amber had already left the car. She homed in on the entrance that combined natural elements with sophisticated design. An obviously classy and expensive home, Amber was drawn like a magnet. When Uncle Walter opened the door, she set down the leather messenger bag she'd been carrying since she entered Reflections. She gracefully shook his hand and dipped, almost as though giving him a curtsy. "Love, love, love your work," she gushed.

"Thank you."

"I mean, I saw a display at the VanDusen in Manhattan that was fabulous."

The handsome elderly gentleman braced himself on a hand-carved ebony cane and smoothed the groomed line of his white beard. His gray fleece vest and jeans were spattered with clay, which meant he must have been working on the wheel in his back room rather than trekking to the studio in the snow. Keeping busy had always been Uncle Walter's way of dealing with problems. No matter how cool he pretended to be, Mallory knew he was worried about Gloria. He looked away from Amber and turned to Mallory. "Who is this?"

"Amber DeSilva. I'm Gloria's eldest daughter." She swept past him into the front foyer where four niches held small sculptures of the elements—earth, water, air and fire. Hundreds of reproductions of these artworks had been one of Walter Pulaski's greatest successes. Amber shivered and gasped and moaned as though having an art orgasm. "These must be the originals. Fabulous. These are worth a fortune. Can I touch them? Can I hold them?"

"They're not for you," Walter said quietly.

Mallory was more irritated by Uncle Walter's lack of surprise at Amber's introduction. He must be aware of the secrets in Mom's past. Why had he never told her? Everyone seemed to know more about her mother than she did. Shane had his internet research to keep him updated. Uncle Walter had memories of a different time. And Amber? Well, her sources of information were enigmatic.

Mallory needed to get to the bottom of this. As soon as Walter herded them into his dining room where his housekeeper had placed a coffee service with lox, cream cheese and bagels on a side table, she squared off with Amber.

"Before we go any further," Mallory said, "I think you owe me some evidence. You've made a lot of claims but have given me no reason to trust you."

"You want proof?"

"That's right." Mallory stood toe to toe with her sister,

wishing she was six inches taller so she could look Amber straight in the eye. "I never saw you before this morning. How do I know you're telling the truth?"

Amber scoffed. "Do you mean to tell me…that the thugs who chased us through a blizzard and put a couple of bullets in your boyfriend's car…aren't proof enough?"

"Not my boyfriend." *Not that I'd mind if he was.* "Shane Reilly is a private eye. The chase and the gunfire happened after those people in the Hummer spotted your rental car at Reflections. Which only proves somebody is after you."

"Me?" Amber rolled her eyes and looked toward Walter Pulaski, the man she'd been fawning over. She didn't want to offend him. Even by Aspen standards, the internationally renowned sculptor was Richie Rich. Amber tried to look innocent. "Why would anybody chase me?"

"You're the one talking about stolen diamonds." Mallory backed off a step. "Look, I don't want to fight. But I need proof that Gloria stole the Teardrop, and now—twenty-six years later—she's trying to sell it."

Amber stalked to the end of the satin-smooth teak table with hand-carved legs. The heels of her boots clacked on the polished marble floor. She flipped open the flap on her leather messenger bag. "Mommy's art gallery didn't do well during the pandemic, did it? Reflections is running out of cash, and Gloria needs a great big infusion. Tell her, Pulaski."

Grasping a coffee mug in his calloused hand, he sank heavily into the seat at the head of the table. Mallory studied the scowl on his lined face. Why was he hesitating? What secrets did he know? Years ago, he'd taken over the accounting responsibilities for Reflections because Gloria sucked at math and was somewhat irresponsible. *Some-*

what? Change that to wildly irresponsible. In the circus of life, her mother soared like a spangled trapeze artist while Walter Pulaski was the strongman doing all the heavy lifting, leaving Mallory to play the role of a clown. "Uncle Walter?"

Nervous, he stroked his groomed white beard. "Is it warm in here?"

"Not really. There's nearly a foot of new snow outside."

And yet, he was sweating. He rolled up his shirtsleeves, spread his hands and gestured widely with the muscular forearms of a sculpture artist who chiseled beauty from chunks of granite. "The finances aren't so bad. Even if they were, I promise I'll always take care of you and Gloria. Always. And I'll never let Reflections close down."

Mallory caught the painful undercurrent of what he was saying. They were losing money and the gallery might go out of business. "We're broke."

She left the table, went to the wide triple-paned window and stared into the continuing snowfall. She should have paid more attention to the business end of the gallery. Her mom had never turned down a request for a new expenditure and had run up outrageous costs of her own by bringing in exhibitions from Chihuly, the glass blower, and a graffiti show featuring Banksy, who Gloria claimed to have dated. Maybe she really did have sex with the famously anonymous artist and many, many others. Mallory wasn't often shocked by anything her mom did, but she expected Walter to be straight with her.

As soon as she found her mom, Mallory intended to hire a real lawyer to replace the current guy who traded legal advice for the opportunity to show his paintings of oddly crossbred animals, like a turtle-ostrich or a camel-zebra.

Then she would gently ease Uncle Walter out of his job as an unqualified accountant. Everything would be okay when she found Gloria. If she found Gloria…

Tears tickled the backs of her eyelids. More than anything—the money, the art, the diamonds from Africa—Mallory missed her mother.

"Here's proof." Amber pointed to the screen of the laptop she'd taken from her bag. "This is a screen grab, shot three days ago from surveillance outside a pawnshop in Brooklyn. The owner of the shop, Ben Hooker, is a well-known fence, specializing in blood diamonds from Africa."

Staring at the screen, Mallory saw a red-haired woman on the sidewalk. She wore a long beige trench with a scarf in a vivid blue, orange and green pattern—a scarf just like it should be hanging in Gloria's closet. In the screengrab photo, the redhead had just taken off her sunglasses and was staring directly into the camera. There was no mistaking her identity.

"Three days ago," Mallory said.

"That's correct."

Mallory had found her mother.

Still missing but not dead.

Chapter Five

Shane tramped up the neatly shoveled sidewalk with Elvis bouncing beside him, trying to catch snowflakes on his long pink tongue. They paused at the sculpture of the giant woman in a turban rising from the earth and reaching for the sky. Though snow draped across her brow and the bridge of her nose, he saw Mallory in her ecstatic expression. Loving the sky. Open to nature. Had she been the model for this statue? Or had it been Gloria?

Elvis had the good taste not to pee on the artwork. Instead, he went to a clump of leafless aspens near the entrance.

From what Shane had learned online over the past few days, he saw beyond the similarities of mother and daughter and recognized their differences. Both possessed vitality, willingness to take risks and joy in living, but Mallory was more mindful. Though reaching for the stars, her feet remained firmly rooted. She'd organized the search for her mother with the skill of a general deploying troops for battle. Mallory set goals and fulfilled them. Unlike Gloria, she avoided being the center of attention and hid from the spotlight. During the time he'd spent with Mallory, Shane hadn't heard her talk about herself. Not once did she mention her own dreams and desires.

He wanted to open that Pandora's box, to know her on a deeper level, to understand what went on inside her head behind the breathtaking turquoise eyes. But he wasn't sure he could continue along this path, ignoring the glaring fact that Gloria had broken the law when she faked her death twenty-six years ago and stole a fortune in precious gems. Not unless he knew why she'd done it.

For sure, this was the most interesting investigation he'd had since getting his PI license, but he knew better than to sidestep the law, especially since they were being pursued by thugs in ski masks. He had to assume a firm stance, had to take control, to tell Mallory no. He couldn't work for her. Not unless she talked to the authorities. Though he liked to believe he could provide all the protection she needed, he wanted to be able to call for backup.

As he approached the carved entryway, the door whipped open. Mallory jumped out, threw her arms around his neck and planted a powerful kiss on his mouth. Too shocked to do anything but react, his arms coiled around her and lifted her feet off the floor. Not light as a hummingbird but solid and real, her slender body pressed tight against his chest. She was toasty warm and smelled like coffee. He allowed himself to accept and savor her wild burst of passion while it lasted, which wasn't long. She bounced away from him.

Beaming, she said, "She's alive. Gloria is alive."

When Mallory reacted on a purely emotional basis, she was ferocious and unstoppable. He couldn't say no to her. His resolution to immediately talk to the police melted like an ice sculpture in a sauna. He cleared his throat and said, "What brought you to this conclusion?"

"Amber has a photo, taken three days ago."

"And you're sure it's Gloria."

"As if I don't know my own mother."

He stepped into the foyer and closed the door. "I didn't mean to suggest—"

"Never mind." She dashed into a lavish dining room to the right of the entrance where she confronted Walter Pulaski, who stood at a side table filling his coffee mug. Mallory jabbed her finger at his chest. "You knew about Mom. Her history."

"I did," he admitted as he hobbled to the chair at the head of the long teak dining table. "I met her when she was in her teens. We hit it off, stayed in touch. Then she came to me when she was in her early twenties. Right before she changed her name."

"More proof." Amber pumped a fist in the air. "Walter is a witness to our mother's name change from Ingrid DeSilva."

Shane could think of several valid and sensible reasons for a name change. This bit of evidence represented the least devastating piece of the puzzle. He faced the white-haired man whom he'd met once before and liked. "Nice to see you again, Walter."

"Same to you, Shane. A devoted skier like yourself must be happy about the snow."

"The start of the season is always a cause for celebration." He'd think about skiing later. Right now, he concentrated on being a private eye. "What happened all those years ago when you saw Gloria?"

He nodded slowly, remembering. "She came to me here in Aspen and asked for help. I hardly knew her, but I couldn't refuse this fascinating creature. She was a goddess—a pregnant goddess. I might have been in love with her."

"I thought you were gay," Amber said.

"I'm an artist, fascinated by the female form. Gloria was my muse. And we had a good partnership. We both benefited. After she took over the sale of my sculptures, I began to profit royally. And she earned enough in commissions to open Reflections."

"You were royally successful," Shane said. "And Gloria had savings of her own."

"Quite a healthy nest egg."

Shane had heard this story before, but he recalled that Mallory mentioned current financial problems. "What happened to the money?"

"That was twenty-six years ago. Things change." Walter shrugged. "When the economy suffers, the purchase of art is one of the first things to go. I'm fortunate. My sales—especially the reproductions—are still doing well. But gallery owners, like Gloria and Mallory, take a risk with every new artist they spend money on to promote."

Elvis sidled through the door to the dining room. Before the dog could shake, rattle, roll and splatter snow all over the place, Shane dropped a towel he'd been carrying over the Lab's back and gave him a rub down. "Sorry, Walter, I should have done this the minute we came inside. He smells like wet dog."

"Perfectly natural."

Shane turned to Mallory. "In case you're wondering, my Navigator wasn't seriously damaged. Only four bullet holes in the left rear fender. The guys in the Hummer aren't great shots."

Walter Pulaski turned his chair, leaned forward with his elbows braced on his knees and smiled at Elvis. "I've been thinking about getting a dog."

"I recommend it," Shane said. "Forgive me for bringing this up, but the last time we visited I noticed you have a limp."

"Knee surgery."

"I'm no stranger to PT and rehab. That's where Elvis and I met. He was my therapy dog—the only one who believed I'd learn to walk and ski again."

"How does a dog help you to walk?"

"There's a whole range of AAT, Animal-Assisted Therapy. Much of the procedure is based on motivation. Working with a dog makes the boring repetition of therapy exercises less tedious. A larger dog like Elvis can be fitted with a special harness and trained to hold a position and provide a solid base for you to balance. They can help in all kinds of ways. Let me give you a quick demonstration."

Shane waved Elvis toward the chair where Walter was sitting and introduced them. With an expression that seemed both friendly and compassionate, Elvis held up his paw to shake hands.

"After you pet him for a while," Shane said, "have a conversation using his name. Be sure to tell Elvis that he's smart and good-looking. Flattery will get you everywhere."

Amber elbowed her way into their conversation. "Excuse me, but I have more evidence, important evidence."

"Not now." Shane held up his hand, signaling her to stop. Amber had inherited her mother's love of center stage, but he refused to be sucked into a conversation with her as the star, not until he was ready. "We're in the middle of something with Elvis."

"Really?" She huffed. "You'd rather pay attention to your dog?"

So true. Shane nodded to Walter. "I saw your cane

hanging near the front door. In a conversational way, tell Elvis to get it for you."

Uncle Walter looked into the dog's attentive face and said, "Elvis, I'd like to go for a little walk. Would you, please, be so kind as to fetch my cane for me?"

"Repeat the important words," Shane said.

"Please. Bring me the cane."

Elvis cocked his head to one side as though logging the information into his brain. Then he turned in a circle, raised his nose in the air and pranced toward the entry where Walter's cane hung on a coatrack. Delicately, Elvis lifted the cane in his teeth, carried it across the room and placed it on Walter's lap.

Mallory, Walter and Shane applauded while Elvis thumped his tail on the polished marble floor, tossed his head and gave his trademark sneer.

"Thanks, Elvis," Walter said. "You're a champ. I'm definitely going to look for a dog like you. Any suggestions for where I should start?"

"I'll hook you up," Shane said. "Not that I'd try to influence you, but Elvis is partial to lady poodles—long-legged standard poodles with curly hair."

Amber groaned. "Are we done setting up a dating service for your dog? Do you think we can get back to the multi-million-dollar business at hand?"

"Fine." Mallory pulled out a chair, set her coffee mug on the table and sat. "It seems that you've had zero contact with Gloria over the years. How did you know she'd gone missing? Why did you come looking for her and for me?"

Amber sat opposite. She reached out with a manicured fingernail and pointed at the laptop screen photograph of Gloria with red hair. "I received this picture with a message to contact Ben Hooker, the pawnshop owner I mentioned earlier. Though I hadn't seen her in person since I was a child, I recognized our mother. She still looks very much like the old photos from Sierra Leone that Felix showed me. I barely knew her. Thought she was dead. The pictures were all I had."

Though he didn't like Amber, Shane was touched by the story of an abandoned child who had lost her mother. When he saw the tears brimming in Mallory's eyes, he knew she felt the same. "Amber, have you stayed in touch with Felix?"

"Of course. He's more like family than my blood relatives. He lived with us almost full-time until I was eighteen and went off to college. As I got older, I realized that he paid for many things that my dad or grandma said were too expensive for a young girl. As if they had any idea what was suitable for me. Felix knew. He gets me. He understands."

"Is he wealthy?" Shane asked.

"He inherited," Amber said. "And he earns a decent amount of money from his original artwork, especially the carved painted masks based on traditional tribal designs."

Mallory's spine stiffened. "Felix Komenda. I know him. We handle his sales at Reflections."

"It's the least our mother could do for him. From what I understand, she never would have gotten away from Sierra Leone without his help."

"So Felix knew all along that Gloria wasn't dead. And he never told you. Or me."

"He was loyal to Gloria."

Walter spoke up. "Your mother was in danger. If certain people found out she was still alive, they would have come after her."

"Like this Conrad person," Shane said. This complicated, intriguing story had taken them very far afield, and he reminded himself that the entire yarn hung on the childhood memories of Amber, who couldn't be trusted as a reliable source. "What happened after you contacted the fence?"

"Ben Hooker promised top dollar if I delivered the African Teardrop to him. After Ingrid or Gloria or whatever she's calling herself visited him, she pulled another vanishing act."

"Did she ever show him the Teardrop?"

"No."

"Did she tell him where it was?"

"No."

This series of events had taken an illogical turn. If Gloria had the diamond, it made sense for her to hand it over to Hooker when she first met with him or make arrangements to deliver the Teardrop shortly thereafter. Was it possible that she'd lost the precious stone? "Did Hooker demand proof? Why look for a buyer if he wasn't one hundred percent sure she had the stone?"

"She showed him photos on her phone with the diamond resting on a newspaper. You know, like kidnappers do with ransom victims."

He wondered if the pictures were taken in New York. "Which newspaper?"

"*USA TODAY.* The date was proof. The location could be anywhere."

Mallory pursued their interrogation from a totally different direction. "You've got me worried again. We know

Mom was okay in that photo with the red wig, before she disappeared again. How do we know she's still all right?"

"She calls Hooker. And she sent a photo of herself in Denver to prove she's still alive."

Mallory perked up. "So she's in Colorado."

"I suppose." Amber scowled. "She's doing this wild dance to keep Hooker on the line, but he's not amused. He'd rather deal with me than her or any of the other dangerous people after the diamond."

"So you made friends with Hooker," Mallory said, summarizing. "How did that lead to me?"

"Like I told you before, once I had the name Gloria Greenfield, I tracked you down. Your website is absolutely full of inquiries about your missing mother, which backed up Hooker's story. And there were also pictures of you. Well, I took one look and—" Amber framed her own face with her fingers "—I knew. You were the fetus our mother was carrying when she disappeared from Sierra Leone."

Shane still had questions. Why would Gloria keep checking in with a pawnbroker in Brooklyn? Had she come to Denver? Where was the diamond? He looked to Walter for explanations. "Does this sound plausible to you?"

He gave a slow sad nod. "It's not reasonable but utterly possible. Gloria has never been known for making well-considered plans. She's impulsive."

"If she has the diamond, why doesn't she move forward to sell it?"

"She might have lost it." Walter spread his hands, palm up, as if making an offering to the gods. "It seems inconceivable, but I can think of dozens of other scenarios. Maybe she gave it to a friend to hold. Or buried it and forgot where she dug the hole. She might have decided not to sell it, after all, and return it to its rightful home. At one time, the Teardrop was considered a national treasure belonging to Sierra Leone."

"What?" Amber shrieked. "Give it back? Never!"

"That's what we should do," Mallory said. "Return the stone to the rightful owner."

"Don't be absurd."

"First we need to find it." Shane struggled to bring order to the chaos that seemed to infect Gloria's plans. "We'll start with the safe-deposit box. Mallory, show Walter the key."

She reached into her jeans pocket and pulled out the key they'd found at Gloria's house. "Uncle Walter, do you know which bank this belongs to?"

Frowning, he studied the key. "She uses Fidelity United Bank here in town. She chose it for the initials."

"FU," Shane said.

"Exactly," Walter responded. "And there's another bank in Denver. Can't recall the name but I can look it up."

"We'll start here with FU." Shane was glad to have some kind of direction. "Then we'll go to Reflections and make a more thorough search."

Amber stood and looked down her nose at them. "Aren't you forgetting something? We have a gang of armed thugs in ski masks chasing after us."

"I sure as hell haven't forgotten." Shane's wary brain sent out constant warning signals, keeping him on edge. "I'm still in favor of calling the police for protection."

"Can't do it," Mallory said. "Mom would end up in jail."

"Absolutely can't," Amber chimed in. "Not that I particularly care about Gloria being arrested. But I'm sure the police would confiscate the Teardrop, and we'd be out millions of dollars."

"One of you stands for love. The other for greed," Shane said. "Two powerful emotions. Neither of you will give in."

"Not a chance," the two women said with one voice.

"I have one nonnegotiable condition." Disregarding Amber, he concentrated on Mallory. "Until this is resolved and Gloria is found, I will act as your bodyguard. All day and all night."

An enticing little grin curved her mouth. "I accept your terms, Shane. It's you and me, together. Twenty-four hours a day."

Bring it on.

Chapter Six

Wondering if Shane was worried about what he'd just gotten himself into, Mallory held his gaze. His dark eyebrows and thick lashes emphasized the honey-brown color of his eyes. His cheeks were still ruddy from being out in the snow. He radiated confidence. No matter what life threw at him, Shane came out a winner.

She enjoyed looking at him, and the prospect of having him with her day and night was super appealing, especially at night when they'd have to stay close together. Sharing the same meals, the same bed or the same shower. Her breath caught in her throat. She had to change her focus before she slid all the way down the rabbit hole into an impossible wonderland. Too many other issues to consider. His undeniable charm didn't count for much when dealing with her mother's disappearance and the loss of the African Teardrop. More than anything, he had to be a good enough detective to solve this puzzle.

The phone in her pocket chimed. When she saw the name *Sylvia* on caller ID, Mallory cringed. Should have called Sylvia earlier. Her good friend and coworker for the past six years tended to be easily excitable, a trait that her new husband found adorable. Mallory wasn't so delighted with semi-hysterics. With a resigned sigh, she answered the phone. "I'm sorry that I didn't—"

"There's blood on the kitchen floor," Sylvia shouted in a high nervous voice, nearly a banshee shriek. "Blood. Both doors are unlocked, front and back. A tray of coffee mugs is scattered on the floor, displays in the front are messed up."

Though Sylvia might be overreacting, a bolt of fear shot through Mallory. What if the bad guys were still there? It hadn't occurred to her that they might stick around or come back to Reflections, but that was a definite possibility. "Listen to me, Sylvia. It's best if you get out of there. Right away."

"Did I mention the blood!"

"Lock up and go home."

"I'm calling Brock."

The police chief. "No, please don't do that."

"Something terrible has happened."

"You're right about that, and it's connected to Mom's disappearance." Mallory heard a string of unintelligible curses from her friend who wasn't one of Gloria's greatest fans. "Getting the authorities involved will only make things worse. Trust me on this. Please."

"I'm not going to turn tail and run, and I won't drag the police into this. But I'm calling Damien. He can be here in ten minutes, and he'll protect me."

Damien Harrison, her husband of four months, stood as tall as Shane and was forty pounds heavier. His extra weight was solid muscle. He managed a horse ranch and was a professional cowboy. He'd won the bronco busting competition two years running at Frontier Days in Cheyenne. For sure, Damien could keep his wife safe.

"We'll be there as soon as we can," Mallory promised.

"We? Who's with you?"

"Shane Reilly, the private investigator." How could she explain Amber? "And someone you've never met before. See you soon. Be careful."

She disconnected the call before Sylvia could ask more probing questions. Explaining Amber was going to be a problem. Uncle Walter had accepted her without hesitation, which might be because he was more familiar with Gloria's checkered past. Sylvia would be judgmental, as would most of Mallory's friends and associates who considered Gloria to be an irresponsible twit. They didn't see her as a single mother who had struggled to establish a business in a highly competitive field while raising a daughter. Mallory couldn't waste time worrying about other people's opinions.

She turned toward Shane and Amber. "We need to get back to Reflections. Sylvia showed up for work, and she's there alone."

"I heard you tell her to leave," Shane said.

"And she refused. Her husband, Damien, is coming to protect her and ought to be there in just a couple of minutes."

"Damien Harrison," Shane said. "He's a big guy and tough as they come, but the men who attacked us were armed."

If something happened to Sylvia or any of her other employees, Mallory would be devastated. "What should I do?"

"Close Reflections until this is over."

Though it went against her instincts as a business owner to shut down, especially after their forced time off during the pandemic, she knew he was right. She immediately called Sylvia back and told her to go home because she was shutting down Reflections for the immediate future. She'd send out an email blast to everybody who worked there, making an excuse for the lockdown. Something about repairs or plumbing. She ended with, "Please don't tell anybody about the blood."

"Not even Damien?"

"Only if he promises not to tell anybody else."

"As if he's some kind of gossip?" Sylvia laughed at the idea of her macho husband chitchatting with the other cowboys at the ranch.

"You're right. My secret is safe with him."

"Before I go, I'll post a closed sign at the door and turn out the lights."

"Thanks, I'll stay in touch."

When she ended her call, she saw that Shane already had his phone in hand. "Just in case, I'm calling Damien. He'll make sure his wife is tucked away safely."

"How do you know Damien Harrison?"

"We've got a lot in common. Until Damien started dating your friend, we were both single guys in Aspen."

Mallory caught the gist of his comment. Many of the hot local guys ran in the same circles, drank in the same taverns and dated the same women. She shuddered. Not a pleasant thought.

He continued, "We're both athletes. Different venues, but we'd run into each other doing weight training."

"Of course." A skier and a rodeo cowboy had more similarities than differences. Maybe they were working on different sets of muscles, but they both needed to stay in shape. Aspen was that kind of town: obnoxiously healthy.

Mallory followed her own physical regimen—jogging, weights, yoga and tai chi—even though she wasn't a competitive sportswoman.

Turning away from him, she concentrated on shutting down Reflections for what she hoped would be a limited time. She changed the message on the phone and with the answering service to say they'd be closed for a while and wouldn't be able to return calls for a few days. Next, she contacted her employees. Using her phone she sent out a text and an email saying that Reflections would be closed for a few days, maybe a week, due to repair work. She added that they'd be paid for their time off and ended with, Enjoy the snow.

Collapsing in her chair at Uncle Walter's dining table, she checked the time. It was only 9:52 a.m., but she felt like she'd already put in a full day's work. She glanced toward Amber, who perched on a chair near Uncle Walter and lavished him with praise while he sat sipping his coffee and sketching in a five-by-eight notebook. Mallory really didn't want to drag Amber along with them while they searched at Reflections and went to the bank to check the safe-deposit box. Her complaining and superior attitude were a drag, to say the least.

She looked over at Shane. "Earlier this morning, you said you'd dug up more information on Mom."

"Knowing about her change of identity pretty much explains my online investigating. I found no records for Gloria Greenfield before you were born. A shallow attempt was made to create an alternate background with a high school and art school, but it didn't take much research to figure out that her alleged history was bogus. I'll go back and search for info on Ingrid DeSilva. That might give us a clue for where she's hiding."

"What kind of clue?"

"She could be staying with friends or family she knew before she became Gloria." He went to the side table and poured himself another cup of coffee. "I'll check it out."

"Really? Do you think I have more family that I'm not aware of?"

"Maybe."

The idea shocked her. Finding out about her missing sister had been a major surprise, but a whole family? Mallory had grown up with no reference to grandparents, aunts, uncles or cousins. According to Gloria, the two of them were alone in the world. "Why wouldn't Mom tell me about them?"

"My guess? She thought she was protecting you. The less you knew about her criminal past, the better."

So many emotions churned inside her. Mallory couldn't sit still. She rose from the dining table and returned to the wide bay window that looked out at the giant statue of Gloria reaching for the sky through the continuing snowfall. Elvis sat beside her, and she stroked his still-damp fur. Had Mom lied to her about everything? Mallory paced toward the corner where a white marble statue on a pedestal—Gloria breastfeeding—greeted her. In Uncle Walter's house, Mom was inescapable. She dominated his art and his memories. Had friends and family from her earlier life felt the same way? Would they welcome her home with open arms?

Mallory struggled to regain her balance and pull herself together. When she heard Amber giggle, she turned her head and saw her alleged sister preening for Uncle Walter. Obviously, she wanted him to use his renown and talent to sculpt her. *Too obviously.* If Amber had asked for her advice, Mallory could have told her that nobody coerced Uncle Walter into taking on a project that didn't interest him. Not even commissioned jobs. His last major project was a life-size memorial for his good buddy, Hunter S. Thompson, with a cigarette dangling from the corner of his mouth and a Colt .45 revolver held close to his vest. Mallory loved the statue. The whirling grain of the stone suggested the hazy thinking of the gonzo journalist. The lenses on his glasses were mirrors that reflected the viewer in a disturbing way.

Amber giggled again. "What are you drawing, Walter? Is it me?"

He frowned, ran his fingers through his beard and gave a noncommittal grunt.

"It is." She clapped her hands. "You're making a sketch of me."

"Not you." He turned his drawing pad around so she could see the picture he'd been working on. "It's the dog."

He'd captured the bright intelligence of the Lab and the Elvis-like smirk on his upper left lip. "I love it," Mallory said.

"I have a chunk of black marble I've been itching to use."

His focus on the sketch told her that his attention had shifted to his art, which didn't work well for her. She needed his thoughts and memories tied to Mom. "You knew Gloria when she was Ingrid DeSilva. Did she mention family or friends?"

"Don't think so. And she wasn't married to DeSilva when we first met. Her name was Ingrid Stromberg or something like that. No family. There was a young man with her, but he faded quickly from sight. I don't even re-call his name. Why are you asking about long ago?"

"She could be contacting people from her past. People she might have kept in touch with over the years. She did a lot of traveling. Business trips, you know. And she went to New York twice a year."

"Where I live," Amber said without her usual bluster. Knowing that Walter preferred the dog over her had deflated her ego. "I can promise you that she wasn't visiting me."

"What about our, um, father?" Mallory steeled herself for what might come next. She'd spent her entire life be-lieving her father was dead. "Would she turn to him?"

"Not unless she had a death wish," Amber said. "He hated her. Cursed her memory."

Mallory couldn't blame her for the harsh tone. She'd grown up motherless, abandoned by Gloria. "I'm sorry for what you went through."

"Save your pity for someone who needs it. My life wasn't bad at all. I lived with my grandpa and grandma DeSilva in a tall narrow Manhattan townhouse that had been in the family for generations. Like your mother, Dad traveled a lot, but Felix was always there for me. He lived on the fourth floor and had a studio where he did his painting."

Mallory made a mental note to track down Felix Ko-menda. "What else can you tell me about our father? How old is he? What does he look like?"

"There's not much more to tell." Genuine emotion tugged at the corners of her mouth. For a moment, she showed her grief. "He died in Africa a few years ago. Murdered."

Her voice softened to a husky whisper as though telling

this story to herself. But the others were paying rapt attention. Shane, Walter and even Elvis watched her as she continued, "The thug who killed Dad worked for Conrad Burdock."

"The man who's after Gloria," Shane said.

"My, my, you catch on quick." Her hostile attitude was back in full force. "Burdock is a terrible human being, a mercenary who fled to Africa to avoid prosecution in the United States, and I'm certain he was behind Dad's murder. The guy who actually committed the crime claimed he was hired by Burdock."

"Do the police have the murderer in custody?" Shane asked.

"He's dead." She flashed a hard satisfied smile. "The worm got what he deserved."

Mallory had the wretched feeling that Amber had arranged for the death of the assassin hired by Burdock. Maybe she'd even pulled the trigger.

Amber spun the laptop around and tapped on the keys. The screen showed a snapshot of a handsome man wearing a custom tuxedo. His dark hair was combed straight back from his high forehead and streaked with gray at the temples. His eyebrows and mustache were black. His hazel eyes stared with a ferocious intensity that some women would find sexy. Not Mallory. To her, he looked mean.

Amber gestured gracefully as she introduced him. "This is Raymond DeSilva."

Their father. Mallory saw nothing of herself in his features. His mouth sneered. His angry eyes accused her of doing something wrong before she'd even said hello. Still, she wished she'd had the opportunity to meet him, to hear his voice and discover why her Mom had found him attractive.

Amber took the laptop back and punched in a new code. Another photo came up. "This is Conrad Burdock."

This time, Mallory recognized the face on the screen. A few days ago, just before she hired Shane, Conrad Burdock came to Reflections and spoke to her about purchasing one of Uncle Walter's sculptures of Gloria.

Chapter Seven

Their search had swerved into a disturbing new direction, and Shane didn't like the look of the road around that corner. Danger pointed directly at Mallory. Her encounter with Burdock—a man he was beginning to think of as some kind of evil mastermind/supervillain—represented a clear threat. He wanted to bring in the Aspen police, the Pitkin county sheriff and maybe the National Guard—whatever it took to protect her. But she refused. Her logic: Burdock hadn't harmed her when he'd had the chance, which meant she wasn't really in danger. Shane thought otherwise.

With Mallory in the passenger seat and Elvis in the back, he drove his Navigator through the sputtering end of the storm. Fat white flakes fell in batches and swirled through the air rather than joining together in a nearly impenetrable curtain. They were headed toward Reflections to search for the Teardrop among the art displays.

He cleared his throat. "I'm going to call my brother in Denver."

"The cop?" Her eyes widened in alarm.

"Don't worry. I won't tell him about the stolen diamonds or any of your mom's other crimes. I need his help with research."

"What kind of research?"

"The local police and I worked together to track the usage of Gloria Greenfield's credit cards. Not a difficult task because we had access to all her records, identification numbers and passwords. As you know, we found nothing. The day your mom disappeared, she stopped charging her expenses and left no record of buying plane, train or bus tickets."

"You think she might be using an alternate identity, like Ingrid DeSilva," Mallory said. "If not DeSilva, Uncle Walter said her maiden name might be Stromberg."

"If we get a nibble on those aliases, we'd have a clue as to her whereabouts. Unfortunately, I don't have the legal authority to quickly put my hands on confidential records."

"But your brother does."

"Logan has helped me before." And wasn't happy about skirting the edges of the law for his private eye brother. Still, both Logan and their father would do just about anything to encourage Shane's pursuit of a more stable profession than "former professional skier who might be talked into extreme life-threatening adventures." The fact that they considered private investigating to be a relatively safe occupation said a lot about his family's values.

He drove his 4WD Navigator past Reflections where the only vehicle in the parking lot was Amber's snow-covered rental SUV. Fading tire tracks showed where Sylvia had come and gone. There was no sign of the men in ski masks.

After circling a few blocks, he maneuvered the Navigator through the accumulated snow outside Mallory's house where he managed to park in the driveway. In addition to searching, they had a number of other projects, and he was glad they'd talked Amber into staying at Uncle Walter's house. Hadn't taken much convincing; she was delighted to lounge in the lap of luxury while they schlepped through the storm.

"Bring a small suitcase," he said. "Pack enough for a couple of days at my place."

"I still don't understand why we can't stay here."

"Do you have an alarm system on your house?"

"No."

"How about weapons and ammo?"

"I used to have a hunting rifle. But now? *Nada*."

"What kind of search engine do you have on your computer?"

She threw up her hands. "Okay, I get it. Your place is better prepared for detective work and more well-protected."

"Also there's space for Elvis to roam, plus all his food and other supplies."

"Fine," she agreed with a resigned sigh. "We'll stay at your cabin."

He didn't usually have this much trouble convincing women to come home with him, and he very much wanted to have her willing consent. Though she sounded annoyed about spending the night with him, he wondered, *Was she, really?* A couple of times, he'd caught her watching him from the corner of her beautiful turquoise eyes. She often smiled and laughed at his silly jokes. And then, there was that kiss. She'd planted one on him, supposedly because she was happy to discover her mom was alive, but he sensed a deeper connection between them.

"You'll like my house." He made direct eye contact. "And I'll like having you there."

An impatient whine from the back seat reminded him that Elvis wanted out. Pulling his watch cap over his hair, Shane stepped out of the Navigator and opened the door for his dog. Much as he loved the snow, he wasn't a fan of the cold that came with it. Not one of those guys who scampers around in a blizzard wearing board shorts and a tee, his winter clothing—from head to toe—was insulated and flexible, designed to keep him toasty and warm. He followed Mallory up the sidewalk.

Standing under the small gable roof over her front porch, she picked up a snow shovel and handed it to him. "While you're waiting for me, make yourself useful."

He grabbed the handle and muttered, "Shoveling the sidewalk isn't usually covered by my detective fee."

"Don't forget the driveway. Otherwise I'll have trouble getting out of the garage." She pivoted, unlocked the door and darted inside. "Should I bring anything from the kitchen?"

"I have food." His cabin was secluded but only a couple of miles away from an excellent organic grocery, and they delivered. "Just pack clothes and your lady bathroom products. I don't keep lotions and potions in stock."

"No scented candles for the bathtub?"

"I'm a shower guy. My tub is for hydrotherapy." Though the last remnants of the storm tumbled around them, his imagination filled with steam from the bath and Mallory rising naked from the water. Under his layers of clothing and parka, he began to sweat. "Twelve massage jets and a whirlpool. I'd be happy to show you how it works."

"And I'd be happy to let you."

Before she closed the door, she flashed a sexy smile and winked. Definitely, she was flirting. He couldn't be misreading these signals. Mallory liked him.

That conclusion kept him energized while he cleared the snow from the short sidewalk leading to the porch, the sidewalk in front and some of the driveway. Elvis bounded across her yard, burying himself in the snow and then standing and shaking it off. In a sudden change of pace, the dog stiffened the way he did when he'd made a find while doing search and rescue.

"What is it, boy?"

The dog sneered, growled and stared across the street.

Dropping the shovel, Shane looked in the direction Elvis indicated. He didn't see what had caused the reaction but feared there might be a threat. "Elvis, heel."

The Lab moved into position, standing at Shane's left hip and still staring. If the guys in the ski masks were back, Shane was in big trouble. The bad guys had gotten the drop on him, which was why bodyguards didn't do things like shovel walkways.

He should have concentrated on the task at hand, which was to protect Mallory. Should have gone into the house with her. Why was she taking so long? He tore off his glove to unzip his parka and reach for his gun.

Though Elvis stayed in the "heel" position, he wiggled and wagged his tail—too friendly for danger. He wasn't cool and determined like his namesake when he sang the lyric, "Are you looking for trouble?" Elvis the dog yipped. Across the street, a malamute appeared, took a stance and barked a greeting of his own.

"Are you kidding me?" Shane muttered. "Dude, we're not here to make friends."

Elvis gave him a skeptical look.

"You're right, I'm lying. I want to be friends with Mallory. More than friends." He stuck his gun into the holster, picked up the shovel and tramped back to the porch.

"Maybe then I'll stop trying to have meaningful conversations with a Labrador retriever. No offense."

Walking close beside him, the dog bobbed his head.

Shane entered without knocking. He'd visited Mallory's house before and liked her eclectic mix of classic and modern, similar to her mom's decor but not so chaotic. Some of the oil paintings were compelling, rich and beautiful. Others had been done by kids with finger paints and watercolors. In a seemingly unplanned manner, all the pieces fit together and created a charming whole. She was a master at setting up interesting little displays in ignored corners, using ceramics, origami, dried branches and yarn sculptures. Her home felt lived in. "Hey," he called out.

"In the dining room," she responded.

As he and Elvis went through the front room into the attached dining area, he asked, "Did you search for clues in your house?"

"First thing I did." Mallory sat at the head of the table and plucked at the keys on her laptop. "Mom bought this house when I was a baby, and she had plenty of time to hide grown-up stuff so I couldn't get my sticky little fingers on it."

"Find anything interesting?"

"Mostly keepsakes, like a shell from a beach in San Francisco and crystals from a cave on the Continental Divide. And jewelry, lots of costume jewelry."

"The African Teardrop? You were only a kid. Wouldn't know the difference between cubic zirconia and the genuine stone."

"That's not the way I was raised," she said. "Mom knew a lot about precious gems, and she taught me how to tell a real diamond from a fake."

"How?"

"You can tell by looking at it. Diamonds have more sparkle in a brighter spectrum. They don't get scratched but usually have flaws deep inside. You can see through a fake as though it was glass. And there's the water test."

"Tell."

"Fill a glass halfway with water. Drop the naked stone into it. If it sinks, it's a diamond. If it floats, it's fake."

And she'd learned all this when she was a kid. "You had an interesting childhood."

"There are advantages to having a weirdo mom."

On the floor beside her chair was an extra-large, expandable backpack. The thing looked big enough to carry the uniforms for the Colorado Avalanche hockey team, including their skates. "You're packed," he said.

"I should have come outside and joined you, but I had a few emails I needed to send."

He didn't believe that excuse. "More likely you wanted to stay inside while I finished shoveling. Otherwise, you could have taken the laptop with us, and we'd be on our way."

"Or I'm such a good employer that I feel an immediate obligation to the people who work for me and the suppliers who come every day—rain, shine or blizzard—with supplies for the coffee shop. Maybe I'm such a good teacher that I needed to notify the kids in my afternoon classes that we wouldn't be meeting for the rest of the week."

Elvis rubbed his red leather harness against the backpack, which was easily large enough for him to fit inside. Usually Shane was careful not to allow Elvis to drip all over somebody else's house, but he was irritated at her. "You teach?"

"Four classes with different age groups. We have a showing scheduled for next week at Reflections. All the parents come, and the kids show off for their friends from school. We have cheese and crackers and juice while we talk about colors and shadows."

He pointed to a framed picture on the wall that appeared to be a man on horseback who had lassoed a rocket ship. Everything was painted in shades of blue and purple. "Tell me how you'd analyze this technique."

"An outsize talent. Great metaphor." She grinned. "It's an astronaut cowboy reaching for a blue moon."

While she talked, the tension at the corner of her eyes relaxed, and the tone of her voice mellowed. He could tell she honestly enjoyed working with these kids. "Can anybody come to this showing? Or do I need a special invite?"

"I'd love to have you there. Elvis, too. He's well-behaved, and I know he'd be a hit with the kids." She stood and slipped into her parka. "I guess we ought to get going."

His natural instinct was to pick up her giant backpack and carry it for her, but he needed to be a bodyguard instead of a boyfriend. If weighed down by her luggage, he couldn't reach his gun quickly. And so he straightened his shoulders and walked unencumbered to her front door.

"I'm going onto the porch first," he informed her. "As your bodyguard, I want to check out the neighborhood and make sure it's safe before you come out."

She hefted her pack and nodded. "Whatever you say."

"When we leave here, I think we should go to the bank first."

"I'm with you. Even a total flake like Mom would have the good sense to keep something as precious as the Teardrop in a safe-deposit box instead of a hidey-hole at Re-flections."

He didn't point out that the key to the box had been dis-covered in a secret cache at Gloria's house. "Let's hope so."

"We can only hope that this is the right bank."

On the porch, he stuck his Ray-Bans onto the bridge of his nose and scanned the street from left to right and back again. Two houses up the hill, a teenager shoveled the sidewalk. A Wagoneer chugged down the neighbor's driveway to the street. He saw no sign of the men in black ski masks or their massive Hummer, but he wouldn't let down his guard. It was too much to hope that supervillain Burdock had given up the hunt.

FIDELITY UNITED BANK occupied the first floor of a red-brick building with windows across the front, parking in back and a drive-through. Mallory had been here hun-dreds of times before. They used FU for deposits from Reflections, and she'd established a savings account for college when she was ten and Uncle Walter had given her a check for two hundred bucks. Several of the tellers and the bank manager knew her by name. Born and raised in Aspen, Mallory's roots went deep. She'd gone to high school here and was prom queen in her senior year. Prac-tically all the locals had participated in the search for Glo-ria, and Mallory didn't anticipate any trouble accessing the safe-deposit box.

The snowfall had lessened, and people were getting started with their day while the plows cleared the main thoroughfares. According to weather reports, the upper slopes had gotten over eighteen inches of new snow. In town, they were looking at eight to ten inches overnight, which wasn't considered too hazardous. In the high Rockies, a minor blizzard didn't amount to a major threat.

On the other hand, her life was a nightmare and getting scarier by the minute. In the past few hours, she'd learned that her mother faked her own death, stole a precious diamond and was on the run. Mallory had confronted a sister who resented and hated her. As if that weren't enough, she'd been shot at, chased and stalked. At the moment, she could only think of one positive aspect, and that was Shane.

During the drive from her house, he acted like a professional bodyguard, diligently checking his rearview and side mirrors to make sure they weren't being followed. She also kept watch. He drove into the mostly empty parking lot, which had already been plowed, and parked near the entrance. "Before we go inside, Elvis needs a wardrobe change."

"Why?"

"Well, he's wearing his badass studded leather and looks like a tough guy. To go into the bank, he needs his service dog harness."

"Are you and Elvis coming with me to open the safe-deposit box?"

"I'm going to stay in the lobby so I can cut off any threat before it gets close to you. Also, I'm armed and don't intend to hand over my weapon."

He went around to the far back of the Navigator and rummaged until he found a red harness and matching leash, which he handed to her so she could help Elvis get changed. Shane posted himself at the back bumper and kept watch. Though she suspected this extreme level of vigilance might be over the top, Mallory appreciated her bodyguard. Never before had anyone devoted themselves to watching over her. With his dark sunglasses and alert posture, Shane looked like one of those secret service agents who protected VIPs and diplomats. She was neither but liked the attention.

While she unfastened Elvis's leather harness and put on the other, she was impressed with how the supposedly tough, fierce dog behaved. He wagged his tail and licked her cheek. When he was outfitted in his service dog vest, she picked up his leash and slung the small knapsack she used as a purse over her shoulder. "We're ready."

Shane escorted her through the front door and waited by the bank guard's post with Elvis while she strolled past the teller stations and went to an office at the rear of the bank. She peeked inside the open door and waved to the heavyset man with thick brown hair and heavy eyebrows. "Hey, Mr. Sherman."

"Howdy-doody, Mallory." The bank vice president bounded to his feet and came around his carved mahogany desk to envelope her in a hug. "Knock-knock."

"Who's there?"

"Could be a skier. Snow telling unless you open the door." He immediately launched into another one. "When the skier's car broke down, how did he get around?"

"Don't know."

"By icicle."

"Good one." She rewarded him with a quiet chuckle. He had a dozen jokes for every occasion, each worse than the one before, but he meant well. Their acquaintance went back several years to the time when she'd dated his son, Josh—a wide receiver for the Aspen High School football team, appropriately named the Skiers.

The banker gave her a concerned smile. "Any news on your mother?"

"Nothing definite."

"She dropped by my office just about a week ago."

To look into her safe-deposit box? Mallory waited for him to continue, but he was silent. She added, "I hired Shane Reilly to investigate."

Mr. Sherman shook his head and frowned. "Poor guy, how's he holding up?"

The clear inference was that Shane's injury and subsequent loss of his career as an Olympic athlete should have left him broken and devastated. She resented the attitude but understood where it was coming from. Josh Sherman blew out his knee in college and ended what might have been a chance to play in the NFL.

Still, she defended Shane. "He might turn out to be a better detective than a skier. Did you know that both his dad and his brother are Denver cops?"

"Well, I hope he finds Gloria for you."

"And that's why I'm here." She dug into the front pocket of her knapsack, pulled out the flat silver key with six digits and held it toward him. "Is this for a safe-deposit box at the bank?"

"Looks like one of ours, and isn't that a co-inki-dink? Your Mom wanted to open the box, too."

This was it! Mallory felt certain she'd solved the mystery of the diamond worth twenty million dollars. Mr. Sherman took the key from her trembling hand and returned to the swivel chair behind his impressive desk. "Let's check the number."

While he searched the screen of his desk computer, she concentrated on keeping her breath steady and her pulse calm. This could be momentous. The air in the bank seemed to press in around her. When she swallowed, her throat felt tight.

"Okey dokey," Mr. Sherman said. "I verified this is Gloria's key. And you are an authorized person to open the safe-deposit box."

Her heart thumped hard against her rib cage. "Can we do it now?"

"Sure thing." He beamed at her. "I need to have you sign a couple of standard forms, and then we can go into the basement."

A terrible thought occurred to her. "If I find something of value in the box, can I take it home with me?"

"That's an excellent question." He rose from his chair and moved toward her. "Since Gloria designated you as an authorized person—a surrogate for herself, if you will—whatever is in that box belongs to you. I might have even given it to you without the key, being as you're a friend of the family."

After signing a few forms, Mallory followed Mr. Sherman down the stairs into a windowless basement where she'd never been before. In spite of the carpeted floor and cheery yellow walls, it felt cold amid the many file cabinets. The few employees working in this area wore thick sweaters, which wasn't all that unusual considering the weather. At the far end of the room, she saw a metal vault door that required two special keys and a digital code to open. The young woman at the desk nearest the door joined Mr. Sherman while he went through the required procedures and chatted about his son whose real estate business was doing very well. "But he still hasn't settled down, never saw fit to get married and give us grandchildren. I seem to recall that you're single, too."

"Yes, sir, I am."

"Josh's mother and I surely wish something had developed between the two of you. You'd make a handsome couple."

Borderline inappropriate, but she smiled anyway. Though she and Josh had dated for several months, she'd never felt the breath-taking connection to him that had overwhelmed her from the moment she laid eyes on Shane. Mr. Sherman pulled open the door to the safe-deposit vault. Together with the clerk from the nearby desk, he stepped inside.

Mallory caught a glimpse of a large room with floor-to-ceiling lockers of various sizes. "Wow," she said. "I didn't think there'd be so many."

"We have more than average for a bank our size. Aspen is a small but wealthy community. Now, I'll have to ask you to wait here while we retrieve the proper container."

"Can you tell me when Gloria got this box?"

"I could look up the exact date for you, but it was about ten years ago. I remember because you and Josh had just started dating."

When he returned to the vault door, he was carrying a metal container, almost two feet long, which he passed to the clerk who had accompanied him. He relocked the vault and escorted her to a small room with a long table and three chairs. Mr. Sherman centered the long box that looked to be about fourteen inches wide on the table and stepped back.

"I have to lock you in, Mallory, but don't worry. When you're ready to leave, push the button by the door and someone will let you out." He patted her shoulder. "It was good to see you. Don't be a stranger."

As soon as the door closed, she flipped open the lid. The box appeared to be stuffed with nine-by-twelve brown envelopes marked with dates from twenty years ago to the present. *No diamond.* She fished around the envelopes, feeling around at the edges for a relatively small piece of jewelry. *Nothing but paperwork.* Carefully, she lifted each envelope out and felt the inside contents. *Damn it, Mom, what's this all about?*

Mallory opened the most recent envelope and found a letter addressed to Gloria. Dated a week ago, the letter ended with *I will see you in Colorado, my friend.* Signed with a flourish by Felix Komenda.

Chapter Eight

Against his better judgment, Shane gave in to Mallory's wishes and agreed to return to Walter Pulaski's chalet so she could talk to Amber. Driving through downtown, he noted the efficient snow removal from the streets and the sidewalks outside shops and businesses. Everything seemed to be returning to normal after the semi-blizzard. Blue sky peeked through the clouds above the slopes. On a typical weekday in Aspen, it should have been easy to solve the complicated human drama playing out in Mallory Greenfield's life. *Not so.* They had a lot to figure out before they put things right.

From what she'd told him, the letters from Gloria's safe-deposit box had been written by Felix Komenda. Most of them provided a narrative of Amber DeSilva's childhood and early teens, including details a mother would want to know. Apparently, Felix had performed more than nanny duties, and his talents extended beyond his artwork. He was a biographer.

Mallory shuffled through the file box given to her by a bank official to carry the brown envelopes. "The latest letters, especially the one from a week ago, don't mention Amber at all. Felix talks about returning a precious treasure."

"The African Teardrop," Shane said. "Returning it?"

"Doesn't make sense. Seems more like she intended to sell it," she said. "He also mentions a trip to Colorado."

"Has he been to Reflections before? Maybe to discuss the sale of his artwork."

"I've met him once or twice." While she pondered, Mallory absentmindedly twirled the loose tip of her long golden braid. "He's about as tall as you are and very thin. Shaved head. Tattoo sleeves on both arms. Across his chest is a huge tattoo of the famous Cotton Tree in Freetown, the capital of Sierra Leone. His skin is a light mocha, and the orange and green colors of his tats really stand out."

"Impressive," he said. "With that detailed description, I could pick him out of a lineup."

"Yeah, I'm not an artist, but I've got a good visual sense."

"Does the letter say when he'll arrive?"

"It's vague. He also mentioned the Museum of Nature and Science in Denver. Specifically, he talks about the gem exhibit and a guy who works there. His name is Ty Rivera. You've got to admit that these letters are the best leads we've gotten so far."

"The fact that your mother was planning to meet Felix somewhere in Colorado is a whole lot more specific than her cryptic departure note."

"I'll be back?" Mallory chuckled.

Finding the cache of correspondence had brightened her mood. But Shane wasn't amused. Gloria was hiding something from her daughter. In Shane's experience, secrecy led to lies and lies meant trouble. He needed to figure out how to control the threat.

She pulled an envelope from the middle of the box,

opened the flap and reached inside. "Seems like I shouldn't look at these."

"Why not?"

"Most of the stuff from earlier years is about Amber. It's intimate and private. She ought to be the person going through them."

"We're not prying," he said. "The letters are evidence. Besides, Gloria wanted you to find them. She designated you as an authorized person to open the box."

"Apparently, I signed a form." Under her knitted blue cap, her smooth forehead wrinkled. "I don't remember. Since I'm a part owner of Reflections, Gloria used to routinely give me a bunch of business-related stuff to review and sign. Did I ever take a look at it? Not really."

"I used to be the same way about paperwork. Not anymore."

"What happened?"

"After my ski accident, I was in a coma for three days. My brother was there when I woke up. As soon as the nurse gave the okay, he hugged me and blubbered like a baby. The first coherent thing Logan said was, 'Dude, you never changed your will.'"

Her eyebrows raised. "I don't mean to criticize your brother, but that's a little bit mercenary."

"No, he was smart to check it out. In the will, I left everything to a former girlfriend. That's *former* with a capital *F*. To say we had a bad breakup would be like calling World War II a minor altercation. I always meant to update the will but never got around to it." Logan was right about a lot of things, and Shane still needed to call him for help in tracking credit cards for his private eye work.

"Anyway, don't worry about violating Gloria's privacy. She saved that stuff for a reason."

Mallory lifted a photograph from the envelope. "So adorable. It's little Amber blowing out candles on a birthday cake. Eight candles. Her eighth birthday. I can't wait to show her. She's going to love it."

"What makes you think so?"

"These letters and photos prove that Gloria didn't just turn her back and walk away. She had Felix keeping an eye on her daughter. Mom cared about Amber. When she reads these letters, she'll know. And she'll be happier."

His impression of her prodigal sister was way more cynical. Not once had he heard Amber speak fondly of their mother. She'd come looking for Gloria with a loaded gun, which didn't strike him as the attitude of a person who was longing to make a connection.

While Mallory pored over the letters, pointing out Amber's good qualities, he scanned the winding road leading to Pulaski's château, looking for the Hummer and considering what else they could accomplish today. A search at Reflections was on the agenda. Also, they needed to track down some of Gloria's clients, close friends and former lovers—people she might have told about her plan to disappear. He added doctor and lawyer to the list. The number one, most important contact had to be Amber's former nanny, Felix.

When they approached the entrance where the gatekeeper kept watch, Shane glanced over at Mallory, who chirped a friendly greeting to Henry. He beamed and waved back. Everybody who knew her loved her. Apart from hair color and matching turquoise eyes, she was very different from her sister. Amber was colder than a blizzard and hard as granite, while Mallory was warm, sweet and kind without being saccharine. The best part of his plan for the day would be taking her home with him tonight.

He parked his SUV in the shoveled driveway outside Walter Pulaski's house. The last time they were here, he'd caught a glimpse of the housekeeper who laid out the breakfast spread and coffee before vanishing. He guessed that Pulaski's other employees—like the person who cleared the snow—were also ubiquitous and silent. When Shane first came home after rehab, he'd required that kind of assistance. He'd had a part-time physical therapist and a live-in housekeeper who cooked and cleaned. Both had done their jobs well, but he couldn't wait to get rid of them and have the cabin to himself. Just him and Elvis against the world, that was the way he liked it.

Amber answered the front door as though she was mistress of the house, but she didn't look happy. "Walter locked himself in the small studio at the back of the house," she said.

Smart man. "And left you in charge?"

"No need to sound so surprised. I've been running households since I was a kid. I've just been chatting with the housekeeper about lunch."

"Great," Mallory piped up. "I'm starved."

Shane gestured with the file box from the bank. "May we come in?"

Amber stepped out of his way. "Walter told me that when you returned, he wanted to see Shane and the dog."

A perfect excuse for a getaway. He carried the box of letters to the dining room table, set it down and turned toward the sisters. "I know how to get to the small studio. I'll take Elvis and leave you two with this."

Amber scowled and flicked her fingers against the cardboard. "What's in there?"

"The contents of Mom's safe-deposit box. Something she considered precious." Mallory took off the lid and pulled out one of the brown envelopes. "I think you're going to be happy to see these letters. They're all about you."

"Why would that make me happy?"

"Well, it shows she cares about you."

"Ha! More likely she felt guilty, which is exactly what she deserves. What kind of person abandons her only child? Letters aren't enough."

"In her letters, she mentions seeing you from a distance on her trips to New York."

"And never saying hello."

Shane stepped into the hallway and made his escape with Elvis following close behind. He tapped on the door to the working studio behind the home office and the kitchen. "It's us, Shane and Elvis."

The door opened inward. Braced on his ebony cane, Walter peered around the edge. "Are you alone?"

"Amber isn't with us if that's what you're asking."

Breathing a sigh of relief, the old man stepped aside and let them enter. The rest of the house was pristine and polished. In here, splashes of dried paint decorated the concrete floor, and the walls held dozens of rough sketches. A potter's wheel stood in one corner and an easel in another. Shelves and tables held supplies and models for future work in the big studio beside the garage. The earthy smell of dried clay mingled with the scent of burnt wood from the potbellied stove. Sunlight filtered through the many windows.

On a heavy center table, he'd been experimenting with

small canine figures in modeling clay to use as a basis for his sculpture of Elvis. He hobbled to a sink, leaned his cane against it and washed his hands. "Haven't found the pose I want yet. Do you mind if I take photos?"

"Elvis loves being the center of attention, like Amber... but in a good way."

Pulaski settled himself on a special stool with a back he could lean against. "Hard to believe she's Mallory's sister. They resemble each other physically and both have a lot of Gloria in them, but being with Mallory always makes me happy. Amber's a bitch."

Shane couldn't have said it better himself. "At the bank, a vice president found paperwork showing Mallory as a designated person to open the safe-deposit box. No diamonds inside, but there were hundreds of letters written by Felix Komenda to Gloria and talking about Amber as a child."

"She saved those?" He rolled down his sleeves and buttoned the cuffs. "I knew she kept in touch with Felix and trusted him to take care of the kid. She also sent money and made several trips to New York to see for herself how Amber was doing. Nearly broke her heart to leave that little girl behind."

"Is that so?" Shane still didn't have the impression that Gloria was a caring mother.

"You don't know the whole story," Walter said. "Felix told me that Gloria had been physically and mentally abused by her husband. If she hadn't run when she had the chance, he suspected Raymond DeSilva would've killed her."

His explanation put a different slant on Gloria's motivations, but Shane wasn't sure he could take her friend Walter's word for her mothering skills. "According to the letters, Felix planned to be in Colorado, which probably means Gloria will join him. I'd like to check in with some of her associates and find out if she's contacted them."

"Got any names?"

Shane rattled off the two that Felix had mentioned specifically. "Her lawyer might know something. And her doctor."

"Dr. Freestone." He grinned and reached over to stroke Elvis's square forehead. "He's known Gloria since Mallory was born. Far as I know, she doesn't have any medical problems, but he's a person she trusts."

"And the lawyer?"

"Don't bother. He's barely competent, and we've been talking about replacing him."

From the dining room, he heard the angry voices of Mallory and her sister. So much for the idea that Amber would be pleased about the letters from Felix. Shane took his phone from his pocket and prepared to contact his brother in Denver. "If you'll excuse me, I need to make a call."

Walter rose from the stool and used his cane to walk to the door. "You stay here. I'm going to check with Constance about lunch and have her bring it in here."

"Thanks, I've been thinking about food. Do you mind if Elvis comes with you to the kitchen?"

"I'd be honored."

Shane called his brother's cell phone and caught him at his desk in DPD's Major Crimes Division where he'd recently been transferred. Logan sounded happy to hear from him. After a quick update on his two kids in grade school—Shane's niece and nephew—and his bright, beautiful CPA wife, he tossed out the usual query. "So, baby brother, any closer to finding a lady and settling down?"

"I've been busy." He kept his attraction to Mallory to himself, not wanting to get his brother's hopes up. Besides which, lusting after a client was highly unprofessional. "I could use your help on an investigation."

"Why am I not surprised? Tell me what you need."

Without explaining any of the details about Gloria's disappearance, he asked his brother to check into possible aliases on credit cards or travel documents. "On a related issue, I'm trying to locate a man named Felix Komenda, originally from Sierra Leone."

"Is this about diamonds?"

"What?" Surprised by his brother's conclusion, Shane cleared his throat and forced himself to remain calm. "Why would you think that?"

"Conflict diamonds, buddy. West African countries are known for using those gems to fund insurrections. Come on, you ought to know that. You're the one who traveled the world."

"But you've got more experience in crime solving."

"Neither one of us Colorado boys need to get involved in international intrigue."

"Felix doesn't have anything to do with that." *At least, I hope not.* "He's been living in the US for over twenty years. He's an artist."

Logan agreed to make the inquiries for him, and Shane ended the call just as Mallory and Amber stormed into the studio like a double-edged blonde tornado. Both were talking. Loudly.

"Where's Walter?" Amber demanded.

Mallory appealed to Shane, "Don't you think it means something that Gloria kept track of Amber for all these years? She loved her daughter."

He recalled Walter's statement about Gloria being heart-broken, but he wasn't about to step into the middle of this sister versus sister argument. "It's hard to know what's going on in another person's mind."

"That's for damn sure," Amber snapped. "Connect the dots on this bit of illogic. She decided to fake her death and steal diamonds. Because she loved me? No way."

"Look at these photos. She kept them all."

Amber picked up the picture of herself and the birthday candles. "I remember my eighth birthday. Felix gave me a two-wheeler. All the DeSilva cousins were so jealous."

"And the bike was probably paid for by Gloria."

"Which doesn't make it right," Amber said. "Tell me about your eighth birthday."

"It was special." Mallory's turquoise eyes took on a gentle sheen and she smiled. "Mom took me and two of my friends for a ride in a hot-air balloon."

"Compare an idyllic balloon ride floating through the clouds with a messy party, surrounded by cousins and family while Felix snapped photos. Doesn't feel special, does it?" She pushed the box of letters away from herself. "I would have traded a dozen bikes for the chance to spend actual physical time with the woman who gave birth to me."

"It's not too late," Mallory said. "You could still have a relationship."

"Don't give a damn about Ingrid or Gloria or whatever she's calling herself this week. All I want is my share of the payoff. I never want to see her or hear from her."

Before Mallory could pipe up with another defense of her beloved Gloria, Shane stopped their argument. "I want to know more about Felix Komenda. Those first letters indicate that he's in Colorado. Amber, has he contacted you?"

"No, and I tried his phone and sent a text. He didn't answer."

"Does Mallory have his number?"

"I do," she said. "When Felix came to Aspen to discuss the sales of his artwork, he usually moved into Mom's extra bedroom. Once, he stayed at the Hotel Jerome. I'll check there and find out if he's registered. In the meantime, we can go to Reflections and look for more clues."

"Seems like a huge waste of time for all of us to poke around at the gallery," Amber said. "Felix used to talk about the gemology exhibit at the Museum of Nature and Science in Denver. I could go into the city and talk to the guy in charge."

"Ty Rivera," Mallory said. "One of Felix's letters mentioned him."

Shane loved the idea of sending Amber off on a quest of her own. "It's a plan," he said. "We'll take you to Reflections where you can pick up your rental car. You go to Denver, and we'll talk to each other tonight to compare notes."

"Can I trust you?" Amber scowled. "If you people stumble across the Teardrop, why would you contact me?"

"Because you're my sister, and I want the best for you."

For a moment, both were smiling. But Shane didn't believe the hostilities were over. They'd had twenty-six years of separation, and that distance wouldn't be erased in one day. Still, he was willing to accept this temporary truce between the two sisters.

Chapter Nine

After they wolfed down a quick but hearty lunch at Uncle Walter's place, Mallory and Shane dropped Amber off at her rented SUV outside Reflections. While he helped her clear the accumulated snow off her vehicle and Elvis dashed around the uncleared parking lot in lopsided figure eights, Mallory sat back in the passenger seat and put through one of the phone calls suggested by Uncle Walter.

Though she'd expected to get the nurse/receptionist Olivia or a recorded message, a familiar male voice answered on the third ring. "Dr. Freestone here."

"Hi, Doc." She'd known him literally since the day she was born, and he always made her smile. "How about this snow?"

"I'm looking forward to hitting the slopes, but the storm played havoc with my schedule. Olivia didn't make it in, and all my morning appointments canceled. Have you heard anything about your mother?"

"I know she was in Brooklyn three days ago."

"New York, eh? She didn't tell you she was going there?"

"She left a note. All it said was, I'll be back."

"Erratic behavior." He hummed to himself. "Even for Gloria, it's erratic."

"That's why I'm calling," she said. "Walter Pulaski suggested that you might know something about her state of mind. Is she sick? Does she have amnesia? Maybe she mentioned travel or visiting a friend."

"State of mind, yes." He hummed some more, and she could almost see him tapping his pencil to the tuneless beat. Freestone fancied himself a musician and had played in a band of nurses and interns called The Infarction in the '80s. "I really can't talk about her medical issues. Patient-doctor confidentiality, you know."

"Of course."

"But I wonder if Gloria had ever spoken to you about, um, you know. About the change?"

"What change?"

"I'm talking about menopause. Some women her age start thinking of rejuvenation and plastic surgery. Maybe breast augmentation. Maybe she'd considered expanding to a D-cup."

Mallory's jaw dropped. *Mom had gone shopping for a boob job, what?* Had she run off to New York to find a specialist plastic surgeon? "Can't believe it."

"In my experience, women who seek augmentation…" He picked up with his humming again. "Well, they often have a new boyfriend."

She stumbled through the rest of their conversation and thanked Dr. Freestone for his insights before she ended the call. Looking through the windshield, she saw that Shane was done helping Amber and making sure her rental car started. Mist from breathing in the cold surrounded him as he returned to the Navigator. He opened the rear door for Elvis and got behind the wheel. "I'll park in that stand of pines around back. The trees will camouflage the car, and nobody will get the idea that Reflections is open."

When she dropped her hand onto his parka above the wrist, the light dusting of snow melted against her flesh. The cold braced her. No matter how confused she was by Amber's hostility and Gloria's erratic behavior, Mallory couldn't allow herself to go numb. She had to keep her head in the game. "New theory," she said. "Dr. Freestone suggested it."

"Okay."

"Mom took off because she has a new boyfriend."

He started the engine. "That's a hell of a theory. Her disappearance and the search involving every rescue team in Pitkin County is because of a guy she's romancing?"

"The Doc told me Gloria was thinking about having a boob job. In his mind, that particular surgery equals boyfriend. Maybe she'll turn up in a couple of days with a new body and ask why we were worried."

Though they needed to consider every possibility, she doubted this scenario. Gloria was famous for her positive body image, didn't mind disrobing to pose as an artist's model. Uncle Walter had sculpted her nude from dozens of angles.

"There's a quick way to eighty-six that theory," he said as he drove to the back entrance of Reflections. "The Aspen police obtained her phone records. I'll check with them and find out if she's been calling plastic surgeons."

"And Hooker, the pawnbroker in Brooklyn. See if she talked to him."

He snugged the Navigator among the pine trees and turned toward her. "When we get inside, I want you to lead me through the search. Think like Gloria. Don't waste time running around and peeking in obscure corners."

"This won't be the first time I've searched Reflections."

"But now you're looking for a diamond that can be hidden in a small space."

"Got it." She noticed that he already had his door partially open. "Are we in a hurry?"

"Let's just say that I trust Amber about as much as she trusts us, which is not at all. She might be working with Burdock. If she locates the diamond, I doubt she'll share with us. I hope we find the jewel before she does."

She nodded. "I'm ready."

"After we're done here, our investigation will move to my cabin where I can make phone calls and launch computer searches. More crimes are solved by research than by action." He shrugged. "My dad told me that."

"Then you'd better listen."

He shot her a quizzical look. "Why would you say that?"

"I did some research of my own after I hired you."

"And what did you find out?"

"Enough." She'd learned that his father and brother, who he casually referred to as cops, were high-ranking officers in the DPD. His father was a deputy chief with half a dozen commendations including a Medal of Honor, and his brother was a sergeant in the Major Crimes Division. Needless to say, his family wouldn't get along with Gloria. Not a topic she wanted to delve into.

Inside the kitchen at Reflections, she was struck by the faint lingering scent of fresh baked goods: breads, muffins, cinnamon coffee cake and rolls. A shame to let this food go to waste. She put in a call to Sylvia Harrison and arranged for her and her cowboy husband to come over and take the food—as well as anything else perishable—to someone who could use it.

"What's going on?" Sylvia asked.

"Shane and I might have to go into Denver for a few days. I want to leave Reflections locked up tight with the alarm system set. We'll be closed for at least three or four days."

"Don't worry. I'll come by tonight to pick up the baked goods. Over the next few days, I'll check on things."

"Bring your big strong cowboy husband with you." If anything bad happened to Sylvia, Mallory would never forgive herself. "No risks. Understand?"

"I know it's dangerous. Don't you remember? I was the one who found the puddle of blood on the kitchen floor."

And she must have mopped it up because the kitchen was clean and clutter cleaned away. Mallory was lucky to have such a smart efficient person as her second-in-command. After she ended the call, she glanced around the large room with high windows and tried to decide if Gloria would have hidden anything in here. Not likely. There was a distinct lack of privacy. Too many others—employees and delivery people and suppliers—came and went.

Skirting the area on the kitchen floor where she imagined the blood had pooled, she strode through the swinging door into the coffee shop. Shane stood at the cantilevered window, gazing out at the gentle snowfall on the sculpture garden. He'd shed his parka, and his thermal turtleneck and vest outlined his muscular upper body and wide shoulders. His sun-streaked brown hair fell across his forehead in rumpled waves. He was as handsome as the artworks in the gallery. Plus, Shane had the added advantage of being warm-blooded and mobile. When he turned to face her, a spark of electricity zipped through the air and struck her nerve endings like a lightning bolt. Paralyzed, she continued to stare.

Elvis padded toward her and nudged her thigh. When she glanced down, she noticed the dog looking up with eyebrows raised. Never before had she seen a dog roll his eyes, but Elvis managed to convey a nonverbal urging for her to "get it together."

Shane came closer, moving as confidently and smoothly across the travertine tiles as when he whooshed down a ski slope on his way to an Olympic medal. When he was near enough, his golden-brown eyes linked with hers, and the electricity accelerated to a high-intensity whirr. She saw his lips move but couldn't make sense of the words. "What?"

"Let's get started," he repeated.

The sooner they launched into this search, the sooner they'd be finished. Then they'd drive to his cabin where they'd spend the night. Just the two of them, with him guarding her body. They'd be alone, except for the smart aleck dog.

SHANE APPRECIATED THE clever use of space in the gallery. Gloria might be an irredeemable wing nut, but she showed a touch of brilliance in the way she curated art. The walls and partitions on the main display floor kept to neutral tones—soft white, cool gray and beige—to avoid clashing with the paintings. The arrangement of partitions with wide-open areas and sharp corners felt like a labyrinth drawing him deeper into the array of passionate oil paintings, airy watercolors and intense abstracts. Around random corners, sculptures of all sizes and shapes were lurking.

He trailed behind Mallory as she wove through the displays, pointing out the way artists were grouped with several of their paintings together. "On the lower level, we have storage for more of their work. If a patron shows serious interest, we might take them down to the cellar for a more in-depth display of the artist's work."

He paused in front of a huge oil painting of a sunset, five by seven feet. Beside it were two smaller paintings of dawn and high noon. "Tell me about these."

"The artist is local. He only paints sky." She stood in front of the sunset and took a few steps back for a better perspective. "Makes sense, I guess. He's a pilot, Steve Fordham."

"Does he have a private plane?"

"He has several, the Fordham Fleet. Two choppers, three little Cessnas and a midsize executive jet. I think it's a Gulfstream."

"The sort of aircraft that could easily make a flight to Brooklyn."

When she whirled around to face him, her long blond braid flipped over her shoulder. "You think Gloria convinced him to take her to New York. But why wouldn't he tell me? Everybody in Aspen knows I'm looking for her."

Offhand, he could think of several reasons. The guy might still be in New York. Or Gloria could have convinced him that it was a secret. Or he could be in love with her. Maybe he was the new boyfriend. "Put him on your list of people to call. Catching a private flight would explain why her name never showed up on a passenger manifest."

She leaned forward and pulled an orange sticky note from a wall plaque with the name of the artist and the artwork. She held it for him to see Gloria's familiar scrawl.

He read the words. "Out of kombucha."

"It's a health drink. Gloria's latest craze."

"Does she leave many of these notes to herself?"

"All the time. She carries a pad of stickies in her pocket." Mallory exhaled an exasperated sigh, probably thinking of the cryptic note her mother had dropped before she disappeared. "I don't think she'd give directions to the Teardrop in a sticky note, but we should probably try to read most of them."

Once he'd become aware of the notes, he saw them everywhere. The messages ranged from trivial reminders to pick up the dry cleaning to scribbled phone numbers to dinner invitations. Disconnected pieces of Gloria were scattered throughout the gallery. Nothing pertained to the African Teardrop. As far as he could tell, there were no hints about the location of the gem. In the far corner of the gallery, he reached for the doorknob on an office.

"Don't bother," Mallory said. "I've gone over both offices with a fine-toothed comb. Those were the first place I searched."

"You're sure?"

"Absolutely."

She led the way to a circular metal staircase, and he followed. While she lectured about the addition of this narrow loft that was twelve feet above the floor of the main gallery and ten feet down from the open beam ceiling, his gaze slid lower on her body. He focused on the swell of her hips and her delicious, round bottom. Her jeans were a perfect fit. The Vibram soles of her hiking boots clunked on the metal steps, and yet her ascent flowed gracefully. Mallory in motion was a sight to behold.

The displays in the long narrow space beside the wall were small paintings, individually lit, and cases of original jewelry—mostly silver and turquoise—which Mallory studied carefully, peering into corners to find the diamond. He didn't follow her gaze. Instead, his attention riveted to her. He watched every gesture and the way her arms moved. Her slender throat. The tilt of her head when she glanced over her shoulder to make eye contact.

Shane forced himself to look away so he could sever this connection and end his fascination with her body. He rested his elbows on the iron railing at the edge of the loft and gazed down into the displays. Though there wasn't anything in the PI rule book forbidding him from hitting on a client, he knew it would be inappropriate. *Even though she'd kissed me first.* He needed to concentrate on his job, namely finding Gloria.

Mallory joined him at the railing, and he felt her warmth, heard the gentle whisper of her breathing and smelled the citrus scent of her shampoo. Instead of looking at her and being sucked into fantasy again, he gestured wide to encompass the displays on the floor below them. "Someday in the far distant future, all this will be yours."

"The gallery is Mom's passion. Not mine. Don't get me wrong, I love Reflections. But running a gallery isn't my dream."

"Tell me what is."

"I'll show you."

She pivoted and stalked the length of the loft to the metal staircase. Descending, he didn't have the distraction of watching her hips. Instead, he gazed at the swing of her braid and imagined unfastening that gleaming plait, strand by strand.

At the opposite end of the gallery, she paused outside a closed door beside the coffee shop. "When Mom bought this place, it was a fully functioning restaurant with a huge wine cellar in the basement. We transformed that space into storage for artwork."

He nodded. "You mentioned that some of the artists on display had other pieces for special clients' viewing."

"And the former wine cellar can be kept at sixty-five degrees with a humidity level of forty-eight percent. Perfect for maintaining the art in prime condition."

He doubted that primo storage conditions had anything to do with Mallory's dreams. "What else is down there?"

She pushed open the basement door and led him down into her lair. "This is my part of Reflections, which is why I don't think Mom would hide her treasure down here. The idea just wouldn't occur to her."

Subtle but well-placed lighting illuminated a long room with thick colorful rugs on the carpeted floor. Beanbag chairs mingled with regular seating and tables. The chalkboard had lettering in various hues. Corkboards in a rainbow array of frames, ranging from violet to red, decorated the walls and were filled with lively, imaginative paintings.

He'd seen a similar display at her house and drew the obvious conclusion. "These are from your students."

"Yes."

"You want to be a teacher."

"Yes."

Her dream seemed readily attainable, but he didn't make the mistake of thinking her ambitions were easy. Obstacles arose when you least expected them. He knew from experience that when everything seemed to be going well, disaster could strike.

Chapter Ten

By the time they left Reflections, the sun had begun to dip behind the low-hanging remnants of snow clouds. Roads were mostly cleared, and people were out and about, celebrating the first decent snowfall of the winter season. Mallory gazed through the windshield at the winding road that climbed the rugged hills above the Roaring Fork Valley.

Today's intense concentration on Gloria had been exhausting, and she set aside her fear, frustration and confusion. Instead, she thought about Shane. She'd never been to his cabin and didn't know what to expect. During his pro-skiing years, he must have been raking in the dough from prize money, endorsements and private lessons. He'd been famous for hosting extreme, off-piste skiing trips for wealthy clients. Did he squirrel away every penny? Or spend lavishly on a mountain mansion? Was he modern or traditional? Fancy or rustic? They'd spent a lot of time together, but she didn't really *know* him.

She needed to *know*. They'd be spending the night together and *anything* could happen. Her instincts urged her to take their simmering attraction to the next level, but she needed to figure out what to expect from him on the morning after. A cynical, clinical way of forming an opinion about sex, but she'd been hurt too many times to risk her heart.

After years of dating, she'd come up with guidelines to decide potential compatibility. Her categories for bachelor pads ranged from "elite," which was decorator glam with every detail perfect, to "slob" for apartments with empty pizza boxes as the predominant decor. Elite guys usually picked her apart and found her lacking. Slobs were too cluttered to think of anything but themselves. She hoped Shane fell somewhere in between.

Nearing his home, she checked out the view. *Spectacular.* His property stretched along the edge of a cliff, overlooking a scenic snow-covered valley with snow-capped peaks in the distance. His cabin—twice as large as her house—had log siding, a peaked roof over a covered porch, a partial second floor and a tall stone chimney. Classy but not pretentious.

Was he secretly a slob? Or, equally problematic, obsessively tidy? As he guided the Navigator into a neatly shoveled driveway leading to a three-car garage, she asked, "Did you clear the snow this morning before you left?"

"I've got a guy who shovels in the winter, rakes in the fall and mows in the summer. I hired him when I got back from rehab and all my physical energy needed to go into therapy."

"But you're recovered now."

"It's a luxury," he admitted. "But he's worth it. I've also got a twice-a-month cleaning person and an office assistant who I call when necessary."

He scored another plus by recognizing that sometimes he needed help. Also, she liked the responsible way he took care of the things he owned and didn't have a full-time housekeeper to fuss over him. *Not an entitled rich guy.*

The interior of his extra-large garage was well lit with shelving across the back wall. He parked in the slot nearest the entry to his house. A Ford truck—older model, beat-up but clean—was next to that. The rest of the space was filled with sporting equipment, including an ATV. Not surprising. She'd known from the moment she met him that Shane was the athletic type, which suited her just fine. Mallory loved mountain sports. Hitting the slopes in winter. Rock climbing and kayaking in summer. Jogging year-round.

Before they left the garage, he reset the digital alarm. "This system is separate from the interior of the house. If you come in here, you've got thirty seconds to disarm it."

"Then what happens?"

"A screaming alarm and a security firm is alerted. They call. If I don't give them the correct password, they'll be here inside of fifteen minutes."

He didn't sound paranoid, but still she wondered. "Why separate systems?"

"Some of the equipment in the garage is valuable."

Shane slung the giant backpack over his shoulder and scooped up the box of letters from Felix. In the mudroom behind the kitchen, he hung his parka and stomped the last bit of snow off his boots. She did the same. Elvis scooted past them, and she followed the dog into an efficient-looking kitchen with hardwood floors, walnut cabinets and black granite countertops. Elvis trotted past a circular breakfast table and proceeded directly to his water bowl in front of the sliding glass door leading onto a snow-covered deck. Through the windows, a red and gold sunset streaked the sky.

Elvis nudged her thigh. When she looked down at him, he sashayed over to his water bowl and tapped the empty food dish beside it. "I understand," she said. "You're hungry."

He gave her an Elvis-like sneer and used his snout to push the food dish toward her.

She called to Shane. "I think your dog is trying to tell me that he's starving."

Shane joined her, shot a glance at Elvis and shook his head. "You ain't nothing but a hound dog, but I'll get your kibble."

"What about you and me?" she asked. "What should we do for dinner?"

She'd already had plenty of opportunity to watch him eat and knew that he preferred healthy options. But a gander inside his shiny double-door refrigerator would tell her if he was gourmet curious or solid meat-and-potatoes.

While he filled the dog's bowl, he asked, "What can I get you to drink? Coffee or tea? Wine or something stronger?"

"Water is fine."

"I've got fizzy and flat, but I usually drink whatever comes out of the tap. One of the reasons I bought this house was the excellent well water."

He earned a double thumbs-up from her. Real mountain people were concerned first and foremost about their water situation. "Tap water sounds great."

"For dinner, I'm thinking honey-glazed pork chops with acorn squash and a balsamic reduction on a caprese salad."

A menu that sounded both delicious and fascinating. *Like him?* "Do you do your own cooking?"

"I got into the habit after my accident. Before then, I never had time. Now, making dinner is how I unwind. I come in here, turn on some music, call up a recipe online and cook."

Music was another area for consideration. Mallory was open to many different styles but definitely had favorites. "What do you listen to?"

"Depends on what I'm doing. I like a heavy beat when I'm running or exercising."

"Are you a country-western fan? Do you prefer classical?"

"Both." He took two glasses down from the shelf beside the sink and confronted her with a steady gaze. "You're asking a lot of questions."

"Just curious."

"Ever since we met, you've been focused on Gloria. Now you've turned the spotlight on me." He turned on the tap and filled the glasses. "What's going on?"

"You're very perceptive." Another point in his favor. But she didn't want to tell him that she'd been judging him. "Have you ever been in therapy?"

"All kinds of therapy. Physical and psychological. And I went to a psychic once."

"You have an open mind. That's good." She took the water glass and swallowed a couple of long gulps. Maybe she ought to abandon her questions. She liked him and vice versa. Shouldn't that be enough to decide where their relationship went? Still, she wasn't sure what skeletons he had in his closet. "Aren't you going to show me around your house?"

He escorted her through the living room, furnished with comfortable modern furniture in shades of blue and gold. The stone fireplace held a long mantel where he'd chosen to display framed photos, Navajo pottery and geodes. He showed her a picture of two kids, a boy and girl. "My nephew and niece. He's seven, and she's five."

"Your brother's children." The warmth in his voice told her that he liked kids. *Another plus.* "How long has he been married?"

"Almost ten years. Cops are famous for having difficult relationships. But not Logan. He and Cheryl are still crazy about each other. They keep trying to fix me up with the perfect mate."

This was a big topic. *Huge.* "Have you been married before?"

"I've come close. Had a couple of long-term relationships, but nothing worked out. In the early years of my career, I was too preoccupied with skiing. After the accident, I had to rebuild myself before I dragged someone else into my messed-up life."

Though she was curious, probing into his breakups was too nosy, even for her. She gestured to the mantel. "I expected to see trophies. Where do you keep your Olympic medal?"

"Another question." He ducked into the kitchen, retrieved her giant backpack and strode down the hallway. Gesturing to an open door, he said, "This is my office."

She peeked inside. The large space held a desk, file cabinets and a long sofa behind a coffee table. The bronze third-place medal in giant slalom hung in a frame on the wall beside a photo of Shane and the rest of the US team in their uniforms. The placement told her that he wasn't egotistical about his win but treated the accomplishment with respect. *Perfect*.

He went down the hall to a bedroom. After placing her pack on an antique-looking steamer chest at the foot of the queen-size bed, he turned to face her. "I usually sleep upstairs but I'm moving down here for the night. I'll be right across the hall."

"You're taking the bodyguard thing seriously."

"Hell, yes." He stepped back into the hall. "We'll be sharing a bathroom."

In addition to the sink, toilet and shower, the outer wall of the pearl-tiled room held a whirlpool bath that was eight feet long. Her analysis of Shane came to a screeching halt as she perched at the edge of the tub. Any guy who owned a whirlpool with twelve—she counted them—jets went to the head of the line. "Loving it."

"The controls are over here. The jets have two different actions. And this one is for a chromotherapy function that turns on pastel lights."

"Water churning. And lights, too?" Better than a ride at the amusement park.

He leaned against the tiled wall. "About all those questions. What's the deal?"

"Do you really want to know?"

"That's why I asked."

"You've been around me long enough to understand a few things about Mom and the way I was raised." She glided her fingertips along the high-gloss white acrylic of the tub. "Gloria didn't give me many rules. She always said if it feels good, do it. I had to make my own decisions and come up with my own boundaries."

"Okay, but I need more explanation."

"When I get interested in a man, I have a series of questions that tell me if he's a good bet for a relationship."

"You've been testing me?"

"In a way."

The easygoing grin fell from his face, and the light in his caramel-colored eyes faded. The temperature in the bathroom dropped by several degrees. "What's the decision, Mallory? Am I good enough for you?"

"When you say it like that, my perfectly rational process sounds creepy."

"You bet it does." He pushed away from the wall and headed for the bathroom door. "Dinner will be ready in an hour and a half."

BEFORE HE GOT started in the kitchen, Shane grabbed the box of letters, went to his office accompanied by Elvis and closed the door. Didn't slam it, though he wanted to. He dropped the box by the couch, then flung himself into the ergonomic swivel chair behind the desk—a chair which Mallory would probably disapprove of because the design with special back support had cost a bundle. She'd think he wasn't practical. And where did she get off judging him? Why did he have to justify himself? Prove himself worthy? He glanced down at Elvis who rested his head on Shane's knee and waited for a pet.

"Why do I care?" He scratched behind the Lab's velvety ears. "She's a client. It ought to be enough that she's paying me for my time."

He wondered if dogs had the same kind of problem with mating. Did Elvis ever approach a female in heat who rejected him? Probably had. Sooner or later, some hot poodle would turn up her nose at him. Just like a bitch.

That description didn't apply to Mallory. She was different. At least, he'd thought so. Sure, she looked like a typical Colorado blonde with long straight hair, a sun-kissed complexion and a tight athletic body, but she lacked the snotty attitude that usually accompanied that natural beauty. Mallory seemed sweet, hardworking, considerate and genuinely concerned about others. He'd wanted to protect her. Not only from physical danger but from the slings and arrows of gossip. Growing up with someone like her mother must have been a challenge, which still didn't justify her system of making a list of requirements for her friends and lovers. He paused. Had she been considering him for the latter role?

A lover, her lover? Shane felt himself smiling through his anger. Most certainly, he'd been looking at her that way. Was she on the same page? *This had to stop. Now.* He had to quit mooning over Mallory and get down to the business of being a competent private eye. "That's right, Elvis. Isn't it?"

The Lab bobbed his head, which meant he either agreed or he wanted more pets.

Shane rose from his comfortable desk chair and went to the leather sofa by the wall and sat beside the box of letters from Felix. Logic told him that somewhere in that stack of memories was a clue. At random, he pulled out a brown envelope and sorted through the contents, noting Felix's excellent penmanship and his attention to detail. He had described Amber's birthday party dress with incredible clarity. He chatted about weather, writing vivid descriptions of the skies over Manhattan and the foliage in Central Park. When it came to clues, nothing jumped out.

Though not really hungry, Shane needed to get started

with dinner. There would definitely be wine, something to take the edge off. Later tonight, he'd check in with his brother and launch into computer research into Gloria's possible aliases. If she'd used a credit card, he could analyze where she'd gone and what she was doing.

For now, his only reference points came from these old letters. Felix had mentioned Ty Rivera in the gemology displays at the Museum of Nature and Science in Denver. And there were references to other friends who Gloria might contact. He and Mallory might need to take a trip into the city.

Shoving the letters back in their envelopes, he rose from the sofa, stretched his arms over his head and yawned. As long as he concentrated on detective work, he could avoid thinking about Mallory in a more intimate, personal, delectable way. Just a client, she was only a client. No matter how much he wanted to run his fingers through her silky hair and carry her into his bedroom, that wasn't part of their bargain. All he owed her were answers about her mother.

Chapter Eleven

When she took her place at the table, Mallory inhaled the rich aroma of perfectly grilled chops and vinaigrette. The stoneware plates were caramel and slate blue. Stemmed wineglasses held an enticing splash of ruby pinot noir. Streaming music in the background featured lovable divas, like Adele, Lady Gaga and Elton John. A perfect dinner, except for one thing. Shane's mood was stiffly polite, almost cold.

She hadn't meant to make him angry, but that was the end result of her questioning and judging. Did that mean he was too proud or too sensitive? Or was it a reflection on her? The first time she'd met him, she'd been attracted. Who wouldn't be? He was a handsome, athletic man with a good sense of humor who talked to his dog. *Adorable*.

But she had to be cautious when it came to relationships. The therapist she'd gone to for a while suggested that because she'd never known her father, she had subconscious daddy issues that made her crave attention from men. Whatever the reason, she often fell too hard, too fast.

She couldn't stand to be hurt again. And so, she accepted the awkward silence that fell between them, making his cozy dining area seem as dismal as a dungeon.

After dinner, Shane retired to his office to do computer research on Gloria. Mallory also had phone calls to make, but she insisted on cleaning up the dishes, which only seemed fair because he'd cooked. While she tidied the countertops, rinsed and stacked the plates in the dishwasher, Elvis kept her company. The black Lab's attentive gaze encouraged conversation, and she said, "I hope Shane doesn't stay mad."

Elvis gave a snort.

"Yeah, I deserve it. I should have thought of how insulting it was before interrogating him. Is it really such a big deal? People judge each other all the time. It makes sense to base decisions about relationships on past experiences."

When the dishes were done, Elvis followed her down the hallway to her bedroom where she grabbed her basic toiletries and a long flannel nightgown. Hoping to sweep the broken fantasies about Shane from her mind, she ducked into the gleaming white bathroom, started the hot water and found a fluffy blue bath towel that she placed within easy reach beside the tub. Before she disrobed, she scampered back to the kitchen and poured herself another glass of red wine, which she took to the bathroom. Elvis followed her inside.

With a barrette, she fastened her braid on top of her head, undressed and slid into the water. Steam rose in thick clouds that fogged the corner windows overlooking a cliff. No one could see inside unless they had the ability to hover like a helicopter. Even with all this glass, the bathroom wasn't cold. Shane had assured her that the panes were triple thick for good insulation, which also meant bulletproof.

Tapping buttons and turning dials on the control panel, she adjusted the high-pressure action on the jets, starting a swirling, churning motion around her legs and feet. With her upper arms resting on the smooth edge of the tub, she positioned her back against the jets and sighed contentedly as the water pummeled and massaged. Her muscles relaxed, releasing the tension she'd been carrying since Mom ran away.

The heat from the bath opened her pores, and the earthy red wine warmed her on the inside. She fiddled with the control panel, discovering that she could dim the overhead lights and then turn them off entirely. In the dark, she gazed through the windows into the snow-covered forest. Distant mountains framed a cloudy night sky sprinkled with stars. She sipped the wine and tried to forget her worries, but as soon as she erased one crisis, another arose, then another. *Stop thinking.* She programmed the lights to sequentially go through the colors of a spectrum from blue to green to yellow to red. The tub water changed from a deep magenta to purple. *More wine.* Her art classes of elementary school kids would love this whirlpool.

She heard a knock at the door and bolted upright in the tub, nearly sloshing the pinot noir into the pulsating light show. She pressed buttons on the control panel. In her confusion, she plunged the bathroom into total darkness.

"Mallory, do you mind if I come in?"

"Maybe later." She didn't want him to see her wallowing in the dark and sucking down wine. "Not right now."

"Don't worry." He sounded irritated. "I promise not to look."

As if I care about modesty. She couldn't figure out the controls. Another button sent the jets into high speed like the mythical zx threatening to swallow her whole. Water splashed out of the tub, and the room was still dark. "Just a minute."

Elvis tilted back his head and howled, which she supposed was better than having the dog burst into laughter.

"What's Elvis barking at? What's going on?" Shane asked. "I'm coming in."

The bathroom door cracked open, and light from the hallway spilled inside. She saw his tall silhouette. Still wearing jeans, he'd changed into a long-sleeved flannel shirt rolled up at the cuffs. Elvis trotted over to his master and sat, thumping his tail on the floor. The two of them exchanged a glance, then looked in her direction. She'd never felt so utterly, totally naked.

"Before you come any closer," she said, "I just want to tell you that I'm sorry for prying and judging and not trusting you."

"Can we turn on the lights? I won't peek."

"There's nothing shameful about the human body." She'd been posing in the nude for art classes since she was sixteen. "I didn't mean for it to be dark in here. I was hitting buttons and accidentally turned off the lights."

"It's kind of nice like this." He crossed the bathroom and approached the tub. "There's just enough moonlight from the window to outline the shape of your head and shoulders."

"Do you forgive me?"

"Oh, yeah." His husky voice soothed her fear that he'd despise her, but she was still tense. He hunkered down by the tub so he was eye level with her. "I can't stay mad at a water sprite, if that's what you are. More likely a wood nymph."

Or a wood nymphomaniac. His nearness combined with

the wine, churning water and her nudity set her hormones on fire. Looking away from him, she watched Elvis come closer with his toenails clicking on the tile floor. She gave the dog a fake scowl. "Now you're my friend, huh? After setting up a howl and making Shane think I was in trouble. You threw me under the bus."

The dog raised his eyebrows as if to say, "Who, me?"

"Yeah, you." She splashed him, and Elvis stepped back.

"Hey, don't take out your frustration on the dog."

She aimed a second splash at Shane. "Who says I'm frustrated?"

He wiped droplets of water from his cheek and forehead. In the glow of moonlight through the windows, he looked cool and calm, almost businesslike. As for Mallory? Not so much. She was nude and her pulse was racing—the opposite of unperturbed. "Why was it so important for you to come in here? Is there something you wanted to tell me?"

"I heard back from my brother and have information. Your mother has been using a credit card and identification from her youth when her name was Ingrid Stromberg."

"Whoa." *More wine.* "She went back in time."

"Ingrid Stromberg is a legitimate person. She has a bank account in Denver, files taxes and uses the credit card often enough to keep the account active, usually during her travels to New York and beyond."

"Why would she do that?" Mallory managed to dial the whirlpool jets back to a reasonable level. "What's the point?"

"A second identity can come in handy. Makes it easy to go incognito."

Which made her think that Mom had been planning all

along to disappear and start another new life by selling the Teardrop. Her work at Reflections was only a stopping point along the way and Mallory could be abandoned... like Amber. "What else?"

"She also has a cell phone in that name. My brother tracked the numbers she called and those who called her."

"Is anybody from Aspen on that list?" Mallory wanted to know if she'd been played for a fool. "How about Uncle Walter?"

"The only names I recognized were Ben Hooker, the fence, and Felix. I tried calling them both and leaving messages mentioning your name. Neither has returned my call."

"I almost hate to ask." A shudder wriggled down her backbone. "Has she been in contact with Conrad Burdock?"

"Her supposed enemy?" His fingertips dangled in the water, and she fought the urge to grab his hand and pull him into the tub with her. He continued, "Actually, he's the first name I looked for. We only have Amber's word that Burdock engineered the attack on Reflections, and I thought he might be one of your mom's phone contacts. But no."

"Can't your brother trace her whereabouts using her phone?"

He gave her a questioning look. "For somebody who doesn't want police involvement, you seem very willing to take advantage of their resources."

"Hey, I watch crime shows on TV. I know about tracking phone signals."

"Not as easy as it looks," he said. "My brother tried, but Gloria has a very old model and has either figured out a way to turn it off or she's thrown it away. There's been no activity on that phone since she got to New York."

Thanks to modern technology, they'd located her, but she'd slipped away before they could catch her. Mom had spent a lifetime evading notice and had gotten good at it. "What about travel? Did Ingrid Stromberg make plane reservations to New York?"

"He couldn't find any of her aliases on passenger manifests," Shane said. "I'm guessing she used her friend the pilot. What's his name again?"

"Steve Fordham."

"The good news," he said, "is that early this morning her credit card pinged at a restaurant in Denver. She's in Colorado. Didn't Amber say that she'd sent Hooker a photo of herself in Denver?"

"She did, and I guess I should call her with this new information." But it might not be wise to share with her sister. Though Mallory didn't want to imagine a conspiracy, it was possible that Gloria and Amber and Felix were working together and not telling her. If so, why would Amber contact her in the first place? "I'm confused. Too many secrets. Too many lies."

"I know."

"I should finish my bath and start driving to Denver."

"Not tonight. We're both tired. And we need a game plan."

"Smart. Logical." Denver was a four- to five-hour drive and a huge city. They couldn't just wander up and down every street calling her name. "I guess we need to do more research. Make a few more phone calls. Check the computer."

He pushed up his shirtsleeve, stretched his long arm

across the whirlpool to the control panel and adjusted the overhead lights to a dim glow. From his vantage point, he had a clear view of her naked body in the lightly swirling water, but she didn't care. In fact, she welcomed his gaze. They'd been ogling each other since the moment they met. It was time to take it to the next level. She was ready. Or was she?

She rested her forearms on the side of the tub and looked into Shane's eyes. Only inches from his face, she studied the pale brown, burnished gold and hazel facets of his iris beneath his dark brows. Light stubble shadowed his cheeks and emphasized the cleft in his chin.

Gently, he caressed her cheek and tucked a loose strand of hair behind her ear. Reaching up, he unhooked the barrette holding her long braid out of the water. The blond plait fell across her shoulder. "What are you doing?" she asked.

"Helping you unfasten your braid."

"Okay."

She swiveled around in the tub and sat with her back against the side while he took her braid in hand and gave a light tug. "Soft."

"Well, sure. It's hair."

"How long did it take to grow this length?"

"A while."

She covered her breasts with her palms, not because she was embarrassed but it seemed like a comfortable position. What else was she going to do with her hands? As he untwined her braid, she felt the length of it tickling her back and shoulders.

"I've got to admit," he said, "I'm kind of obsessed with your hair. It's mythic, like a mermaid."

"And what does that make you?"

"The hapless dope who can't resist your siren song."

She turned her head to face him. The whirlpool swirled around her legs, but he wouldn't let her float away from his grasp. Shane lifted her from the water and enclosed her in his arms. His kiss was liquid and sensual. His tongue slid between her teeth, exploring and then demanding. When she pressed her wet body against him, he rose to his feet, pulling her from the tub. Cool air raised goose bumps on her backside. He draped the fluffy blue towel around her shoulders.

"Wait," she said. "I have to wash my hair."

"Let me help. It'll be easier in the shower."

"Yes."

Though the distance from the tub to the shower was only a few feet, he guided her protectively across the white-tiled floor. Inside the glass enclosure, a rainfall showerhead splashed a steady flow upon her long hair. She turned her face up toward the hot water and allowed the rivulets to sluice down her throat and over her breasts. The dizzying effects of the wine lingered in a gentle buzz.

Then he was beside her in the shower, naked and muscular. She pushed the rising steam aside for a better view of his hard athletic body. He did not disappoint. Shane could have been one of Uncle Walter's sexy marble sculptures, except for the scars on his legs from his many surgeries after the skiing accident.

They soaped and rinsed and kissed. He paid particular attention to her hair, ending the shower by piling the long tresses under a towel on top of her head. After they dried off, he carried her—still naked—into the guest bedroom. When he tried to place her onto the comforter,

Elvis had already claimed the bed and sprawled posses-
sively across it.

Shane dropped her feet to the floor and shooed the dog.
"Sorry, buddy. Off the bed."

Elvis sneered and grumbled under his breath.

"You heard the boss," she said.

The dog hopped down and slouched out of the bedroom.
Shane closed the door behind him and turned to her. "Do
you really think I'm the boss?"

"Of the dog."

She threw aside the comforter and slid between the
dark blue sheets. He joined her and they embraced until
their damp flesh was warm. They made love throughout
the night.

THE NEXT MORNING, Mallory wakened slowly. She replayed
the night before, remembering one amazing climax after
another, crashing like waves against a distant shore. She
recalled a gentle moment when Shane had sung to her, and
she to him. Elvis had returned to the bedroom and joined
in. Happily exhausted, she'd slept.

Through the window, she saw blue skies. Elvis danced
between the bed and the bedroom door as if heralding the
arrival of breakfast. The aroma of fresh brewed coffee
rose from a large bed tray table where Shane had placed
two mugs and a plate of cinnamon rolls. His wide smile
emphasized his dimples. Oh, my god, he was handsome.

Before she could even say good morning, her phone
rang and she answered. The voice on the other end was
light and cheery. "Have you missed me?"

Mallory stared at her phone screen in disbelief. Caller
ID showed the name Hannah Wye, an attorney and a mid-

talent watercolor artist from Denver, but the voice definitely belonged to her mother. Mom's chuckle rippled through Mallory's memory, sparking the recall of a million jokes and sweet, silly games.

"What's the matter, honey pie?" Gloria asked. "Cat got your tongue?"

"Mom, where are you?"

"I'm so sorry if I upset you. It was never ever my intention to hurt you. You understand, don't you? That's why I left a note."

As she recalled the scribble, Mallory clenched her jaw. The note read, *I'll be back.*

"Mom, that's a tag line for a movie. Three damn words aren't an explanation for why you took off and disappeared for over a week without any other communication."

"A dear friend needed my help, and I simply couldn't say no to him."

"What friend?"

"Felix. You've met him. Tall, skinny, shaved head and tattoos up and down both arms. He's Black."

"Felix Komenda. Is he here in Colorado? Can I meet him?"

"Don't worry. Everything's going to be all right."

Just like that. Gloria expected the intense efforts of an all-out search to be forgiven. Never mind the risks and the long hours put in by the sheriff's office, Aspen police and Aspen/Pitkin County Search and Rescue teams. Mallory forced herself to remain calm. "Tell me where you are, and I'll pick you up."

"Not yet, munchkin. There's one more thing to do, then I'll come home."

"When?"

"Gotta run." Another musical chuckle. "When I get back, I'll answer all your questions."

"Will you? Will you, really?" Mallory had a lot more to say, but her throat choked up. She shoved the phone toward Shane.

He turned the volume up so she could hear, then he spoke into the screen. "May I ask a few questions?"

"Who the holy heck are you?"

"Shane Reilly. I'm a private investigator your daughter hired to locate you, Mrs. Greenfield."

"There's no need for further conversation. I was lost, but now I'm found. Like it says in the song." Her tone had changed. Mallory could tell that she was on the verge of an argument. "And I'm not a Mrs., for your information."

"Okay." Shane's shoulders tensed. "Would you prefer I call you by your maiden name? Or your prior married name? Ingrid DeSilva."

"How did you know?" Rage underlined her words. It went against her free-spirited, live-and-let-live attitude to get angry. But when she did, the effect was terrifying. "This is none of your damn business."

Mallory grabbed the phone. "Please don't hang up."

"How could you hire some creepy private eye to poke around in my life?"

"I was desperate, scared that you were hurt or even dead."

"I'd never die without letting you know."

"Please, Mom, tell me where you are."

"I'm so sorry, but I have to do this my way."

"Wait!"

"Goodbye, Mallory."

She couldn't let her go, couldn't let it end like this. "When were you planning to tell me about Amber? Did you fake your own death? Answer me, Mom. What happened to the priceless African Teardrop? Did you take it from your safe-deposit bank?"

The phone went dead.

Chapter Twelve

Gloria needed to put distance between herself and Hannah Wye's downtown Denver art studio/law office on Blake Street before her daughter and the private investigator sent someone to find her and drag her back to Aspen to face the consequences. Why were all these people getting in her way? She was trying to do the right thing, damn it. Ben Hooker in Brooklyn had turned out to be a Greedy Gus, which made her grateful that she hadn't brought the diamond with her to New York. Felix had been annoyingly uncooperative, and she could only hope that Ty Rivera at the museum would have better contacts. Then there was Mallory. How had her daughter discovered the theft of the Teardrop and how had she deduced that the diamond had been in her safe-deposit box at the bank? Worse, how had she learned about her sister?

Amber, dear little Amber. At the remembrance of the spunky blond child with turquoise eyes, an unexpected pain stabbed Gloria so hard that she doubled over. Her first baby, her darling Amber had been bright, athletic and strong. Even at four years old, she'd known her mind. Leaving Amber behind was the greatest regret of Gloria's life. She never could have done it if Felix hadn't been there to protect the child and keep her safe.

She stepped away from the landline phone, slung her backpack over her shoulder and stalked out the door, grateful that Hannah Wye had seen fit to give her a key of her own so she could pick up artwork even if the artist was out of town. Gloria hadn't been ready to return to Aspen last night, especially after she heard about several inches of snowfall in the mountains.

The city sidewalks had been spared from the storm. The air felt dry and relatively warm on this October morning. There was something good to be said for living at a lower elevation.

As she strolled past Coors Field and headed toward Larimer Square to the bistro where she'd meet with Felix for a breakfast of chai tea and muffins, Gloria remembered when she had lived at sea level. It had been twenty-six years ago...

AFTER SIX O'CLOCK, she had shuffled through the open-air marketplace of Freetown in Sierra Leone. The sunlight had begun to fade, and the night violence commenced. Tall modern buildings loomed over the colorful street where most of the stalls were vacant. The few people she saw shouted at her and told her to find safety. A futile warning.

The dangers of a civil war that had been ongoing since the early '90s seemed distant compared to the daily threat of living with her husband, Raymond DeSilva. Whenever his diamond-brokering business took them to Sierra Leone, he drank Jameson like it was water. And he blamed her for every little thing that went wrong. Even now, when she was seven months pregnant, he lashed out.

Thinking of his latest assault, she stumbled in her ill-fitting leather sandals. Raymond had shoved her to the floor, bruising her knees. That dull ache was nothing compared to the throbbing pain in her left wrist from when he'd twisted her arm and demanded that she admit to mishandling a computer entry about their inventory.

To end the pain, she admitted to a wrong she'd never committed and decided, at the same time, to leave the abusive monster. His violent attacks came more and more frequently. And he'd started drinking when they were home in Manhattan where Amber was being cared for by Raymond's parents. The thought of her daughter spiked tears. She hadn't asked to be dragged into this life, watching her father inflict painful punishment on her mother, hearing her mother's sobs. True enough, Raymond adored the child. His love for Amber was the only reason she'd stayed with him during these long painful years. She'd endure anything, absolutely anything, to be certain that Amber was protected.

Her long dress in a bold pattern of dark green, orange, yellow and brown flowed over her pregnant belly and brushed the pavement. Her long blond hair was piled on top of her head and wrapped in a yellow-and-green-striped turban. In spite of the tropical heat, she pulled a shawl around her shoulders, trying to become invisible and unnoticed. She wished she could disappear. Not for the first time, she wished she was dead.

At the end of the street, she saw a dozen young men with rifles. They shouted wildly and fired into the air. If she stood right here and faced them, she might be killed. Her nightmare would be over.

But that was not to be. Her friend Felix emerged from an alley, caught hold of her uninjured wrist and guided her away from the crossfire on the street. In his soothing accented voice, he said, "Come with me. This shall not be the end of you."

"I can't stay with him." She staggered down the narrow alley between sunbaked brick and stucco walls. When she protectively cradled her belly, pain knifed from her wrist down to the tips of her fingers and up to her elbow. "I can't bring another child into this hell."

"Divorce him."

A bitter laugh fell from her lips. Raymond would never agree to a divorce, and not because he loved her. "He'd rather kill me than pay alimony or child support."

"Your husband has enemies. They seek to destroy him."

According to Raymond, the aura of hatred surrounding him was her fault. Though she sat quietly in a corner and said not a word, she had offended people and turned them against him. "Felix, do people hate me?"

"Not at all."

"But I don't have friends."

"My country is at war. Friendship is a luxury few can afford."

He was a kind man, the only person she trusted. And she believed him when he told her about the plans of Raymond's enemies. They intended to set off a bomb in the dingy two-story office building where DeSilva Gems kept a small office in Freetown.

She knew they were close to the plain ugly building with bars on the windows and double locks on every door. They needed to go there, to warn her husband. She hated Raymond but wasn't a murderer.

"He is not there," Felix said. "He does not work late."

She knew as much. She knew he was at their rented apartment where she'd left him with his half-empty bottle of whiskey. He'd ordered her to go out into the streets where she was supposed to go to the office and pick up one of the ledgers. Her husband had sent her directly into the line of fire.

In the destructive orange flare of multiple explosions on the streets of Freetown, she saw her future. The cries of victims and attackers urged her forward. This was her chance to run.

If she could clean out Raymond's diamond inventory before the building was destroyed, she'd be presumed dead in the explosion. There would be no reason to come after her, to chase a ghost. With the sale of the precious gems, she could finance her escape from Africa.

Raymond wouldn't care that she was gone. Insurance would cover his loss from the stolen gems. And she would disappear into a new life of freedom and safety...and heart-wrenching sorrow. She would have to leave her beloved Amber behind.

Chapter Thirteen

Shane approached Mallory carefully. Fragile as a porcelain statue, she sat motionless in the center of the bed with her legs tucked beneath her and her head drooping forward. A curtain of straight blond hair hid her face. Still naked, she clutched the dark blue sheet over her breasts and shivered. But when she lifted her chin, he didn't see tears. Though the call from Gloria had obviously left her shaken, her eyes remained dry. How could a mother treat her child with such callous disregard? So wrong, so very wrong.

Carefully, he moved the tray with two mugs of coffee off the bed and placed it on the floor. Then he reached for her cell phone. From the corner of his eye, he saw Elvis sneaking toward the tray and warned him off. "Don't even think about eating those cinnamon rolls."

The dog sneered.

"I mean it," Shane snapped. He didn't have time for games. "Don't touch. Step away from the breakfast pastries."

With a shrug, the dog obeyed. Shane joined Mallory on the bed and glided his arm around her. She melted into his embrace and exhaled a sigh. "I shouldn't be surprised by Mom's refusal to talk to me. Everybody has secrets."

No wonder she didn't give her trust easily. Her father

couldn't be counted on; he'd never been around. Her sister was hostile, cold and completely out for herself. As for her mother? Her mom's whole life was a lie. He wasn't inclined to let Gloria get away with this. If she didn't face the illegality of her actions, she should at least acknowledge the damage done to her children. He whispered, "We'll find her."

"Yeah, sure." She nuzzled her head under his chin. "Please don't tell me everything is going to be all right. I can't take another lie."

"No promises, but I'll do whatever I can."

She tilted her head back and looked into his eyes. The line of her cheekbone and chin formed a delicate silhouette. "We need to get moving," she said. "And that's kind of a shame."

"Why?"

"Another disappointment. Like the fact that you're completely dressed. You know, I'd hoped we'd have some time this morning...time for us."

"I'm glad you feel that way." Last night had been outstanding, both in the shower and in the bed. Did he want more? Hell, yes. But they had to wait. He dropped a light kiss on her forehead and on the tip of her nose. "Before we go, there's something we need to do."

"Something fun?"

"Something necessary." He picked up her phone. "We need to turn this thing off and take out the battery."

"But you already made the signal untraceable."

"This is an extra precaution."

"Just let me call Sylvia and check on Reflections." She clutched the phone to her breast. "Then you can turn it off."

"Don't forget. Those guys in ski masks who chased after us in the Hummer worry me." He stroked her silky hair. "I don't want them to be able to find you. So, call Sylvia and hand over your phone. We'll have our coffee and get rolling."

When he reached down to pick up the bed tray, he saw that the coffee mugs were undisturbed but the pastries were gone, and Elvis had smears of frosting on his nose. "Bad dog."

"What did he do?"

"Ate the cinnamon rolls, didn't you?" The Lab ducked his head. His brow wrinkled, and he looked totally ashamed. "Oh, man, I can't believe you."

When she leaned forward, the sheet slipped lower and gave him an even more enticing view. She reached toward the dog who crawled toward her, rested his chin on the bed and whimpered. "It's okay, sweetie. Shane's being mean."

"I can't let him get away with stuff like this." And he couldn't indulge her by allowing her to keep her phone. His job was to protect both of them. "It's not good for him to eat sugary stuff, especially rolls with raisins."

"Then you shouldn't have left the cinnamon rolls so close. You can't blame Elvis for giving in to temptation."

Shane handed her the coffee mug. "Have some caffeine."

"You're right. We have to get going. It's a long drive to Denver."

"Who said anything about driving?"

She cocked her eyebrows. "What did you have in mind?"

"I know a guy," he said. "We used to work together when I took rich tourists on extreme skiing excursions to remote terrain. Long story short, he'd drop us off in the backcountry."

"By helicopter?"

"We're supposed to meet him at nine thirty, which means we've got to hurry. I've already contacted SAR to let them know I'll be out of town. And my answering service."

He left her to get dressed and drink her coffee while he dashed upstairs to his primary suite, grabbed a dark blue cashmere sweater from his closet and pulled it over his button-down shirt and khakis. His brown leather jacket could transition from snow in Aspen to the warmer weather in Denver, and his lightweight hiking boots worked for either climate. After he slid his second Glock into a shoulder holster, he went downstairs to get his laptop.

Before they joined his friend at the Roaring Fork private airfield, they needed to make a stop at Uncle Walter's place, where Shane had already arranged to drop off Elvis. He couldn't very well drag the dog into town. Though his black Lab had a harness proclaiming his training as a therapy dog, a lot of places didn't make exceptions for any canines. Besides, the only other time he'd taken Elvis on the chopper, the dog had been "all shook up" for a week.

It felt like he'd covered all the bases. Since he'd kept Mallory safe overnight, he figured he was doing a decent job as a bodyguard. His phone calls and PI investigating had made progress toward finding her mom. Best of all, he and Mallory had gone deeper in their connection. *To the deepest level, the mermaid level.* He imagined her long silky hair streaming behind them as they joined together in a warm soothing sea. No more need to wonder if there was a future for them.

At the foot of the staircase, Elvis dashed toward him, nervously woofing and panting and spinning in a circle.

"What's wrong, dude?"

Then he heard Mallory shout, "How did you get my phone number?"

Shane charged past the dog and went into her bedroom. She'd promised to hand over her phone after one more call to Sylvia—a promise that came too late. She held up her phone and hit the speaker button so he could hear both sides of the conversation.

"How, indeed. You gave me your card and your personal number when I visited Reflections." The speaker had a baritone voice with an unusual accent, a combination of British and Middle Eastern. "You sound upset. Why is that?"

"You've had dealings with my family in the past. You should have told me." She looked at Shane and whispered, "It's Conrad Burdock."

"I fear you have drawn some unfortunate conclusions, young lady. I mean you no harm. In fact, I have a proposition for you."

"Why would I ever hook up with you? Your thugs charged into my gallery with guns blazing. They chased us through the streets in a Hummer and put bullet holes in my friend's car."

"Do not be absurd. It was never my intention to injure you or frighten you. The opposite is true. I hope to catch more flies with honey."

"What are you talking about?"

"Listen to me, Mallory. I believe, sincerely believe, we can work together. You and I can find the African Teardrop and return the gem to the people of Sierra Leone."

Shane noticed a softening at the edges of Mallory's turquoise eyes, and he could tell that the idea of returning the stone to its rightful owners appealed to her. In spite of Burdock's melodious voice, he recognized the words of a con man who'd say anything to get what he wanted.

"Why should I trust you?" Mallory asked.

"I have lived in Africa for most of my life. I love the land and the wildlife. I understand the people, their customs and their ways. With proceeds from the sale of the Teardrop, we could fight the extreme poverty afflicting Sierra Leone. We could provide wholesome food and medicine for the children. We could build schools."

Shane gripped her free hand and whispered, "Don't fall for his pitch."

But her tender heart had been touched. "Suppose I agree to go along with you, what do you want me to do?"

"We must get your sister out of the way. I am sorry to inform you, but Amber DeSilva is a liar and a cheat. If you and I talk to your mother, she will see things my way. She will want to do the right thing."

"Give me a minute." She muted the phone and made eye contact with Shane. "I believe what he's saying. Mom would want to help the starving children."

"Hey, I'm the last person to say your sister is trustworthy, but I believe her more than this crook. Don't forget the guys in ski masks with guns."

"Right." She unmuted the phone. "You said the men who attacked us at Reflections weren't connected with you."

"Correct."

"If they aren't working for you, who sent them?"

"Once again, I must be the bearer of sad tidings. Forgive me." He cleared his throat. "I have every reason to believe that the culprit is none other than Raymond DeSilva. Your papa."

"But he's dead."

"And so is your mother, Ingrid Stromberg DeSilva." A low chuckle. "Yet, she appears to be extremely active."

Was he suggesting that both Mallory's mother and father faked their deaths? Not a chance! The odds against two faked deaths in one family were astronomical. Shane vigorously shook his head and gestured for her to mute the call again.

"Please excuse me," she said.

"I am out of time. Must dash. Think of all I have said."

"Wait!" Mallory's voice rang with urgency. "Amber said you killed my father."

"Consider the source," he said darkly. "Farewell, Mallory. I shall be in touch."

The call ended. She sank onto the unmade bed and waved the blank screen of the phone in Shane's direction. "This is a perfect illustration of why I need to keep my phone with me."

"So you can get calls from murderous international liars?"

He took the phone away from her and pulled out the battery, hoping he had disabled Burdock's ability to trace their location. They needed to get rid of the phone as soon as possible.

"What if he's telling the truth?" She'd already dressed in jeans and a forest green sweater. Sitting on the edge of the bed, she stuck her feet into her hiking boots. "I like the idea of giving the Teardrop back to Sierra Leone."

"Let me look into the background for Raymond DeSilva.

When Amber told us he was dead, I crossed him off my list of suspects."

She flopped back on the bed. "When I was just a kid, I used to dream about having a real father. A handsome prince or a dashing explorer like Indiana Jones or a rock star. In the screen photo Amber showed me, he's almost handsome with his black hair and mustache. Maybe I can still meet him."

And maybe that wasn't such a good idea. If her father was still alive, he had a stronger motive than anyone else to come after her mom and reclaim the Teardrop. Twenty-six years ago, Gloria had faked her death and stolen a fortune in precious gems from him.

Shane knelt before her and finished tying her bootlaces. When he stood, he pulled her into his arms. Keeping Mallory safe was becoming more complicated by the minute.

AT THE ROARING FORK private airfield outside Aspen, the runways and tarmac surrounding several hangars were cleared of snow. Sunlight glistened on the white wings of the small aircraft and the blades of helos. Mallory and Shane had been rushing since they left his house. She looked down at his laptop, which she held on her lap. The minute when Burdock had claimed her father was still alive, she'd wanted to do a computer search for Raymond DeSilva. As soon as she got a chance…

First, they'd dropped off Elvis. Not an easy task. Though the dog had politely accepted treats from Uncle Walter and allowed himself to be petted, he kept firing sad pathetic looks in their direction. She'd assured him that they'd be back. If he was a good boy, he'd have a lovely time with sweet, kindly Uncle Walter. Then Shane had taken her phone away and given it to Walter for safekeeping. She felt naked without it.

When they'd returned to the Navigator, she'd used Shane's phone to make a few calls and ascertained that Steve Fordham, the pilot who might have given Mom a ride to Brooklyn kept his fleet at the Roaring Fork facility. He wasn't in his office, but she hoped she could talk to someone who worked for him.

They were making progress. Slowly.

Shane parked the Navigator outside an arched metal hangar that was the size of a small warehouse. Under the curved roof, she could see two helicopters with green bodies and striped yellow and black blades. Though she'd gone on helo rides before, Mallory wasn't really comfortable with flying. Not that there was anything to fear with Shane at her side.

She looked toward him, appreciating his confident grin and steady gaze. Once again, he held his phone toward her. "Give Amber a call. Find out where she's staying and if she's uncovered any new information."

"I don't want to talk to her."

His smile didn't falter. "Don't tell me you trust that Burdock weasel more than your long-lost sister."

"Okay, I won't tell you." She snatched the phone from him. "After this, I want to run over to Fordham's hangar and see if somebody can verify his trip to New York with Mom."

"I can do that while you talk to Amber."

She patted his cheek, not intending to notice how fine-looking he was in the clear, sunny morning light. But she couldn't help herself. A warm sexy feeling started in her belly and spread through her body. "Fordham's office staff will be more willing to talk to me because I'm Gloria's daughter."

"And I'm an Olympic skier." He stroked her hair, tucking a strand back into the messy bun on the top of her head. "In most places, nobody cares about my rep, but here in Aspen I'm kind of a superstar."

"You might want to check that ego before you talk to anybody."

"I think Fordham's people will understand." He gestured to three nearby hangars with the name Fordham written in oversize wildly egotistical letters. He opened the car door and stepped out. "Wish me luck."

"Don't break a leg."

Watching him jog toward the Fordham hangars, Mallory decided that Shane had made a full recovery from his injuries. No limp. No hitch in his step. He seemed to be a man at the peak of his physical powers, but she knew that wasn't true. Before his accident, he'd been an elite world-class athlete. Being merely "above average" had to be disappointing. Last night, she'd been blown away by the perfect proportions of his naked body. Never would she forget the way he strutted across the bedroom like the king of the castle. But she'd noticed the scars from operations on his legs. Were they imperfections or badges of courage that came from overcoming adversity?

She hoped to have a long time to figure Shane out, but now she had more pressing issues. She flipped open the laptop. Though it would probably be best to wait until she had some quiet time to explore on the internet, she just couldn't wait any longer. She typed in the codes he'd shown her to bypass his cyber security and access the Internet. The browser lit up. Entering her father's name brought up several possibilities. While she sorted through them, she called her sister, hoping to be able to leave a message. Unfortunately, Amber picked up after the fourth ring.

"It's me," Mallory said. "Did you find a place to stay?"

"Brown Palace Hotel in downtown Denver. It's old-fashioned, surprisingly charming."

"Why surprising?"

"Well, it's Denver, after all. Not a place I associate with class."

"You're showing your ignorance." Mallory hated the way some people put down the city. Denver hadn't been a backwoods cow town for decades. "Denver is very sophisticated."

"Whatever."

She sounded like a spoiled eye-rolling teenager. Amber epitomized many attitudes Mallory disliked, and she'd already decided not to tell her sister about Burdock. There was no problem sharing her conversation with Mom. "She called earlier this morning."

"Ingrid?"

Mallory didn't bother correcting her. "It seems that Mom stayed with a Denver artist. Her name is Hannah Wye."

Amber verified the spelling and promised to look her up. "What else?"

"She mentioned her good friend Felix." Only half concentrating on her talk with Amber, she sorted through computer entries until she found a likely thread to follow. "Have you contacted him?"

"Matter of fact, I have." There was a hesitation in Amber's voice. Was she lying? "Felix and I made an appointment for a one o'clock lunch at the Ship Tavern at the hotel. Too bad you won't be able to get to Denver in time for that meeting."

Mallory smiled to herself. *Oh, yes, I will.* "What about the guy from the museum? Ty Rivera. Have you spoken to him?"

"I left a message. I'll check back later. When do you expect to get here?"

"We haven't left Aspen yet," Mallory said truthfully. The laptop screen filled with a photograph of Raymond DeSilva—a dashing gent with distinguished silver streaks at his temples. "I'll call when we're near the Brown. I have a good feeling about our investigation. We might find her today."

"Forget her," Amber said. "We might find the diamond."

At least her sister was consistent. Her priority had always been to find the Teardrop, and she'd never pretended to care about their mother. For her, the investigation was all about the money.

When she ended the call, Mallory concentrated fully on her internet search and read her father's biography. Raymond DeSilva was very much alive, living in Johannesburg. Why had her sister lied to her? Amber had to know about Raymond DeSilva. He didn't seem to be making any attempt to hide. Photos of his estate showed a gleaming modern mansion constructed of geometric shapes, similar to the facets on a diamond. His trophy wife couldn't have been much older than Mallory.

She had a father. Should have been good news. She should have been excited, happy, fascinated. Truthfully, she just didn't care.

Chapter Fourteen

Shane couldn't say she hadn't warned him. Mallory had told him about her phobia regarding air travel. During the hour and a half helicopter flight from the airfield outside Aspen to a small airport south of Denver, she'd gone from clutching his hand in a finger-crushing grip to a somewhat more relaxed state of panic. Two or three times, she'd peered through the plexiglass bubble of the helo at the earth below. Together, they'd watched the snow-topped mountains recede into valleys and rocky foothills, which morphed into houses and streets and highways packed with vehicles. Her momentary fascination faded quickly, and her eyelids squeezed shut. Not sleeping but denying the queasy fear that churned in her gut.

Her phobia might have been worsened by the unsettling discovery that Amber had lied and Mallory's father—the father she'd never met—was alive. When Shane saw the computer article about Raymond DeSilva, he kicked himself for not taking the time to research the guy when his name first came up. But it didn't make sense for Amber to pretend she didn't know he was alive. Why tell them a fairy tale that could be so easily disproved?

He wondered if Amber arrogantly assumed he and Mallory were idiots and would never figure it out. Or she might be keeping Raymond DeSilva out of the picture to protect him from his enemies like Burdock. Speaking of that devil, Burdock had offered a reasonable explanation for Amber's deception: she and her father were working together to get the Teardrop. By claiming he was dead, she'd hoped to divert suspicion from them both.

When they climbed out of the helo and stepped onto the airport's tarmac, Mallory flung herself into his arms and squeezed with all her strength. "Sorry to be such a baby."

"You did fine." He held her close, pleased by the way they fit together. He enjoyed being her rock—the guy who protected her, even though she was far from helpless. "All the same, I wouldn't mind driving back to Aspen when we're done here. Instead of flying."

"I'd like that." She pivoted, gave their pilot a less emphatic embrace and thanked him for the ride.

"No prob." He shrugged his narrow shoulders and adjusted his aviator shades to deal with the brilliant Denver sunlight. "I've got a couple of things I need to do in the city, and I already lined up a vehicle. You guys need a ride into town?"

"I've got it covered." Shane had ordered a rental car to be delivered to the small terminal with attached offices, a lounge and coffee shop. "There's somebody I need to talk to before we head out."

While Mallory and the pilot walked to the terminal, Shane made his way to Hangar D where Steve Fordham rented space for his planes when he was in Denver. His assistant in Aspen had told Shane that Fordham would be at this airport from ten o'clock until noon, and he wanted to meet this guy in person. It seemed obvious that Fordham had given Gloria a ride to New York, but Shane sensed there was more to the story.

In the small lounge attached to the hangar, he found the CEO of Fordham Aviation sprawled on an uncomfortable-looking love seat with metal arms. His long legs stretched out in front of him, and a blue baseball cap with his logo—a huge *F* and smaller *ordham*—shaded his eyes.

Shane sat in the chair opposite. "Steve Fordham," he said.

"Who wants to know?"

"Shane Reilly. I'm a PI working for Mallory Greenfield."

"And you want to know if I gave Gloria a ride to New York." Fordham sat up straight, took off his cap and stared at Shane with intense blue eyes that contrasted his dark leathery tan. "I took her there. She called me about a week ago and asked if I could give her a lift. It's a trip we've made a couple of times before, and I don't mind helping her out."

The aviator didn't seem like the sort of guy who did favors out of the goodness of his heart. "Are you and Gloria dating?"

"I wish." He flashed an over-whitened smile and licked his lips suggestively. "She's a fine-looking woman. A little old for my taste but still hot. Like her daughter. Am I right?"

Shane wasn't amused by the creepy playboy attitude. "You must have heard about the search for Gloria in Aspen. It's big news."

"Yeah, I guess. Everybody thinks Aspen is so sophisticated, but it's really just a small town where everybody gets up into everybody else's business. Some of my passengers are movie stars and royalty, but they're no different than you or me. Do you remember that Swedish super-model who plays a space cop? Bang, bang, bang, she's a real tasty meatball. And then—"

Before he could list all the famous people who had flown with Fordham Aviation, Shane got back on topic. "Why didn't you notify the police? Let them know Gloria was okay."

"She asked me not to tell anybody."

"You don't seem like the kind of guy who lets somebody else call the shots." Shane took a jab at Fordham's ego. "I'm guessing Gloria has some kind of leverage over you."

His gaze slid sideways, evading direct eye contact. "She's my agent."

Shane had all but forgotten the artist-to-agent part of their relationship. "Gloria must have a lot of contacts in New York."

"You bet she does." He stood and stabbed at Shane with his index finger. "The woman represents Walter Pulaski, and he makes big bucks. If she could get a couple of my paintings into galleries in Manhattan, my work might catch on. I'm a pilot who paints the sky. That's a good hook, right?"

"Not exactly unexpected."

"As if you're an expert." He took two angry strides toward the exit. "Besides, I figured the guy who drove her to the airfield would be responsible and talk to the sheriff."

Finally, he'd said something interesting. Shane jumped to his feet. "What guy?"

"You know who." He reached for the doorknob.

Much as he hated chasing Fordham, Shane dodged around the chair and blocked the exit. Gloria's disappearance might be a joke to this flyboy who was a legend in his own mind, but Mallory was nearly devastated. And there was a twenty-million-dollar diamond involved. He pinned Fordham with a gaze. "I want a name."

"Okey dokey." He scoffed, mocking the lighthearted word. "That's how he talks. Howdy-doody and diddly-do and great googly-moogly."

"A name."

"The vice president at Fidelity Union, Drew Sherman."

Everybody in town knew Sherman. The husky man with heavy black eyebrows had a smile for every patron of the bank and an encyclopedic memory for jokes. He played Santa at the Christmas Carnival and was known as a family man. "What was he doing with Gloria?"

"Not sure," Fordham admitted. "He didn't come into the hangar to say hello, but I saw him arguing with her outside his car. When she came inside, I asked about Sherman, and she told me that they'd been associates for years."

His inflection when he said *associates* made Shane wonder if there was more to the story. It seemed like Gloria had a lot of male friends, ranging from Uncle Walter to Fordham to Felix to the local banker. "Do you know anything else about their relationship?"

"I'd say they were palsy-walsy." He smirked at the corn-ball phrase, which he obviously intended to make fun of Sherman. "She's known him for years, ever since Mallory dated his son in high school. Get your mind out of the gutter, Shane."

"Occupational hazard." Private investigators tended to see the worst in everybody, and they were often correct when it came to cheating spouses and lying businessmen. Shane missed the more straightforward world occupied by his police officer brother and father.

"Anything else?" Fordham asked.

Shane figured he might as well tie up loose ends. "You flew Gloria back to Denver from New York."

"That's right."

"Will you be taking her back to Aspen?"

"She's not on my schedule. I dropped her off a couple of days ago and haven't seen her since. I suppose if her timing worked out, I'd give her a lift. No point in alienating an agent, right?"

His body language didn't indicate deception, but Fordham had folded his arms across his chest, which usually meant a closed-down or unfriendly attitude. No surprise. The pilot walked a shaky tightrope between civil and hostile. He never actually said anything offensive but implied a lot.

Figuring he had nothing to lose, Shane introduced the multimillion-dollar question. "Did Gloria mention a special object that she was taking to New York?"

"Like what?"

His gaze turned shifty. Shane wondered how involved Fordham was in Gloria's disappearance. Was he more than a hapless dupe who wanted to get on his agent's good side? "Forget I said anything."

"Come on, man. You can tell me. Are you talking about some kind of artwork?"

"You might call it that." Again, Shane studied the other man's body language, looking for clues. "When I think about this object, I want to cry. To shed a teardrop."

Fordham looked confused. Apparently, the word *teardrop* meant nothing to him. "Have it your way. I don't care what kind of game she's playing. Are we done here?"

"Afraid so."

After this little talk with Fordham, Shane didn't feel much closer to finding the elusive Gloria Greenfield or the diamond she'd stolen twenty-six years ago. He'd ask Mallory about Drew Sherman but doubted there was anything more than a friend giving another friend a lift to the airport. Maybe they'd have better luck with Amber.

AT TEN MINUTES past one o'clock, she and Shane dropped off their rental car at the valet station and strolled into the Brown Palace Hotel in downtown Denver. As she crossed the luxurious lobby, Mallory flashed back to her junior year in high school when she attended the Rocky Mountain Debutante Ball at the Brown. The event was an unaccustomed splash of glamour in her super-casual lifestyle. For her, getting dressed up meant wearing clean jeans, which was what she had on right now—black jeans, hiking boots and a cashmere sweater set in deep burgundy. Her simple pearl necklace was a gift from a boyfriend and couldn't have possibly come from the stash Mom had supposedly stolen.

"The first time I came into this hotel," she said as she fingered the pearls, "I was wearing a coral chiffon gown. Long and ruffled in the back. Short in the front. With a halter neck because I didn't have the boobs to hold up a strapless. Still don't."

"There's nothing wrong with your boobs," Shane said. "Was it a debutante ball?"

"How'd you guess?"

"I got roped into escorting girlfriends to a couple of those things. Always wore the same black suit."

"Men have it easy when it comes to fancy events. My date for that dance was Josh Sherman, the football star."

Her family had known his for nearly ten years, and it came as no surprise when Shane told her that Mr. Sherman gave Mom a ride to the airfield. But why hadn't he mentioned it to her when she stopped by the bank? Or to the sheriff when he was involved in the search? Mr. Sherman wasn't the sort of person who kept secrets unless he had a very good reason. The obvious inference was an affair, but she couldn't imagine the straight-arrow banker cheating on his wife of thirty years.

She straightened her shoulders when they paused at the hostess desk in the Ship Tavern. Like the prow of a galleon, the restaurant was located at the front of the triangle-shaped red sandstone hotel. The decor and the long bar suggested a vintage pub with polished wood and leather booths. The ship fixtures—such an odd metaphor for Denver—included a thick mast and crow's nest with an old-fashioned ship's clock. She spotted Amber and Felix at a table halfway across the floor. Her sister was blithely sipping a margarita.

Amber's carefree attitude lit the fuse on Mallory's anger. She felt a red flush rising on her cheeks, and she clutched Shane's hand, needing his self-control before she confronted her sister, who had lied about the death of their father and had done nothing to help in the search for Gloria.

"Hey." Shane summoned her attention. "Don't explode until after we find out what she knows."

"Don't worry. I can control myself."

He looked doubtful. "Maybe I should do the talking."

"I've got this." She set her mouth in a rigid smile as she approached Felix Komenda, who rose politely from his chair to shake her hand. "We met at Reflections in Aspen. I'm Mallory."

"Of course." He was as tall as Shane—slender, poised and graceful. Under his blazer, Mallory knew he had full-sleeve tattoos. "Even if I did not remember our first meeting, I would know you ladies are sisters."

True, they resembled each other. Today, they both happened to be wearing similar shades of mauve. Mallory had pulled her long hair up into a knot on top of her head. Amber's neatly styled hair was a nearly identical blond. The sisters glared at each other with matching turquoise eyes.

Amber stated the obvious. "You're here."

"Surprised?"

"I thought it would take longer to drive."

"Which is why we decided to fly," Mallory said. "Shane's friend runs a helicopter service."

The two men shook hands like civilized human beings while the sisters faced off like a couple of lionesses sizing each other up before going in for the kill. Mallory had never been this furious. Her sister had done more than subtly betray her trust. Amber had outright lied.

"I am so very pleased to see you," Felix said in an accented melodic voice. "Please sit down. Would you care for a drink?"

When Shane pulled out her chair and guided her into it, she was grateful for his assistance. Her legs and arms were tense and stiff, nearly immoveable. "I'll stick to water."

"An upset stomach, perhaps?" Felix regarded her with what appeared to be genuine sympathy. "Your mother mentioned that you are an anxious flyer."

Not allowing herself to be distracted from her outrage, Mallory's glare at her sister intensified. "I'm fine."

Under the table, Shane took her hand, holding her back from the hostility that simmered so near the surface. "We have a few questions."

"Right," Mallory snapped, ready to get down to business. They had an investigation to pursue, and she didn't intend to waste time. "Mr. Komenda, have you spoken to my mother recently?"

His gleaming smile highlighted his mocha brown skin. The last time Mallory had seen him, his head was shaved. Now his hair was closely trimmed, and he wasn't bald. His onyx eyes held a depth of unreadable expression. "Gloria and I met for brunch."

"Her name is Ingrid," Amber said. "I don't know why you people insist on using her alias. She is now and has always been Ingrid DeSilva."

"For purposes of clarity," Felix said, "I will refer to her as Gloria, the name she chose for herself rather than the one she was given. I believe it is a woman's right to name herself."

"Absolutely," Mallory said. "I like the way you think."

"You would." Amber turned to Felix and stuck her tongue out at him like an angry kindergartner. "You're never on my side."

"My dear child, I have watched over you from when you were an energetic four-year-old. I documented your life in hundreds of letters to Gloria and—"

"Ingrid," she interrupted.

When he stretched his long arm and touched her hand, his collar—which was open four buttons—spread wider, and Mallory caught a glimpse of the topmost branches of the Cotton Tree in Freetown tattooed on his chest. When he spoke to Amber, he was gentle. "You must trust me, child. I will always do what is best for you."

"Then tell me…" In contrast, her voice was harsh. "Where is the African Teardrop?"

"I do not know."

"Don't know?" She flung his hand away from her. "Or won't say?"

"I speak the truth."

"You've always been on Ingrid's side. Never on mine," she snarled. "You've been lying to me since I was a little girl."

Mallory surged to her feet. "You're a fine one to talk about lies. You claimed my father was dead. Not so. Raymond DeSilva is living with his new wife in South Africa."

"She's a bitch. And so are you." On the opposite side of the small table, Amber stood to confront her. "I never should have contacted you. You and your broken-down-skier-turned-investigator have been useless. He and his ugly mutt are a joke."

"I can believe that you think I'm a bitch. Making an allowance for rudeness, I can accept your snide comment about Shane. But nobody, and I mean absolutely nobody, insults Elvis." Mallory snatched the water glass from beside Felix's place setting and flung the contents into her sister's face.

Gasping, Amber stared as water dripped down her chin onto her silk blouse. She huffed and puffed, unable to speak. Nose in the air, she stalked away from the table.

Mallory had no regret for what she'd done. In fact, she wished she'd ordered a cocktail to throw. Something big and messy like a Bloody Mary.

Chapter Fifteen

When Felix took a step toward the exit from the Ship Tavern to follow Amber, Shane gestured for him to return to the table. "Stay with us."

"I must be certain that she is all right."

"She'll recover. It was only water."

Much as Shane might have hoped that Amber had been drenched in goop or splashed with permanent dye, Mallory's attack had been benign—wild and a little bit shocking but still harmless. It was time for him—the so-called broken-down skier/investigator—to take charge and start tying up loose ends. He waited for Felix to sit, then signaled the waiter who had been hovering nearby, waiting for their drama to fizzle. "I'll have a Guinness on tap."

The waiter nodded to Mallory. "And for the lady?"

"A Bloody Mary."

"Very well." The waiter glanced at the vacant chair. "Will she be returning?"

"Don't know," Shane said. After the waiter left, he leaned across the table toward Felix. "We have questions that will be easier for you to answer without Amber hanging over your shoulder."

Felix nodded. "Perhaps."

"From what I understand, you've been watching over

her since she was four and her mother faked her own death."

Felix affirmed the somewhat outrageous statement, and Shane had to wonder why this seemingly sane, sophisticated man would accept Gloria's criminal intentions. Why would he agree to watch over a child he barely knew? There must be some way he benefited from this relationship. "Why?"

"Of course, I cared about the child. Amber can be endearing. However, she has not outgrown a habit of throwing tantrums and making ridiculous demands."

A lovable child abandoned and needing help was a partial explanation, but Shane sensed a more compelling, more personal reason. He couldn't believe that Felix—a man of the world—would dedicate his life to Amber because he liked the kid. Maybe he was looking for a way to escape Sierra Leone. "You stayed with her family in New York. Was it difficult to get a green card?"

"I have United States citizenship. I was born in Atlanta, Georgia. My parents moved to Sierra Leone when I was a toddler. I consider both countries to be my home."

Immigration hadn't been an issue, but there were other advantages to living in America. "When you came here, did you go to college?"

"Oh, yes, I attended several art schools and academies in New York. Also, I worked in galleries, like Reflections." He beamed at Mallory. "I was pleased when Gloria told me what she was doing in Aspen."

Everything he said made sense, but Shane wasn't close to satisfied. The story lacked important connections. "Tell me about Amber's father. Are you close to him?"

He exhaled a weary sigh and shook his head. "Raymond DeSilva paid me to act as Amber's nanny and body-guard—"

"Excuse me," Mallory interrupted. "Why does she need a bodyguard?"

"Much as I hate to bear more bad news, your father has enemies, legions of enemies. Need I remind you of Conrad Burdock?"

"I guess not," she said.

"I worked for DeSilva, but we were never friends. His lying, cheating, thievery and violence disgusted me. I hated him for the way he abused Gloria."

"Physically?" Mallory asked in a voice shaking with anger or grief or both. "Did he physically hurt her?"

"Yes," Felix said. "Gloria tried to make her marriage work, but she could not change her husband. Leaving him was the best decision she ever made. She is a strong, wise woman."

Shane heard the anger in his voice when he talked about DeSilva, which was counterbalanced by affection when he mentioned Gloria's name, and that explained a lot. The puzzle pieces were falling into place. Felix had taken care of little Amber because he had deep, intimate feelings for her mother, maybe even loved her.

A familiar pattern began to form. Shane couldn't explain, but he recognized intuitively what was happening. *Gloria Greenfield is magic.* As she floated through life being irresponsible and creative, she cast magical spells that drew people, mostly men, to do her bidding. Walter Pulaski called her his muse. Fordham, the misogynist pilot, rearranged his schedule to fly her to New York, free of charge. And Felix Komenda had devoted over a decade of his life to babysitting her daughter.

When the waiter returned with their drinks, he glanced

over at Mallory as she tucked a long strand of gleaming blond hair behind her ear. The crimson flush of anger that colored her cheeks had faded to a pinkish hue, and her mouth curved in a smile. *She's magical, too.* He'd do anything for another taste of those soft full lips.

They tipped their glasses toward each other and sipped. In unison, they turned toward Felix. Shane hated to leave the relationship part of this complicated story behind, but they might not have much time before Amber came charging back into the Tavern. "I have to ask about the Teardrop."

Felix laced his long slender fingers together and rested his hands on the tabletop. "This story covers many, many years. I shall try to condense my narrative. At 521 carats, the African Teardrop ranks among the finest stones found in Sierra Leone. The pale blue gem—with the color and glitter of a perfect teardrop—is worth more than twenty million and symbolizes the dichotomy between the natural wealth of the nation and the poverty of the people who live there. Shortly after the Teardrop was discovered in 1968 and displayed to the world, it disappeared. Everyone assumed it was stolen and sold as a blood diamond or hidden in the private vault of a wealthy collector."

Shane knew a little bit about the tragedy of blood diamonds, also called conflict diamonds. During his prime, he'd skied off-piste in the Atlas Mountains of northern Africa and had been approached by warlords and terrorists who offered to sell him gems at cut-rate prices—a heinous, tragic bargain. The real cost came in the suffering of the people who were forced to give up these treasures and barely had enough to feed their families. The United Nations and the Kimberley Process system were involved in regulating the sales of gems and marketing them as "conflict-free."

This history didn't explain what had happened to the Teardrop. "How did the gem fall into the hands of Raymond DeSilva?"

"We will never know," Felix said. "When Gloria scooped up Raymond's inventory before his shop in Freetown was bombed and burned to the ground, she did not know the Teardrop was among the other stones. After she left Sierra Leone, she discovered the treasure. And this is where I come into the story."

"You had an interest in the gem," Shane said.

"Of course." He winced at a distant but still remembered heartache. "The African Teardrop is a national treasure in addition to the monetary value. Gloria was aware of this heritage. She wished to return the gem, making sure that it went to the right people. I offered my help, and she accepted."

"A hell of a huge responsibility."

"Yes."

"How old were you at the time?"

"Twenty-six." He nodded to Mallory. "The same age as you."

"And my mom when she left Africa," she said. "I hope I can step up the way you both did and make things right. The Teardrop could provide funding for hospitals and schools, alleviating suffering and truly helping the people of Sierra Leone."

"The opposite is equally true," Felix warned. "For decades, conflict diamonds have financed warlords and terrorists. The Teardrop might be used to pay for a slaughter. This is a most delicate political situation."

Shane wanted to get back to his narrative. "When you realized that Gloria had the Teardrop, what did you do?"

"I was young and needed guidance. My parents had many contacts, but they were spending more time in the United States because of the civil war in Sierra Leone. Government officials were corrupt. Some of the rebels were admirable. Others were pure evil. No one seemed worthy. None could help me. I didn't know who I could trust."

"I understand," Mallory said. "Not knowing who to believe can paralyze you."

"When it came to the Teardrop, you and Gloria were faced with difficult decisions," Shane said. "You didn't want to make a mistake."

Felix paused to take a sip of his beer. "And so, we did nothing."

"You told no one about the Teardrop?"

"Gloria's escape from DeSilva seemed to be successful. No one knew where she had gone. They weren't following her. They believed her to be dead."

A miracle. Again, Shane thought of Gloria's secret weapon—a magic that caused criminals to provide her with perfectly forged identification and gemologists, like Ty Rivera at the Museum of Nature and Science, who helped her sell the precious stones. Uncle Walter got her settled in Aspen, which couldn't have been an easy proposition. And she'd made a living for herself and her infant daughter with an art gallery. Not the most lucrative or stable occupation.

Felix continued, "She hid the Teardrop. For twenty-six years, we kept the secret."

With rapt attention, Mallory asked, "What changed?"

"DeSilva."

"Did he find her?"

"To be honest, I do not know." Felix lifted his beer mug to his lips and took another taste. "She started receiving odd emails and texts. On the street outside Hotel Jerome, she thought she saw him. More than once, she heard his voice, threatening her. And she found objects in her house missing or misplaced, including mementos that DeSilva would know were important to her. Frightened, she believed she must return the Teardrop before DeSilva got his hands on it."

The new revelation opened other doors for investigation, namely he needed to track the location of Raymond DeSilva. Shane had several questions, but he caught sight of Amber at the entrance to Ship Tavern, and knew they were about to be interrupted. He asked Felix, "Who is Hannah Wye and how does she fit in?"

"She's a watercolor artist."

"And also an attorney," Felix added. "Her services might be needed while dealing with the return of the Teardrop. And she offered Gloria use of her downtown loft last night."

Shane pressed forward. "Why did Gloria go to the fence in Brooklyn?"

"A mistake." Felix shook his head. "I suspect she planned to easily sell the gem and be done with it. Instead, her actions alerted Amber and Conrad Burdock."

"What can you tell me about Ty Rivera at the museum? Can he be trusted?"

"I hope so. Gloria went to see him at lunchtime. I wanted to accompany her, but she insisted on talking to Rivera alone."

"Mallory has an appointment with him," Shane said. "In less than two hours."

"Rivera has excellent contacts in Sierra Leone. His advice would be highly beneficial."

Keeping his voice low, Shane asked, "How can I reach Gloria?"

"I fear you must wait for her to contact you."

"Is she returning to Aspen?"

"I do not know."

"Stay in touch, Felix. I'll do the same."

Amber stormed around the table and returned to her seat. With a nasty smirk, she stared at Mallory and lifted her stemmed margarita glass. The tip of her tongue licked salt from the rim. Mallory did the same with her Bloody Mary, which was a much more destructive drink than the water she'd flung before. It seemed apparent that neither of these women was inclined to apologize for the prior argument. He would have liked to probe into Amber's relationship with her father but doubted she'd tell him the truth. When the people in this dysfunctional family took sides, she was firmly on Team DeSilva.

He pushed back his chair and stood. "We should be going."

"Oh, I don't think so," Amber said. "You won't get away from me that easily. I want to know what you've found out about the Teardrop. I've waited a lifetime for that inheritance, and I deserve every penny."

Mallory stood tall and straightened her shoulders. "You and your father stay away from me and Gloria. We owe you nothing."

Shane tossed a couple of twenties on the table and took Mallory's hand. Together, they left the Ship Tavern and went to the valet station on the street. He glanced over his shoulder at the charming old hotel. "Should I make a reservation? We could stay here tonight."

"With Amber down the hall?" She shook her head, and another strand of hair slipped out of her loosely knotted bun. "This hotel isn't big enough for the both of us."

"Still, I hate to pass up a night without Elvis. Just you and me."

"I miss the dog."

When their rental car pulled up to the valet station, he held the door open for her. "We're early for our appointment with Rivera, but I wouldn't mind taking a walk around Ferril Lake at City Park."

"Perfect." She turned her face up to the sun, unfastened her bun and let her silky golden hair cascade down her back. "When we get back to Aspen, we're looking at snow and cold. While we're here, it's nice to enjoy the autumn."

He slipped behind the steering wheel and drove east on Seventeenth Avenue. Brilliant sunshine glistened on the red maples and golden aspens that still had their leaves. He'd grown up in Denver and loved the temperate October weather, perfect for jogging, biking and football.

After he parked near the lake, he noticed a commotion in the parking lot outside the Museum of Nature and Science that overlooked a fountain and rose garden. Though there was no sound from sirens, red and blue police lights flashed against the granite walls of the four-story rectangular building that housed dinosaur skeletons, dioramas of hundreds of animals and impressive rocks and mineral displays.

"I have a bad feeling about those police lights," he said.

"Me, too."

His cell phone jangled. A call from Logan.

His brother got right to the point. "Last night, you asked me to research credit cards for Ingrid DeSilva, Ingrid Stromberg and Gloria Greenfield."

"And I appreciate your help." Already he didn't like the direction of this conversation.

"Did you find the woman?"

"I haven't laid eyes on her," Shane said truthfully. "What's the problem?"

"This woman—let's call her Gloria—had a lunch meeting at the Museum of Nature and Science with the gemologist in charge of the precious stones exhibits. She was last seen in his company at the café in the museum. His name is Ty Rivera. Do you know him?"

Once again, Shane could be completely honest without implicating Mallory or her mom. "Never met the guy."

"I have another name for you," Logan said. His voice sharpened, and Shane recognized the tone from when they were kids and Logan was about to give him a hard time. "Mallory Greenfield."

No way to sidestep that one. "I know her. Why do you ask?"

"I made some phone calls to the cops in Aspen and found out that Mallory is the daughter of Gloria, the woman you asked me to trace. She's been missing for seven days."

"Right."

"I was thinking that maybe, just maybe, Mallory hired you to find her mother. Is she your client?"

As a cop, his brother ought to recognize the confidentiality issues involved in being a private investigator. "Can't tell you," Shane said.

Life would have been easier if he could have honestly

talked to Logan, confided everything they'd learned about Gloria and the African Teardrop. He wanted his brother's help in tracking down Gloria and DeSilva and Conrad Burdock. But he couldn't betray Mallory. He refused to be the person responsible for sending her mom to jail.

"Your friend Mallory also has an appointment scheduled with Ty Rivera. At half past three." Logan paused, waiting for him to fill the silence. When Shane didn't speak, his brother continued, "If you have contact with her, you can tell Mallory Greenfield that Mr. Rivera won't be able to meet with her."

Dreading the answer, Shane asked, "Why is that?"

"Your client is knee-deep in a stinking pile of trouble, buddy. I know you're trying to protect her. I get it. But you're both going to get hurt. You've got to tell me whatever you know."

"Why can't she meet with Rivera?"

"He's dead. Murdered. His throat slashed by an ancient Mesoamerican obsidian blade from one of the museum exhibits."

Chapter Sixteen

A loud disorderly gaggle of Canadian geese waddled along the paved path encircling Ferril Lake at City Park. Mallory tried to disregard their raucous honking and eavesdrop on Shane's phone call. His part in the conversation sounded noncommittal, but still she worried. His brother was a cop, an occupation which represented a heavy-duty threat to Mom. Never mind that her crimes didn't hurt anyone except her abusive husband. For twenty-six years, she'd paid her taxes and been a model citizen notwithstanding her eccentricity. None of that mattered. Because she'd faked her death and assumed a false identity, she was considered a criminal, and it was Logan's job to arrest her.

When Shane ended his call, he stood for a moment, staring at the screen on his cell phone, giving her a chance to appreciate his tousled sun-streaked hair and tanned complexion. His ridiculously long eyelashes drew her attention to his caramel-colored eyes. The way he'd looked at her last night set off a chain reaction unlike anything she'd felt before. If he wanted to turn Mom over to the police, Mallory didn't think she could bear it.

He tried to smile, but his mouth was tense. "I just got a text from Pulaski. Gloria called your phone, and he's passing on the message."

Her heart skipped a beat. "Is she all right?"

"Yes."

"What did she say?"

"She wants you to call her back. But before you do, I need to tell you something. Let's walk."

"Why?"

"I can't think when I'm standing still." As he moved along the paved path beside the lake, static energy fizzed around him. "We were right to be worried about the police lights at the museum."

She kept pace with his long-legged stride, fearing the worst. "Is this about Ty Rivera?"

"He's dead."

Shocked by the unexpected news, she sucked in a sharp breath. Though she'd never actually met Rivera, she'd spoken to him on the phone and had an appointment this very afternoon. "An accident?"

"His throat was cut."

"How did—"

"You don't want to know," he said. "I don't mean to be blunt, but there's no time for a sensitive explanation. And you might want to brace yourself. From here on, the story gets worse."

When he unintentionally started walking faster, she nearly had to jog to keep up with him. "I'm ready."

"According to Logan, your mom met Ty Rivera for lunch. It's likely Gloria was one of the last people to see him alive." He shook his head. "Logan recognized her name from when I asked him to trace her credit cards. And he knows you have an appointment with Rivera."

She digested the information and immediately recognized the possible consequences. Gloria could be a murder suspect. "Is your brother going to arrest her?"

"He wants me to put him in touch with you and with Gloria."

She came to a halt, gazed across the lake where geese and ducks swooped and chased along the calm water. At the eastern end was the Band Shell and Pavilion, sunlit and glowing amidst a canopy of trees and lawns, which were still green in October. The scene was idyllic, but she was gripped by dread. This was the moment she'd feared, the moment when Shane had to choose between his law-abiding upbringing and her edgy family. "What are you going to do?"

"He's my brother, Mallory. I can't lie to him."

"What did you tell him?" She shot a nervous glance over her shoulder at the museum where police lights continued to flash. Shane had been guiding her in that direction. Did he intend to leave her in his brother's custody? Had he already decided to abandon her?

"I didn't lie," he said.

When he clasped her hand, she jerked away from him. Last night, she thought she'd finally found a man she could trust, but she was wrong. He'd betrayed her. "Let me go."

"I'll never hurt you, Mallory. Sure, I'd feel better if I could tell my brother the whole truth. And I'd welcome the police for backup. We're talking about murder here and need all the help we can get. You and I are running around with nothing but my Glock for protection, and I'm not a great marksman."

"But we have Elvis."

In spite of his tension, he laughed. "The dog is fierce."

She met his gaze. "What exactly did you say to Logan?"

"I sidestepped. When we were kids, I got out of fights by telling nothing while using a barrage of words. Here's how it works. One time I borrowed his favorite baseball glove without asking and left it at the park. I never actually lied to him but never admitted that I lost his dumb glove. After dinner, I crept out of the house and found it. All was cool."

The current situation was far more complicated than a piece of missing sports equipment. "How much did you say about Mom?"

"I could honestly say that I've never met the woman. Then I tap danced around the topic, avoided telling him about the Teardrop and our investigation. I didn't even mention that I was in Denver, probably standing a couple of hundred yards away from where the murder took place."

A gust of relief whooshed through her. She stepped toward him and collapsed against his chest, welcoming the shelter of his arms. "What did you tell him about me?"

"He already knows about your search for Gloria and has spoken to the Aspen sheriff and the Pitkin County sheriff. Until this is over, we've got to avoid all the local cops."

"I wish it didn't have to be like this. I had hoped that the first time I met your family, we'd be sharing a dinner, reminiscing over pot roast and mashed potatoes."

"Wrong picture. My family are decent people, but we're not a wholesome Norman Rockwell painting."

"Who?"

"As part owner of an art gallery, you ought to know." He tightened his embrace. "We'll head back to Aspen. Gloria mentioned to Walter that she was returning home."

"Should we drive?"

"Yeah." He kissed her forehead. "I want to keep my

Glock with me, so we can't fly commercial. And I can't count on my buddy with the helo."

She glanced back at the museum. "It's probably for the best that I can't talk to your brother. I mean, there isn't really anything I can tell him about the murder."

"Begging to differ." Using his thumb and forefinger, he lifted her chin so she was looking up at him. "Tell me, Mallory. Who do you think killed Ty Rivera?"

"Conrad Burdock is a shady character. And Felix told us that Mom suspected my father was following her. He could be a murderer."

"Those are two suspects my brother doesn't have. You know a hell of a lot more than my brother."

But she didn't want to know. She wished her mind could be blissfully empty of all these terrible details of what had happened long ago before she was born. Her lighthearted mother had been an abused wife. She'd stolen a fortune in precious gems and changed her identity. Mallory had to wonder if she'd ever contacted her birth parents. Did Gloria have brothers and sisters? Someday, Mallory might wake up to find she had a dozen cousins. *But I can't complain*. Throughout her life, Mallory had enjoyed being with Mom, who was fun and funny, always attentive and encouraging. She'd made a great single mother. The best. And she wanted to stay in that world where they were happy and…innocent.

She wanted to build her future with sweet, sensual fantasies about her and Shane, joined together in the shower, talking and laughing. She longed for a real relationship, maybe more, maybe children. Ironically, she knew that Gloria would adore him—the man who claimed that he'd never hurt her. Deeply, deeply, deeply, Mallory wished she could follow this beautiful new path.

THE RENTAL CAR wasn't nearly as comfortable as Shane's Navigator, but Mallory was glad to be leaving the city and zipping along I-70 into the foothills, leaving rush hour behind. Denver was great, but Aspen was home. Before she made her phone call to Gloria, she needed to organize her thoughts. First, she needed to know what kind of arrangements Mom had made with Ty Rivera. Second, Gloria was undoubtedly returning to Aspen to pick up the Teardrop, and Mallory needed to know where she'd hidden it.

She glanced over at Shane. "You're sure Fordham recognized Mr. Sherman."

"Absolutely. Fordham even did his own parody of the way Drew Sherman talks. Phony-baloney, if you know what I mean."

"Are we thinking that she left the Teardrop with him for safekeeping?"

"It's a place to start looking, assuming she won't tell you."

The third thing she ought to bring up with Mom was Hannah Wye, the attorney. Mallory didn't know if Hannah was a legit lawyer or a flaky artist who dabbled in lawsuits. Gloria was going to need a criminal attorney to defend her against possible murder charges as well as the whole faking-her-death thing.

Last but not least, Mallory had to convince Mom to tell her where she was. She and Shane could pick her up and eventually turn herself over to law enforcement. Though Gloria had spent the past twenty-six years hiding from the authorities, that had to change. The murder of Ty Rivera sounded an alarm that couldn't be ignored. *Danger, danger, danger.* Someone—possibly Burdock, possibly her father or maybe even Amber—was willing to slash a man's throat to get what they wanted. If they got ahold of Gloria, it would be light's out.

In the meantime, she and Shane would keep Mom safe. Again, she looked toward him. Though she didn't trust him one hundred percent, she was beginning to depend on him. "Somehow, we've got to make her come with us so we can protect her."

"I have an idea."

"Shoot."

"Back in the old days when I had fans and groupies, especially in Aspen, I sometimes needed a place to go where I could be totally alone. I bought a tiny cabin in the middle of nowhere. It came in handy when I was in recovery and didn't want anybody to see me limping around."

"You have a secret hideout?"

He shrugged. "Call it a safe house. We can take Gloria there and barricade the doors."

With her seat belt fastened, she couldn't lean close enough for a real kiss. So she settled for stroking his cheek. "You're a genius."

"I know." Shane handed her a phone. "Call your mom. I already plugged in the number that Walter gave me. You can talk as long as you want on this. It's a prepaid mobile phone."

"A burner. Why do you have one?"

"I have several. They came with my how-to-be-a-great-private-eye kit," he said. "Burners are handy for all sorts of things. Use it. Then pitch it. Untraceable."

She dialed the number and listened to six rings before

Gloria answered with a squeaky, nasal voice that wouldn't fool anybody. *"Bonjour,"* she said, "this is zee wrong number."

"Mom, it's Mallory. We need to talk."

"Me first," Gloria said without the phony voice. "I called to let you know that I finally have everything worked out. By this time tomorrow, I'll be able to explain everything."

Tomorrow might be too late. Hoping to get Mom's attention, Mallory held her reaction and switched focus. "Does Mr. Sherman have the Teardrop?"

"How on earth did you figure that out? I'm impressed or, as Drew Sherman would say, I'm hob-nob-gobsmacked." She gave a raucous chuckle. Clearly, Gloria thought she'd solved all her problems and was sitting pretty. "Did his son tell you? I didn't know you and Josh were still friends."

"Are you going to pick up the diamond from him?"

"Well, I can't do that until tomorrow morning when the bank opens. He put it into his personal safe-deposit box, and it requires two keys to open the vault."

"And then what happens?"

"I made arrangements with a guy at the Museum of Nature and—"

"Ty Rivera," Mallory said. "He's a friend of Felix's."

"Well, you know everything, don't you? Anyway, Ty set me up for a meeting with an important person from Sierra Leone to hand over the Teardrop."

"I need details, Mom." Rivera hadn't been killed for a vague indication of a handoff. "What is this important person's name? Does Felix know him or her? Where will the meet take place? When?"

"None of those things are any of your concern."

As if she could keep from being concerned? Late afternoon was fading into twilight, a hazardous time to be on the road. "Are you driving, Mom? Maybe you should pull over while we talk. I have some bad news."

"Not about Amber, I hope. I've always felt terrible about leaving her behind. Do you think she can ever forgive me?"

Not unless you give her the diamond. "Just pull over."

"I could say the same to you, Mallory. Are you driving?"

"I'm not behind the wheel."

"Who is?"

Now wasn't the time to introduce her to Shane, though she'd technically already met him by phone the last time they talked. "Please, listen to me. I don't want you to drive while you're distracted."

"I'm hanging up now."

"Wait, wait, wait. Okay, we'll do this your way." *Was there ever any doubt that Gloria would wear me down?* "So, Mom, answer this for me. After all these years of hiding, why are you suddenly willing to trust the word of Rivera?"

"Recommendations from other gem dealers," Gloria said.

"Like who?" Despite an effort to stay cool, Mallory's temper was rising. "Fences? Thieves? Conflict diamond warlords? Criminals?"

"Don't be overdramatic, dear. Felix knows Rivera and can vouch for him."

Mallory didn't want to lapse into a futile argument but needed for Gloria to understand. "I want to help you. There's no need to do this by yourself."

"I have everything under control."

"Ty Rivera is dead. Murdered."

"No."

Gloria gasped. Mallory cringed. Maybe, just maybe, she finally realized what kind of risk she was taking. "Are you okay?"

"We had lunch together. I thought he might be flirting with me but more likely he was thinking about the Teardrop. Damn that stone. It brings nothing but pain and sorrow." She rambled, avoiding the difficult topic. "The food wasn't even that good. Some limp salad. Ty had the vegetarian chili."

"I get it. You ate at the T-Rex Café in the museum." Gently, Mallory reined her in. "There were witnesses. You were one of the last people to see Rivera alive."

"You make it sound like I'm a suspect."

"It might be smart to put a good attorney on retainer. Does Hannah Wye handle criminal cases?"

"Don't be ridiculous. I'm not a murderer."

"You can't pretend like this isn't happening." Desperation crept into her voice. "Mother, you're in danger."

"I can handle it."

"Let me help." She glanced over at Shane. "I know a safe house where you can hide out until this is settled. Where can we meet in Aspen?"

"That's not going to happen, especially not now. I'm not going to put you in danger."

Mallory flopped back against the seat. *Talk about a giant reversal.* All this time, she'd been protecting Gloria. Now the tables turned. "Trust me."

"You listen to me and pay attention. It's true that I messed up with Amber, but I did a good job raising you, and I'm not going to let a murderer attack you. Stay away from me. I forbid you to contact me again."

Taken aback, Mallory stared at the phone. Her mother wasn't the type of parent who forbade her from doing anything. When Mallory wanted to go on an overnight trip or skip school or try vodka, Mom had stepped aside and allowed her to make her own mistakes. Gloria was a cool mother, not the type to tell her she couldn't do something.

Gloria continued, "My way of parenting worked. You graduated at the top of your class with scholarship offers for college. You were popular, mostly drug-free and strong. Now, I'm giving you an order. Leave me alone."

"Don't you dare forbid me. I'm not going to stand around with my thumb up my nose while some diamond hunter attacks you."

"Goodbye, Mal. I love you."

The phone went dead.

"She hung up on me." Not a big surprise. Mom had decided not to cooperate and nothing would change her mind. Mallory looked to Shane. "Now what are we going to do?"

"Gotta find her," he said.

"In Aspen? Offhand, I can think of dozens of places she could hole up until tomorrow morning when the bank opens. Not to mention that there might be a killer tracking us down. As if that isn't enough, the police are going to be looking for us." One complication piled on top of another. "How are we going to search?"

"We have a secret weapon."

"What's that?"

"He ain't nothing but a hound dog." Shane tapped the side of his nose. "But Elvis can find anybody, anywhere."

Even when they don't want to be found.

Chapter Seventeen

By the time they drove the rental car into Walter Pulaski's gated community and parked in his triple driveway, twilight had merged into dark. The huge marble sculpture of a woman emerging from the snow in his front yard with her head tilted back and her arm extended was artistically lit. Revolving lights created the illusion that her long hair rippled in the breeze as her delicately sculpted hand reached for the stars. The effect mesmerized Shane. He thought the statue's impossible quest to grasp the heavens made her oblivious to the mundane concerns of everyday creatures. Much like Gloria, Pulaski's muse.

Starting twenty-six years ago, Mallory's mom had made a series of bad decisions. The latest—refusing their help—was risky for her and for them. Though he understood her pride and her unshakeable belief that she had life under control, her current decision impacted Mallory. He couldn't let things slide or pretend nothing was wrong, which seemed to be Gloria's default position. He needed to find her and the Teardrop.

Right now, things were about to get a whole lot better because Elvis would be rejoining the team. While in Denver, Shane had missed his canine partner. As he and Mallory walked up the shoveled sidewalk to the front door, he saw the black Lab bouncing up and down as if his feet were on springs. At the high point of each bounce, he peeked through the beveled glass window in the door.

As soon as Pulaski unlocked the door, Elvis leaped outside. Though the dog was trained not to jump on people, Shane had a signal to override that command. He went down on his good knee and held out his arms, which meant it was okay for Elvis to dive into his embrace, to lick his face and make all kinds of weird growls and joyful yips. His sleek furry body wriggled happily against Shane's chest. Was there anything better than the greeting from a loyal dog after being apart? Still excited, Elvis danced in a circle, shaking his shoulders and wagging his tail like a metronome gone wild.

Mallory copied Shane's pose, and Elvis pounced on her. Since she wasn't very large, the dog toppled her into the snow beside the shoveled walk. She let out a giggle and a shriek. Unapologetic, he stood over her, nudging her with his nose and licking while she laughed.

"I missed you," she said to the dog. "Our trip to Denver was terrible."

"Sorry to hear that," Pulaski said. "Come on in. I've got a pot of beef stew and homemade bread."

On the front stoop, Shane caught a whiff of the stew from the kitchen and realized that the sisterly fight had caused him and Mallory to skip lunch. "Great timing. I'm hungry."

She gave Pulaski a giant hug. "I'm so glad to see someone I can trust."

Could she? Shane had slotted Pulaski in the "good guy" column but intended to be careful in what he said and did.

The multi-million-dollar diamond made a powerful incentive for switching over to the dark side.

Before he entered the house, Shane glanced over his shoulder at the street and considered the imminent threat. Though Pulaski's house featured top-notch security and he employed two husky assistants who could also act as bodyguards, danger still existed. Pulaski's friendship with Mallory's mom was well-known. He'd been pulling that lady out of trouble ever since she moved to Aspen.

Following him inside, Shane asked quietly, "Any other contact from Gloria?"

"Only the one phone call to Mallory's number. You?"

While Mallory and Elvis went to the kitchen to dish up bowls of stew, Shane confided, "I suppose it won't come as a shock to you that she's being unreasonable."

"I'd expect no less." In a thoughtful gesture, he stroked his white beard. "Can you give me a recap?"

"She made an arrangement with Ty Rivera at the Museum of Nature and Science. Gloria was the last person to see him before he was killed—his throat slashed by an ancient Mesoamerican obsidian blade from one of the exhibits."

Pulaski exhaled a sigh. His eyes were weary and worried. "Are the police looking for her?"

"My brother's a cop. The Denver PD views her—and Mallory—as persons of interest in the murder. The Aspen police and Pitkin county sheriff have also been informed."

"Sounds to me like you and Mallory have nowhere to turn." He took his usual seat at the head of the table where a half-full snifter of brandy awaited his return. "What's next?"

"First, we eat. And then we locate Gloria and try to talk sense into her."

"Good luck with that."

When Mallory returned to the dining room with a bowlful of stew and a chunk of fresh bread, Elvis made his presence known. He rubbed against Shane's leg and looked up at him with a happy smirk as if to say, "Glad you're back. Don't ever leave me again." Then he went to Pulaski and rested his chin on the old man's knee.

As soon as she was seated, she asked, "Uncle Walter, how well do you know Felix Komenda?"

"The guy who sent those letters to Gloria? We've met. On one of his visits to Aspen, I spent some time with him. A lean handsome man," he said with a sigh. "And a sophisticated artist who modernizes themes and colors from folk art. On his chest, he has a tattoo of a kapok tree that stands in the middle of Freetown. When I asked about it, he told me the Cotton Tree is over two hundred years old and symbolizes freedom for the Black settlers of Sierra Leone."

Shane didn't ask how Pulaski knew what tattoo imprinted Felix's bare chest. These guys were entitled to their privacy, and Shane liked both of them. But he couldn't ignore the many connections Felix had with the Teardrop. He raised Amber, worked for her father and corresponded with Gloria. With roots in Sierra Leone, he might know Burdock, Ty Rivera and the mysterious person who would help Gloria deliver the diamond to those who needed it.

Felix seemed like a "good guy," but Shane had to wonder. He looked toward Mallory. "Why are you asking about Felix?"

"Trying to get my bearings and figure out what we do next. I'm thinking we should first visit Mr. Sherman."

Pulaski gave her a disbelieving look. "Drew Sherman the banker?"

In the kitchen, Shane filled a bowl with chunky beef stew containing potatoes, carrots, onions, parsnips and peas. He listened to Mallory explain how Fordham had seen Gloria with Sherman at the airfield. It seemed obvious that she'd given the Teardrop to the banker. But why hadn't he contacted the police when Gloria was reported missing? At least he should have told Mallory. Why was Sherman keeping that secret? Though it was hard to believe a man who claimed everything was hunky-dory could be part of a plot to steal the jewel, Shane needed to treat Sherman with the same level of suspicion as everyone else.

He took his place at the table opposite Mallory and dug into the hearty stew. He gave a long low moan that must have sounded like one he'd make while having sex because Mallory was staring at him with her eyebrows raised and a smart-aleck grin. He allowed pleasant memories to penetrate his mind and arouse his senses before speaking. "I don't think we should bother with Sherman tonight. Gloria said that he promised to keep the Teardrop in his personal safe-deposit box at the bank. Which means he can't access it until tomorrow."

"He might have lied to Gloria."

"Sure, but if he's being a loyal friend and hiding it for her, why lie? On the other hand, if he's aware of the danger associated with the gem, why keep it at his home?"

She dipped the heel of her bread into the last of her stew, soaking up the dark, rich mushroom gravy. "Where should we start searching?"

Though he wanted to drive out to the airfield and pick

up his Navigator, the anonymous rental vehicle offered more protection. "Your mother mentioned seeing Raymond DeSilva at the Hotel Jerome. Let's go there and show his photo around."

"Hold on." Pulaski waved his hands. "I thought DeSilva was dead."

"So did we," Mallory said. "Amber lied."

"A terrible deception. I'm so sorry, dear heart."

"It's just as well." She tossed her head and lifted her chin. "Amber and I want very different things. She's after the big payoff for selling the diamond, and I feel that it ought to be returned to Sierra Leone to benefit the people."

Elvis circled the table and sat by her, offering a sure signal of approval. Shane agreed. As far as he was concerned, the Teardrop was cursed until it was used for good.

THE MIDSIZE RENTAL sedan didn't meet with Elvis's approval. Shane had spoiled the diva dog by refurbishing the back of the Navigator into a cozy nest with an excellent view. Though he'd spread a couple of towels to protect the rear seat upholstery, Elvis couldn't get comfortable. Growling to himself, he paced from one side to the other and nudged the windows, an indication that the only way he'd like this mode of transportation was if he could hang his head out the window.

"Not gonna happen, buddy." Sitting behind the steering wheel, Shane craned his neck around to see into the back. "It's too cold to drive with the windows down, and we're supposed to be incognito. Everybody in town knows you."

Mallory reached between the seats to scratch the parallel worry lines between the Lab's eyebrows, if he'd had eyebrows. "You're too famous for your own good."

Elvis already wore his harness emblazoned with the words *service dog*, which ought to be enough to get him in the front door when they reached the downtown hotel. Shane had already called ahead to make sure his friend was working tonight and would be willing to talk about current guests. This interview couldn't be conducted over the phone since Shane had identification photos to show from his computer. The bad guys probably checked in using aliases.

He'd debated with himself about whether or not Mallory should be involved in this part of the investigation. His number one priority was to protect her from certain danger. If the police were involved, she'd be tucked away in a safe house with armed guards protecting her. Instead, they were on their own with little more than Shane's two Glocks to hold off the threat.

Leaving her with Pulaski hadn't been an option. Not only would she have refused to sit quietly on the sidelines, but Shane didn't feel right about putting her trusted old friend in peril. As he drove through the plowed but still snow-covered streets of Aspen toward Hotel Jerome, he considered asking her to stay in the car while he went inside. *Not a good solution.* If Mallory was alone, she made an easier target.

"I have a question," she said.

"Shoot."

"Well, I would. But I don't have a weapon." From the corner of his eye, he saw her smile before she said, "Har-de-har-har."

"Are you channeling Drew Sherman?"

"Making a point," she said. "You have two guns. One

in a shoulder holster and the other hooked to your belt. I should have one of those in my pocket."

Inwardly, he groaned. "You told me Gloria didn't approve of firearms. Have you ever even held a gun before?"

"I'm not a hunter, but I know the basics."

"I'll keep that in mind. For right now, I need you to concentrate on managing Elvis." Actually, the dog made a more intimidating weapon than a Glock. "His attack command is *g-e-t-e-m*. Drop his leash, point, give the command and watch this handsome rock star turn into Cujo."

At the hotel, he pulled up to the valet station, handed the guy a twenty and told him they'd be back in fifteen. Mallory held the leash as they entered the lobby. Hotel Jerome didn't have the high ceilings and ornate design of the Brown Palace, but the historic Aspen hotel had a uniquely Western charm with polished wainscoting, heavy furniture and mounted trophy heads of elk and deer on the walls. With Mallory and Elvis at his side, Shane approached the reception desk and nodded to his friend Kevin, who motioned for them to come around the desk into the office area. The front-desk clerk stood taller than Shane's six feet two and had an athletic build. Years ago, he'd come to the mountains as a ski bum. Now this was his home. He greeted Shane, gave Mallory a hug and hunkered down to shake paws with Elvis.

"We appreciate this," Shane said.

"Always happy to help my favorite private eye and his fur-ball sidekick." Kevin straightened his vest and stood. "What do you need?"

"These guys might be registered under fake names." He opened his tablet screen and showed the first photo.

"That's Felix Komenda. I don't remember seeing him

recently, but he stays here often. He's friends with Gloria. Good tipper." He gave Mallory a skeptical look. "I can't believe he did something bad."

"Neither can I," she said. "We're just covering all the bases."

Shane held up a photo of Raymond DeSilva, a handsome older gentleman with a groomed mustache and silver streaks at his temples. "How about this guy?"

Kevin nodded. "Yeah, he was here for a couple of days. Checked out this morning."

The timing struck Shane as being too coincidental. Amber and her father had arrived in Aspen at approximately the same time. "What name was he using?"

"I remember because it was an obvious alias. Raymond Chandler, like the guy who wrote the detective books. You know, Phillip Marlowe."

"I didn't know you were a reader."

"At night, it gets boring," Kevin said. "And I like a good *noir*."

Shane pulled up a snapshot he'd found of Conrad Burdock. Since Mallory actually saw Burdock, she had verified the identification. Hadn't been an easy search. Supervillains, like Burdock, didn't like to have their pictures taken. He showed the screen to Kevin.

"Whoa, you know him?" Kevin's surprise was genuine. "The ambassador?"

"Tell me more."

"He checked in five days ago with an entourage—all big guys who looked more like bodyguards than butlers. The ambassador is all class but friendly. Nice to the little people. He stopped at the desk himself to pick up a special delivery package and opened it right there. A bunch of muffin-type things from a bakery in Denver. The ambassador called them street cakes and offered me one."

"Nice," Shane said. Was Burdock a supervillain or a superhero?

"Totally delicious. And he's a handsome dude. In this job, I see a lot of beautiful people, but the ambassador was right up there at the top. His dark brown Versace jacket fit perfectly, and he had a humongous diamond pinkie ring."

"A diamond?"

"Huge diamond."

Shane exchanged a glance with Mallory before looking back at Kevin and asking, "Where is the ambassador from?"

"Someplace in Africa. He has a lapel pin with a blue, white and green flag. And a circle pin with a stylized picture of a tree."

"Freetown," Mallory said. "The Cotton Tree. And those are the colors of the Sierra Leone flag."

"Is he here?" Shane asked.

"Not on a Friday night. He and his entourage are out and about. The guy who pays all their bills asked where they could hear jazz and eat sushi. I made reservations. He tipped me a hundred bucks and passed on his thanks from the ambassador. Like I said, a class act."

And maybe a murderer.

Chapter Eighteen

Back in the rental car on their way to pick up the Navigator from the airfield where Shane had left it, Mallory hunched over the computer. In spite of occasional jostling in the passenger seat, her search of the internet quickly led to the ambassador to the United States from Sierra Leone. His multi-syllable British-sounding name wasn't Conrad Burdock, but his face belonged to the guy she'd met at the gallery.

"Everybody's got some kind of false identity." She leaned back in her seat and stared through the windshield at the cloudless night. "My father is pretending to be somebody else. My mother faked her death, and I can't begin to guess where she came up with the Gloria Greenfield name."

"Suits her," Shane said. "I've never met her, but the name makes me think of something bright and natural."

"That's her, all right." She continued her list of phony names. "The ambassador from Sierra Leone—with the last name of Lewiston-Blankenship—has his own alias."

"The first time we heard about Burdock was through Amber, right?"

"She claimed that he'd killed our father. Obviously, not

true. She also said the guys who chased us away from Reflections worked for him which he denied. Another lie?"

"Absolutely," Shane said. "Kevin's description of an entourage built like bodyguards fits the thugs in ski masks who came after us and made bullet holes in my car."

"An ambassador." She shook her head and sighed. Truly, there was no one or nothing she could trust.

"The fact that Burdock and your father were both staying at Hotel Jerome at the same time is suspicious. They might be working together."

"How does Amber fit into that picture?"

"She doesn't." He shrugged, but his tense grip on the steering wheel told her he was anything but nonchalant. "I think Amber is about to get the rug pulled from beneath her feet. One or both of those men are going to cut her out of the profits when they sell the Teardrop."

Mallory almost felt sorry for her sister. Amber dreamed of a vast fortune, enough wealth to live like a princess. Not much chance of that. By placing her trust in her slimeball father, she'd bet on the wrong horse.

Not that Mallory's loyalty to Gloria had paid off. "Do you think the ambassador is the person Ty Rivera arranged for Mom to meet?"

"I do."

She noticed how he kept checking the rearview mirrors, making sure they weren't being followed. Fortunately, there weren't many headlights on the road to the airfield. The major activity on a weekend would be in town with everybody yakking about the new snow and wondering when the slopes would open. The Hotel Jerome had just been starting to get busy when they left. "If Ty Rivera was working with the ambassador, why was he killed?"

"Loose ends," Shane said. "Rivera was a witness. Maybe he knew the ambassador was after the Teardrop and expected to receive a payoff. Or maybe Rivera honestly believed a high-ranking official from Sierra Leone would do the right thing. Either way, he'd be a liability...if and when these crimes come to light."

"What do you mean? What crimes?"

"Let's start with fraud. Who owns the diamond and how can they prove it? There's smuggling involved to get the jewel in and out of the country. Don't even get me started on political ramifications. In the worst-case scenario, violence erupts and somebody else gets killed. I don't need to remind you that the ambassador's thugs shot at us."

"Do you think they'd hurt Mom?"

A long moment of silence stretched between them. In a quiet voice, he said, "Yes."

Deep in her gut, she knew he was right. Her mother could be killed. Mallory's eyes squeezed shut. She turned off the computer and clenched her fingers into fists, holding onto fragile hope. Sensing her distress, Elvis poked his nose between the front seats and bumped her elbow, demanding a pet. She loosened her hand to stroke the soft fur on his head. The warm friendliness comforted her, though she was far from calm.

From the moment Gloria went missing, Mallory feared dire consequences, even before she knew the whole story. Mom shouldn't have gone off half-cocked, should have looked to Mallory for help, should have engaged a lawyer. Was it too late to make things right? "What can we do?"

A few more ticks of silence passed. "I know you don't want to hear this, but the murder of Ty Rivera makes the threat to your mom even greater. We should call the police. I can coordinate their actions through my brother."

"Sensible."

"Safe."

But she couldn't betray Mom's confidence, couldn't be the person to send her to prison. "Before we call in the cops, we have to find her."

"The cops can make our search easier. When you first discovered she was missing, you activated the entire town of Aspen, from forest rangers to the Pitkin County sheriff."

"That effort didn't turn out well," she reminded him. "I know Mom better than anybody else. With a little help from Elvis, I can find her."

He turned left onto the road that led to the hangars at the airfield. "I'm worried about you, Mallory. You could be next on the list of people who need to be eliminated."

Once again, his reasoning made sense. Another complication she didn't want to face. "I hadn't considered the threat to myself."

"I have." He parked beside his Navigator and killed the engine on the rental sedan. "You're the main thing I think about."

She unfastened her seat belt and twisted in her seat to embrace him. The midsize sedan had insufficient room for maneuvering, and Elvis got between them. But she managed to join her lips with his. His mouth tasted warm and familiar but exciting at the same time. Fighting the dog for Shane's attention, she pressed her upper body against his.

Though she didn't agree with everything he'd said, she understood his logic. And she actually appreciated his law-abiding attitude. Gloria had taught her the difference between right and wrong. "She's not really a criminal."

"A lot of decent people step outside the rules from time to time." He kissed her again. "Most of them don't get involved in international intrigues with twenty-million-dollar gems."

"Go big or go home." That was what Mom always said.

Elvis disentangled himself from their threesome, bounded into the back seat and ran to the window. Peering through the glass at the Navigator, he raised his chin and howled like a coyote seeing the moon.

"I think he wants to go back to your car," she said.

"You bet he does. It's cozy, and he's got a great view. The Navigator is like home on wheels." He unfastened his seat belt and opened the car door. "Let's go find Gloria."

SHANE POINTED THE 4WD Navigator—a vehicle both he and Elvis loved—back toward town. Their starting place had to be Gloria's house. Neither he nor Mallory thought her mom would be dumb enough to make that her hideout, but they needed to pick up an article of her clothing for Elvis to sniff before he got into serious tracking.

In the passenger seat beside him, Mallory was making plans, listing places her mom liked to hang out, including the back room of her favorite restaurant, an ex-lover's house and a mountain cave at the bottom of the towering cliff beside Reflections. She mumbled, "I doubt she'll go there in this weather."

"Probably not, but don't scratch anything off the list." If they found Gloria, he could convince mom and daughter to abandon the lone-ranger act and go to the police. His brother would be hacked off at him for not leveling with him, but Shane's loyalty rested with his client. Even if he wasn't falling for Mallory, he'd follow her wishes, which seemed to be coming into sync with his. Finally, he'd almost convinced her to seek help from the police. With full-on protection from law enforcement, they might all survive.

As he drove into the hills outside Aspen, he watched Mallory in a series of quick glances as she combed her fingers through her hair, pulled it together in a long tail and twisted it into a knot on top of her head. He looked forward to the moment when he would unfasten her barrette and allow her blond hair to tumble over her creamy white shoulders.

"Almost there," she said. "You remember the house, right?"

"Hard to forget."

"Mom has wild taste, and that's an understatement. She claims to be utterly nonjudgmental with a unique ability to recognize when an art object or a painting is inspired or skillfully done."

Gloria's logic was shaky, but she must be doing something right. Reflections had been successful in a competitive market. "Tell me more about the house."

"When she bought the half-acre property twenty-six years ago, she got a great deal. It was just a small A-frame in a clearing surrounded by pines."

"You were a newborn."

"And she was raising me by herself. A single mother starting life over with a new identity. You'd think that would be enough for her to handle, but noooo. Gloria never could sit still. Almost immediately, she started adding rooms to the house. A totally new kitchen. A playroom for me. A giant bedroom with a walk-in closet for her. The A-frame was always under construction."

He remembered his first impression of Gloria's house. Chaotic but warm. "How did you feel about the constant renovation?"

"Why are you asking? Are you my psychotherapist?" She shrugged. "I don't mean to sound defensive, but it seems like I've spent most of my life explaining Mom to people."

Taking care of Gloria. He didn't say those words out loud because he wasn't a shrink and didn't want to criticize or analyze Mallory. If she was okay with her Mom revamping the house, so was he. "Home improvement and DIY is a way of life for a lot of people."

"Nothing wrong with that."

After he drove the scary stretch of road at the edge of a cliff and rounded a few more curves, they arrived. The porch light was on as well as other strategically placed lights to emphasize the multilevel architecture that sprouted with inconsistent styles, materials and colors. A deep purple wall melted into a rock silo bordered by a modernistic cedar cube. A barn-sized structure with a southwest wall of glass looked like an artist studio. The overall effect, even at night, was kind of breathtaking.

More than the wild design, he noticed light shining from one of the lower windows and most of the second floor. "Somebody's here."

She pointed to a rental car. A black SUV. "The ambassador?"

The other car had parked in the driveway, which had been shoveled earlier in the day. Shane pulled in behind the other vehicle. Moving cautiously in case anybody inside was watching, he approached the SUV and slashed the rear right tire with a four-inch blade he kept in his glove compartment. This time, nobody would be able to chase them. Then, he went to the back of the Navigator, opened the door for Elvis and gave a single command. "Quiet."

The Lab hopped out and stood beside him in a silent alert stance. In the brief time he'd been separated from Elvis, Shane had missed this level of unflagging obedience. "Good dog."

When Mallory stepped out of the door, he warned, "Don't slam it."

She carefully closed the door and tiptoed through the snow toward him. "Now might be a good time to give me a weapon."

"Not yet. You're in charge of Elvis. Do you remember the command for attack?"

"It's *g-e-t-e-m*."

"Follow me."

Reaching inside his parka, he drew the Glock from his shoulder holster and held it at his side as he followed a shoveled sidewalk to the front porch of what was probably the original A-frame. The front door showed no signs of being broken into, and the handle twisted easily. Unlocked.

Mallory stayed behind him with Elvis at her side. For her, this had to be a weird way to enter the house where she'd spent much of her life. The black-and-white-tiled foyer reflected another era—maybe the roaring '20s—with deco statues, ornate framed paintings and two small antique oak tables. Shuffling noises could be heard and seemed to be coming from the second floor. The intruder or intruders made a lot of noise, opening and closing doors and drawers. They didn't seem to care about being overheard.

Exchanging a look with Mallory and with Elvis, Shane

raised his weapon and ascended the carved oak staircase to the peaked second floor of the A-frame where lavish Persian rugs covered the floors. A dusky rose paint covered the upper walls in a sitting room with a peaked ceiling at the top of the "A" and dark oak trim.

He followed the noises to a door beyond the original A-frame. If he had to guess, he'd say this was Gloria's bedroom with the walk-in closet. Before entering, he assessed the possibilities. With no idea how many people he might be facing or whether they had guns, he wanted to protect Mallory and Elvis. First disarm the enemy.

With a hard shove, he pushed the door. It swung wide and crashed against the wall. In a two-handed stance, Shane took aim. "Show me your hands."

The man stood beside a long dresser with the top drawer open. He wore a gray parka and a black knit cap. He whirled, dropped to one knee and raised his handgun. Felix!

Before Shane could react, Mallory shouted the command. "Get 'em, Elvis."

The dog flew past him. Though Felix lifted his hands in immediate surrender when he recognized Shane, Elvis had been given his order. He bashed into Felix, knocking him flat on his back. His jaws closed around the wrist that had been holding the gun.

"Down." Shane stalked across the room. "Down, Elvis. It's okay. You're a good boy."

The black Lab released his grip and lowered himself onto the floor with his chin on his front paws. A low growl rumbled in his throat.

Mallory rushed to Elvis and knelt beside him. She cooed and kissed the dog's smooth furry head, lightening his mood and causing his tail to thump. "Such a good boy. You're a star."

Straightening her spine, she glared at Felix. "And you're an ass. Did you break in? You could have been shot and killed."

"The dog is fierce," Felix said.

"Only when he needs to be." Shane studied the sleeve of Felix's parka where Elvis had chomped down just hard enough to tear the fabric. He'd been trained to take down the enemy and neutralize them, not to harm them unless commanded to do so. Shane had never needed to test his dog's lethal instincts.

"I did not break in. Gloria gave me a key a long time ago."

"Which still doesn't give you the right to come and go without permission." Mallory jabbed an index finger at his chest. "Have you spoken to her?"

"I have not. Many times, I tried to reach her by phone. She will not answer." His gaze darted around the room. "I must warn you. I did not come to this house alone."

Bad news. Shane looked over his shoulder toward the door. Of all the villains who could have accompanied Felix, the most toxic was the woman who strode through the door with her Beretta clutched in her manicured hand but not aimed at him. Her turquoise eyes—so like Mallory's—narrowed in a hostile glare.

"I'm not here to hurt anybody," she said, "especially not your stupid dog, but Ty Rivera's murder freaked me out."

Shane figured he might as well try to get some useful info from Mallory's sister. "Who do you think killed him?"

"That's obvious." She waved her gun impatiently. A

gesture that made him nervous. "The killer had to be Conrad Burdock. Or one of his hired thugs."

"You're referring to a man who was staying at Hotel Jerome with his entourage. The ambassador from Sierra Leone."

Felix's expression showed confusion and concern. Amber—who was a much better actress—protested loudly that she didn't know what he was talking about. "Burdock is a thief, a criminal. He followed me here and has been trying to—"

"No more lies." Shane had just about had it with Amber. "The ambassador checked into the hotel five days ago. I'm guessing it was shortly after Gloria visited the pawnbroker in Brooklyn. That's what inspired you to take up the chase for the Teardrop, and it must have done the same for Ambassador Lewiston-Blankenship."

"You're the liar," Amber said.

She pointed her gun at his chest, and Shane had to wonder if prodding Amber was the best strategy. "The man you call Burdock was in Aspen before you."

"Put down your gun and stop threatening us." Mallory stepped into the argument. "We know you arrived in town at almost the same time as your father, Raymond DeSilva."

"He's here?" Amber's fuss and bluster turned into tears. She lowered the gun. "He didn't tell me."

"Maybe you aren't his favorite person, after all."

"I don't have to listen to this." She swabbed moisture from her cheeks. "The Teardrop belongs to me."

"Is that why you're here? To search?"

"Duh! Isn't that why you're here?"

"We came to find something with Mom's scent. For Elvis to use in tracking."

"Cute." Amber pivoted and stalked away.

"She'll be back," Shane said to Felix. "I slashed one of your tires."

He exhaled a weary sigh. "Is it true? Burdock and the ambassador are one and the same."

"You knew Rivera, right?"

"Yes."

"Do you think he intended to refer Gloria to the ambassador?"

"I believe so," Felix said. "But Rivera is a respected gemologist. I find it unlikely that he would associate with Burdock. I fear this mistaken identity was engineered by someone very clever, namely Raymond DeSilva."

Shane had come to a similar conclusion.

Chapter Nineteen

Leaving Amber and Felix to deal with the flat tire at Mom's house, Mallory and Shane set out to track Gloria using a couple of T-shirts from the dirty clothes hamper. One featured a logo for Save the Whales. The other advertised the Jimi Hendrix Experience. Sitting in the passenger seat of the Navigator, she sniffed the unique scent of Gloria Greenfield, a mixture of oil paint, turpentine, the balsamic vinegar she often used on salads, lavender and a hint of patchouli. She hoped these faint fragrances would be enough to do the job. "Do you really think Elvis can find her?"

"Like I told you before, his sense of smell is ten thousand times more sensitive than ours." Shane drove toward a more populated area of Aspen. "I think we should start at your house. Gloria might seek places that are more familiar."

"Agreed. All she needs is a hideout until tomorrow morning when she can pick up the Teardrop from the bank."

"Is the bank open on Saturday?"

"Until noon," she said.

"What's going to happen after she has it?"

She'd been considering possibilities. Mom had held the Teardrop in her possession for twenty-six years and kept it, fearing the valuable gem would fall into the wrong hands.

Also, she realized that as soon as her story was known, she had to face the consequences. Mallory didn't like her answer but realized it had to be. "We go to the police."

"My brother can help."

"Maybe."

She appreciated that Shane didn't gloat. Instead, he seemed genuinely concerned about what would happen to Mom, a woman he'd never met. Mallory sighed. "I'll stand by her, no matter what. And I'll make sure she has a terrific attorney."

Though she hoped and prayed that everything would turn out all right, she couldn't count on happily-ever-after. Mom's vanishing act had overturned her life. She didn't know what to believe or which way to go. Nothing made sense. Her carefree mom had been an abused wife who undertook desperate measures to save herself. Unbelievable! Her past held so much sorrow. It seemed impossible for a loving person like Gloria to abandon her child. Which pointed out another big change in Mallory's life. She had a sister! And a father who was still alive and, by all accounts, an evil, vicious, malevolent human being.

She gazed through the darkness at Shane and allowed herself to smile. Meeting him signaled a change in the right direction. For a long time, the idea of a significant relationship didn't fit into her future. She'd put romance on the back burner, allowing it to simmer like an ex-boyfriend stew and never really expecting to find a mate. Then she'd tumbled into Shane's embrace, and she never wanted to leave. Happily-ever-after? Maybe so.

He parked the Navigator in front of her house. The porch lamp lit on a timer as it always did after sunset. Same for a lamp in the dining room. Her sidewalk hadn't been shoveled since this morning but was clear enough to walk on without slipping. There didn't appear to be any indication that Gloria had been here.

When Elvis climbed down from the back of the Navigator, he was all business. Shane poured water into a collapsible bowl for the dog and changed his harness to the search-and-rescue vest he'd been wearing the first time she saw him. He looked to Mallory as though awaiting some instruction.

"Okay, Elvis. Here's the deal," she said. "We're searching for Gloria. She's the person you were looking for at the base of the cliff near Reflections. I have a couple of her shirts. Hope that's enough to give you the scent."

Though she knew the Lab didn't understand most of the words she spoke, Elvis was a better listener than most people she knew. At least he paid attention.

While she unlocked the front door, Shane gave Elvis a chance to get familiar with Gloria's scent before entering the house. He also talked to the dog, much the same way she had. Elvis was the third partner in their little team, their family.

Shane gave the command. "Elvis, search."

Inside her house, she noticed that Shane held the Glock he'd taken from his shoulder holster, ready for return fire if they were attacked. She followed Elvis into the kitchen. On the countertop, she saw a newly opened package of chocolate and macadamia cookies, Mom's favorite. "Good boy, Elvis. That's a clue."

"He's good at his job."

"So are you," she said.

"Glad to hear you say that." He caught hold of her hand

and pulled her toward him. "I might need for you to write me a recommendation."

She glided toward him and wrapped her arms around his middle. With her head tilted back, she gazed into his golden-brown eyes. "I'd definitely recommend you. You're so good at so many things. Maybe too good. Maybe I shouldn't tell anybody else about you and hire you for a permanent position."

He kissed her, starting with a gentle pressure and escalating. At the same time, he tightened their embrace, until she felt like they were joined together. A happy ending and a new beginning at the same time.

The kiss ended, and he loosened his hold on her. With a grin, he said, "I'll take the job."

In the upstairs bedroom, they spotted a note in the same place she'd left her original "I'll be back" message. Mallory picked it up and read, "I love you, Mallie Monster. Don't want you to be hurt. Please, please, please don't try to follow me."

Mallory talked at the sheet of paper torn from a spiral notebook. "Too late, Mom. We're already on the trail, and we're going to rescue you. Whether you like it or not."

Shane signaled to her. "Let's go, Elvis is on the move."

The dog had returned to the front door where he stood, apparently waiting for them to catch up. "What's going on?" she asked. "Does he want to go out?"

"We need to follow him." Shane gave Elvis another whiff of Mom's shirts and opened the door. "I'm guessing Gloria left the house."

"Sharp deduction, Sherlock."

"Just try to keep up."

She found it hard to believe that Elvis could track

Mom's scent through the snow, but the dog kept his nose down and his tail pointed straight up. He moved swiftly while she and Shane struggled to keep pace. A gust of chill wind slapped her cheeks. Her boots tread carefully on the cleared but icy sidewalk.

Elvis led them down the street to the corner and from there to nearby Reflections. The parking lot hadn't been shoveled. Tire tracks of various sizes crisscrossed the snow, but no vehicles were parked there. It made sense for Mom to come here. Reflections probably would have been next on their list of places to search.

Elvis stood at the back door, looking at them over his shoulder. He gave a woof, as if telling them to hurry up.

Stumbling across the ridges of ice and snowdrifts, a sense of anticipation ratcheted up inside her. They might come face-to-face with her mother. No matter the final outcome, the drama that had started twenty-six years ago might finally grind to a conclusion.

Shane reached the door first, twisted the handle and shoved. It opened with a squawk, and Elvis immediately poked his nose inside. Mallory was right behind him.

"Wait," Shane said softly. "We don't know who or what is inside. I should go first. Down, Elvis."

The dog obeyed.

Though her heart revved at high speed, she agreed. Shane had the weapon and could protect them. She took a step backward and watched as he entered the mudroom where she'd changed from her boots to her green clogs almost every day. Using the Maglite from a shelf by the door, he checked out the room, then gestured for her and Elvis to follow him into the kitchen, where the overhead lights were already turned on.

Considering all the time she spent at Reflections, the place ought to be as familiar as her own home. But tonight, she saw the kitchen through different eyes, influenced by fear and apprehension. The pans hanging on a circular rack above the butcher-block table glinted brightly. An anxious, ceaseless hum from the refrigerator and meat locker stirred the air. The cutlery betrayed sharp edges. So many things could go wrong.

Elvis circled the prep tables in the kitchen, still sniffing. After a brief pause at the industrial-size oven, he went to the swinging door that led into the gallery and coffee shop. Out there, the gallery display area was huge, filled with nooks and alcoves. Following Mom's path, Elvis had his work cut out for him.

Before going through the swinging door, Shane whispered to her, "Lights on or off?"

"I can find my way around in the dark," she said, "and there ought to be enough glow from moonlight through the windows in the coffee shop."

"Elvis can search without lights, but can you?"

Good point. If Mom was determined to hide, she could make herself invisible in a shadowy corner. And if the bad guys had already arrived, they could be anywhere. "Lights on."

Passing through the swinging door, she flicked the switch that illuminated the coffee shop and the front area. The aroma of fresh brew told her that Gloria had been here. Three used cups sat in the middle of a table by the window. *Three cups.* She'd had company.

Bracing for the worst, Mallory hit the light switches by the front door. At first glance, nothing seemed out of place. Gloria might have already come and gone. If bad

guys were here, she'd probably already alerted them by
turning on the lights.

"Mom, are you here?" Her voice stayed at a conversational level. She cleared her throat and called out more
loudly, "Gloria? Where are you? Mom?"

"Let's keep moving." Shane gave her a hug. "We'll find
her."

Following Elvis saved them a lot of time. The dog
didn't bother with the basement area where Mallory taught
classes and paintings were stored. Elvis skirted most of
the displays and went directly to the staircase leading to
the narrow upstairs gallery outside the offices. From that
vantage point, they could look down on the entire gallery.

With her boots clanging on every step, she charged up
the metal stairs with Shane following. He'd moved from
the front of the pack to the rear, and she noticed that he
held his Glock at the ready and was constantly scanning,
looking for threats. On the balcony, she leaned against
the iron railing and looked down on the displays of paintings, photographs and sketches. She saw the garish sky
paintings by Fordham, the pilot, and dainty watercolors
of hummingbirds by Hannah Wye, the lawyer.

Mom was nowhere in sight. Elvis went down the cor-
ridor leading to offices but didn't pause outside any of the
closed doors. Instead, the dog returned to the staircase
and descended. His toenails clicked against the metal.
He loped around the edge of the displays and returned to
the coffee shop.

"Where's he going?" she asked Shane as she chased
after the dog.

"Not sure, but we better follow."

Elvis paced back and forth in front of the tall window

panels that looked out on the sculpture garden where several of Uncle Walter's pieces were on display, ranging from an abstract grizzly bear to his trademark goddesses to several baby bunnies. Not that they could see details. The bright light in the coffee shop obscured the darkness beyond the windows, and moonlight didn't provide enough illumination to see anything more than vague shapes of white marble.

Squinting hard, Mallory could make out the two-foot-tall stone retaining wall at the edge of the garden, meant to be a barrier to protect unwary hikers from the seven-hundred-foot drop. In years past, it hadn't proven effective. At least five climbers had fallen to their deaths.

"What is it, Elvis?" Shane hunkered down to talk face-to-face with his search dog. "What did you find?"

The dog stood up on his hind legs and pressed his nose against the window glass. Something must be out there. At the far end of the windows near the coffee maker, Mallory flipped several light switches to activate spotlights in the sculpture garden. Much of the snow had melted on this western-facing patch of land that spread to the edge of the cliff.

She saw Gloria, tied to a life-size sculpture of Artemis, goddess of the hunt. A heavy rope around Mom's waist bound her to the white marble statue, but one hand had broken free. Visibly trembling, she reached toward the window.

Mallory gasped. Paralyzed by shock, her feet rooted to the floor. Her hand thrust forward as if she could break through the glass and rescue Mom.

Gloria's hand fell limply to her side. Her head drooped forward.

Chapter Twenty

Shane squeezed Mallory's shoulders and whispered, "Stay here with Elvis. I'll bring her inside."

She ought to go with him. This was her fight, not his. But it took all her strength to remain standing and not collapse in a heap on the floor. Her fingertips touched the ice-cold glass. Her gaze riveted on Mom. She must be so terribly cold, wearing only a light windbreaker and no mittens. When she raised her hand, her fingers clenched into a grotesque claw.

Stumbling toward a table, Mallory sank into a chair beside the window. Beside her, Elvis paced back and forth, expelling nervous tension, and then the dog halted and stood at attention, staring through the glass. Shane had entered the sculpture garden. Gun in hand, he made his way through the snow toward Gloria. He reached her and enfolded her in a hug. Mallory leaped to her feet, knocking over the chair where she'd been sitting. She couldn't hear what he was saying but knew he was speaking to Mom, offering reassurances.

Gloria nodded. Her eyes opened to slits. Mallory could tell that she was in pain. But still alive, damn it, she was still alive.

Shane had to put down his weapon to untie the knots

on the rope that held Gloria against the sculptured hunt-ress with her bow and arrow. Though his fingers worked quickly, the minutes felt as slow as hours.

Gloria pointed. Shane twisted to look over his shoulder. A shot rang out.

A man dressed in black and wearing a ski mask aimed his handgun at Shane and Gloria. He must have missed because neither appeared to be injured. Shane dove to the ground to pick up his Glock. He rose to one knee, aimed and fired.

The masked man let out a yelp, loud enough for Mallory to hear through the triple-paned glass. He ducked behind a sculpture of a buck with an intricate eight-point rack and fired again.

Shane was on the move, drawing fire away from Mom, who had loosened the ropes and fallen to the snow-covered earth. Shane was in greater danger. From the time they first met, he'd warned her that he wasn't a sharpshooter, but he'd hit the attacker on the first try and now he nicked the antlers on the marble deer.

At the retaining wall on the edge of the garden, Shane angled for a better shot.

The masked man fired three times in rapid succession. Shane flinched. He was hit.

Helpless, she watched as his legs gave out. His body twisted. He fell over the retaining wall and disappeared from sight.

A guttural scream tore from her throat. With both hands, she banged against the window. Shane was gone. *This can't be happening.* She couldn't believe the cliff had claimed another victim, but she'd seen him fall. The man who shot him went to the retaining wall, looked over and shrugged. Shane's death meant nothing to him.

Elvis took off running. She didn't know which way he'd gone, couldn't remember the command that would stop him. Her only thought was revenge. If she couldn't have Shane back, she wanted to destroy the men who'd killed him. Under her breath, she muttered, "Get 'em, Elvis. Get 'em."

Through the window, she watched as another masked man lifted her mother and threw her over his shoulder like a sack of potatoes. Did he mean to fling her over the cliff?

"No!" she yelled. "Don't hurt her."

"Calm down," said a smooth baritone voice behind her. "We're not going to kill Gloria. That would be foolish. We need her to collect the diamond."

She turned and faced the man she'd known as Conrad Burdock. "You must be the Ambassador."

"I suppose I am." He went to the coffeepot and poured himself a mug. "It's unfortunate you discovered that connection. I can't have you talking to the Sierra Leone Embassy, can I?"

"You're a monster." Rage overwhelmed her sorrow. She wanted this man dead. "Why would you force my mother to stay out in the snow?"

"As I mentioned before, I don't want to kill Gloria, but I need her to work with me. She was being uncooperative, and I thought the cold might change her mind." He sipped his coffee. "This is a very nice brew."

"Choke on it."

"I'm so glad you're here. Your mother couldn't be convinced to work with me in spite of pain and cold. But I think she'll feel differently about threats to you, her darling daughter."

"You don't scare me."

"Then, you are a fool."

Mallory returned to the window. Elvis had gotten outside and positioned himself at the edge of the retaining wall where Shane had fallen. When one of the men in black approached the dog, Elvis bared his teeth and growled. The masked man backed off.

Elvis sat beside the wall. He tilted back his head and howled, long and low, commencing a loyal dog's vigil for his fallen master.

CLINGING TO THE granite face with one hand, Shane tried to recall details from when he had been here before, standing at the base of the cliff, looking up and thinking about the good old days when he'd guided groups on extreme skiing adventures that sometimes required him to do rock climbing. He had a knack for discovering the best route across a supposedly impassible wall of stone. If he hadn't been shot in the left shoulder, making his arm useless, and had been wearing better shoes for climbing, he could have easily maneuvered his way to the top. The snow didn't bother him. He was a skier and had dressed for the cold.

When he fell over the retaining wall, survival had been topmost in his mind. He'd skidded down the rock face over an outcropping that hid him from view from above. And he slowed his fall by grabbing every rocky protrusion and dangling root until he found purchase on a ledge about twelve feet from the lip and wide enough for him to stand flat-footed. He caught his breath and took stock of his situation.

In the garden above him, he heard Elvis setting up a howl. If he continued, one of the thugs would undoubtedly shoot him. Shane whispered the command, "Down, boy. Get down."

The howl ended immediately. Shane imagined the dog with his belly on the ground and his head resting on his front paws. But when he looked up, he saw the face of the black Lab peering down at him. "You heard me, Elvis. Get down."

He figured Elvis would prevent any of the masked men from coming closer to look for him. If they did, he wasn't helpless. True, he'd lost one of his guns in the fall. But he had another in his belt holster. Not that he wanted to get into a shoot-out. Blood seeped from his wound, and his shoulder felt numb. Plus, he didn't know how many of the enemy he'd be facing. Earlier, they'd encountered four attackers who worked for the ambassador, who made five. And there was Raymond DeSilva to consider.

The best option for his survival and that of Mallory and her mom meant calling for backup. Balancing precariously, he dug into his pocket and pulled out his phone. Activating the screen took some tricky maneuvering, but he got it working only to discover that his phone was fully charged but there were no bars. Not a big surprise. Not many people tried to make calls while dangling off the edge of a seven-hundred-foot cliff in the high Rockies above Aspen.

The irony struck him. Finally, he had a legitimate reason to call in the police, but his phone didn't work. If he hadn't been losing blood and feeling dizzy, he would have laughed.

Only one thing to do. He had to climb up a vertical rock face, crash into Reflections and overwhelm an unknown number of armed thugs. Not the first time in his life that he'd faced an impossible challenge. He could do it. He had great motivation, and her name was Mallory.

MALLORY HUGGED HER MOM, sharing bodily warmth. Cold as ice, Gloria shivered in her arms. Mallory took off her parka and wrapped it around her. Still not enough. Gloria's fingers showed signs of hypothermia.

Mallory snapped an order at one of the men who worked for the ambassador. "Go to the mudroom behind the kitchen and get me a couple of blankets. And take off that stupid ski mask. You look like a joke."

The ambassador nodded to him. "Do it."

She glared at him. "Leave us alone."

He swept a bow to Gloria. "I apologize for the inconvenience, but I must insist on your cooperation. Where is the diamond?"

Obstinately, Gloria shook her head.

"You're stoic when it comes to your own safety. But how do you feel about punishment inflicted on your child?" He snatched Mallory's long hair and yanked her toward him. His arm snaked around her middle, and he squeezed her upper arm so tightly that she yelped.

"Stop it," she snapped. "I'll be happy to tell you where the Teardrop is."

"No," her mom said.

"It doesn't matter. He can't get to it." She faced the ambassador. "In a safe-deposit bank at Fidelity Union Bank. The box belongs to Drew Sherman, a bank vice president. If you threaten him, the police will be involved."

"I don't believe you."

"Call Mr. Sherman. Before you start threatening him,

consider the potential charges for bank robbery." She took the blankets from the guy who'd gone to the mudroom and tucked them around Mom's legs and shoulders. "By the way, did you murder Ty Rivera?"

He cleared his throat. "Certainly not."

"I'll rephrase," Mallory said. "Did you or one of your hired goons take a blade from a museum exhibit and slash his throat?"

"Why would anyone do such a thing?"

She knew the answer. "Because he thought you were the ambassador. But Gloria could identify you as your alter ego, Conrad Burdock, a criminal. I'm guessing you've used your political status to stay out of trouble with the law. Rivera could have ended that deception."

"And now," he said coldly, "you and Gloria know my secret. I arranged for the death of Ty Rivera."

Their chances for survival looked slim. She had to think fast, to come up with something that would cause him to hesitate and allow them to escape. "Earlier, you called me and suggested that we work together against Amber. Do you remember?"

He refreshed his coffee without offering any to her or Mom. "You should have accepted. There was no need for us to be enemies."

"We can still be partners."

She went to the coffee machine. Standing this close to the ambassador, Mallory struggled to restrain herself. There were weapons at hand. Hot coffee. The glass carafe. She might even find a knife in one of the drawers. But that revenge would be a short-lived pleasure. She kept herself under control, dumping the used grounds and brewing a fresh pot of coffee. While learning how to make sales at

Reflections, Mom had taught her about bargaining. Wait for the other person to speak first.

"What do you propose?" the ambassador asked.

"In the morning, Mom and I will go to the bank. You'll have to trust us to fetch the Teardrop and bring it to you. After that, we'll trust you to grant us our freedom."

"Why wouldn't you turn me over to the police?"

"Because we'd also go to jail. Mom stole the Teardrop." He still looked dubious, so she added, "And you'll pay us $200,000, which is about one percent of the worth."

The criminal alter ego of the ambassador understood her plan. "You have a deal."

"Now I'd like to take Mom home so she can rest and recover."

Mallory exchanged a grin with Mom. Truly, the acorn didn't fall far from the tree. She had no problem lying and making a deal with a criminal. She'd been born to it.

WITH A FINAL burst of strength, Shane hauled himself over the edge of the retaining wall and lay flat against it, breathing heavily while Elvis licked his face. The spotlights in the garden had been turned off, and he doubted anyone could see them in the shadows. The frozen night surrounded him. Snow permeated his clothing, but his shoulder wound flamed with dark wet heat. He was still losing blood. Not much time left before he passed out.

With his back leaning against the wall, he pulled the Glock from his belt holster. Staggering to his feet, he peered through the windows at the interior of the coffee shop. Mallory served a mug of coffee to her mom, who was swaddled in mismatched blankets. The ambassador, alias Burdock, strutted through the tables and chairs.

Shane saw two armed men who no longer wore masks. One of them must have been the guy he shot in the garden. Both his right leg and right wrist were bandaged. Shane figured the other two had been assigned to protect the front and back doors of Reflections, which meant he only had to get past one guard. And then what?

He took out his phone, glad to see the screen light up and he had bars indicating he could make a call. He tapped speed dial for his brother. The call went through.

Shane's strength was fading. He had to talk fast while his brain was still working and he made sense. "Logan, I'm at Reflections in Aspen. There are at least five men holding Mallory and her mom hostage. One of them probably killed Ty Rivera. I need backup."

"I'm on it, bro. I know the chief of police in Aspen. They'll be there pronto."

"Hostage situation," he repeated. "They can't go in with guns blazing."

"Got it," Logan said. "Mallory Greenfield is the woman you're working for, right? You care about her. I get it. Just don't do anything stupid."

"Count on it."

Shane ended the call and headed toward the rear door with Elvis following close behind. He didn't intend to do anything dumb but hoped to disarm the situation before the police arrived and everything got crazy. Mallory needed him. Now.

At the rear entrance, he saw a guy in a ski mask standing under the porch light, almost as though waiting for Shane to sneak up to him and knock him unconscious with the butt of his Glock, which was exactly what he did. Shane dragged the guy into the mudroom. In the masked man's pocket, Shane found a zip tie and used it to fasten his wrists behind his back. He turned the ski mask into a gag.

He crept through the kitchen and stopped at the swinging door. His shoulder wound began to throb. Still bleeding, he needed for this to be over. But he couldn't charge into the coffee shop while outnumbered and outgunned. He needed a distraction.

As if on cue, Amber slammed the front door and entered Reflections. In a loud near-hysterical voice, she demanded to know where the diamond was. "When will I get my share?"

He heard Gloria's faint voice. "My beautiful daughter, can you ever forgive me?"

"No. Never."

"I tried to do what was best."

"Best for you," Amber said. "Not for me."

He wondered where Felix was. He must have changed the tire and given Amber a ride here. Felix would be on Shane's side. He might even the odds.

Shane opened the swinging door enough that he could see when another person entered from the front. An older man, tall and handsome with silver streaks at his temples. Raymond DeSilva.

He swaggered toward the coffee shop and held his arms wide open. "Daddy's home."

Shane needed to take advantage of the chaos, but he didn't want Elvis involved. Even though the dog was trained to attack, he couldn't stop a bullet. "Stay," Shane ordered. "Elvis, you need to stay here."

The dog looked up at him with a wise, patient gaze that told Shane he understood. At the same time, Elvis gave a low dangerous growl. He was ready for a fight.

Shane crept toward the coffee shop where Amber argued with her father about how they should handle the situation. She seemed to think the plan hatched by Mallory and the ambassador would cut them out of the money. He was more inclined to take absolute control. When Gloria piped up, DeSilva whirled and slapped her hard, knocking her from the chair where she'd been huddled in blankets.

To his surprise, Amber responded, "It's true what Felix said about you. You're abusive, a predator."

"I'm the guy who paid your bills, little girl. You'll give me the respect I deserve."

"What happens if I don't? Are you going to hit me, too?" Amber whipped out her handgun. "Don't even think about it."

Mallory helped her mom back into the chair and placed herself in the middle of the argument. "Everybody settle down."

"Don't push me," DeSilva said with a sneer as he drew his gun.

"Go ahead and shoot," she confronted him. "You think you have a lot to lose, but it's only money. Tonight, I had everything taken away. My heart is broken. The man I love is dead."

Shane entered the coffee shop. His Glock aimed at DeSilva. "Drop it."

Before he could react, Amber fired her weapon. The bullet hit her father's gun, causing him to drop it. Amber laughed. "Daddy did an excellent job of teaching me how to handle firearms."

Shane turned his weapon on the ambassador and his men. "I've got you covered. No false moves."

From outside, he heard police sirens wailing. So much

for the subtle approach from the Aspen cops. The threat was enough to disarm the ambassador's men, who would all be arrested.

Mallory found her place beside him with his one good arm wrapped around her. Her incredible turquoise eyes filled with tears as she looked up at him. She whispered, "When I thought you were dead, I knew. You're the love of my life. I want to be with you forever."

"Yes," he said.

Forever and ever.

TEN MONTHS LATER in late summer, Mallory made good on her proposal. The wedding would be held in the sculpture garden at Reflections, where she thought she'd lost Shane forever. Mom had served a six-month sentence in a low-security prison in Englewood and would be on probation for five years. The light sentence came as a result of intervention from the Sierra Leone government, which was thrilled to once again have possession of the African Teardrop. The plans were to sell it and use the proceeds for schools. The new ambassador from Sierra Leone planned to attend the wedding.

Amber would serve as maid of honor. She still wasn't happy about losing out on the millions from the sale of the Teardrop but received a regular paycheck for opening a Reflections gallery in Brooklyn and handling uncle Walter's sculptures.

Logan Reilly would act as Shane's best man.

Standing at the edge of the garden, Mallory held Drew Sherman's elbow. He would escort her to the minister who stood before a bower of flowers. He leaned down to kiss her cheek. "You look real fancy-schmancy in that lacy white dress."

"Okey dokey."

Elvis in his red leather harness with the silver studs pranced down the aisle ahead of her, carrying their rings in a pouch. She had to admit that the dog was pretty cute, but her entire field of vision was filled by Shane, who looked amazing in his tuxedo. Shane Reilly was the best thing that had ever happened to her, and it was almost worth going through the tribulation of nearly losing her mother to find him. *Almost worth it.*

* * * * *

INTRIGUE

Seek thrills. Solve crimes. Justice served.

Available Next Month

Keep reading for an excerpt of a new title
from the Intrigue series,
CONARD COUNTY: MURDEROUS INTENT
by Rachel Lee

Prologue

Krystal Metcalfe loved to sit on the porch of her small cabin in the mornings, especially when the weather was exceptionally pleasant. With a fresh cup of coffee and its delightful aroma mixing with those of the forest around, she found internal peace and calm here.

Across a bubbling creek that ran before her porch, her morning view included the old Healey house. Abandoned about twenty years ago, it had been steadily sinking into decline. The roof sagged, wood planks had been silvered by the years and there was little left that looked safe or even useful. Krystal had always anticipated the day when the forest would reclaim it.

Then came the morning when a motor home pulled up beside the crumbling house and a large man climbed out. He spent some time investigating the old structure, inside and out. Maybe hunting for anything he could reclaim? Would that be theft at this point?

She lingered, watching with mild curiosity but little concern. At some level she had always supposed that someone would express interest in the Healey land itself. It wasn't easy anymore to find private land on the edge of US Forest, and eventually the "grandfathering" that had left the Healey family their ownership would end because of lack of occupancy. Regardless, it wasn't exactly a large piece of land, unlikely to be useful to most, and the Forest Service would let it return to nature.

Less of that house meant more of the forest devouring the eyesore. And at least the bubbling of the creek passing through the canyon swallowed most of the sounds that might be coming from that direction now that the man was there. And it sure looked like he might be helping the destruction of that eyesore.

But then came another morning when she stepped out with her coffee and saw a group of people, maybe a dozen, camped around the ramshackle house. That's when things started to become noisy despite the sound baffling provided by the creek.

A truck full of lumber managed to make its way up the remaining ruined road on that side of the creek and dumped a load that caused Krystal to gasp. Rebuilding? Building bigger?

What kind of eyesore would she have to face? Her view from this porch was her favorite. Her other windows and doors didn't include the creek. And all those people buzzing around provided an annoying level of activity that would distract her.

Then came the ultimate insult: a generator fired up and drowned any peaceful sound that remained, the wind in the trees and the creek both.

That did it. Maybe these people were squatters who could be driven away. She certainly doubted she'd be able to write at all with that roaring generator. Her cabin was far from soundproofed.

After setting her coffee mug on the railing, she headed for the stepping stones that crossed the creek. For generations they'd been a path between two friendly families until the Healeys had departed. As Krystal crossed, she sensed people pulling back into the woods. Creepy. Maybe she ought to reconsider this trip across the creek. But her backbone stiffened. It usually did.

She walked around the house, now smelling of freshly cut wood, sure she'd have to find *someone*.

Then she found the man around the back corner. Since she was determined not to begin this encounter by yelling at the guy, she waited impatiently until he turned and saw her. He leaned over, turning the generator to a lower level, then simply looked at her.

He wore old jeans and a long-sleeved gray work shirt. A pair of safety goggles rode the top of his head. A dust mask hung around his neck. Workmanlike, which only made her uneasier.

Then she noticed more. God, he was gorgeous. Tall, large, broad-shouldered. A rugged, angular face with turquoise eyes that seemed to pierce the green shade of the trees. The forest's shadow hid the creek that still danced and sparkled in revealed sunlight behind her.

This area was a green cavern. One she quite liked.

Finally he spoke, clearly reluctant to do so. "Yes?"

"I'm Krystal Metcalfe. I live in the house across the creek."

One brief nod. His face remained like granite. Then slowly he said, "Josh Healey."

An alarm sounded in her mind. Then recognition made her heart hammer because this might be truly bad news. "This is Healey property, isn't it?" Of course it was. Not a bright question from her.

A short nod.

"Are you going to renovate this place?"

"Yes."

God, this was going to be like pulling teeth, she thought irritably. "I hope you're not planning to cut down many trees."

"No."

Stymied, as it became clear this man had no intention of beginning any conversation, even one as casual as talking about the weather, she glared. "Okay, then. Just take care of the forest."

She turned sharply on her heel without another word and made her way across the stepping stones to her own property. Maybe she should start drinking her morning coffee on the front porch of her house on the other side from the creek.

She was certainly going to have to go down to Conard City to buy a pair of ear protectors or go mad trying to do her own work when that generator once again revved up. *Gah!*

Josh Healey had watched Krystal Metcalfe coming round the corner of his new building. Trouble? She sure seemed to be looking for it.

She was cute, pretty, her blue eyes as bright as the summer sky overhead. But he didn't care about that.

What he cared about were his troops, men and women who were escaping a world that PTSD and war had ripped from them. People who needed to be left alone to find balance within themselves and with group therapy. Josh, a psychologist, had brought them here for that solitude.

Now he had that neighbor trying to poke her nose into his business. Not good. He knew how people reacted to the mere idea of vets with PTSD, their beliefs that these people were unpredictable and violent.

But he had more than a dozen soldiers to protect and he was determined to do so. If that woman became a problem, he'd find a way to shut her down.

It was *his* land after all.

Chapter One

No.

Nearly a year later, that one word still sometimes re-sounded in Krystal Metcalfe's head. One of the few words and nearly the last word Josh Healey had spoken to her.

A simple question. Several simple questions, and the only response had been single syllables. Well, except for his name.

The man had annoyed her with his refusal to be neigh-borly, but nothing had changed in nearly a year. Well, ex-cept for the crowd over there. A bunch of invaders.

At least Josh Healey hadn't scalped the forest.

Krystal loved the quiet, the peace, the view from her private cabin at the Wyoming-based Mountain Artists' Retreat in the small community of Cash Creek Canyon. She was no temporary resident, unlike guests in the other cabins, but instead a permanent one as her mother's part-ner in this venture.

She thought of this cabin and the surrounding woods as her Zen Space, a place where she could always center herself, could always find the internal quiet that unleashed wandering ideas, some of them answers to questions her writing awoke in her.

But lately—well, for nearly a year in fact—this Zen

Space of hers had been invaded. Across the creek, within view from her porch, a fallen-down house had been renovated by about a dozen people, then surrounded by a rustic stockade.

What the hell? A fence would have done if they wanted some privacy, but a stockade, looking like something from a Western movie?

Well, she told herself as she sat on her porch, maybe it wasn't as ugly as chain-link or an ordinary privacy fence might have been. It certainly fit with the age of the community that had always been called Cash Creek Canyon since a brief gold rush in the 1870s.

But still, what the hell? It sat there, blending well enough with the surrounding forest, but weird. Overkill. Unnecessary, as Krystal knew from having spent most of her life right here. Nothing to hide from, nothing to hide. Not around here.

Sighing, she put her booted feet up on her porch railing and sipped her coffee, considering her previous but brief encounters with the landowner, Josh Healey.

Talk about monosyllabic! She was quite sure that she hadn't gotten more than a word from him in all this time. At least not the few times she had crossed the creek on the old stepping stones.

The Healey house had been abandoned like so many along Cash Creek as life on the mountainside had become more difficult. For twenty years, Krystal had hoped the house's steady decay would finally collapse the structure, restoring the surrounding forest to its rightful ownership.

Except that hadn't happened and she couldn't quite help getting irritated from the day a huge motor home had moved in to be followed by trucks of lumber, a noisy generator and a dozen or so men and women who camped in tents as they restored the sagging house. A year since then and she was still troubled by the activity over there.

The biggest question was why it had happened. The next question was what had brought the last owner of the property back here with a bunch of his friends to fill up the steadily shrinking hole in the woods.

No answers. At least none from Josh Healey. None, for that matter, from the Conard County sheriff's deputies who patrolled the community of Cash Creek Canyon. They knew no more than anyone: that it was a group residence.

The privacy of that stockade was absolute. At least the damn noise had quieted at last, leaving the Mountain Artists' Retreat in the kind of peace its residents needed for their creative work.

For a while it had seemed that the retreat might die from the noise, even with the muffling woods around. That had not happened, and spring's guests had arrived pretty much as usual, some new to the community, others returning visitors.

Much as she resented the building that had invaded her Zen Space, Krystal had to acknowledge a curiosity that wouldn't go away. A curiosity about those people. About the owner, who would say nothing about why he had brought them all there.

Some kind of cult?

That question troubled her. But what troubled her more was how much she enjoyed watching Josh Healey laboring around that place. Muscled. Hardworking. And entirely too attractive when he worked with his shirt off.

Dang. On the one hand she wanted to drive the man away. On the other she wanted to have sex with him. Wanted it enough to feel a tingling throughout her body.

How foolish could she get?

Across the creek, Josh Healey often noticed the woman who sat on her porch in the mornings drinking coffee. He knew her name because she had crossed the creek a few times: Krystal Metcalfe, joint owner of the artists' retreat. A pretty package of a woman, but he had no time or interest in such things these days.

Nor did he have any desire to share the purpose of his compound. It had been necessary to speak briefly with a deputy who hadn't been that curious. He imagined word had gotten around some, probably with attendant rumors, but no one out there in the community of Cash Creek Canyon, or beyond it in Conard City or County, had any need to know what he hoped he was accomplishing. And from what he could tell, no one did.

Nor did anyone have a need to know the reentry problems being faced by his ex-military residents.

Least of all Krystal Metcalfe, who watched too often and had ventured over here with her questions. Questions she really had no right to ask.

So when he saw her in the mornings, he shrugged it off. She had a right to sit on her damn porch, a right to watch whatever she could see…although the stockade fencing had pretty much occluded any nosy viewing.

But sometimes he wondered, with private amusement, just how she would respond if he crossed that creek and questioned her. Asked *her* about the hole in the woods created by her lodge and all the little cabins she and her mother had scattered through the forest.

Hah! She apparently felt she took care of her environment but he could see at least a dozen problems with her viewpoint. Enough problems that his own invasion seemed paltry by comparison.

As it was, right now he had more than a dozen vets, a number that often grew for a while, who kept themselves busy with maintaining the sanctuary itself, with cooking, with gardening. And a lot of time with group therapy, helping each other through a very difficult time, one that had shredded their lives. All of them leaving behind the booze and drugs previously used as easy crutches.

Some of his people left when they felt ready. New ones arrived, sometimes more than he had room for but always welcomed.

Most of the folks inside, male and female, knew about Krystal Metcalfe, and after he explained her harmless curiosity to them, they lost their suspicion, lost their fear of accusations.

Because his people *had* been accused. Every last one of them had been accused of something. It seemed society had no room for the detritus, the *problems*, their damn war had brought home.

He sighed and shook his head and continued around the perimeter of the large stockade. Like many of his folks here, he couldn't relax completely.

It always niggled at the back of his mind that someone curious or dangerous might try to get into the stockade. Exactly the thing that he'd prevented by building it this way in the first place.

But still the worry wouldn't quite leave him. His own remnant from a war.

He glanced at Krystal Metcalfe one last time before he rounded the corner. She appeared to be absorbed in a tablet.

Good. Her curiosity had gone far enough.

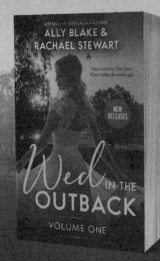
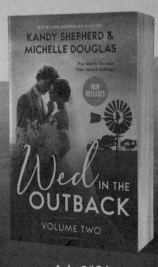